All Kinds
of Courage

Selected by Sidonie Matsner Gruenberg

Favorite Stories Old and New
Let's Hear a Story
Let's Read a Story
Let's Read More Stories
More Favorite Stories Old and New
All Kinds of Courage

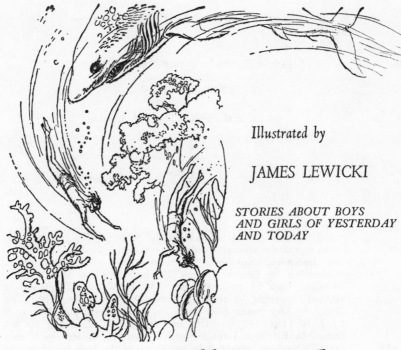

Illustrated by

JAMES LEWICKI

STORIES ABOUT BOYS
AND GIRLS OF YESTERDAY
AND TODAY

All Kinds
of Courage

Selected by

SIDONIE MATSNER GRUENBERG

DOUBLEDAY & COMPANY, INC.
Garden City, New York

Grateful acknowledgment is made to the following for granting permission to reprint the selections which appear in this book:

American Junior Red Cross News, for permission to use "Giovanni and the Narrowback" by Edward Fenton. "Elephant Ears" by Ruth Holberg; copyright 1942 by Ruth Holberg. "An Extra Indian" by Marion Holland; copyright © 1955 by Marion Holland. "The Wish Book Dress" by May Justus; from *Cabin on Kettle Creek,* published 1941 by J. B. Lippincott, copyright by May Justus. "Rounding up the Sheep" by Elizabeth Yates McGreal. "Adventure on Ice" by Wanda Neill Tolboom. All reprinted by permission of the authors and *American Junior Red Cross News.*

Erick Berry, for permission to use "Ashu and the Whirlwind."

Hugh Cave, for permission to use "Two Were Left." Copyright 1942 by the Crowell-Collier Publishing Company.

Childhood Education Association. "Hatsuno's Great-Grandmother" by Florence C. Means, from *Told under the Stars and Stripes.* Reprinted by permission of the Association of Childhood Education International, Washington, D.C.

Elizabeth Coatsworth, for permission to use "The Attack."

Doubleday & Company, Inc., for permission to use "Gloucester Boy" by Ruth and Richard Holberg. Copyright 1940 by Ruth and Richard Holberg; "The Desirable Shawl" by Grace P. Moon, from *Chi-Weé: The Adventures of a Little Indian Girl.* Copyright 1925 by Doubleday & Company, Inc.

Ann Durell, for permission to use "A Red-Handled Sheath Knife" reprinted from *Trailblazer,* copyright 1955 by W. L. Jenkins.

Ginn & Company, for permission to use "The Sampler" from *Young Americans* by Cornelia Meigs, published 1936 by Ginn and Company, owners of the copyright.

Harcourt, Brace & World, Inc., for permission to use "The Hundred Dresses" from *The Hundred Dresses* by Eleanor Estes, copyright 1944 by Harcourt, Brace & World, Inc.

Harper & Brothers, for permission to use "Deep Water" from *On the Banks of Plum Creek* by Laura Ingalls Wilder. Copyright 1937 by Harper & Brothers.

5

Acknowledgment

I want to thank my friend and colleague, Bella Koral, whose knowledge of children's literature has been of great help in five of my anthologies. I am especially grateful for her assistance in the demanding research that the selections in this book represent.

For our grandchildren

Peter Barnard
Daniel Barnard
Nicholas Benjamin
Elizabeth Allee
Richard Joseph
Ann Matsner
Kathryn Mary
Jean Allee
Judith Sidonie
Joel William
Matthew Alan
Richard Matsner

Contents

CONTENTS

12

Foreword

Over the years I have been gathering into books all kinds of stories for boys and girls, but this collection has been the hardest. I have read hundreds of stories in search of some that are not only interesting, but also related to modern life. Most of these stories tell us about heights that girls and boys of today and yesterday could reach under special circumstances.

Most of us think of courage as the absence of fear in the face of physical danger, or perhaps as the control of fear in confronting danger. Yet sooner or later most of us discover that there are many kinds of courage, some that are not at all spectacular—or even obvious.

Everybody knows that it takes courage to risk one's life in order to save another—we hear about Medals for Heroism being awarded; spectacular rescues are widely publicized. But it also takes courage to struggle alone for hours against fatigue and hunger and sleepiness to protect other people from danger, people one does not even know. Or to give up a beloved stray dog that one has trained, on discovering the rightful owner. Or to stand up for a classmate who has been plagued or humiliated by your friends. Or to admit frankly and without trying to explain that you have been in the wrong.

We cannot count the various ways in which young people of all races and all nations demonstrate their courage. I hope that these stories will entertain you and inspire you.

Sidonie Matsner Gruenberg

All Kinds
of Courage

Commando Charles

JEAN MACCALLUM SWEET

Charles climbed a rock, slippery with wet kelp that oozed around his toes. By clinging with both hands to the kelp that hung from above, he could just manage it. Then he stopped to look around. The fog had come in thick, and though he couldn't see the sun, he thought it must be almost suppertime, time to go home.

He took a minute to decide which way to go. His island wasn't a very big one. He could go around the slippery rocks to the little wharf and then up the path, or he could go back to the Landing and then up through the field.

The Landing was the only bit of sandy beach on the island. It was the one spot where a small boat could be pulled quickly out of the surf without being dashed to pieces on the rocks by the roaring breakers. In the last few years nobody had used it, of course, since there was the wharf, but the old fishermen called it the Landing and nobody ever thought of it as a beach. Maybe it was just too small.

His sea-trained eye studied the water line. The tide was rising. Around the wharf way he'd have to climb higher now, and the going would be hard. He turned back toward the Landing, slipping and sliding down the rock he had just climbed.

Charles knew every rock on that shore. Ten of his eleven years had been spent on the little island where the Fundy surf sang him to sleep every night. He had had the fishermen's children to play with, and no bored city child, sitting in a movie, could dream of the living adventure that life held on the island. At the Landing they played Pirate and Explorers, beaching their driftwood rafts and leaping ashore with daggers in their teeth. Sometimes they took sides and battled it out on the beach.

But today Charles was alone; nowadays he was almost always alone. When he was eight the war had come and the fishermen and their children had gone. They were banished to the mainland as the soldiers moved to the island. Charles was left behind, one boy without a playmate, because his father kept the lighthouse at the point. And the lighthouse had to be kept on that dangerous rocky coast to guide ships.

He hurried a little now. His mother would want him to be at home before it started to get dark. He didn't mind being alone, and don't think for a minute that he was ever sorry for himself. Oh, no. Life on his island was more of an adventure now than ever. Soldiers swarmed all over it, building and building and changing everything. The island was a very special military secret, and no civilian was allowed to set foot on it, but Charles lived right there and just *had* to know all about it! The soldier boys were friendly, and when they had time they talked and played with him. It wasn't like having other children, but it was exciting, especially knowing the secrets and feeling the size and reality of the war.

Charles passed the cave without stopping. It wasn't a very big cave, but they used to have fun playing smugglers in it a long time ago. You had to be careful and watch the tide. Up to about half tide you could easily get in by climbing around the rocks at the entrance. But at high tide the waves broke over those rocks and washed far up into the cave, leaving only a little dry place at the very end. Charles still remembered the day he was caught in the cave. He was burying treasure and didn't notice, and by the time those who were supposed to surprise him had arrived they couldn't get in and he couldn't get out. They climbed the cliff above and ran for his father who soon came around, grumbling, in his small boat. And because he was so clever about boats and about tides he managed to work it in between the angry breakers on the rocks and over the surf into the cave. They were both soaked, and Charles was forbidden ever to play in the cave again.

So this night he passed the cave. He knew the Landing was just around the next big rock. It didn't seem

such a good place for pirates or explorers now that he was alone. But sometimes lately he had played Commando, or Defense of English Coasts, there. It was easy to imagine an enemy, and often when he made a landing himself, the sentry who passed every few minutes would really capture him and search him and pretend to send him to the guardhouse. It was great fun and good practice for the sentry too.

This time Charles decided he would leap off the big rock into the surprised center of a circle of raiders. This time he would capture the lot singlehanded! It was a fine leap. He landed far out on the tiny beach and whirled, pointing his revolver, which was his finger, at the half-dozen desperate men who weren't there. His jaw stuck out fearsomely to frame the growl, "I've got you, you—" when he froze, really froze, his finger pointing, his legs apart. He was looking into a very real and very ugly revolver. He was hearing a strange voice, low and harsh, commanding, "Don't move. Don't speak!"

A man was sitting in the sand close to the big rock. Charles had leaped right over him. The stranger had dropped his blouse when he stooped to pick up his gun. He had stiff blond hair and small blue eyes. A limp heap of rubber lay beside him.

It seemed a long time that Charles stood there, cold and still. Then slowly his mind began to work. This must be a spy. This was the enemy, right here in front of him and holding a gun that most certainly was loaded. That bunch of rubber must be a boat, an awfully small one. The U-boat he came from must be near, very near. But how had he ever landed? Only the smartest fisherman could make the Landing, and then just at one time of tide. Oh, his clothes—Charles suddenly realized that when the spy got to the breakers he swam and pushed his rubber boat in.

The few seconds that it took Charles to figure this out had helped him. His mind was clear now and racing. The man had come to spy on the island defenses. He'd go back and tell them where to place their shells. But he wouldn't go back—he wouldn't—HE WOULDN'T! There must be some way. Now he, Charles, must play to the hilt the game he had played here so often alone. Now he was a real Commando and he must use his wits. The first thing was to gain time until he could think of a plan.

His whisper was thin and hoarse, but he hoped it was as bold as he tried to make it. "You don't dare. The guard would hear the shot!"

The man's face hardly changed when his thin lips moved.

"There is a very good silencer."

Charles swallowed. "But," his voice was firm and strong, "they'd find—the body—soon. The sentry will come here any minute now."

"Ah, what I wished to know. You will help me much, my little man." Still holding the gun ready, and without moving his eyes, he was picking up things and smoothing the sand. "Now you will show me where I hide until dark." He slipped on a khaki blouse and stood in battledress, Canadian battledress, exactly like every other soldier on the island! "Remember," he added, "you call or lead me wrong, and before anything can happen you get it first. Now, where do I hide?"

Charles didn't have to look frightened. He was more terrified than he had ever been in his life. But he was not frightened about himself. He was terribly afraid that the man would get away. He was desperately afraid that he wasn't big enough or wise enough to formulate the right plan and to watch for the right moment. But he tried to keep from showing that he was capable of planning anything. He wanted to look like a boy simply scared stiff when he said slowly, "The only place I know is a cave. It's back there a short distance."

"Good, a cave, very good. Go now, and I will be close behind you. You will try no tricks, remember."

Charles went as quickly as he could, over and around the slippery rocks, jumping the wet gullies between. His eyes were on the tide, rising rapidly now. It wouldn't be very near the cave. They must get there in time to get in. It was all he could think of. He had no other plan.

The German, trained to be nimble as a cat, was close behind all the way. They reached the cave just as the wash from the big waves was licking around the entrance. The fog was lifting a bit in patches, but darkness was coming on.

"Stop!" The man looked carefully at the rock formation around the entrance. He studied the rocks farther out that were disappearing under the rising tide. "Yes, I can get my boat out here. She is a very light boat. The cave is dry inside?" Charles nodded and they went in, up the steep, wet beach into the darkness ahead. The German watched carefully for the high-tide mark which soon showed on the walls, clearly outlined by the mound of dead, grayish-brown seaweed left by the last wave of each tide. There the cave, a small one at best and narrow, took a turn and ended in cold darkness out of sight of the darkening sea. The sand here was fairly dry, and they sat down in silence to wait.

Charles was getting hungry. He felt very tired and cold. His nerves twitched, but he waited and waited. It must not be too long or too soon. At last he spoke. "I'm cold."

"I, too, am cold." The spy laughed. "But you will be much colder, my little man. You will be all night here alone when I am gone. Ah, you have found me a wonderful place. I do not need to kill you. You are lucky, yes? You will be safe here until early morning when I shall be gone, and your beautiful island—very much of it—will be gone too!" He laughed again. "You are so lucky; you have a good bomb shelter for what will come!"

Charles said, "I was thinking we might have a little fire—just a small one to warm our hands. Even without the fog no one will see, because the cave turns."

The spy was silent a moment. Then he carefully struck a match and looked around. A few bits of driftwood lay on the sand. "Yes, I think you are right. It will be very small, but I can warm my hands and perhaps watch you better. There must be no tricks."

Charles collected the small bits of wood and started the fire. It was just beginning to give a little heat when there was no wood left. Charles did not need heat now. Although burning from head to foot, still he was trembling. "That's all the wood, but this seaweed is nice and dry," he said.

The German only nodded.

Charles gathered a good armful of the weed and started feeding it to the glowing sticks. It cracked and curled, and he suddenly piled it all on. The glow disappeared. Charles poked aimlessly. Here and there a spark showered, and the cave was filling with smoke.

The German coughed; then he started up, "See here, what are you doing? That stuff is wet! Put out the fire!"

Charles stamped and scattered it, raising a lot more smoke while he worked. They were both coughing now. The German grumbled and scrambled to fill his cap with water. Finally he killed the little fire completely. He settled down again, growling and muttering at the stupidity of the boy and of all Canadians in general. Charles was silent and taut. He tried to remember every line of the pitch-dark cave. He was glad the man talked so much; it showed he was not moving. The tide had risen so that the waves were breaking within the cave, and the voice became harder to hear in the crashing echoes. The smoke had cleared wonderfully.

In the lull of sound between waves Charles strained his ears and waited. The time seemed endless. At last he heard what he had hoped for so desperately. He coughed loudly to cover the sound. Another wave broke. He gathered himself to spring, and as the echoes died away he shouted, "One man! With a gun!" and leaped to the back of the cave. He threw himself on his face as the German's gun blazed and a bullet struck the rock where he had been.

The rest was a daze—the soldiers, the spy bound and thrown into the boat, the rush through the surf with his father, the only man who could have guided the boat between those rocks. Then came his hot supper in bed, with the Commanding Officer himself sitting there asking questions, and a man writing down everything he said.

"It was easy," Charles told them, "once I remembered about the cave. You see, we kids found that cleft, or crack, above the cave in the back of the roof one stormy day. It was a terrible storm, and we were looking for the best place to watch the waves on the rocks. Right in the middle of the raspberry bushes back of the old Simpson house we saw a kind of fountain that came and went. We ran over, and it was just the smallest opening. The waves were big enough in the cave that day to dash right up and spray out above. It was fun to watch it! After that we looked for the crack in the cave, but you can't really see it because of the way the rocks are formed."

"But how did you manage the smoke signal?" The Commanding Officer and the other men waited.

"That was just seaweed. I knew the opening was right near the East Gate where the bushes had been cleared away, and the guard is always there. I knew he'd see the smoke. But I had to take a chance that the German wouldn't know. They say lots of places don't have this kind of seaweed on the shore. I guess Germany must be one of those places, because all kids know what an awful smoke seaweed makes if you throw it on a fire."

"Well, son." The Commanding Officer stood up, and the soldier put away his pencil. "If a boy of eleven can do a job like this, then Canada is well defended. And don't think for a minute that we believe it was easy. We know how much real courage it took, and you'll be hearing more about it. But right now I'll give you your first reward by trusting you with a military secret. Our corvettes are out there after that U-boat. They haven't far to look, because it's waiting around for your friend. You may be sure they'll get it before morning. Good night, Commando."

And a happy, tired hero turned over and went to sleep.

Elizabeth Ann Fails
in an Examination

DOROTHY CANFIELD FISHER

Something perfectly dreadful had happened in
school that day. The Superintendent, the all-important,
seldom-seen Superintendent, came to visit the school,
and the children were given some examinations so he
could see how they were getting on.

Now, you know what an examination did to Elizabeth
Ann. Or haven't I told you yet?

Well, if I haven't, it's because words fail me. If there
is anything horrid that an examination didn't do to
Elizabeth Ann, I have yet to hear of it. It began years
ago, before ever she went to school, when she heard
Aunt Frances talking about how she had dreaded examinations when she was a child, and how they dried up
her mouth and made her ears ring and her head ache
and her knees get all weak and her mind a perfect blank,
so that she didn't know what two and two made. Of

28

course Elizabeth Ann didn't feel all those things right off at her first examination, but by the time she had had several and rushed to tell Aunt Frances about how awful they were and the two of them had sympathized with one another and compared symptoms and then wept about her resulting low marks, why, she not only had all the symptoms Aunt Frances had ever had, but a good many more of her own invention.

Well, she had had them all and had them hard this afternoon when the Superintendent was there. Her mouth had gone dry and her knees had shaken and her elbows had felt as though they had no more bones in them than so much jelly and her eyes had smarted, and oh, what answers she had made! That dreadful, tight panic had clutched at her throat whenever the Superintendent had looked at her, and she had disgraced herself ten times over. She went hot and cold to think of it, and felt quite sick with hurt vanity. She who did so well every day and was so much looked up to by her classmates, what must they be thinking of her! To tell the truth, she had been crying as she walked along through the woods, because she was so sorry for herself. Her eyes were all red still, and her throat sore from the big lump in it.

And now she would live it all over again as she told the Putney cousins. For of course they must be told. She had always told Aunt Frances everything that happened in school. It happened that Aunt Abigail had been taking a nap when she got home from school, and so she had come out to the sap house, where Cousin Ann and

Uncle Henry were making syrup, to have it over with as soon as possible. She went up to the little slab house now, dragging her feet and hanging her head, and opened the door. Cousin Ann, in a very short old skirt and a man's coat and high rubber boots, was just poking some more wood into the big fire which blazed furiously under the broad, flat pan where the sap was boiling. The rough, brown hut was filled with white steam and that sweetest of all odors, hot maple syrup. Cousin Ann turned her head, her face red with the heat of the fire, and nodded at the child.

"Hello, Betsy, you're just in time. I've saved out a cupful of hot syrup for you, all ready to wax."

Betsy hardly heard this, although she had been wild about waxed sugar on snow ever since her very first taste of it. "Cousin Ann," she said unhappily, "the Superintendent visited our school this afternoon."

"Did he?" said Cousin Ann, dipping a thermometer into the boiling syrup.

"Yes, and we had examinations!" said Betsy.

"Did you?" said Cousin Ann, holding the thermometer up to the light and looking at it.

"And you know how perfectly awful examinations make you feel," said Betsy, very near to tears again.

"Why, no," said Cousin Ann, sorting over syrup tins. "They never made me feel awful. I thought they were sort of fun."

"Fun!" cried Betsy indignantly, staring through the beginnings of her tears.

"Why, yes. Like taking a dare, don't you know? Somebody stumps you to jump off the hitching post, and you do it to show 'em. I always used to think examinations were like that. Somebody stumps you to spell 'pneumonia,' and you do it to show 'em. Here's your cup of syrup. You'd better go right out and wax it while it's hot."

Elizabeth Ann automatically took the cup in her hand, but she did not look at it. "But supposing you get so scared you can't spell 'pneumonia' or anything else!" she said feelingly. "That's what happened to me. You know how your mouth gets all dry and your knees . . ." She stopped. Cousin Ann had said she did not know all about those things. "Well, anyhow, I got so scared I could hardly stand up! And I made the most awful mistakes—things I know just as well! I spelled 'doubt' without any b and 'separate' with an e, and I said Iowa was bounded on the north by Wisconsin, and I—"

"Oh, well," said Cousin Ann, "it doesn't matter, if you really know the right answers, does it? That's the important thing."

This was an idea which had never in all her life entered Betsy's brain and she did not take it in now. She only shook her head miserably and went on in a doleful tone, "And I said thirteen and eight are twenty-two! And I wrote March without any capital M, and I—"

"Look here, Betsy, do you want to tell me all this?" Cousin Ann spoke in the quick, ringing voice she had once in a while which made everybody, from old Shep up open his eyes and get his wits about him. Betsy

31

gathered hers and thought hard; and she came to an unexpected conclusion. No, she didn't really want to tell Cousin Ann all about it. Why was she doing it? Because she thought that was the thing to do. "Because if you don't really want to," went on Cousin Ann, "I don't see that it's doing anybody any good. I guess Hemlock Mountain will stand right there just the same, even if you did forget to put a b in 'doubt.' And your syrup will be too cool to wax right if you don't take it out pretty soon."

She turned back to stoke the fire, and Elizabeth Ann, in a daze, found herself walking out of the door. It fell shut after her, and there she was under the clear, pale blue sky, with the sun just hovering over the rim of Hemlock Mountain. She looked up at the big mountains, all blue and silver with shadows and snow, and wondered what in the world Cousin Ann had meant. Of course Hemlock Mountain would stand there just the same. But what of it? What did that have to do with her arithmetic, with anything? She had failed in her examination, hadn't she?

She found a clean white snowbank under a pine tree, and setting her cup of syrup down in a safe place, began to pat the snow down hard to make the right bed for the waxing of the syrup. The sun, very hot for that late March day, brought out strongly the tarry perfume of the big pine tree. Near her the sap dripped musically into a bucket already half full, hung on a maple tree. A bluejay rushed suddenly through the upper branches of the wood, his screaming and chattering voice sounding like noisy children at play.

Elizabeth Ann took up her cup and poured some of the thick, hot syrup out on the hard snow, making loops and curves as she poured. It stiffened and hardened at once, and she lifted up a great coil of it, threw her head back, and let it drop into her mouth. Concentrated sweetness of summer days was in that mouthful, part of it still hot and aromatic, part of it icy and wet with melting snow. She crunched it all together into a delicious big lump and sucked on it dreamily, her eyes on the rim of Hemlock Mountain high above her there, the snow on it bright golden in the sunlight. Uncle Henry had promised to take her up to the top as soon as the snow went off. She wondered what the top of a mountain would be like. Uncle Henry had said the main thing was that you could see so much of the world at once. He said it was too queer the way your own house and big barn and great fields looked like little toy things that weren't of any account. It was because you could see so much more than just the . . .

She heard an imploring whine, and a cold nose was thrust into her hand! Why, there was old Shep begging for his share of waxed sugar. He loved it, though it did stick to his teeth so! She poured out another lot and gave half of it to Shep. It immediately stuck his jaws together tight, and he began pawing at his mouth and shaking his head till Betsy had to laugh. Then he managed to pull his jaws apart and chewed loudly and visibly, tossing his head, opening his mouth wide till

ELIZABETH ANN FAILS IN AN EXAMINATION

Betsy could see the sticky, brown candy draped in melting festoons all over his big white teeth and red gullet. Then with a gulp he had swallowed it all down and was whining for more, striking softly at the little girl's skirt with his forepaw. "Oh, you eat it too fast!" cried Betsy, but she shared her next lot with him too. The sun had gone down over Hemlock Mountain by this time, and the big slope above her was all deep blue shadow. The mountain looked much higher now as the dusk began to fall, and loomed up bigger and bigger as though it reached to the sky. It was no wonder houses looked small from its top. Betsy ate the last of her sugar, looking up at the quiet giant towering grandly above her. There was no lump in her throat now. Although she still thought she did not know what in the world Cousin Ann meant by saying that about Hemlock Mountain and her examination, it's my opinion that she had made a good beginning of an understanding.

She was just picking up her cup to take it back to the sap house when Shep growled a little and stood with his ears and tail up, looking down the road. Something was coming down that road in the blue, clear twilight; some-

thing that was making a very queer noise. It sounded
almost like somebody crying. It was somebody crying!
It was a child crying. It was a little, little girl . . . Betsy
could see her now . . . stumbling along and crying as
though her heart would break. Why, it was little Molly,
her own particular charge at school whose reading lesson
she heard every day. Betsy and Shep ran to meet her.
"What's the matter, Molly? What's the matter?" Betsy
knelt down and put her arms around the weeping child.
"Did you fall down? Did you hurt you? What are you
doing 'way off here? Did you lose your way?"

"I don't want to go away! I don't want to go away!"
said Molly over and over, clinging tightly to Betsy. It
was a long time before Betsy could quiet her enough
to find out what had happened. Then she made out
between Molly's sobs that her mother had been taken
suddenly sick and had had to go away to a hospital,
and that that left nobody at home to take care of Molly,
and she was to be sent away to some strange relatives
in the city who didn't want her at all and who said so.

Elizabeth Ann knew all about that! Her heart swelled
big with sympathy. For a moment she stood again out
on the sidewalk in front of the Lathrop house, with
old Mrs. Lathrop's ungracious white head bobbing from
a window, and knew again that ghastly feeling of being
unwanted. She knew why little Molly was crying! And
she shut her hands together hard and made up her
mind that she would help her out!

Do you know what she did, right off, without thinking about it? She didn't go and look up Aunt Abigail.

She didn't wait till Uncle Henry came back from his round of emptying sap buckets into the big tub on his sled. As fast as her feet could carry her she flew back to Cousin Ann in the sap house. I can't tell you (except again that Cousin Ann was Cousin Ann) why it was that Betsy ran so fast to her and was so sure that everything would be all right as soon as Cousin Ann knew about it; but whatever the reason was it was a good one, for though Cousin Ann did not stop to kiss Molly or even look at her more than one sharp first glance, she said after a moment's pause during which she filled a syrup can and screwed the cover down very tight: "Well, if her folks will let her stay, how would you like to have Molly come and stay with us till her mother gets back from the hospital? Now you've got a room of your own I guess you could have her sleep with you."

"Oh, Molly, Molly, Molly!" shouted Betsy, jumping up and down, and then hugging the little girl with all her might. "Oh, it will be like having a little sister!"

Cousin Ann sounded a dry, warning note: "Don't be too sure her folks will let her. We don't know about them yet."

Betsy ran to her and caught her hand, looking up at her with shining eyes. "Cousin Ann, if you go to see them and ask them, they will!"

This made even Cousin Ann give a little abashed smile of pleasure, although she made her face grave again at once and said: "You'd better go along back to the house now, Betsy. It's time for you to help Mother with the supper."

The two children trotted back along the darkening wood road, Shep running before them, little Molly clinging fast to the older child's hand. "Aren't you ever afraid, Betsy, in the woods this way?" she asked admiringly.

"Oh, no!" said Betsy protectingly. "There's nothing to be afraid of except getting off on the wrong fork of the road near the Wolf Pit."

"Oh, ow!" said Molly, scringing. "What's the Wolf Pit? What a name!"

Betsy laughed. She tried to make her laugh sound brave like Cousin Ann's, which always seemed so scornful of being afraid. As a matter of fact, she was beginning to fear that they had made the wrong turn, and she was not quite sure that she could find the way home. But she put this out of her mind and walked along very fast, peering ahead into the dusk. "It hasn't anything to do with wolves," she said in answer to Molly's question. "Anyhow, not now. It's just a big, deep hole in the ground where a brook had dug out a cave . . . Uncle Henry told me all about it when he showed it to me . . . and then part of the roof caved in; sometimes there's ice in the corner of the covered part all the summer, Aunt Abigail says."

"Why do you call it the Wolf Pit?" asked Molly, walking very close to Betsy and holding very tightly to her hand.

"Oh, long, ever so long ago when the first settlers came up here they heard a wolf howling all night, and when it didn't stop in the morning they came up here on the mountain and found a wolf had fallen in and couldn't get out."

"I hope they killed him!" said Molly.

"Gracious! that was more than a hundred years ago," said Betsy. She was not thinking of what she was saying. She was thinking that if they were on the right road they ought to be home by this time. She was thinking that the right road ran downhill to the house all the way, and that this certainly seemed to be going up a little. She was wondering what had become of Shep. "Stand here just a minute, Molly," she said. "I want . . . I just want to go ahead a little bit and see . . . and see . . ." She darted on around a curve of the road and stood still, her heart sinking. The road turned there and led straight up the mountain!

For just a moment the little girl felt a wild impulse to burst out in a shriek for Aunt Frances and to run crazily away, anywhere so long as she was running. But the thought of Molly standing back there, trustfully waiting to be taken care of, shut Betsy's lips together hard before her scream of fright got out. She stood still, thinking. Now she mustn't get frightened. All they had to do was to walk back along the road till they came to the fork and then make the right turn. But what if they didn't get back to the turn till it was so dark they couldn't see it . . . ? Well, she mustn't think of that. She ran back, calling, "Come on, Molly," in a tone she tried to make as firm as Cousin Ann's. "I guess we have made the wrong turn after all. We'd better . . ."

But there was no Molly there. In the brief moment

Betsy had stood thinking, Molly had disappeared. The long, shadowy wood road held not a trace of her.

Then Betsy was frightened and then she did begin to scream at the top of her voice, "Molly! Molly!" She was beside herself with terror, and started back hastily to hear Molly's voice, very faint, apparently coming from the ground.

"Ow! Ow! Betsy! Get me out!"

"Where are you?" shrieked Betsy.

"I don't know!" came Molly's sobbing voice. "I just moved the least little bit out of the road and slipped on the ice and began to slide and I couldn't stop myself and I fell down into a deep hole!"

Betsy's head felt as though her hair were standing up straight on end with horror. Molly must have fallen down into the Wolf Pit! Yes, they were quite near it. She remembered now that big white birch tree stood right at the place where the brook tumbled over the edge and fell into it. Although she was dreadfully afraid of falling in herself, she went cautiously over to this tree, feeling her way with her feet to make sure she did not slip, and peered down into the cavernous gloom below. Yes, there was Molly's little face, just a white speck. The child was crying, sobbing, and holding up her arms to Betsy.

"Are you hurt, Molly?"

"No. I fell into a big snowbank, but I'm all frozen and I want to get out!"

Betsy held on to the birch tree. Her head whirled. What should she do! "Look here, Molly," she called down, "I'm going to run along to the right road and back to the house and get Uncle Henry. He'll come with a rope and get you out!"

At this Molly's crying rose to a frantic scream. "Oh, Betsy, don't leave me here alone! Don't! Don't! The wolves will get me! Betsy, don't leave me alone!" The child was wild with terror.

"But I can't get you out myself!" screamed back Betsy, crying herself. Her teeth were chattering with the cold.

"Don't go! Don't go!" came up from the darkness of the pit in a piteous howl. Betsy made a great effort and stopped crying. She sat down on a stone and tried to think. And this is what came into her mind as a guide: What would Cousin Ann do if she were here? She wouldn't cry. She would think of something.

Betsy looked around her desperately. The first thing she saw was the big limb of a pine tree, broken off by the wind, which lay half slantingly against a tree a little distance above the mouth of the pit. It had been there so long that the needles had dried and fallen off, and the skeleton of the branch with the broken stubs looked like . . . yes, it looked like a ladder! That was what Cousin Ann would have done!

"Wait a minute! Wait a minute, Molly!" she called wildly down the pit, warm all over in excitement. "Now listen. You go off there in a corner where the ground makes a sort of roof. I'm going to throw down something you can climb up on, maybe."

"Ow! Ow, it'll hit me!" cried poor little Molly, more

and more frightened. But she scrambled off under her shelter obediently while Betsy struggled with the branch. It was so firmly imbedded in the snow that at first she could not budge it at all. But after she cleared that away and pried hard with the stick she was using as a lever she felt it give a little. She bore down with all her might, throwing her weight again and again on her lever, and finally felt the big branch move. After that it was easier, as its course was downhill over the snow to the mouth of the pit. Glowing and pushing, wet with perspiration, she slowly maneuvered it along to the edge, turned it squarely, gave it a great shove, and leaned over anxiously. Then she breathed a great sigh of relief! Just as she had hoped, it went down sharp-end first and stuck fast in the snow which had saved Molly from broken bones. She was so out of breath with her work that for a moment she could not speak. Then, "Molly, there! Now I guess you can climb up to where I can reach you."

Molly made a rush for any way out of her prison and climbed, like the practiced squirrel that she was, up from one stub to another to the top of the branch. She was still below the edge of the pit there, but Betsy lay flat down on the snow and held out her hands. Molly took hold hard, and digging her toes into the snow, slowly wormed her way up to the surface of the ground.

It was then, at that very moment, that Shep came bounding up to them, barking loudly, and after him Cousin Ann striding along in her rubber boots, with a lantern in her hand and a rather anxious look on her face.

She stopped short and looked at the two little girls covered with snow, their faces flaming with excitement, and at the black hole gaping behind them. "I always told Father we ought to put a fence around that pit," she said in a matter-of-fact voice. "Someday a sheep's going to fall down there. Shep came along to the house without you, and we thought most likely you'd taken the wrong turn."

Betsy felt terribly aggrieved. She wanted to be petted and praised for her heroism. She wanted Cousin Ann to realize . . . oh, if Aunt Frances were only there, she would realize . . . !

"I fell down in the hole, and Betsy wanted to go and get Mr. Putney, but I wouldn't let her, and so she threw down a big branch and I climbed out," explained Molly, who, now that her danger was past, took Betsy's action quite as a matter of course.

"Oh, that was how it happened," said Cousin Ann. She looked down the hole and saw the big branch, and looked back and saw the long trail of crushed snow where Betsy had dragged it. "Well, now, that was quite a good idea for a little girl to have," she said briefly. "I guess you'll do to take care of Molly all right!"

She spoke in her usual voice and immediately drew the children after her, but Betsy's heart was singing joyfully as she trotted along, clasping Cousin Ann's strong hand. Now she knew that Cousin Ann realized . . . She trotted fast, smiling to herself in the darkness.

"What made you think of doing that?" asked Cousin Ann presently as they approached the house.

"Why, I tried to think of what you would have done if you'd been there," said Betsy.

"Oh!" said Cousin Ann. "Well . . ."

She didn't say another word, but Betsy, glancing up into her face as they stepped into the lighted room, saw an expression that made her give a little skip and hop of joy. She had pleased Cousin Ann.

That night as she lay in her bed, her arm over Molly cuddled up warm beside her, she remembered ever so faintly, as something of no importance, that she had failed in an examination that afternoon.

Giovanni and
the Narrowback

EDWARD FENTON

That afternoon when school was out, Johnny
Rossi found himself standing on the corner beside Hugh
Lathrop. Hugh was a new boy at school. The other
boys were pelting past them. "Hi, Johnny!" some of
them called, and he called back. He thought that he
ought to say something to Hugh, but he didn't know
how to begin, and they stood there silently watching
the traffic on the New York City street rush by as they
waited for the light to change.

It finally switched to green.

"Well," Johnny said, "I go this way." And he jerked
his dark head in the direction of the crowded tenement
section that began beyond the Avenue.

"I've never been that way," Hugh said, "but I guess
it wouldn't be too hard to find my way home from
there. I'll go along with you for a while." He grinned.
"That is, if it's all right with you."

45

"Sure," Johnny said dubiously. "Why not? Come along then." All the same he wondered what there could be in his part of the city that might interest anyone like Hugh.

As they crossed, Johnny couldn't think of anything to talk about. But there didn't seem to be much need for conversation. Hugh appeared content to look curiously around him at this part of the city.

Johnny Rossi stole a glance at his companion. Hugh was slightly taller than he was, with rangy arms and legs. His hair was sandy and straight, and his looks were what Johnny enviously thought of as "American." Johnny thought a little bitterly that if he had looked like that himself he would never have had to face the taunts of the other boys when he first came to school. The color rose in his face when he remembered the jeering shouts of "Wop" and "Hey, Spaghet!" that had greeted him during the first days of the term. No one called him that any more. He had been accepted at last, but it had cost him several scuffles and torn shirts.

He didn't know very much about Hugh Lathrop. None of the boys in their class did. But then, Hugh was very quiet and kept to himself. It was as though he was waiting to see which of his classmates he really wanted for friends. He had only been in their school for a week. All Johnny knew was that Hugh's family had just moved to New York from somewhere in Vermont.

"He's just a stuck-up Narrowback, like all those New Englanders," Buddy O'Connor had said the first day.

And from then on all the other boys had referred to the newcomer as the Narrowback. If Hugh had noticed, he did not seem to mind. Finally Buddy had called him that to his face, but instead of making an issue of it and fighting it out, Hugh had simply turned a slow, amused grin toward Buddy; which strangely enough had earned him a certain respect. That had been one of the things that made Johnny decide that he would like to get to know this new boy better.

But now, with Hugh beside him, Johnny felt an odd constraint. How could they ever be friends, Johnny thought, with things the way they were? Hugh came from a real American home. He really belonged here, whereas Johnny could still remember, although only vaguely, the big ship on which he had crossed the ocean with his parents when he was a very small boy.

They had been trudging steadily along. The streets were more crowded now and full of cheerful noises. People stood on the steps of the building, calling out to each other. The shopwindows displayed food that to Hugh's American eyes must seem strange and outlandish. Women sat leaning on cushions at the open windows of their tenement apartments, enjoying the warm spring air and calling down to their friends in the street from time to time in a foreign language.

Hugh peered at everything. "What do you call this part of town?" he asked at last.

Johnny darted a quick glance at Hugh's face. Then he lowered his eyes. In a low voice he replied, "They call it 'Little Italy.'"

He was sure that Hugh lived in one of the blocks on the other side of the school where the buildings were all well kept and immaculate, where no one sat at the windows, where there were no shouting peddlers, and where most of the apartment houses actually had doormen in uniform.

And then suddenly from overhead there was a familiar voice, calling "Giovanni! Giovanni!"

It was his mother.

How many times had he begged her to call him Johnny, in the American way!

"That's my mother," he muttered to Hugh. Then reluctantly he looked up.

Mrs. Rossi was smiling down at them from the kitchen window. "Giovanni," she called, "you bring your friend upstairs for some milk and *biscotti.*"

Giovanni! he thought savagely; that name! All he needed was to have one boy know about it, and it would be all over school, and he wouldn't have any peace.

He turned to Hugh and said helplessly, "Would you like to come upstairs?"

He hoped that Hugh would have sense enough to refuse and go off home to the apartment house where he lived with his parents who spoke English all the time.

But Hugh only smiled and said, "Sure, I'd like to very much."

And now, Johnny thought, the Narrowback would look at everything in a patronizing way. He would say to himself that the Rossis were only foreigners. Johnny asked himself between clenched teeth why people like Hugh Lathrop couldn't stay in New England where they belonged.

They climbed the shabby stairs. With each step Johnny wished that Hugh would think of some reason for turning back, some important errand that he had to do before he went home. And then they were at the door and Mrs. Rossi was there waiting to let them in, a smile of welcome on her face.

But after they had entered the apartment Hugh seemed full of eager interest as Mrs. Rossi showed him all the things she had brought with her from Italy. "He's not interested in all that stuff, Mamma," Johnny kept saying.

"Be quiet, Giovanni," she replied. "Of course he is interested."

And then Hugh came to the Madonna framed in gold that Johnny passed a hundred times a day without really looking at it. Hugh cried out, "Gosh, Mrs. Rossi, we have this picture home too. My mother bought it in Italy when she was a girl. It's her favorite picture."

Mrs. Rossi's dark eyes shone. "That Madonna comes from my city," she said. "When you go to Italy you will see for yourself how beautiful she is!"

Then they had their milk, with crunchy biscuits that tasted faintly of licorice. After that Johnny sat open-mouthed, listening to his mother tell stories about her childhood in Italy; stories he had never heard before. Sometimes he would break in saying, "But I don't remember that, Mamma." And she would shake her head and say, "Ah, *poveretto*, you were so small when we left, how could you remember? But one day I will take you back and you will see for yourself with the eyes of a grown boy, and you will understand how beautiful it is in my city."

Johnny was amazed, too, that Hugh didn't mind his mother's broken English. Whenever she finished one story he would ask for another. At last it was time for Hugh to go.

"I'll walk you downstairs," Johnny said.

"You come for supper next time, Ugo," Mrs. Rossi said. "I'll make spaghetti with a sauce that I cook for at least five hours! And you will meet Giovanni's papa. Maybe, if he feels good, he will play his violin."

When they reached the street, Hugh said, "Gosh, I envy you!"

Johnny looked blank. "Envy me?"

Hugh nodded. "It must be wonderful," he said in a thoughtful voice, "to have two countries to belong to! Well, see you tomorrow at school, Giovanni!"

Johnny Rossi hardly heard the sounds of Little Italy all around him. The sound of his own name was ringing in his ears. Giovanni sounded fine.

As for calling Hugh Lathrop a Narrowback, he'd settle that with Buddy O'Connor as soon as he got to school in the morning.

The Grandest Hero

WILLIAM MACKELLAR

Duncan watched his grandfather as he sat motionless in his chair by the window. It wasn't fair, the boy thought wearily, it just wasn't fair.

The old man stirred and his pale blue eyes fastened on his grandson, who stood by the coal bunker next to the fireplace.

"Let's see now, the King's Birthday Parade will be tomorrow?"

As though he doesn't know as well as I, thought Duncan. Aloud he said, "Aye, tomorrow."

The old man nodded. "And the grandstands will be up by the Green?"

"Aye," Duncan said again, "and they've hung the flags and banners." He had a horrible feeling he was going to cry, and hurriedly crossed and placed himself behind his grandfather's chair.

52

"It would be grand to be there," the old man said wistfully. "It's been a long time since I was able to get oot and see one. To hear again the wild skirl o' the bagpipes, and to see the brave Scots laddies marching, and the bonnie kilts swinging . . ." He swallowed, and the words stopped, but not before Duncan had noted the sadness and the loneliness.

I must do something, he thought. I must, I must. The words squirmed and turned in Duncan's mind in a dull, gray confusion, so that it was hard for him to think at all. He's got to see the parade tomorrow, but how? How?

Suddenly Duncan's heart skipped a beat. The idea was so fantastic, and yet . . . and yet . . .

"I've got it!" he cried, whirling around in the chair and facing his grandfather. "A motorcar!"

The old man stared in amazement at the boy. "A motorcar?" he repeated slowly. "What for?"

Duncan cut in, his voice tense with emotion. "I'll go doon to the village and see Sandy MacPhail. He's the Chairman o' the King's Birthday Parade. And I'll say to him, 'Mister MacPhail, a motorcar if ye please for my grandfather, ex-sergeant Jock Thompson of the 42nd Highlanders. A soldier of the King for forty years from India to Africa, and him crippled now and canna see the parade unless ye get a car for him.'"

"Ye've gone daft, Duncan," snapped the old man angrily. "Plain daft. A motorcar, indeed. Dinna ye understand there's nobody in the village got one, and even if someone had, would they be likely to lend it to the likes o' me on the King's birthday?"

"Aye, they would," cried Duncan fiercely, "for ye're the grandest hero in the Highlands, that's why."

"Tosh, tosh," grumbled the old man, waving his arm impatiently in the air. "The world's full o' heroes these days."

"Aye, but there's none like ye, and if ye'll be excusing me, I'll be on my way to Mister Sandy MacPhail." Putting an old Balmoral tam over his brown hair, Duncan set off on the three-mile hike to the village and the home of Mister Sandy MacPhail himself.

The Chairman of the King's Birthday Parade gazed uneasily for the third time that afternoon at the boy who sat so determinedly in the chair across the kitchen from him. Duncan knew Mister MacPhail's reputation as a very cautious man, and he waited while the Chairman coughed and cleared his throat.

"I dinna know what to tell ye, lad," he muttered not unkindly. "It's myself would like to help ye and poor Jock Thompson, but a motorcar . . ." He shuddered and closed his eyes.

"He canna see the parade if ye don't get one," Duncan pointed out. "I told him ye would, and surely ye wouldna be letting him doon, him the grandest hero in the Highlands, and it the King's birthday?"

In the face of this devastating logic Mister MacPhail puffed his red cheeks in embarrassment and carefully tugged at his right ear. Finally he sighed and looked unhappily over Duncan's head at the bare kitchen wall.

"Duncan, we're poor people here in Bridie," he began gently, "and we've no motorcars, and so I'm thinking that old Jock Thompson will no be seeing the parade." His eyes clouded and he patted Duncan awkwardly on the shoulder. "I'm sorry, lad," he said gruffly. "Right sorry."

There was a numbness deep in Duncan's stomach as he turned to go. In some mysterious way all the brightness seemed suddenly to have seeped out of the world, and only the room was real; only this and the grave, deliberate face of Mister MacPhail.

With unseeing eyes Duncan followed his hand as it groped for the doorknob. His fingers found the cold metal, and then the door was open and the heavy scent of freshly cut grass from the garden was in the room. He must have stood there, unthinking, for a few moments before he was suddenly aware that Mister MacPhail had been speaking.

". . . and I'll do my best, Duncan. More than that no man can do."

Duncan spun around. His eyes were wide with wonder.

"Ye'll do what, Mister MacPhail?"

"I said I'll do my best to arrange for the renting of the motorcar in one of the nearby towns. It'll not be easy though, for few cars there are for hire, and on the holiday tomorrow the demand is sure to be considerable. But I'll do my best, Duncan, that I will."

Duncan stared at him, his eyes bright in the corners

where the tears were. He wanted to laugh and sing with the great happiness that filled him. As for the Chairman of the King's Birthday Parade, he shifted uneasily from foot to foot as though suddenly aware that he had said something which should have required additional thought. He opened his mouth, but before he could speak Duncan poured out his thanks and rushed off to tell his grandfather.

The old soldier stared at his grandson in amazement after the boy had burst into the room and poured out his story.

"Say that again, Duncan, a wee bit slower," said the old man.

Duncan desperately tried to curb the excitement that made the words stumble over each other. He took a deep, deep breath and began again.

"I said Mister MacPhail's hiring a motorcar so ye can go down and see the parade tomorrow." He paused dramatically to let the full importance of the message sink in.

Almost a full minute passed before Jock Thompson spoke.

"A motorcar?" he murmured wonderingly. "For me?" He was silent while he studied his grandson from under brows heavy with white.

"Ye would not be mocking me, Duncan?" he said sharply.

Duncan grinned. It was fine, this bringing good news. "Why, it is the Chairman of the King's Birthday Parade himself who is hiring the car," he said. "He just had to when I told him how ye are the grandest hero in the Highlands—"

"Ye didna say that, Duncan?" The old man looked stern, but Duncan could tell by the way his lips twitched that secretly he was pleased.

"Aye, I did," Duncan said proudly. "I told him that a hero like yerself just had to hear the pipes again, and Mister MacPhail, he agreed."

For the first time a look of hope stole into the old veteran's eyes. Slowly his shoulders lifted, his back straightened, and then suddenly with a quick tilt of his head he was sitting erect, bold and proud and handsome, in his chair.

The words came slowly to the old man's lips but they rang out clearly in the kitchen. "Thank ye, Duncan. Thank ye kindly."

A hot flush of pleasure stained Duncan's face. Aye, it was fine, this bringing good news.

The next morning when Duncan arose, the mist from the hills was thick around the cottage, but he knew that soon the wind would be stirring to brush the swirling eddies of fog into the shallow places, and then the sun would shine and make the flat rocks warm against his hand. Truly it was going to be a glorious day for the parade!

When Duncan had finished his chores in the village he rushed to take a final look at the gaily decorated reviewing stand by the Green. The lampposts were bright with the Union Jack and the ancient blue-and-white St. Andrew's Cross of Scotland. The chairs had been carefully arranged for the reviewing officials, and a large bowl of ripe black grapes had been placed beside a huge pitcher of water. In his mind's eye Duncan could see old Jock Thompson sitting stiffly at attention, popping grapes into his mouth, pausing delicately now and then to bring a glass of water to his lips. Somehow the idea was so ridiculous that Duncan giggled helplessly all the way home.

He had hardly opened the door of the cottage when he stopped, amazed at the sight that met his eyes. A gay Glengarry bonnet was cocked at a jaunty angle on his grandfather's head. Around his body and held at the shoulder by a huge Cairngorm brooch was flung a green-and-black tartan plaid, while a pair of handsome silver-buckled shoes encased his feet. On his chest was a row of bright-colored ribbons, and the medals pinned on his dark velvet jacket winked and glistened in the sunlight that poured through the window.

"How do I look, Duncan? No so bad?"

The old man tried to sound matter-of-fact, but there was an anxious catch in his voice.

"Ye look grand," whispered Duncan, his heart nigh breaking with pride.

His grandfather nodded, pleased. "What time will it be now, Duncan?"

The boy turned and glanced at the clock. "Eleven," said he. "They should be here soon with the motorcar."

The old soldier nodded again, and his fingers wandered to the ribbons on his chest. "A grand day for it," he said.

"A grand day, indeed," Duncan replied. He was too excited to eat the broth and the thick scones and marmalade on the table, too excited for anything except to rush to the window every half minute to see if the car was coming along the country road that wound past their cottage.

Slowly the minutes ticked away, and Duncan found himself watching the big broad hand on the clock as it doggedly chased and finally passed the slim hour hand. For the last thirty minutes Duncan had not spoken, or had his grandfather. They sat very silent and waited, and the ticking of the clock grew louder and ever louder in Duncan's ears.

When he heard the solitary boom that told that one o'clock was here and gone, the last faint flicker of hope died in his heart. The parade had started at twelve, and there wasn't going to be any motorcar for old Jock Thompson, or any parade either.

It's all my fault, thought Duncan miserably. I should never have led him to believe he would see the parade, and now look at him sitting there in all his fine clothes.

Suddenly the old man looked up, startled, and his knuckles whitened where his gaunt fingers clung to his chair. "Did ye hear that, Duncan?" he whispered.

Duncan listened, but no sound came to his ears, and he shook his head.

Jock Thompson sighed. "For a minute I thought it was . . ." He stiffened and held up his hand. "Did ye hear it?" he said in a hushed voice.

Wonderingly, Duncan stood and listened. Then far

away, faint but quite clear, rising and falling in a thin wail of triumph, came the unmistakable sound of bag-pipes.

"It's the pipes," he said in an awed voice, and his grandfather nodded and there was a quiet glory in his eyes.

In a daze Duncan found himself standing by the window. Nearer and nearer came the insistent throb of the drums and the shrill screech of the pipes. And then suddenly around the turn of the little country road that ran past the cottage burst a sight that took Duncan's breath away. It was beyond his dreams.

Gallant in bright Highland costume, their sporrans swinging rhythmically and their white spats gleaming, swept the biggest pipe band Duncan had ever seen. Behind them in perfect formation came a company of the 42nd Highlanders, stiff-armed and proud, and the pleats in their dark kilts were as one as they marched.

After that came a fife band and then another pipe band, and finally around the corner marched all the im-portant people of the community: the Lord Provost and the Town Clerk and the Rector, and why—there was Sandy MacPhail himself! He was waving a red Balmoral tam, and on his usually sober face there was a grin from ear to ear.

How Jock Thompson got to his feet Duncan never did know. He had never seen him stand unaided as long as he could remember. But there he was, straight as a poker, and when the soldiers swept past and the captain snapped the order "Eyes right" he brought his hand up stiffly in the familiar open-palm salute, and there was a look in his eyes that Duncan had never seen.

"Imagine having a parade all to ourselves," he whispered a moment later, "and making a reviewing stand o' this hoose. I just canna believe it."

Duncan looked at him proudly. "It's because we've got the grandest Hero in the Highlands in this very same hoose, that's why."

The villagers were churning past now and cheering gaily as they came abreast of the open window.

"The grandest hero indeed," Jock Thompson said gently, looking down at his grandson, and Duncan thought for a moment that the old soldier was going to cry. Then he smiled and Duncan smiled too.

Danger on the Docks

FLORENCE BRUMBAUGH

Mark loved the busy East River. Almost every day he would run down to the docks after school and watch the boats loading and unloading. His favorite dock was the one where the banana boats were tied up, for often the sailors would show him monkeys or bright-colored parrots that they had brought back from South America. They had many stories to tell the small boy, and Mark's round brown eyes almost popped out of his face as he listened.

Jack, one of the sailors, showed Mark an ugly-looking spider. "It's a tarantula," he said. "You won't see one of these very often. But sometimes a tarantula hides when the bananas are being picked and it isn't found, even though the bananas are looked over carefully before they are loaded."

Mark shivered as he looked at the spider. Legs and all, it was as large as his hand.

"I'm glad that you have it in that big bottle," he said. "Why don't you kill it?"

"I'm taking it to a man who asked me to bring him one," answered Jack. "He's trying to find a cure for the tarantula's bite."

Mark ran away to the playground to tell some of his friends to come to the dock to see the big spider. The girls did not want to come, but some of the boys returned with him. Mark looked for the sailor and his bottle, but he had left the ship for a few hours. So the boys climbed around for a while over the coils of rope and the boxes and crates on the dock.

It began to get dark. One of the boys said, "I can't wait any longer, Mark. It's time for supper." And he ran off toward his home. One by one the others left until Mark was alone.

Maybe Jack will come soon, he said to himself. I'd like to look at that tarantula again before he takes it away. He sat down on a coil of rope to wait for the sailor.

Street lights began to come on. The skyscrapers looked like castles in the air with their windows alight, high up in the sky. Boats began to go down the river, with green and red lights that seemed to float like balloons on the masts. Mark forgot all about Jack and walked to the end of the dock. The other part of the city across the river looked very close, although he knew it really wasn't.

"I guess I might as well go home." He sighed.

63

"Mother will be home from work now and have my supper ready."

He started down the dock, but suddenly stopped when he came near one of the crates. The street light was shining on it, and there on top was a tarantula. Mark started to run. He looked for a policeman, but no one was in sight. He turned and looked back. The tarantula had not moved.

That spider might drop down inside the crate, thought Mark. No one would find it until the crate was opened. Then it might bite somebody.

Mark ran a little farther. Still he could see no one to call to for help. He stopped and tried to think what he should do. He was puzzled. I'm too little to catch a tarantula, he said to himself.

Slowly he walked back to the box, almost hoping that the spider would be gone. But no, it was still there. It looked as ugly as before.

Mark glanced down at his feet. His sneakers were old and had holes in them. He did not dare step on the tarantula.

Sailor Jack had his tarantula in a big bottle, he thought. Mark looked around for a bottle, but he could not find any. At last he found a tin can. It had no lid.

I'll put the can over the spider, he thought. Then it can't get away.

Mark's hand shook, but he dropped the tin can over the tarantula. Then he waited. The can began to move.

What shall I do now? thought Mark. There seemed to be only one thing to do, and Mark made up his mind to do it. He climbed up on the crate and put his hand down hard on the can. Then he sat there holding it. He grew very tired, but he did not move except to wiggle his feet when they went to sleep.

Won't anybody ever come? he wondered. He was tired and lonely. Soon he began to feel sleepy.

I wish I had something to eat, he said to himself. He felt in his pocket with the other hand and found one small piece of chocolate candy. It looked a little dirty, but Mark was so hungry that he did not care about that.

The clock struck again and then again while he sat there. It was getting very late. Just as he thought he would have to go to sleep or get off the crate he heard voices.

"Tim! Tim!" he shouted at the top of his voice. A big policeman came in sight, followed by two of the boys who had been on the dock with Mark that afternoon. The boys shouted with joy when they saw him.

"We thought you must have fallen off the dock or something!" they said.

"Your mother is looking everywhere for you," said Tim. "Now aren't you a bad one to be scaring her like that! Come on down, you little nuisance." Tim's words were cross, but he looked as happy as the boys, for Mark was a friend of his.

"I can't, Tim," answered Mark. "I'm keeping a tarantula from biting people."

The policeman looked sharply at Mark. "And did you

go crazy, sitting here by yourself? Come on now, and get to bed."

But Mark shook his head and would not move until Tim put his hand on the can. Then Mark gladly got off the box and stretched his poor tired legs.

Tim lifted the can a little and looked under it carefully. "Why, you little hero!" he said in surprise. "You're right!" He blew his whistle and another policeman came quickly.

"Go and get a bottle to put this horrid-looking creature in," he said. "We'll show it to the men at the station house. Mark, you're brave enough to be a policeman! How would you like to be a policeman when you grow up?"

But Mark was not there. He was running home as fast as he could, with the other boys following close behind.

Best Friend

GLADYS R. SAXON

Judy Wong heard her mother call from the kitchen but she pretended to be asleep. Two or three minutes later she heard her big brother Tom call her. Again she did not answer.

I don't care if I am late for school, she thought crossly. I won't find a best friend this week any more than I did last week. I hate this new town. I hate school. I. . . .

Now from the kitchen came a deeper, sterner voice. "Judy Wong, get up immediately."

Quickly Judy got out of bed. Quickly she washed and dressed.

When Papa spoke in that tone everybody did exactly what he said. Even the men at the Missile Lab where he now worked did what he said. Judy had noticed that when she visited on Open House Day.

How proudly she had watched her father explain

about the huge wind tunnels to all the visitors! Tom
had been proud, too, but of course he had understood
what Papa was saying. He wanted to be an electronics
engineer, and already knew a lot about such things.

Judy sat at the breakfast table half expecting a scolding. Fortunately, though, her father and Tom were deep
in talk about "re-entry problems" and "blunt nose versus
sharp nose." And her mother was busy at the stove.

"Please hurry, Judy," her mother said, putting a plate
of eggs and toast before her. "My gardening class is
today, you know. Mrs. Rodgers is to pick me up at
eight."

Judy began to eat. Her mother turned to the little
row of African violets at the window table. Judy watched
almost jealously as her mother touched them ever so
gently. As gently as she had held them all the way down
the Peninsula from San Francisco on the day they
moved. Was that only two weeks ago?

"Mama," said Judy. "I wish you would call me Mei
Lon [Beautiful Flower] as you used to. As everybody used to."

It was Papa who answered. "In Chinatown we lived
like Chinese-Americans," he said. "Here in Sunnyvale
we will live like all Americans—but we will not forget to
be proud of our Chinese ancestry."

Tom laughed as he got up from the table. "All-Ameri-
cans! Wouldn't I like to be one of them!"

His father laughed, too, and got up. What was
funny about *that?* Judy wondered, but nobody ex-

plained. Papa and Tom just hurried off—Tom to school, Papa to the Lab.

A few moments later a car honked. Judy's mother gave her a hasty kiss and a final, "Do hurry, Judy." Then *she* hurried out of the house.

Judy stopped eating. Everybody had things to hurry off to. Everybody had nice, interesting things to do and people to do them with. Everybody else, that is.

She began to clear the table. If only I could talk with Grandmother Yee, she thought. And see all my friends again.

In her mind's eye she saw Grandmother Yee's third-floor flat in the old brick building just off Grant Avenue. She imagined herself sitting again on the balcony to watch the funny cable cars clanging up the steep hill and down. She heard the firecrackers and the Chinese band and noisy crowd at the Chinese New Year's parade. It would soon be time for that parade again. She wouldn't see it though. For the first time in her life she wouldn't see it.

From the schoolyard two blocks away Judy heard the first warning bell. She plunged the dishes into the soapy water, rinsed them, and left them in the rack to drain dry. Dashing into the bedroom, she gave her shining black hair a stroke or two of the brush. She put her red barrettes in her sweater pocket, to fix on the way to school.

The warm January sun perked up her spirits as she walked. Maybe, just maybe, she would find a best friend this week. Why, there must be more than one Chinese family moving down from San Francisco to work in electronics or in a flower nursery or in a restaurant, or to be a doctor or a lawyer or something!

Couldn't it be that one girl, just one girl, might be in the fifth grade and therefore in her room?

Along the way, children smiled at Judy or said "Hi!" Judy smiled back but she did not feel equal to talking to them. She did not know how to talk to American boys and girls. She had never really met one before last week. Oh, she had seen them in the curio shops and restaurants of Chinatown, but she did not know what they were like. Did they live in their homes like Chinese families? Did they eat the same foods? Did they talk about the same things?

There *was* a new girl in her class. But she was a very tall blond girl with bright blue eyes. And she had such a strange name—Birdie Watson.

"Birdie," said Miss Parr, the teacher. "Won't you come up here and tell us a little about yourself?"

Judy saw Birdie's fair skin become as pink as a chrysanthemum on a Chinese robe. She saw Birdie's skirt catch as she twisted to get out of her chair. A button fell off the skirt and rolled, rolled, rolled, down the aisle. She saw Birdie put her hands over her face. She heard some of the children giggle.

Judy knew exactly how the new girl felt. Almost without realizing it, she got out of her own seat and went to the front of the room. "I will tell about myself," she said to Miss Parr.

Miss Parr smiled. "Thank you, Judy. We have been wanting you to do that ever since you came. Haven't we, class?"

"Yes," they answered in chorus.

"Before I came here," Judy said proudly, "I lived in San Francisco, in the part that people call Chinatown because so many Chinese people live there. Oh, it was so nice there! On Saturdays my best friends and I would go in and out of the stores looking at the ivory animals and the silk clothes and buying melon rind or ginger to eat. Then we might take the cable car to Fisherman's Wharf, or maybe . . ."

Suddenly Judy stopped. Her lips began to tremble and she couldn't think of another word to say. She went back to her chair.

Smiling, Miss Parr said, "Thank you again, Judy. And do you know? You have given me a wonderful idea, something we all might plan to do together. Can you guess what I mean?"

Judy's breath quickened. What could Miss Parr mean? . . . could she possibly mean the Chinese New Year's Day parade and everything? All during the reading and arithmetic classes she hugged the thought. How wonderful that would be!

At recess she hoped Miss Parr might speak to her, but she did not. So Judy sat at the outdoor tables as usual and began to eat her apple and read her book.

By looking busy like that she didn't feel so bad when the boys and girls chose up sides and played games. It was no fun being chosen last because she was new and had no best friend to do things with.

Today was different, though. Today some of the children ran up to her and teased to know what Miss Parr had meant. Judy decided not to guess out loud. Maybe that *wasn't* what Miss Parr had meant!

It was Birdie who stayed at the table when the others left. "Miss Parr helped me sew on that mean old button," said Birdie.

"That's nice," said Judy.

"Say, thank you for talking instead of me," Birdie went on. "I always get so fussed when everybody sits there and looks at me."

Judy closed the book. It was much nicer to talk than to pretend to read. "So do I," she said with a half smile.

"We came here from Texas," said Birdie. "My daddy is going to drive a bus here. What does your daddy do?"

Judy told her, then said thoughtfully, "If Miss Parr's idea . . . if my idea is the same . . . if your father . . ."

"Tell me, tell me," begged Birdie. "What is the idea?"

Judy shook her head. "I'd better not guess, but we could ask Miss Parr. There she is at the door. Come with me, Birdie."

Quickly the two girls went over to Miss Parr. Judy told her about Birdie's father. "Did you mean the whole class might go to the New Year's Parade?" she asked shyly. "I could get my friends to reserve us really good seats, and we could have supper at my Grandfather

Yee's restaurant, and . . . maybe Birdie's father could take us in his bus, Miss Parr."

Miss Parr stopped Judy's eager planning. "Let's keep it a secret for the present, Judy," she said. "You can bring it up at the next class meeting."

Judy and Birdie lined up with the rest of the class when the recess bell rang. For the first time in this new school she felt at home. Why, Birdie was no different really than Linda Sun. Linda had hated to recite too. And Linda had liked to ask questions one after the other.

That afternoon Judy stopped at Birdie's house on the way home from school. Birdie's mother did exactly what her own mother did—reminded Birdie to change out of her school dress and straighten up her room. Birdie's big sister teased Birdie just as Tom teased her. And Birdie's father, although he was tall and broad and very blond and spoke like a Texas cowboy, ruffled up Birdie's hair the way her own father did hers.

Then the girls went to Judy's house. It was Birdie's turn to be surprised. "I always wondered what a Chinese house was like inside," she said, "but it is practically no different, except it's prettier—at least it's prettier than ours, anyway."

"I think yours is pretty," said Judy politely. Then she said to her mother, who was busy getting supper ready, "Birdie and I are going to be best friends, and do you know what else? Birdie and I and Miss Parr have a big secret, and we can't tell anyone until I present it at the next class meeting. Can we, Birdie?"

Judy's mother smiled. "Welcome to Sunnyvale, my daughter," she said. "Or should I call you Mei Lon?"

Judy did not need to answer in words. She knew that her mother understood. She only said, "Would you like to see my collection of Chinese animals, Birdie? They are all made of ivory and hand carved. There isn't one any bigger than your little finger."

The Attack

ELIZABETH COATSWORTH

Abigail, stopping at the window on her way to the pantry, saw the colt come tearing across the meadow, scattering flying clouds of new turf behind him. It was a fine spring day with a southwest wind and hurrying clouds and a smell of the budding woods beyond the clearings, and Abigail smiled at the little horse's frolicsomeness. But a moment later she frowned. Jenny, the old mare, had appeared at a more ponderous gallop and was wheeling and stamping by the gate.

"Something has disturbed the horses, sir," she said, turning to her father. "Do come and see."

Mr. King moved from the fire to the window and chuckled as he watched Jenny and her colt. He pinched his daughter's cheeks.

"It's the fine gaiety of spring, my child," he said.

75

"Something has disturbed the robins. Hear how they are singing in your mother's lilac bush."

Mrs. King, who had been clearing away the bowls and pewter from the table, hesitated and then spoke.

"You don't think it could be savages, Enoch?"

"The crows have all flown up," said Abigail quickly from her place by the window. Her face was grave.

"You women dream of savages," he said. "If you hear a mouse in the wall it's a savage; if a bullfrog croaks it's a war cry to you. There's no trouble with the tribes—and here is the Prebles' garrison house a stone's throw from our back door. You're as safe as if you were living in Pemaquid Fort."

Mrs. King went softly on with the dishes, and Abigail said nothing more. Her father was one of those large good-natured men who laugh a great deal but who are quickly made angry by any argument.

Abigail slipped out to the woodpile where her brother was splitting firewood.

"John," she said, "something's wrong. The horses are wild, and the crows are flying up. Father says it's high-spiritedness, but the sheep are huddling too. That's not high spirits."

John gave a hasty look, spit on his hands, and went on splitting wood.

"You and Mother are a couple of scare-cats," he said. "Sheep are always huddling about something or other. You don't catch Aunt Phipps worrying over nothing."

John was only fourteen, a year younger than Abigail,

but lately he had taken to aping his father's hearty ways. Aunt Mary Phipps, Mr. King's widowed sister who lived with them, was the same. She had three little children, Eunice and Samson and Lydia, all round-headed and round-eyed and casual. Even down to fat, dimpling Lydia they seemed to go deaf if anyone tried to tell them that they were doing a thing the wrong way.

It might have been a fox, thought Abigail. There is no reasonable reason for my feeling so sure that savages are near.

But all day long she went about her work, more silent than usual, and seemed to be listening for something. Her father and Aunt Phipps, young John and the children, were busy and boisterous all day, but her mother looked tired and anxious.

The other member of the household to seem disturbed was Mittens, the cat, a big gray tom who followed the family about like a dog and would even walk a mile or two with them. This day he mewed about people's feet and seemed unable to keep still, moving from one favorite spot to another.

In the evening while Mrs. King was spinning by the fire and Aunt Phipps and Abigail knitted on the settle, and the little children played a game of Fox and Geese with red and yellow kernels of corn on a square they had marked on the floor with charcoal, and Mr. King and John smoked their pipes, the talk came around to the tawnies.

Aunt Phipps said with a chuckle to her sister-in-law,

"Sister King, your new quilted pelisse will be handy if Abigail's savages take you off to Canada. And I shall wear my red coat."

Mr. King and John laughed, but Mrs. King said, with sudden vehemence, "I pray that God will let me die at their hands before He allows me or mine to be carried away!"

"I was but teasing you," said her sister-in-law, with a touch of annoyance. "Pray you, do not fly off with so much earnestness."

Mittens mewed at Abigail's feet and jumped into her lap. She rubbed his head and ears, but he would not purr. Soon he had jumped off again and recommenced his prowling. She was wondering if she, too, would rather be tomahawked than taken. She had heard such dreadful accounts of the journey to the Indian towns on the St. Lawrence, of death and torture by the way. But some had come back full of praise of the French and even of the Indians. Old Benjamin Glazier, who had been their prisoner for three years, said he preferred tawnies to white people. But then, he was a cross-grained old man fond of taking the opposite side of any and every discussion.

Abigail, in her little room at the head of the stairs, slept all night long, tired out with her anxiety. Once she awoke to feel Mittens jump on her bed, a thing he rarely had done before, but she was soon asleep again. In the morning, however, she was disturbed by finding several footprints in the soft earth under the windows. Aunt

Phipps, her arms full of the wet clothes she was bringing out to spread on the grass, came up to her as she stood examining the marks.

"Bless us, child!" she exclaimed. "You're still fretting over your savages. No, they don't look like moccasin tracks to me. But I did see young John there yesterday morning, cleaning up last year's rubbish. You take my advice, Abigail, and think of something else."

That morning her father announced that he meant to make use of the good weather and take some grain to the town to be ground and a couple of lambs to sell. John was to go with him, and they would not be back until late that night.

"But, Enoch—" began Mrs. King in her anxious voice.

"But nothing, Mary!" cried her husband. "Pluck up heart, my love! Look at Sister Phipps here. She's not afraid. There's no danger, or I shouldn't be leaving you, and that you well know. But if any more of Abigail's crows fly from one field to another you have only to run over to the Prebles' and you'll be perfectly safe at the garrison house."

"There's only the old man and Mr. Preble," ventured Mrs. King, but she stopped at her husband's angry look.

"You two will drive me mad with your whining," he exclaimed, shrugging his shoulders impatiently. "Come, wife, don't play the coward. Give me a cheerful fare-ye-well and no more nonsense."

An hour after Mr. King and John had ridden away the Indians came. They had evidently been watching

from the woods and waited only until the two were well out of hearing of gunshots. There were five of them, their faces streaked and splashed with bright blue, naked except for their breechclouts, but each with a good French gun over his arm. They separated and approached the house from different sides.

Aunt Phipps had time to snatch Eunice from the doorstep and bolt the door. Abigail ran to fasten the shed door and came back to find that her aunt had got the loaded gun down from the mantel.

"I'll fill those tawnies with lead," she was saying. "I never yet was afraid of any man, white or red!"

Abigail's mother snatched at the barrel.

"You must do nothing of the sort, Sister Phipps!" she said quickly and commandingly. "You could never hurt more than one, and they would kill all your children. They can knock a hole in this flimsy house in five minutes and fire through it. I'm going to let them in. It's our only chance."

"You've gone mad with fear!" cried Aunt Phipps, shouldering the lighter woman aside once more.

"Abigail!" said her mother, and Abigail snatched the gun unexpectedly from her aunt and stood with it behind her.

"Quick, Mary!" said her sister-in-law. "Take the babies and get into the kitchen closet. When I let them in, the way to the garrison house will be clear. While I am feeding them, Abigail and you are to get the children over the stockade and into the Prebles'."

"But they'll kill you, for certain, Sister King!" cried Aunt Phipps, wringing her hands.

"If they do, you and the children will still have a chance while they're at it," said Mrs. King.

There was a battering at the door.

"I'll stay with you, Mother," said Abigail. "It will look more natural. But you must promise to go first and help Aunt Phipps with the children. I shall never stir from here while you're in the house."

Her mother gave her a quick look, sighed, and nodded. Aunt Phipps and her brood were gone.

"Bring the rum and mugs, child," she said, and smoothing out her skirts, walked over to the door and opened it with a strained smile. Two savages rushed in, brandishing their tomahawks. At their yell the others ran from behind the house and poured in also.

"Rum," said Mrs. King, smiling still and pointing to the table where Abigail, her heart pounding in her throat, had brought out rum and mugs. As she turned her back she saw one of the savages snatch at the string of gold beads about her mother's neck. The chain that held them broke and the beads fell in a shower over the floor, several rolled about her feet, and at the same moment she heard the sharp slap of her mother's hand on the Indian's arm, but she walked steadily over to the cupboard and came back with a plate of johnnycake. When she turned she saw that the savages were laughing. They grabbed greedily at the bread and began eating it in large mouthfuls. They were hungry.

Her mother went into the next room and came back with a half-eaten leg of cold lamb which she set before them. As she went out again, for an instant her eyes met Abigail's to tell her that she was going to try to make her escape. She had been gone only a minute when one of the Indians made as if to follow her.

Abigail had an impulse to throw herself in front of the door. Instead, she climbed onto a chair to search the upper shelves of the cupboard beside the mantelpiece, smacking her lips. The Indians halted to watch her. She must take as much time as she could, but she must not lose their interest. She rummaged noisily, hoping to cover any creaking of floor boards or the gentle opening of a door. Just as she felt the Indian about to move again for the kitchen she brought down the keg of molasses which she knew was always kept there away from the children and, setting it on the table, brought five wooden plates on which she placed more johnnycake over which she poured the molasses, watched by five pairs of unwinking eyes. She was all alone in the house with the Indians, but by this time she was so excited that she had passed into a sort of calm in the middle of the storm.

"Eat!" she said, smiling as her mother had smiled, and gave each a plate into which they dipped their hands greedily, dripping and sticky.

They had never tasted the stuff before and were lost in the pleasure of the moment. The room reeked with the odor of rum and bear's grease. The girl brought them more corn bread and poured more molasses for them. Surely even heavy Aunt Phipps must be over the stockade fence by now. The black eyes glittered at her from the painted masks of the savages' faces. She could not tell whether they suspected her or not. She walked over to the fireplace and mended the fire. Three minutes more. At any moment they would be wondering what had delayed her mother, and then she would be lost. She took a platter from the dresser as though to bring in still more food and walked into the next room. A glance showed her that the cupboard door was open and the cupboard empty, though the outside door had been closed again, probably to avoid a telltale draught. It would be her mother who would think of that. She put down the platter, opened the door softly, and as she closed it felt something at her feet. It was Mittens, looking terrified. She caught up the cat. He should not be left to those devils if she could help it, and then gathering her skirts with her left hand to keep them from catching in the spring brambles, she ran toward the stockade fence a hundred yards away. She saw her mother's white face in an upper window of the garrison house, then she heard a shout behind her, caught her

foot in a bramble bush, and pitched headlong, flinging
Mittens forward as she fell. She was up in a moment,
stumbling over her skirts. She saw the Indians running
toward her. One was standing, leveling his gun. She ran
forward, ducked suddenly to pick up Mittens, heard a
shot ring over her where her head had been, and ran
on. She saw Mr. Preble's face appear over the stockade
wall.

"Quick, Abigail!" he shouted, reaching down for her.
She threw the clawing cat over the six-foot stockade,
held up her wrists, and in a moment felt herself being
dragged painfully up the rough side of the wall and
hauled to safety.

Once on the ground, Mr. Preble caught her about
the waist and ran toward the garrison house. Another
shot rang out behind them, answered by a shot from
one of the upstairs windows. The door flew open,
women's hands drew them into the semidarkness of the
room, and the door was bolted again.

"Oh, my love!" cried Mrs. King, seizing Abigail in her
arms. "I feared you would never come out of that house
alive."

"It's you two we have to thank for our lives," said
Aunt Phipps, red and serious. "I owe you an apology,
Sister King, for calling you a coward."

"But I *am* a coward," said Mrs. King, trembling and
smiling. "I must get back to making my bullets. You may
have your chance now, Sister Phipps, of shooting a
tawny."

Old Grandfather Preble appeared for a moment at
the head of the stairs.

"Got one, I think," he called. "They're going back into the house."

Abigail followed Mr. Preble up to the second story. Downstairs the shutters had all been closed, but here the light shone sweetly in upon the wide boards of the floor and the quilted covers of the feather beds. Swallows were flying back and forth across the sky, and beyond the pines she caught a curve of the river glistening in the sun.

Let them burn her father's house if they would. It was only flesh and blood that counted. She sat down on the floor, tired out but curiously peaceful.

Perhaps her father would take warning next time, but she knew that he would not. He would build another house, he would cut timber and haul it with oxen, he would take his lumber to the sawmill and raise a rooftree again; he would furnish and furbish; and her mother would spin and weave a new supply of linen and wool; and when all was done her father would forget that he had lost everything once through his own fault.

Perhaps John was young enough to have learned something from all this. No one would ever call her mother a coward again, at least.

Crows were wheeling black against the sky. Something had disturbed them. Yes, there were figures moving out along the lane toward the north. Two of them were carrying a wounded Indian on a litter made of the back of the settle; the other two were laden with the covers of the feather beds filled with loot.

"Mr. Preble!" she called. "The Indians are going!"

"I've been watching them," he said regretfully. "Too

far off to get a shot. Father, you stay here and fire off your gun if you see them turn, and Abigail and I will see if they've set the house on fire."

They found the King place in great confusion, everything pulled about and the feathers flying like snow. The fire had been hauled out onto the floor, but was only charring the stout boards: a couple of buckets of water from the well turned it to black soot and wet cinders. The Indians had taken all the food they could lay hands on, a few knives and ornaments, the gun which Abigail had snatched from Aunt Phipps's hands and rehung over the old mantelpiece.

"You have been fortunate," said Mr. Preble. "If only—"

Abigail understood. The Indians had been in hiding for at least a day before they made the attack; they had watched the family at supper through the windows; they had come, finally, when the women were defenseless. Now although they had seemed to go north, they might still be lying in wait somewhere for the return of Mr. King and John.

Abigail opened the door and looked out. The light was golden with the late afternoon, and two butterflies passed in zigzag flight. Beyond the fields and meadows the crows were beginning to roost, lighting in the tops of beeches and uttering their usual cries. Then a shape moved along the side of the house, and Mittens sat down solidly on the doorstep and began to smooth his ruffled coat with a white paw.

"No," said Abigail, laughing a little hysterically. "I'm sure Father and John are safe and the savages altogether gone. Mittens is washing his whiskers."

Albacore Ahead!

GLADYS R. SAXON

Johnnie Donesa made fast the wire screen of the last rabbit hutch. It was just past suppertime and the sun was making long shadows among the rows of vegetables in his grandfather's garden colony of San Diego.

There, that's done, he said to himself. Next week it's Mary's turn to feed them, and then Rosella's, and then I'll be back.

He walked through the grape arbor to the cage that held his own special pet, the green-and-yellow Mexican parrot that his big brother Joe had brought back from his last fishing trip.

"Say good-bye, Carmelita," he coaxed, reaching to pet her.

"Bye-bye-bye-bye," croaked Carmelita.

Johnny latched the door of the cage and picked his way carefully down the path to his grandfather. He squatted beside him and began to weed the Portuguese horse beans too.

"Well, Joao," said his grandfather, speaking in Portuguese. "Have you your sea bag ready?"

"*Sim*," Johnnie answered in the same language.

Minutes passed and the garden seemed to become a world of its own in the fading light. At last Johnnie found courage to ask the question that had been bothering him since his father had told him he was to go fishing on the *Mary Rosella* again, this time halfway down the coast of Mexico to the San Benito Islands.

"Grandfather, suppose . . . suppose . . . I shame *papai* before his crew?"

His grandfather grunted as he straightened up and looked at Johnnie. "Never has the family of Donesa owned a coward," he said sternly. "But think not that I do not understand," he went on. "I know how strong must be your memory of that other voyage."

Johnnie shivered, then tried to hide it. More than anything in the world he wanted to be a good fisherman like his grandfather used to be and like his father and Joe were now. But every time he thought about those long, cold minutes in the great heaving Pacific Ocean he felt terribly frightened.

Maybe this time they wouldn't be able to rescue him so quickly, he thought. Maybe this time the albacore would knock him overboard at night.

"Remember, my little Joao," his grandfather said gently, "to face fear is to kill it a little."

He patted Johnnie's shoulder. "Now go into the house. Your *papai* wants to cast off by nine."

Johnny ran into the house, picked up his sea bag, said good-bye to his three sisters and his baby brother. A moment later he followed his father and Joe into the car, his mother at the wheel.

Now they turned into Harbor Drive and in a few minutes were parked close to the *Mary Rosella* as she nosed gently against the wharf in her place among the hundred or so other fishing boats.

Quickly Johnnie said good-bye to his mother, and with fast-beating heart, jumped aboard. "*Ate a vista!*" he called back.

The crew of five had everything ready, and almost before Johnnie realized it the boat was moving quietly westward in the Bay of San Diego. The lights of San Diego and North Island grew smaller and smaller. Thirty minutes later they were passing Point Loma Lighthouse and heading due south into the Pacific Ocean.

Why, I'm not afraid at all, Johnnie said to himself. Grandfather was right.

Then he went into his father's cabin and was soon dreaming of rabbits and parrots that could swim and of fish that lived in cages.

Hardly had he fallen asleep, it seemed, than he heard his father calling. "Hit the deck, boy! There's work to be done!"

Quickly he pulled on his shoes and ran into the galley. How hungry the ocean air made him! He ate griddle-cakes and syrup until the cook got tired of making them.

ALBACORE AHEAD!

His father laughed. "Ah, Johnnie, he who eats must pay for eating, so into the galley with you. You're our official messboy and errand boy, you know."

Johnnie laughed, too, though a little wryly. But he felt so good and the day was so blue and the *Mary Rosella* was making her ten miles an hour so smoothly that he really didn't mind much.

When he had finished the dishes and the scrubbing he joined the crew at the stern and helped with the mending of the bait nets and with the rigging of the bamboo fishing poles with their feathered barbless hooks. And as he listened to the men talk of the wonderful albacore haul that was going to make them all rich he felt sure that fishing was the life for him. Some day he'd be the best *pescador* in San Diego!

During the next two days Johnnie did his own work quickly, then worked with Joe and the crew, or helped his father at the wheel, or climbed to the crow's nest. Now the *Mary Rosella* was cruising closer to the Mexican shore, looking for sardines or anchovies to use as chum to lure the albacore close enough to the boat to take the hooks.

On the afternoon of the second day, while the lookout was on deck for a rest, Johnnie searched the quiet waters around the islands more carefully than usual. Suddenly his binoculars picked up a mass of dark spots. Were they birds feeding? He looked more sharply.

Yes! That meant a school of anchovies maybe! *"Ola, BAIT!"* Johnnie shouted down to Joe. Joe called the men. The boat headed toward the birds.

Out came the bait net. Two men took the free end of

it with them into a skiff. Johnnie's father guided the *Mary Rosella* in a big circle around the school of little fish. The crew pulled the sagging net alongside. At top speed, with long-handled dip nets, everyone hurried to get the anchovies into the bait tanks before they injured themselves in the net. Johnnie knew why—knew that albacore wouldn't rise to any but live chum.

The bait tanks filled, the men were in high spirits. "Good bait tonight means many albacore *amanha*," said the chummer. "Maybe eighteen ton; fill the boat and get back soon to San Diego."

Johnnie was glad, too, and went to bed feeling happier than ever about the voyage. He fell asleep knowing he had done a little something for his father. Suddenly he was awakened by the pounding of feet and excited shouts.

"Albacore ahead!"

Johnnie began to shiver, all his old fear coming back. He pulled the blankets over him. He could imagine the bamboo poles jerking up and the lines and the feathery hooks flying as the men landed the twenty- or twenty-five-pound fish on deck. He felt again the cold water close over him. He couldn't face it again; he just couldn't, that's all!

After a time he grew calmer. He looked out of the cabin windows. The sun was almost up. I could make some coffee and sandwiches for the men, he thought, knowing that when a school of albacore is found even the cook becomes a fisherman. I can keep away from the racks.

He pulled on his sweater and boots and ran down into the galley. Soon he had a platter of food ready. He stood beneath the boom amidship and called to Joe, holding the food so Joe could see it.

Joe beckoned to him. Fearfully Johnnie edged to the near end of the bait tanks and shoved the platter within reach of the men. Then he went back to the safety of the boom.

"Good boy, Johnnie," called his father. "Now keep out of the way. We don't want you falling overboard again . . . we'd lose too much time fishing you up." He grinned as he said it, and Johnnie knew he was only joking.

By now the *Mary Rosella* was listing to starboard with the weight of the catch. The men standing in the racks were waist deep in the rough waves, but never once did they stop casting and bringing in the fish.

Johnnie watched Joe landing an especially big albacore. He saw the line break and the pole flip out into the water.

"Throw me down another, Johnnie," Joe yelled to him, pointing to the spare poles.

Johnnie picked up a strong-looking pole already rigged. He started toward Joe with it. Suddenly he realized what he was about to do. He stopped, grabbed the pipe that fed the bait tanks. His knees wobbled. He just couldn't go any closer to that dark, cold water.

"Hurry, Johnnie!" Joe shouted, turning to see why Johnnie was so slow.

Thus turned, Joe did not see the albacore bearing

93

down upon him as one of the men swung back his pole.

But Johnnie saw. He slid across the slanting deck and threw himself at the fish. That changed its direction but did not stop its speed. Down went Johnnie into the flopping, slimy fish piled high against the rail. Grasping blindly for something to hold onto, Johnnie slid over the fish, closer and closer to the racks. The cook saw him and caught him by the legs, stopping his slide.

Joe picked Johnnie up and helped him to the platform just above and out of reach of the poles. "*Obrigado*, Johnnie," he said, "guess you saved me from a swim in the Pacific. Are you all right?"

Johnnie looked down at his sweater and jeans, now smeared and scaly. He rubbed his bruised knees. "Yes, sure," he said.

Joe went back to his fishing. Johnnie gave a long, long sigh. I *am* all right, he said to himself. And I'm not afraid any more!

He saw his father looking at him. He saluted to show he was feeling fine. His father returned the salute, smiling proudly.

Somehow that salute was terribly important to Johnnie. All at once he felt older and happier. Suddenly there was no place he would rather be than right here on his father's boat learning to be a good fisherman like all the other men in the Donesa family.

He picked up the now empty coffee pot and platter and hurried into the galley to refill them.

Deep Water

LAURA INGALLS WILDER

Pa and Ma did not care how much the children played in the creek. Only they must never go upstream beyond the little willow valley. The creek came around a curve there. It came out of a hole full of deep, dark water. They must never go near enough to that hole even to see it.

"Someday I'll take you there," Pa promised them. And one Sunday afternoon he told them that this was the day.

In the dugout Laura and Mary took off all their clothes, and over their bare skins they put on old, patched dresses. Ma tied on her sunbonnet, Pa took Carrie on his arm, and they all set out.

They went past the cattle path and the rushes, past the willow valley and the plum thickets. They went down a steep, grassy bank and then across a level place where the grass was tall and coarse. They passed a high, almost straight-up wall of earth where no grass grew.

"What is that, Pa?" Laura asked.

And Pa said, "That is a tableland, Laura."

He pushed on through the thick, tall grass, making a path for Ma and Mary and Laura. Suddenly they came out of the high grass, and the creek was there.

It ran twinkling over white gravel into a wide pool curved against a low bank where the grass was short. Tall willows stood up on the other side of the pool. Flat on the water lay a shimmery picture of those willows with every green leaf fluttering.

Ma sat on the grassy bank and kept Carrie with her while Laura and Mary waded into the pool.

"Stay near the edge, girls!" Ma told them. "Don't go in where it's deep."

DEEP WATER

The water came up under their skirts and made them float. Then the calico got wet and stuck to their legs. Laura went in deeper and deeper. The water came up and up, almost to her waist. She squatted down, and it came to her chin.

Everything was watery, cool, and unsteady. Laura felt very light. Her feet were so light that they almost

lifted off the creek bottom. She hopped, and splashed with her arms.

"Oo, Laura, don't!" Mary cried.

"Don't go in any farther, Laura," said Ma.

Laura kept on splashing. One big splash lifted both feet. Her feet came up, her arms did as they pleased, her head went under the water. She was scared. There was nothing to hold onto, nothing solid anywhere. Then she was standing up, streaming water all over. But her feet were solid.

Nobody had seen that. Mary was tucking up her skirts, Ma was playing with Carrie. Pa was out of sight among the willows. Laura walked as fast as she could in the water. She stepped down deeper and deeper. The water came up past her middle, up to her arms.

Suddenly, deep down in the water, something grabbed her foot.

The thing jerked, and down she went into the deep water. She couldn't breathe, she couldn't see. She grabbed and could not get hold of anything. Water filled her ears and her eyes and her mouth.

Then her head came out of the water close to Pa's head. Pa was holding her.

"Well, young lady," Pa said, "you went out too far, and how did you like it?"

Laura could not speak; she had to breathe.

"You heard Ma tell you to stay close to the bank," said Pa. "Why didn't you obey her? You deserved a ducking, and I ducked you. Next time you'll do as you're told."

98

"Y-yes, Pa!" Laura spluttered. "Oh, Pa, p-please do it again!"

Pa said, "Well, I'll—!" Then his great laugh rang among the willows.

"Why didn't you holler when I ducked you?" he asked Laura. "Weren't you scared?"

"I w-was—awful scared!" Laura gasped. "But p-please do it again!" Then she asked him, "How did you get down there, Pa?"

Pa told her he had swum under the water from the willows. But they could not stay in the deep water; they must go near the bank and play with Mary.

All that afternoon Pa and Laura and Mary played in the water. They waded and they fought water fights, and whenever Laura or Mary went near the deep water Pa ducked them. Mary was a good girl after one ducking, but Laura was ducked many times.

Then it was almost choretime and they had to go home. They went dripping along the path through the tall grass, and when they came to the tableland Laura wanted to climb it.

Pa climbed part way up, and Laura and Mary climbed holding to his hands. The dry dirt slipped and slid. Tangled grass roots hung down from the bulging edge overhead. Then Pa lifted Laura up and set her on the tableland.

It really was like a table. That ground rose up high above the tall grasses, and it was round, and flat on top. The grass there was short and soft.

Pa and Laura and Mary stood up on top of that

tableland and looked all around at prairies stretching to the rim of the sky.

Then they had to slide down again to the lowland and go on home. That had been a wonderful afternoon.

"It's been lots of fun," Pa said. "But you girls remember what I tell you. Don't you ever go near that swimming hole unless I am with you."

All next day Laura remembered. She remembered the cool, deep water in the shade of the tall willows. She remembered that she must not go near it.

Pa was away. Mary stayed with Ma in the dugout. Laura played all alone in the hot sunshine. The blue flags were withering among the dull rushes. She went past the willow valley and played in the prairie grasses among the black-eyed Susans and goldenrod. The sunshine was very hot and the wind was scorching.

Then Laura thought of the tableland. She wanted to climb it again. She wondered if she could climb it all by herself. Pa had not said that she could not go to the tableland.

She ran down the steep bank and went across the lowland, through the tall, coarse grasses. The tableland stood up straight and high. It was very hard to climb. The dry earth slid under Laura's feet; her dress was dirty where her knees dug in while she held onto the grasses and pulled herself up. Dust itched on her sweaty skin. But at last she got her stomach on the edge; she heaved and rolled and she was on top of the tableland.

She jumped up and she could see the deep, shady

pool under the willows. It was cool and wet, and her whole skin felt thirsty. But she remembered that she must not go there.

The tableland seemed big and empty and not interesting. It had been exciting when Pa was there, but now it was just flat land, and Laura thought she would go home and get a drink. She was very thirsty.

She slid down the side of the tableland and slowly started back along the way she had come. Down among the tall grasses the air was smothery and very hot. The dugout was far away and Laura was terribly thirsty.

She remembered with all her might that she must not go near that deep, shady swimming pool, and suddenly she turned around and hurried toward it. She thought she would only look at it. Just looking at it would make her feel better. Then she thought she might wade in the edge of it but she would not go into the deep water.

She came into the path that Pa had made and she trotted faster.

Right in the middle of the path before her stood an animal.

Laura jumped back and stood and stared at it. She had never seen such an animal. It was almost as long as their dog Jack, but its legs were very short. Long gray fur bristled all over it. It had a flat head and small ears. Its flat head slowly tilted up and it stared at Laura.

She stared back at its funny face. And while they stood still and staring that animal widened and shortened and spread flat on the ground. It grew flatter and flatter till it was a gray fur laid there. It was not like a whole animal at all. Only it had eyes staring up.

Slowly and carefully Laura stooped and reached and picked up a willow stick. She felt better then. She stayed bent over, looking at that flat gray fur.

It did not move and neither did Laura. She wondered what would happen if she poked it. It might change to some other shape. She poked it gently with the short stick.

A frightful snarl came out of it. Its eyes sparkled madly, and its fierce white teeth snapped almost on Laura's nose.

Laura ran with all her might. She could run fast. She did not stop running till she was in the dugout.

"Goodness, Laura," Ma said. "You'll make yourself sick, tearing around so in this heat."

All that time Mary had been sitting like a little lady, spelling out words in the book that Ma was teaching her to read. Mary was a good little girl.

Laura had been bad and she knew it. She had broken her promise to Pa. But no one had seen her. No one knew that she had started to go to the swimming hole. If she did not tell, no one would ever know. Only that strange animal knew, and it could not tell on her. But she felt worse and worse inside.

That night she lay awake beside Mary. Pa and Ma sat in the starlight outside the door, and Pa was playing his fiddle.

"Go to sleep, Laura," Ma said softly, and softly the

fiddle sang to her. Pa was a shadow against the sky and his bow danced among the great stars.

Everything was beautiful and good except Laura. She had broken her promise to Pa. Breaking a promise was as bad as telling a lie. Laura wished she had not done it. But she had done it, and if Pa knew, he would punish her.

Pa went on playing softly in the starlight. His fiddle sang to her sweetly and happily. He thought she was a good little girl. At last Laura could bear it no longer.

She slid out of bed, and her bare feet stole across the cool earthen floor. In her nightgown and nightcap she stood beside Pa. He drew the last notes from the strings with his bow, and she could feel him smiling down at her.

"What is it, little half-pint?" he asked her. "You look like a little ghost, all white in the dark."

"Pa," Laura said in a quivery small voice, "I—I—started to go to the swimming hole."

"You did!" Pa exclaimed. Then he asked, "Well, what stopped you?"

"I don't know," Laura whispered. "It had gray fur and it—it flattened out flat. It snarled."

"How big was it?" Pa asked.

Laura told him all about that strange animal. Pa said, "It must have been a badger."

Then for a long time he did not say anything and Laura waited. Laura could not see his face in the dark, but she leaned against his knee and she could feel how strong and kind he was.

"Well," he said at last, "I hardly know what to do, Laura. You see, I trusted you. It is hard to know what to do with a person you can't trust. But do you know what people have to do to anyone they can't trust?"

"Wh-at?" Laura quavered.

"They have to watch him," said Pa. "So I guess you must be watched. Your Ma will have to do it because I must work at Nelson's. So tomorrow you stay where Ma can watch you. You are not to go out of her sight all day. If you are good all day then we will let you try again to be a little girl we can trust."

"How about it, Caroline?" he asked Ma.

"Very well, Charles," Ma said out of the dark. "I will watch her tomorrow. But I am sure she will be good. Now go back to bed, Laura, and go to sleep."

The next day was a dreadful day.

Ma was mending, and Laura had to stay in the dugout. She could not even fetch water from the spring, for that was going out of Ma's sight. Mary fetched the water. Mary took Carrie to walk on the prairie. Laura had to stay in.

Jack laid his nose on his paws and waggled; he jumped out on the path and looked back at her, smiling with his ears, begging her to come out. He could not understand why she did not.

Laura helped Ma. She washed the dishes and made both beds and swept the floor and set the table. At dinner she sat bowed on her bench and ate what Ma set before her. Then she wiped the dishes. After that she ripped a sheet that was torn in the middle. Ma turned the strips of muslin and pinned them together, and Laura whipped the new seam over and over with tiny stitches.

She thought that seam and that day would never end.

But at last Ma rolled up her mending and it was time to get supper.

"You have been a good girl, Laura," Ma said. "We will tell Pa so. And tomorrow morning you and I are going to look for that badger. I am sure he saved you from drowning, for if you had gone to that deep water you would have gone into it. Once you begin being naughty it is easier to go on and on, and sooner or later something dreadful happens."

"Yes, Ma," Laura said. She knew that now.

The whole day was gone. Laura had not seen the sunrise or the shadows of clouds on the prairie. The morning-glories were withered, and that day's blue flags were dead. All day Laura had not seen the water running in the creek, the little fishes in it, and the water bugs skating over it. She was sure that being good could never be as hard as being watched.

Next day she went with Ma to look for the badger. In the path she showed Ma the place where he had flattened himself on the grass. Ma found the hole where he lived. It was a round hole under a clump of grass on the prairie bank. Laura called to him and poked a stick into the hole.

If the badger was at home he would not come out. Laura never saw that old gray badger again.

Ghost of the Lagoon

ARMSTRONG SPERRY

The island of Bora Bora, where Mako lived, is far away in the South Pacific. It is not a large island— you can paddle around it in a single day—but the main body of it rises straight out of the sea, very high into the air like a castle. Waterfalls trail down the faces of the cliffs. As you look upward you see wild goats leaping from crag to crag.

Mako had been born on the very edge of the sea, and most of his waking hours were spent in the waters of the lagoon, which was nearly enclosed by the two outstretched arms of the island. He was very clever with his hands; he had made a harpoon that was as straight as an arrow and tipped with five pointed iron spears. He had made a canoe, hollowing it out of a tree. It wasn't a very big canoe—only a little longer than his own height. It had an outrigger, a sort of balancing pole, fastened to one side to keep the boat from tipping over. The canoe was just large enough to hold Mako and his little dog Afa. They were great companions, these two.

One evening Mako lay stretched at full length on the pandanus mats, listening to Grandfather's voice. Overhead, stars shone in the dark sky. From far off came the thunder of the surf on the reef.

The old man was speaking of Tupa, the ghost of the lagoon. Ever since the boy could remember he had heard tales of this terrible monster. Frightened fishermen, returning from the reef at midnight, spoke of the ghost. Over the evening fires old men told endless tales about the monster.

Tupa seemed to think the lagoon of Bora Bora belonged to him. The natives left presents of food for him out on the reef: a dead goat, a chicken, or a pig. The presents always disappeared mysteriously, but everyone felt sure that it was Tupa who carried them away. Still, in spite of all this food, the nets of the fishermen were torn during the night, the fish stolen. What an appetite Tupa seemed to have!

Not many people had ever seen the ghost of the lagoon. Grandfather was one of the few who had.

"What does he really look like, Grandfather?" the boy asked for the hundredth time.

The old man shook his head solemnly. The light from the cookfire glistened on his white hair. "Tupa lives in the great caves of the reef. He is longer than this house. There is a sail on his back, not large but terrible to see, for it burns with a white fire. Once when I was fishing beyond the reef at night I saw him come up right under another canoe—"

"What happened then?" Mako asked. He half rose on one elbow. This was a story he had not heard before.

The old man's voice dropped to a whisper. "Tupa dragged the canoe right under the water—and the water boiled with white flame. The three fishermen in it were never seen again. Fine swimmers they were too."

Grandfather shook his head. "It is bad fortune even to speak of Tupa. There is evil in his very name."

"But King Opu Nui has offered a reward for his capture," the boy pointed out.

"Thirty acres of fine coconut land and a sailing canoe as well," said the old man. "But who ever heard of laying hands on a ghost?"

Mako's eyes glistened. "Thirty acres of land and a sailing canoe. How I should love to win that reward!"

Grandfather nodded, but Mako's mother scolded her son for such foolish talk. "Be quiet now, son, and go to sleep. Grandfather has told you that it is bad fortune to speak of Tupa. Alas, how well we have learned that lesson! Your father—" She stopped herself.

"What of my father?" the boy asked quickly. And now he sat up straight on the mats.

"Tell him, Grandfather," his mother whispered.

The old man cleared his throat and poked at the fire. A little shower of sparks whirled up into the darkness.

"Your father," he explained gently, "was one of the three fishermen in the canoe that Tupa destroyed." His words fell upon the air like stones dropped into a deep well.

Mako shivered. He brushed back the hair from his damp forehead. Then he squared his shoulders and cried fiercely, "I shall slay Tupa and win the King's reward!" He rose to his knees, his slim body tense, his eyes flashing in the firelight.

"Hush!" his mother said. "Go to sleep now. Enough of such foolish talk. Would you bring trouble upon us all?"

Mako lay down again upon the mats. He rolled over on his side and closed his eyes, but sleep was long in coming.

The palm trees whispered above the dark lagoon, and far out on the reef the sea thundered.

The boy was slow to wake up the next morning. The ghost of Tupa had played through his dreams, making him restless. And so it was almost noon before Mako sat up on the mats and stretched himself. He called Afa, and the boy and his dog ran down to the lagoon for their morning swim.

When they returned to the house, wide awake and hungry, Mako's mother had food ready and waiting.

"These are the last of our bananas," she told him. "I wish you would paddle out to the reef this afternoon and bring back a new bunch."

The boy agreed eagerly. Nothing pleased him more than such an errand, which would take him to a little island on the outer reef half a mile from shore. It was

ALL KINDS OF COURAGE

one of Mako's favorite playgrounds, and there bananas
and oranges grew in great plenty.

"Come, Afa," he called, gulping the last mouthful.
"We're going on an expedition." He picked up his long-
bladed knife and seized his spear. A minute later he
dashed across the white sand where his canoe was
drawn up beyond the water's reach.

Afa barked at his heels. He was all white except for a
black spot over each eye. Wherever Mako went, there
went Afa also. Now the little dog leaped into the bow of
the canoe, his tail wagging with delight. The boy shoved
the canoe into the water and climbed aboard. Then
picking up his paddle, he thrust it into the water. The
canoe shot ahead. Its sharp bow cut through the green
water of the lagoon like a knife through cheese. And so
clear was the water that Mako could see the coral
gardens, forty feet below him, growing in the sand. The
shadow of the canoe moved over them.

A school of fish swept by like silver arrows. He saw
scarlet rock cod with ruby eyes, and the head of a
conger eel peering out from a cavern in the coral. The
boy thought suddenly of Tupa, ghost of the lagoon. On
such a bright day it was hard to believe in ghosts of
any sort. The fierce sunlight drove away all thought of
them. Perhaps ghosts were only old men's stories, anyway!

Mako's eyes came to rest upon his spear—the spear
that he had made with his own hands—the spear that
was as straight and true as an arrow. He remembered
his vow of the night before. Could a ghost be killed with

a spear? Some night when all the village was sleeping, Mako swore to himself, he would find out! He would paddle out to the reef and challenge Tupa! Perhaps tonight. Why not? He caught his breath at the thought. A shiver ran down his back. His hands were tense on the paddle.

As the canoe drew away from shore the boy saw the coral reef that above all others had always interested him. It was of white coral—a long, slim shape that rose slightly above the surface of the water. It looked very much like a shark. There was a ridge on the back that the boy could pretend was a dorsal fin, while up near one end were two dark holes that looked like eyes!

Times without number the boy had practiced spearing this make-believe shark, aiming always for the eyes, the most vulnerable spot. So true and straight had his aim become that the spear would pass right into the eyeholes without even touching the sides of the coral. Mako had named the coral reef "Tupa."

This morning as he paddled past it he shook his fist and called, "Ho, Mister Tupa! Just wait till I get my bananas. When I come back I'll make short work of you!"

Afa followed his master's words with a sharp bark. He knew Mako was excited about something.

The bow of the canoe touched the sand of the little island where the bananas grew. Afa leaped ashore and ran barking into the jungle, now on this trail, now on that. Clouds of sea birds whirled from their nests into the air with angry cries.

Mako climbed into the shallow water, waded ashore, and pulled his canoe up on the beach. Then, picking up his banana knife, he followed Afa. In the jungle the light was so dense and green that the boy felt as if he were moving under water. Ferns grew higher than his head. The branches of the trees formed a green roof over him. A flock of parakeets fled on swift wings. Somewhere a wild pig crashed through the undergrowth while Afa dashed away in pursuit. Mako paused anxiously. Armed only with his banana knife, he had no desire to meet the wild pig. The pig, it seemed, had no desire to meet him either.

Then ahead of him the boy saw the broad green blades of a banana tree. A bunch of bananas, golden ripe, was growing out of the top.

At the foot of the tree he made a nest of soft leaves for the bunch to fall upon. In this way the fruit wouldn't be crushed. Then with a swift slash of his blade he cut the stem. The bananas fell to the earth with a dull thud. He found two more bunches.

Then he thought, I might as well get some oranges while I'm here. Those little rusty ones are sweeter than any that grow on Bora Bora.

So he set about making a net of palm leaves in which to carry the oranges. As he worked, his swift fingers moving in and out among the strong green leaves, he could hear Afa's excited barks off in the jungle. That was just like Afa, always barking at something: a bird, a fish, a wild pig. He never caught anything either. Still, no boy ever had a finer companion.

GHOST OF THE LAGOON

The palm net took longer to make than Mako had realized. By the time it was finished and filled with oranges the jungle was dark and gloomy. Night comes quickly and without warning in the islands of the Tropics.

Mako carried the fruit down to the shore and loaded it into the canoe. Then he whistled to Afa. The dog came bounding out of the bush, wagging his tail.

"Hurry!" Mako scolded. "We won't be home before the dark comes."

The little dog leaped into the bow of the canoe, and Mako came aboard. Night seemed to rise up from the surface of the water and swallow them. On the distant shore of Bora Bora, cookfires were being lighted. The first star twinkled just over the dark mountains. Mako dug his paddle into the water, and the canoe leaped ahead.

The dark water was alive with phosphorus. The bow of the canoe seemed to cut through a pale liquid fire. Each dip of the paddle trailed streamers of light. As the canoe approached the coral reef the boy called, "Ho, Tupa! It's too late tonight to teach you your lesson. But I'll come back tomorrow." The coral shark glistened in the darkness.

And then suddenly Mako's breath caught in his throat. His hands felt weak. Just beyond the fin of the coral Tupa there was another fin—a huge one. It had never been there before. And—could he believe his eyes? It was moving.

The boy stopped paddling. He dashed his hand across

his eyes. Afa began to bark furiously. The great white fin, shaped like a small sail, glowed with phosphorescent light. Then Mako knew. Here was Tupa—the real Tupa—ghost of the lagoon!

His knees felt weak. He tried to cry out, but his voice died in his throat. The great shark was circling slowly around the canoe. With each circle it moved closer and closer. Now the boy could see the phosphorescent glow of the great shark's sides. As it moved in closer he saw the yellow eyes, the gill slits in its throat.

Afa leaped from one side of the canoe to the other. In sudden anger Mako leaned forward to grab the dog and shake him soundly. Afa wriggled out of his grasp as Mako tried to catch him, and the shift in weight tipped the canoe on one side. The outrigger rose from the water. In another second they would be overboard. The boy threw his weight over quickly to balance the canoe, but with a loud splash Afa fell over into the dark water.

Mako stared after him in dismay. The little dog, instead of swimming back to the canoe, had headed for the distant shore. And there was the great white shark—very near.

"Afa! Afa! Come back! Come quickly!" Mako shouted.

The little dog turned back toward the canoe. He was swimming with all his strength. Mako leaned forward. Could Afa make it? Swiftly the boy seized his spear. Bracing himself, he stood upright. There was no weakness in him now. His dog, his companion, was in danger of instant death.

Afa was swimming desperately to reach the canoe. The white shark had paused in his circling to gather speed for the attack. Mako raised his arm, took aim. In that instant the shark charged. Mako's arm flashed forward. All his strength was behind that thrust. The spear drove straight and true, right into the great shark's eye. Mad with pain and rage, Tupa whipped about, lashing the water in fury. The canoe rocked back and forth. Mako struggled to keep his balance as he drew back the spear by the cord fastened to his wrist.

He bent over to seize Afa and drag him aboard. Then he stood up, not a moment too soon. Once again the shark charged. Once again Mako threw his spear, this time at the other eye. The spear found its mark. Blinded and weak from loss of blood, Tupa rolled to the surface, turned slightly on his side. Was he dead?

Mako knew how clever sharks could be and he was taking no chances. Scarcely daring to breathe, he paddled toward the still body. He saw the faintest motion of the great tail. The shark was still alive. The boy knew that one flip of that tail could overturn the canoe and send him and Afa into the water where Tupa could destroy them.

Swiftly, yet calmly, Mako stood upright and braced himself firmly. Then murmuring a silent prayer to the Shark God, he threw his spear for the last time. Downward, swift as sound, the spear plunged into a white shoulder.

Peering over the side of the canoe, Mako could see the great fish turn over far below the surface. Then slowly, slowly, the great shark rose to the surface of the lagoon. There he floated, half on one side.

Tupa was dead.

Mako flung back his head and shouted for joy. Hitching a stong line about the shark's tail, the boy began to paddle toward the shore of Bora Bora. The dorsal fin, burning with the white fire of phosphorus, trailed after the canoe.

Men were running down the beaches of Bora Bora, shouting as they leaped into their canoes and put out across the lagoon. Their cries reached the boy's ears across the water.

"It is Tupa—ghost of the lagoon," he heard them shout. "Mako has killed him!"

That night as the tired boy lay on the pandanus mats listening to the distant thunder of the sea, he heard Grandfather singing a new song. It was the song which would be sung the next day at the feast which King Opu Nui would give in Mako's honor. The boy saw his mother bending over the cookfire. The stars leaned close, winking like friendly eyes. Grandfather's voice reached him now from a great distance, "Thirty acres of land and a sailing canoe . . ."

Two Were Left

HUGH B. CAVE

On the third night of hunger Noni thought of the dog. Nothing of flesh and blood lived upon the floating ice island with its towering berg except those two.

In the breakup Noni had lost his sled, his food, his fur, even his knife. He had saved only Nimuk, his devoted husky. And now the two marooned on the ice eyed each other warily—each keeping his distance.

Noni's love for Nimuk was real, very real—as real as the hunger and cold nights and the gnawing pain of his injured leg in its homemade brace. But the men of his village killed their dogs when food was scarce, didn't they? And without thinking twice about it.

And Nimuk, he told himself, when hungry enough would seek food. One of us will soon be eating the other, Noni thought. So . . ."

He could not kill the dog with his bare hands. Nimuk

was powerful and much fresher than he. A weapon, then, was essential.

Removing his mittens, he unstrapped the brace from his leg. When he had hurt his leg a few weeks before, he had fashioned the brace from bits of harness and two thin strips of iron.

Kneeling now, he wedged one of the iron strips into a crack in the ice and began to rub the other against it with firm, slow strokes.

Nimuk watched him intently, and it seemed to Noni that the dog's eyes glowed more brightly as night waned.

He worked on, trying not to remember why. The slab of iron had an edge now. It had begun to take shape. Daylight found his task completed.

Noni pulled the finished knife from the ice and thumbed its edge. The sun's glare, reflected from it, stabbed at his eyes and momentarily blinded him.

Noni steeled himself.

"Here, Nimuk!" he called softly.

The dog watched him suspiciously.

"Come here," Noni called.

Nimuk came closer. Noni read fear in the animal's gaze. He read hunger and suffering in the dog's labored breathing and awkward, dragging crouch. His heart wept. He hated himself and fought against it.

Closer Nimuk came, wary of his intentions. Now Noni felt a thickening in his throat. He saw the dog's eyes and they were wells of suffering.

Now! Now was the time to strike!

A great sob shook Noni's kneeling body. He cursed the knife. He swayed blindly; flung the weapon far from him. With empty hands outstretched he stumbled toward the dog, and fell.

The dog growled ominously as he warily circled the boy's body. And Noni was sick with fear.

In flinging away his knife he had left himself defenseless. He was too weak to crawl after it now. He was at Nimuk's mercy, and Nimuk was hungry.

The dog circled him and was creeping up from behind. Noni heard the rattle of saliva in the savage throat.

He shut his eyes, praying that the attack might be swift. He felt the dog's feet against his leg, the hot rush of Nimuk's breath against his neck. A scream gathered in the boy's throat.

Then he felt the dog's hot tongue caressing his face.

Noni's eyes opened, staring incredulously. Crying softly, he thrust out an arm and drew the dog's head down against his own. . . .

The plane came out of the south an hour later. Its pilot, a young man of the coastal patrol, looked down and saw the large, floating floe with the berg rising from its center. And he saw something flashing.

It was the sun gleaming on something shiny which moved. His curiosity aroused, the pilot banked his ship and descended, circling the floe. Now he saw, in the shadow of the peak of ice, a dark, still shape that appeared to be human. Or were there two shapes?

He set his ship down in a water lane and investigated.

There were two shapes, boy and dog. The boy was unconscious but alive. The dog whined feebly but was too weak to move.

The gleaming object which had trapped the pilot's attention was a crudely fashioned knife stuck point first into the ice a little distance away and quivering in the wind.

A Red-Handled Sheath Knife

ANN DURELL

Joey sat on the back steps counting earthworms as she transferred them from a rusty tin can to a Mason jar filled with good wet dirt. It was hard work because the worms could slip through her fingers and be hidden in the loose dirt before she knew it. Donny and Mac, Joey's big twin brothers, paid five cents for fifty worms, and they wanted their money's worth, so the counting had to be pretty accurate if Joey didn't want to cheat them—or herself.

"Forty-six, forty-seven, forty—ouch!"

The screen door behind her swung open, and Joey—worms and all—pitched forward on the concrete walk.

"I'm so sorry, Joey dear," cried her mother. "I was in such a hurry to get to the car that I didn't see you. Are you hurt?"

"Not much," said Joey, "but these old worms are getting away and I sure would hate to dig more."

"Oh, dear, so they are. Here, I'll help you catch them. At least they can't burrow into a concrete sidewalk." Mrs. Finch, who was a good sport and didn't mind worms at all, got down on her knees and began scrambling after the wigglers.

"There," said Joey finally, "we've got them all, I think." She sat back on her sneakers. "But, gee, Mom, you've got white streaks all down your skirt."

Mom gasped and jumped up in horror. She brushed her skirt with both hands, and Joey helped by giving a couple of good whacks to the back.

"That will just have to do," Mom decided finally. "I haven't time to change. Thanks for the brushing, Joey. I'm rather surprised that you noticed. Maybe you're turning into a girl-type after all."

"Not me!" said Joey disgustedly.

"I," corrected her mother, climbing into the car. "Can I get you anything in town?"

"Not this time, but I'll be asking you to get my sheath knife soon. I only need a quarter more, after Donny pays me for these worms."

"Well, that's good news, but I wish you were saving your money for something a little more feminine. A locket, maybe?"

"Huh!" snorted Joey as she walked toward the house, balancing the jar of worms carefully. Mom was so much fun most of the time, but she just didn't understand how a girl could want a hunting knife. Donny and Mac had been given knives on their joint birthday, and right after that Joey had seen just the one she wanted in a store in town. It had a red plastic handle and a leather sheath that was slit so that you could run your belt through it. The knife was seven and a half inches long and it cost just ninety-seven cents. Joey had asked for it right away for *her* birthday in August, but Mom had put her foot down. Ten was plenty old enough to start thinking about girl things like clothes and jewelry, she said, and too old for a boy thing like a sheath knife.

Donny came loping across the back yard toward her, and Joey looked at him enviously. He had a sheath knife *and* a hatchet in the belt of his dungarees.

"Give me my worms quick," he yelled. "Old John Rufus says that big granddaddy pike is jumping down 'n the creek again."

"Not till you give me the nickel," said Joey, putting the jar behind her back. Once her brother got the worms he would never pay till Dad made him.

Donny was mad at that but he was also in a hurry, so he threw her a nickel and grabbed the jar. Then he was off down the driveway, his red hair streaming in the wind. Joey grinned. She didn't think there would be any fish, even cantankerous old granddaddy pike, biting in the middle of October, though this had been a very warm fall and today was like summer. But Donny was fishing crazy, and the worms he had bought during the summer had practically paid for her knife.

I don't think I'll ever earn money that way again, though, Joey thought. It takes too long. Maybe I'll raise chickens next summer and sell the eggs. She began planning a chicken farm, and by the time she got into the cool, dark front hall she was so busy thinking about wire mesh and chicken feed that she didn't notice that Grandmother was talking to Daddy in his study with the door ajar, until the sound of her own name caught her attention.

"Joanna is a disgrace to the family, Frederick," Grandmother was saying, "and there is no excuse at all for the way you and Louise put up with her appearance."

Joey sneaked quietly toward the front door. She didn't want to hear any more about what a dreadful tomboy she was, and if Grandmother caught her now she'd really be in trouble, with that rip in the seat of her dungarees and dirt all over her face and hands. She slid out the door and bumped into Mac, who was sneaking in.

"Can't you watch where you're going?" he snapped. "I'm trying to keep out of Grandmother's way, and you have to go crashing into me and making a big noise."

"How did you know Grandmother was here?" asked Joey.

"I saw her car out front, dopey. I came home to get my shotgun because a big flock of ducks came in on the Deer Head bog this morning, and I want to go hunting after work tonight, before Donny hears about them. And now I won't be able to because Grandmother will see me with the gun and raise a rumpus. Of all the luck!"

Joey knew how badly Mac wanted to get the first duck of the season. Donny had beat him three years running, and Mac didn't get much chance for hunting any more, either, because he was working with the men on Dad's cranberry bogs on Saturdays to earn some extra money.

"I wish I could help," she said generously.

Mac brightened up. "Maybe you can," he said quickly. "Listen, Joey, why don't you get the gun and bring it up to me at the Deer Head this afternoon? That's where we're working."

"But Grandmother would see me," she objected.

"Not if you left while she was taking her nap, dopey!"

"That's not until four o'clock and it's nearly dark then."

"Don't be silly. You'd have at least two hours before it got dark."

Joey shook her head. She was scared of the swamps at dusk.

"All right. If you'll bring me my gun I'll give you the quarter you still need to get your hunting knife."

Joey gave in. She wanted that knife more than anything else in the world. "Okay," she said reluctantly.

"Mackenzie Finch," said Grandmother's voice right behind them. "What are you doing home at this time of day?"

Mac bolted, but Joey, who was trapped, went in to wash her hands and listen, with no good grace, to stories of how neat and ladylike Grandmother was when she was a little girl.

Grandmother finally marched upstairs to take her nap in the spare room. Joey waited until she heard Dad close his study door on himself and his accounts, and then went stealthily to the rumpus room where the gunrack was kept. Mac's shotgun was easy to pick out because he scratched his initials on the stock. Joey lifted it carefully out of the rack, and carrying it over one shoulder the way Daddy had taught her, hurried quietly out of the house.

She had a bad moment when Mom's car turned into the driveway just as she came out of the front door, but she dropped down behind the shrubbery quickly, and Mom didn't see her.

The road was plenty light while she was crossing the dams between the bogs which lay right around the house, but in the thick swamps beyond, dusk had settled already and the rustling shadows were pretty scary. Joey tried to hurry but the big gun was heavy and awkward to carry and she often stumbled. Her sneakers made hardly any noise on the narrow sandy road, and every animal crackle magnified in the stillness. It was hard not to think about the awful stories the cranberry pickers told—about lame Uncle Tom-Tom with the humpy shoulder, and one red eye that would put a haunt on you if you met him alone in the woods, or the fierce wild dogs who roamed the swamps in packs, looking for something to eat.

Especially something fat and tender like me! thought Joey, and then wished she hadn't. I sure do wish I had a dog. I think I'll use the money I get from my chicken eggs to buy one. The more she thought about this plan the better it sounded, and she had just about decided on a cocker spaniel when a great thump behind her made her change to a great Dane—the biggest available. The thump turned out to be a dead branch crashing to the earth, but it had scared her so that she was practically running, gun and all. Even conjuring up a vision of the long, shiny sheath knife swinging from her belt was no comfort.

"I wish I was home," Joey moaned, "right in front of the fire."

She had passed the Maple Swamp with its twisted gnarled stumps that all looked like Uncle Tom-Tom, and the Deer Head was practically around the corner, but it was really twilight now and the shotgun was like a ton weight on her shoulder. Her legs dragged in spite of themselves, and each breath hurt. But just as she felt that she couldn't take another step but would have to lie down and curl up like a frightened possum, she saw the patch of treeless sunset sky. She took a fresh grasp on the gun, and sighed with relief. It made her feel braver, just knowing that Mac was so close.

But the breath froze in her throat. Coming down the road between her and the safety of the Deer Head bog was a squat, dark figure, hippety-hopping rapidly toward her with one shoulder twisted above the other. Uncle Tom-Tom!

Joey's heart stopped altogether and then started thumping like a giant woodpecker. Run, it pounded, Run, *run!* Run, *run!* But her legs, with no more strength than melting icicles, refused to obey. She couldn't even scream as he hobbled right up to her, and she waited for the red glare of the terrible eye.

"Joey! Am I glad to see you!"

At the sound of Mac's voice Joey's legs moved. They shook so hard that they let her right down on the ground.

"What's wrong with you?" he asked. "You're like a piece of putty."

"I thought you were Uncle Tom-Tom," gasped Joey. "What's wrong with *you*? Limping along, all hunched up like that!"

"I had an accident," he said sheepishly. "I was trying to fix up a hiding place near that patch of wild rice where the ducks have been feeding at night, and I got too smart. I was sliding down the side of the dam with a big armload of cedar boughs to use as camouflage, and I lost my balance and rolled over about six times. My foot got all twisted up and a great huge cedar splinter went into my hand. It's still there. Every time I tried to pull it out I felt so funny I had to stop. That's why I walked bent over. I was holding that hand with my other one, but it didn't help much."

Joey took hold of his hand and looked at it hard. The splinter was the biggest one she had ever seen. It had gone in at an angle, and was so thick that she could see the course it had followed down into Mac's hand.

"Can you get it out?" he asked anxiously.

Joey could see how much it hurt him. Mac was always brave about pain, and now he looked as if he might cry. The splinter was big and rough, but it had an end sticking out about half an inch which would give her a good grip.

"I'll try," she said, "better grit your teeth." She took a firm hold of Mac's wrist with her left hand and seized the splinter with her right. And then pulled gently because she didn't want it to break off before she got it out. Mac gave one groan and then it was over, and Joey, for the second time, sat down on the ground while Mac dabbed at his wound with a rag he carried around to tie up his rock specimens.

"Are you going to be sick, Joey?"

"I think so," she gulped, but she swallowed hard and after a few minutes she felt better.

"Wait here a second. I've got to go back to the bog and get my lunch box."

Joey jumped up in a hurry. "I'm all right now. I'll come with you."

Mac grinned, and she knew if he hadn't been so grateful just then he would have teased her about being scared of Uncle Tom-Tom. But he helped her pick up the shotgun, and they started off together.

Mac's pile of cedar boughs was lying where the dam curved into the bank which ran around the bog and held in the water which protected the cranberry vines all winter. The patch of wild rice, which always attracted ducks on their trip South, grew nearby, but the dark, cedary water never reached that spot, so it was an ideal place for a duck hunter to lie. The lunch box was lying by the branches, and Mac eased himself gingerly down the side of the dam after it. Suddenly he lifted his head, listening hard. High up in the distance they could hear the busy quacking that meant the ducks were coming home for the night.

"Quick," he whispered, "bring me my gun."

Joey slid down the bank in her turn, holding the gun tightly with one hand and steadying herself with the other. She had hardly touched level ground before Mac had the gun and was loading it from the supply of shells he was hoarding in his lunch box. The quack-quack came nearer, and looking up, Joey could see the first bird coming in against the pink sky. Mac lifted the shotgun to his shoulder and lowered it quickly, wincing with pain.

"I can't shoot," he groaned angrily. "My hand still hurts and it's my right one. And I'll never get a chance like this again."

Joey nodded. She knew that this was the perfect moment, when the sun was so low that the ducks were blinded but not the hunter, and that they had hit it with rare good luck. Suddenly Mac thrust the gun toward her.

"You might as well try it," he muttered.

Her chest swelled. Never, not even for target practice, had she been allowed to borrow Mac's gun. She raised it to her shoulder, bracing the stock firmly and squinting up the sights. A whole line of ducks was streaming by now, and she settled on one toward the rear and lined it up carefully. The duck came steadily closer, and the gun muzzle swung with its progress.

"Now!" shouted Joey's mind, and she squeezed the trigger.

"You got him, Joey," Mac yelled. "Good shot! He's not very far out. I'll wade over and get him." Sprained foot forgotten, he peeled off his socks and sneakers and headed for the dark patch floating on the water.

Joey picked herself up. The kick of the shotgun had knocked her right over, and she felt stunned. Mac had scared off the rest of the ducks with his yells and excited splashing, but she certainly didn't care. Almost before she realized that she had shot her first game he was back, waving her prize triumphantly.

"Here you are," he chortled. "Cleanest shot I ever saw. Boy, will Donny be mad! A girl beating him, and his own kid sister at that."

She looked at the limp bundle of feathers, still shining where the light hit them, the pathetic drooping neck. Her stomach rose in earnest and she tore for the bushes.

Mac was subdued on the way home. Joey had expected an awful ribbing, but though he looked disgusted when she refused flatly to carry the duck and said she would just as soon bury it then and there, he had just picked up the bird and his lunch box and limped off! Joey trudged along beside him, lugging the gun, which she would have liked to heave into the middle of the bog.

Daddy met them just beyond the Maple Swamp. It had been dark for about half an hour and he had come out looking for them with a flashlight. He was almost as excited over the duck as Mac was, so he forgot to scold them. Joey privately thought that nothing had ever looked so good as that big flashlight unless it was the light streaming out of the kitchen windows where Mom was getting supper. She ran right upstairs and took a hot bath, scrubbing herself hard all over with Mom's expensive scented soap, and she put on a plaid dress and tied her hair back with a red ribbon. She tried not to think about the duck, which Daddy was cleaning and plucking on the back porch, having borrowed Mac's sheath knife for the purpose.

Mom didn't say a word, even when she set the table and mixed the salad dressing without being told to. But she gave her a big hug when they were alone in the kitchen, and Joey felt a lot better.

The boys and Daddy were very respectful at dinner. Joey squirmed under their questions about her great achievement. They were treating her as an equal, and she wasn't sure she liked it.

When dessert had been served, Mac delved into his pocket and slowly hauled out a quarter. Mom had put iodine and an intricate white bandage on his hand, and he had a little difficulty using it. He passed the quarter over to Joey.

"Here's your money, kid," he said, and it was plain that he thought she really deserved it.

"You'll be able to get the sheath knife now," said Mom, smiling at her. "It's been a long pull and we all admire you for sticking to it. Do you want me to get it for you in town tomorrow?"

Everyone looked at her affectionately. Joey swallowed hard.

"I don't want a hunting knife," she said finally, with her eyes fastened on her ice cream. "I think hunting is awful. I'm going to start buying chickens."

Nobody said anything, but they kept right on smiling at her, and Joey realized that they had really expected her to act like a girl all along. She grinned back. It was going to be all right, after all.

The Desirable Shawl

GRACE PURDIE MOON
from *Chi-weé: The Adventures of a Little Indian Girl,* 1925

What matters the shade of a little maid's skin
If her heart is the kind that is right within?
If it sings with the song of the Night Hawk's cry,
And leaps to the pink of the pale dawn sky?
There are hearts that are wild, and hearts that are tame
But hearts that are true are ever the same!

It was a beautiful shawl! Chi-weé could see that clear across the Trader's store: dark blue on one side and glowing red on the other, with a fringe of the same two colors, and it looked warm and soft and much to be desired!

Chi-weé saw the look in her mother's eyes as she passed her hand over its surface, and in her heart a fierce little voice said:

"My mother shall have that shawl—the Good Spirit made that shawl to be for my mother!"

It was trading day for Chi-weé and her mother. In the early morning they had come in the wagon of Mah-peé-ti, the sheepherder, with the jars that Chi-weé's mother had made, to trade them at the store for food and clothing.

It was a long ride in the bumpety old wagon from the high mesa town to the canyon store, a ride over the wide desert of many-changing colors and up and down sandy washes, but it was a ride that Chi-weé dearly loved and of which she never tired. There were so many living things to see on the way: prairie dogs and lizards and horned toads; sheep, and sometimes, away in the distance, an antelope or a gray coyote. And then there was always the excitement of wondering, when they bumped down into a very deep wash, whether Mah-peé-ti's old wagon would hold together until they got up the other side. But it always did, and it always had for as many years as Chi-weé could remember, for once a month they had taken this ride in the same old wagon ever since Chi-weé had been old enough to sit by herself instead of being carried in the shawl on her mother's back—and the wagon looked now as it had looked then. Like the desert and the pueblo where she lived, it did not seem to change.

Chi-weé came close to the shawl and felt it with her fingers—it was soft as it looked, and very warm.

"You will buy it, my mother?" she asked eagerly, laying her cheek on the soft wool.

Her mother shook her head a little sadly.

"No, my little one," she said. "We must trade today for food and not for the things we do not need."

"But you need a shawl—this shawl," said Chi-weé. "You know, my mother, that you need it!"

"We will not speak of it more," said her mother, turning away. "We have money for food only, my daughter." And she spoke to the Trader of the flour and sugar and grain that she needed.

Chi-weé stood looking down at the shawl, and queer thoughts were in her mind, but above them all was the firm resolution— My mother shall have this soft, beautiful shawl!

She waited until her mother had carried some of the food out to the wagon and then she went to the Trader. He was a pleasant man and had always spoken kind words to Chi-weé, so she had no fear of him.

"What is the price of that shawl?" she asked him. "The soft blue one with the red underside."

"Six dollars," answered the Trader with a kindly smile for Chi-weé. "It is all wool and very warm."

There was a thoughtful look in Chi-weé's eyes as her little hand went to her throat and opened the collar of her cotton waist.

"Look," she said softly to the Trader, "this is a very beautiful necklace that I have on. See, the shells are the color of the sky when the sun comes up—pink. I—I— think it is a very beautiful necklace."

The Trader stooped and looked at it.

"Yes." He nodded. "I would give you two dollars for the necklace if you cared to sell it."

Her face fell and her fingers touched the pink shells tenderly.

"Two dollars? I—I—thought—you see, it is the shawl I want. . . ."

"I'm sorry," said the Trader gently, "but the shawl is worth more, little girl. No, I could not exchange it for the necklace."

Chi-weé felt her heart grow very heavy, and all the way home in the bumpety wagon she had no eyes for the lizards and little hares and prairie dogs that scuttled out of their way, or for the wonderful colors of the tumbleweed and cactus, or the faraway blue buttes—her mind was busy with plans to earn money for the wonderful shawl—but how?

There were very few ways to earn money in the high mesa town. She could weave a little—an old man in the pueblo had taught her—but that took a long time and money, too, to buy the colored wools; and pottery she could not yet make well enough to sell. She could help pick peaches and apricots, but now was not the time for them, and anyway, they gave her but a few pennies for that. And she had nothing to sell—nothing but the necklace, her one treasure—and the Trader had told her that was worth only two dollars—and the shawl cost six! Oh, but it was a very difficult thing, this earning money— she could not understand how other people did it. But not for a moment did she give up the thought of getting the shawl for her mother—it was just how to get it that puzzled her.

When next they went to the Trader's, Chi-weé looked eagerly for the shawl and she felt that her heart almost stopped beating when she did not see it where it had been before. Of course others would see how beautiful it was and buy it; others who had six dollars and even more—others who did not have to wait and plan; she felt the hot tears stinging her eyelids—never had her heart been so set on anything as on that beautiful blue shawl with its red underside!

"Has it been sold?" she asked the Trader in a voice she could not quite keep from shaking, "that—that beautiful shawl—has it been sold?"

He looked at her for a moment with a little puzzled frown on his face.

"The shawl?" he asked, and then a look of remembrance came into his eyes as he laughed a little. "No, it is still here—did you want to buy it?"

A sudden resolve came into Chi-weé's heart—it almost frightened her.

"Yes," she said quickly, and looked to see that her mother was beyond hearing. "I want to buy it—but I have not the money—not all now. Here!" And with trembling fingers she unclasped the little shell necklace and thrust it into his hand. "I will bring more next time. Could you, oh, could you keep it a little while for me?"

There was such eagerness in the little voice, such a

look in the eyes, and such a tremble all through the small figure that the Trader could not help but see it. From surprise the expression in his eyes softened, and he put his hand on Chi-weé's black head.

"How old are you, little girl?" he asked unexpectedly.

"Seven, I think," answered Chi-weé in a surprised voice. "My mother tells me—yes, she tells me seven."

"Ah," said the man slowly, and the look in his eyes was far away but very tender, "my little girl would have been seven now. . . . Yes," he added, suddenly changing his voice, "I will keep the shawl for you, little girl of the mesa, until you bring the rest of the money." And he turned to the others who had entered his store.

Chi-weé felt as if she walked on air as she went to the wagon. The shawl was hers—hers—almost! And "almost" was such a little word that she nearly forgot it altogether. Those warm, soft folds would rest on her mother's shoulders, and that lovely red would gleam as she walked—and how proud she would feel that she, Chi-weé, had bought and paid for it herself—yes, and her heart dropped a little at the thought—but how was she going to pay for it herself?

The next month was a very busy one for Chi-weé, and a happy one, too, and had her mother not been very occupied with her own work she must have noticed something strange about Chi-weé's actions. She seemed to be hiding something, and there were trips she made into the desert for which she gave no explanation. When the next trading day came there was a bumpy place under the little girl's shawl that had not been there on other trips, and when she handed the Trader a great jar of wild honey her heart was beating fast with excitement and happiness. She did not tell of the labor she had had in getting it, or of the painful lump on her arm that told of the angry stinging of the bee, but there was a deep pride in her voice as she said:

"I have brought this to pay some more for the shawl—next time I will bring something else."

There was a look she could not understand in the Trader's eyes as he took the honey, but he turned quickly from her and spoke to a white stranger who was standing near. She could not catch the words, and when he turned back to her she still could not understand the look in his eyes.

"I have other shawls," she suddenly heard him saying to her. "You will not mind that this gentleman has bought the blue one with the red underside?"

To Chi-weé it seemed as if the world turned black—her shawl—her precious shawl—to go to this stranger! She could not speak—words would not come—and everything began to swim through the sudden tears in her eyes. She saw the stranger man walk to the door with a bundle under his arm, and the Trader turned his back to her to attend to those who waited at his counter. It could not be true—people could not be so cruel as that!

Chi-weé stumbled out of the store and into the waiting wagon, with a storm of anger and grief in her heart. But she did not cry. She sat in silence all the way home and tried to think why white people did things that no Indian could ever do.

At their door her mother called her to help with the parcels in the wagon.

"And take this great one," she said, "that the white stranger said you had bought from the Trader. With what could you buy, little daughter?"

Chi-weé opened her eyes wide and stood still—what could it mean? Her mother placed a great bundle wrapped in white paper in her arms. Soft it felt to the touch—soft, like a baby!

She did not wait to think, but tore open the paper there before her door—and—IT WAS THE SHAWL— HER SHAWL! And tied to one corner was a little card with words printed on it in ink—she could read them with difficulty—she wished now she had taken more lessons from the teacher lady at the Mission school.

"It is your love for your mother that has bought this shawl, little girl of the mesa. And it is my love for another little girl like you that gives you back your precious treasure. White hearts are just the same as Indian ones, inside!"

And there beside the shawl, wrapped in a bit of paper, was her pink-shell necklace!

Now Chi-weé did cry—but the tears were just for happiness as she hugged the shawl—and her mother— who did not yet understand—and the little pink necklace that had come home again!

She did not know then or afterward whether it was the Trader himself or the white stranger who had given

her the shawl, as the Trader would not say, but to Chi-
weé it did not matter, for she had learned a great secret—
one that you and I know already—that "White hearts are
just the same as Indian ones, inside!"

The Sampler

CORNELIA MEIGS

Because the Lloyds's household was a very regular one, Elizabeth sat down every afternoon at exactly the same hour to sew on her sampler. Sewing was no easy task for an active girl who liked to be doing other things. But nobody, of course, ever thought of excusing her from it, or ever dreamed of her growing up without having covered at least one square of linen with neat letters and figures.

The sampler was supposed to give her practice in all the different stitches of embroidery. Below the alphabet and the figures up to ten it showed a small, carefully outlined picture of a willow tree and a tombstone. It was to be finished with her name and a motto such as THE GOOD DIE YOUNG or WASTE NOT, WANT NOT.

There was so much to do in that thick-walled stone house, looking from its low hill out upon the bay, that there was no real time during the day when any older person could say with reason, "Elizabeth, you should be at your sewing." But when candlelight came—when the baking and sweeping, the dressing of chickens, and the curing of hams could not go forward so quickly by the dimmer light, then it was that her mother always said, "Now, Elizabeth," and the girl knew the sampler could not be avoided. It never occurred to her to hate it; she only knew that she liked doing anything else a great deal better.

She had sat down to it this October evening, with a wild wind swinging about the house and making the waves crash upon the shore below the hill. Elizabeth was alone, or almost alone; for her father and mother had driven five miles to the nearest town for the weekly marketing and had left Elizabeth with only deaf old Nora, the cook, who as everyone knew would fall asleep in her rocking chair in the little room above the kitchen the moment the last of the work was finished.

Not even the wind that blew in around the deep-framed windows, setting the candles to flickering—not even the slamming of the shutters—could rouse her. But as Elizabeth paused to slip the end of a thread into the slim eye of her needle there came a sound that, it seemed, would wake any sleeper on earth. *Boom!*

The great crash sounded from out on the water, where just at twilight she had looked out to see the smooth surface of the bay with not even a fishing boat in sight. *Boom!* This time all the windows in the house rattled and the glasses clattered on the dresser. *Boom!* the sound came a third time.

Elizabeth jumped up and ran to the window. What could it be? This was a time of peace, the year of 1810. It had been thirty years since the guns of the Revolution had echoed along those shores, and it would be two more years before another war was to break out between England and America.

She wondered for a puzzled minute if it could be pirates. It was quite true that pirates had landed on this coast within the memory of people not very much older than herself. She pressed her face against the pane, trying to peer out. How black it was outside!

Yet there beyond the point was the ghostly form of a ship, dark against the duller darkness of the water. It was a bigger ship than those which usually came up the bay. She saw a great flash of red flame as once again a cannon crashed, and against its light she could make out, near the shore and struggling on the top of a towering wave, the dark shape of a small boat with three men in it.

The blackness shut down again and there was nothing to be heard except the roaring of the wind. Then in a moment of brief calm there came a sound more surprising than any she had yet heard—a voice, little and distant, calling out, calling her own name.

"Elizabeth! Elizabeth Lloyd!"

She rushed to the door, lifted the latch, and immediately felt the wind snatch it from her hand and swing it wide, letting in a driving splatter of rain. Old

Nora had actually been awakened by the cannon shots, which shook the house, and was thumping down the stairs. Elizabeth stood on the sill, holding back the door so that all the light that was possible would come shining out upon the darkness of the night.

The men in the boat needed a signal to guide them to the strip of beach just below the house. Her flash of light seemed to have shown them the direction; for she was almost certain that she heard, in another quiet moment, the sound of the bow on the gravel. She waited. How the wind roared!

Again there was a crash of the ship's cannon, its report followed a moment later by the splitting of wood. Voices and the tramp of feet were coming up the path. Somebody said, "They got our boat that time." And a deeper voice answered: "It's lucky we were no longer in it. Go easy there, mate; he's too tired to move another step." Three figures came out of the darkness, two of them supporting a third. The little group stumbled across the doorstep and stood blinking in the light of the warm kitchen.

Elizabeth closed the door against the rain and, as is always the duty of a hostess when guests come in out of the cold and wet, bent to put another log on the fire. One did that and then asked questions. But when she straightened up to look at the unexpected visitors she had no need to ask. She cried out quickly, "Why, it's Cousin Nathaniel!"

"We thought this must be my uncle's house and that you at least would hear our hail."

THE SAMPLER

Her cousin Nathaniel Holmes was only a year or two older than her own fourteen years; but he looked like a man indeed with his tall figure, his white, tired face, and his rough seaman's coat.

The broad-shouldered man beside him said in a big, friendly voice, "'Tis a shame to frighten you, young mistress, but men who are fleeing for their lives will take shelter anywhere."

"You did not frighten me," she answered bravely.

They were helping their comrade into the armchair in which she had been sitting. When once the tall man with graying hair had dropped back on the cushions, her cousin Nat stooped, picked something off the floor, and handed it to her.

"Your sampler, Elizabeth," he said with a broad smile. "I know how you love to sew, and I see how prettily you have made the tombstone. I fear you are to be badly interrupted in your favorite work this night. You wonder why we are here? Have you ever heard men speak of the custom of the British Navy—that of taking seamen by force?"

She had indeed, and her cheeks colored angrily as she thought of it. All America was excited over this same matter, which was to end by leading two friendly nations into war with each other. England had need of sailors and gunners for her warships, and since the life on board was hard, cruel, and dangerous, very few men would offer themselves for it. As a result the officers were ordered by their government to take men where they could, and take them they did.

They had fallen into the way of stopping American vessels at sea, searching them, and declaring that certain able seamen were really British and must be carried on board English ships to serve in His Majesty's Navy. It was of little use for the American captains to fight against them. The English battleships always had a row of cannon with which to back up their demands. Many a good man was rowed away and taken on board a proud, tall-sailed English vessel, each looking back to his own ship and to his comrades, whom perhaps he was never to see again. But here it seemed were three, at least, who had dared to refuse and had made this bold effort to escape.

"Yes," Nat said, looking up to answer the question in Elizabeth's eyes, "they took us all three, though Bo'sun Leonard here is an old sailor, and though I am not yet a real seaman, for I sailed only six months ago. We swore to one another that we were not going to fight for the British King."

He held out his thin, cold hands to the blaze, saying no more, for he did not seem to think it was necessary to tell just what they had done. It was the broad-shouldered man, Dan Peters, who finished the account. He gave it in the most matter-of-fact way in the world. It was plain to see that all three were too weary to think of much of anything except that they were warm and safe here, at least for a few minutes.

Peters told of how they were carried away in a boat with four British sailors and a lieutenant, all armed with pistols and heavy swords. They made Peters pull an oar in the middle of the boat; but as they came near the towering side of the British vessel he saw, to his amazement, that Nat had leaped up to seize the officer around the middle, pinning his arms so that he could not draw his sword. The brief, hard struggle ended in the lieutenant's being flung overboard, while the two older Americans each fought with the sailor nearest him.

"We swung them over the side like sacks of gravel," Peters related cheerfully. "They were so taken by surprise that they had no time to fight. The last one jumped to save us the trouble, and we caught up the oars and slipped away into the twilight, for it was just beginning to get dark. All those we dropped overboard got to the ship, and before she could get her cannon aimed at us we were in among the islands. But we didn't dare land anywhere along these swampy shores."

The war vessel had followed, most of the shots from it going wide in the dark, but a few of them were good guesses which almost hit their mark. Higher and higher up the bay they had come, the men in the boat fighting so hard against wind and tide that Leonard, the old sailor, was fainting at the oars, and even the other two could scarcely lift and dip the heavy blades.

"Then we saw your light."

Old Nora, like Elizabeth, had without a word turned herself to caring for the comfort of the guests. She brought a great bowl of stew from the cupboard, poured it into a big iron kettle, and hung the kettle on the swinging hook. Nat helped her to lift it, and she nodded thanks and greeting to him, but asked no questions. She had been deaf so long that she was used to the idea of not having things explained to her. She trotted back and forth, casting curious looks at the weary and dripping guests, but she stirred and seasoned the soup, cut bread from the long loaf, and said nothing. Elizabeth, however, kept no such silence.

"What will you do next?" she asked, looking from one to the other.

They were all three quiet, so that the beat of the rain outside and the harsh voice of the wind were the only sounds. The storm roared, then dropped an instant, and in the stillness there came to all of them the sound which no person who lives by the sea can ever fail to recognize—the creak of oars in their oarlocks. Even Bo'sun Leonard, sitting with closed eyes in the big chair, heard it and raised his drooping head.

"It's only a matter of minutes before they'll be here." It was the first time he had spoken, but his words were quick and very clear. "They can't fail to visit the only house that's in sight. You're to go on, you two. Do you hear me? That's orders. I can't move; but you're to get away, and I will stay here."

It is the habit of every sailor to obey the commands of his superior. Nat and Peters hesitated a minute. Then Nat turned suddenly to the door of the bedroom opening from the kitchen. "Carry him in there," he said. "There's no time even to get him upstairs. And by some chance they may not search the house."

They lifted Leonard, bore him into the room, and laid him on the bed. He did not speak again or even open his eyes, but he made an impatient motion with his hand. They were to go.

"If we could get across the hill to the Mallorys' house," Nat said, "we could get Ephraim Mallory and his three sons to stand by us, that I know. We could make a dash back and get Leonard away safe, even if the British had already laid hands on him. But if harm should come to you, Elizabeth—"

"No harm will come to us—two women who have done nothing," Elizabeth answered boldly, more boldly than she felt. "We will keep them back as long as we can." She put her mouth close to Nora's ear and shouted. "We are going to have still more guests. Pile up the fire and bring out the biggest ham."

Nat hesitated a moment in the doorway. Peters said, as he went through the door: "And if they do follow us, little mistress, would you try to flash a light at the window, maybe, if you could do it without danger? Then we would know where to make a stand." The door banged, and Elizabeth was left in the kitchen, listening.

The wind, roaring over the hill, drowned the noise of their retreating steps, but in the shelter of the house another sound began to be very plain, the heavy, orderly tramp of marching feet coming up from the landing— many of them it seemed, oh, very many. Then there were voices, a thundering knock, and a command, "Open, in the King's name."

They all came in together—a tall officer wrapped in a dripping cape, a file of men behind him, their shoes, their hair, their rough blue coats streaming with the rain.

Elizabeth made her most polite curtsy, just as she had seen her mother do when important guests arrived. "My parents are from home," she said calmly; "but we shall do our best to make you comfortable. You—you look as though you might be in need of refreshment."

The officer—it might possibly have been the same lieutenant whom Nat had thrown out of the boat—swung his rapid glance about the room. The big spotless kitchen was bright with the leaping fire and its reflection in the polished copper pots and pans. Elizabeth was laying a white cloth on the long table. Nora had unwrapped the ham and was already cutting delicate, rosy slices. The officer looked, hesitated, and then sat down in the big chair.

"The men will march better if they have some food," he said. "That was a long row we had, searching along the shore. Dobbs, go out and see that guards are placed around the house. If there is anyone hiding here it will be impossible to get away while they are watching. We may as well give ourselves the relief of a little warmth and food and look for those runaway rascals later on. Well, young woman, let me see what your house has to offer."

It was a splendid feast which the old farmhouse gave its guests that night. The whitest linen out of the great chest in the parlor, the glass dishes and the blue plates that had come from England with Elizabeth's great-grandmother, the polished silver spoons were all brought forth. The choicest preserves, the last vegetables from the garden, the ham cured by a recipe a hundred years old, made a supper fit for King George III himself instead of one of his lower and lazier officers. "Have you this?" the blue-uniformed man would ask now and again. "Do you not have that?"

"In a minute, sir; in just a minute," Elizabeth would answer. She lingered over the serving as long as she dared, she ducked curtsies when she received an order, she did everything to make the meal last a little longer.

Nora went back and forth, waiting on the men who sat humbly upon the benches by the fire while their commander dined alone at the long table. It was fortunate that farmhouses of that day had generous supplies in their storerooms. A large company it was, ten men, with even larger appetites.

The minutes went by, oh, so slowly. Nat and his comrade would be across the farm, Elizabeth was thinking; they would be climbing the hill; once over the top they would be within reach of the Mallorys' house. How long, how very long it took to reach shelter on this stormy night. But time was passing. Triumph colored her cheeks. They were growing safer every minute, safer. . . .

"And now," ordered the British officer, pushing his chair back suddenly, "I have even a mind to lay me down to take a little rest before I start out in the storm again. Light me a candle. I will go into the bedroom yonder and sleep a little."

No! Oh, no! Elizabeth had almost cried out the words

in her terror, but she put her hand over her mouth and held them back. "We have better rooms above," she managed to say, her voice shaking, "if it would please you just to walk up the stairs."

"In an American farmhouse the best bed is always in the spare chamber below," he answered stubbornly. "I have been on shore often enough to learn that." He yawned widely and got up. "In our wandering life we must learn how to sleep comfortably when we can."

He walked across the kitchen. Elizabeth had lighted the candle and stood shaking, holding out her arm to bar the door. How, how could she stop him? She looked hopefully past him to old Nora beside the fire. Could not Nora think of something? But no, what did she understand?

The officer stopped, staring at her as she barred the way. His heavy brows drew together in a suspicious frown. "What is this? You have, after all, something hidden in that room? Out of my way!" He stepped forward.

Old Nora dropped a spoon with a great clatter. She took one limping step across the floor and flung the kitchen door wide open. "Don't waste time," she cried in her trembling old voice. "It was that way they went. Can't you see the marks of their feet beyond the door-stone? Go, if you have any hope of catching them."

There was a thump of heavy feet, a clash of swords drawn, a hail of orders as the men jumped up, seized their arms, and swung toward the door. The officer snatched up his cloak. "Why did you not tell me this before?" he roared at Nora.

"Eh? I'm so deaf, how was I to know your errand? Nobody tells me anything." He was over the sill, but swung around on the doorstep to give a final order.

"Dobbs, stand here and do not let either of these women pass. Keep three men to guard the windows so that they cannot make a signal. Do not follow us until we are well away." He was gone, and the door slammed behind him.

Elizabeth stood for a second trembling, wondering what she should do next. Then she seized a lantern from its hook on the wall, lighted it at the fire, and sped up the stairs. The door as well as the windows was guarded, but the men would not be watching that little round opening, hardly a real window, just above the roof of the kitchen.

She was beside it; she had wrapped her skirt about the lantern to hide its light; and she had climbed out through the space, which was little bigger than the porthole of a ship. The shingles on the roof below were wet and slippery, but she knew how to run across them, knew that she must keep running or she would fall. She ended, with a bump, against the great stone chimney. Steadying herself with one arm against the warm, rough stones, she made her way around the chimney and was on the peak of the kitchen roof, facing the distant hill.

Fearlessly she swung the lantern once, and again and again. A deep voice below shouted to her to stop. She took no notice, and suddenly a humming bullet went

past her and hit against the chimney. The crash of the big pistol would give warning, even if the swinging light was not enough. Nat and his companion would know that the British were coming behind them. The lantern fell from her hand and broke on the stones below, but she had given her wild signal of danger and could do no more.

It had taken but a few seconds to run across the roof, but now it was slow minutes as she crawled back in the wind and the wet. Once inside and downstairs, she stood close to Nora by the fire. Her knees felt suddenly like water and her voice was trembling.

"Nora," she said close to the old woman's ear, "how could you tell them where Nat had gone?"

"It was better to give the old one a chance, even at the cost of a bit of danger to the young ones," answered Nora. "Yes, you told me nothing, but it did not take me long to guess what was going on. I saw the Revolution; I've been by before this when hunted men were hiding from their enemies." She drew a great breath and smoothed her apron. "Sakes, but we have a lot of dishes to wash up. Men do be great ones for messing a kitchen!"

Elizabeth was not of much help in setting the place to rights. Again and again she stood at the back door, straining to hear any sound that the wind might carry. Was that a distant shout and another? What was that? Voices that were far off. They were nearer; they were coming this way. Had they taken her cousin? Would they in the end lay hands on poor Bo'sun Leonard, lying helpless within? Oh, Nat! Oh, Nat!

There was shouting and stumbling before the door. It swung back, and a dripping figure, sword in hand, was on the doorstep. Here was no blue coat or gold lace; here was no heavy British seaman. This thin, long figure could be only one person—her cousin Nat!

Nathaniel threw his weapon down upon the table, where there were still standing the dishes and glasses which had been used for the lieutenant's dinner.

"'Tis the wrong men who have feasted in this house tonight," he said. "Such a dinner! And we out there in the dark, hungry! May the Mallory boys come in?"

There was enough left; for the farmhouse could feed one company and still have plenty remaining for another. Nora, smiling broadly, brought them more and more food; the fire leaped on the hearth, and everyone together tried to give an account of what had happened. Nat and Peters were just coming over the hill with the Mallorys behind them when they saw Elizabeth's signal, and found a favorable place to make a stand against the advancing British.

"They could not guess our numbers in the dark, and they decided, after the first attack, to retreat to their boat," Nat said. "They will have a pretty row out to their ship, for she has had to stand offshore in this wind. Here's a pleasant journey to them, and may they take profit by the lesson they have learned. It is not well to lay hands on American seamen."

"The whole British nation may learn an even better

one in time," Dan Peters added; but most of his remark was lost in the hollow of the cup of cider he had raised to his lips.

It was easy to see by looking at Bo'sun Leonard that he must stay where he was for many days. Perhaps, indeed, he would never be able to go to sea again. But the other two stood up at last and said good night.

"We have to join our ship," Nathaniel said. "Our skipper will be in need of sailors, and he was to stop at Norfolk, where we can meet him." The night's adventures seemed to mean little to men whose days and hours were passed among the dangers of the sea. "No; we can spend no more time except to offer you our thanks, Elizabeth Lloyd."

Two hours later Elizabeth's father and mother came home. Their daughter was sitting by the table, quietly stitching away at the task which she had begun so much earlier. She looked up as her parents came in.

"There is a guest in the spare chamber," she remarked calmly, "and there have been others here to supper. And see, Mother, I have finished my willow tree. Instead of the verse at the bottom I am going to embroider 'Liberty Forever.' And then I am never going to sew another sampler. I think, now that I am fourteen, that I have other things to do besides stitching pictures of tombstones."

Don Pedro's Christmas

ERIC P. KELLY

Madre Marta had said at dinner that Don Pedro simply couldn't go to the midnight Christmas Eve service with Lolla.

"But Don Pedro is good," declared Lolla. "He works all the time, and I don't know what I'd do without him. I would just tie him outside near the door. I know he would be quiet."

"Well . . . ," said her mother finally, "take him along if you must."

Lolla's face was radiant. To be sure, remaining outside the church wasn't so good as being inside, but Don Pedro would be able to hear the music and the sermon and the bells.

She ran out from the little square adobe dwelling and hurried to find her pet, who was calmly eating dried grass.

DON PEDRO'S CHRISTMAS

"My good little burro," she exclaimed, throwing her arms around the shaggy neck, "I just couldn't go to church without you."

Don Pedro said nothing, but continued to eat. His tail, however, flicked merrily and his eyes twinkled; at least so it seemed to Lolla. Certainly his ears twitched.

On both sides of the little New Mexican valley the land rose sharply to high mesas, red in places, in others gray; slopes packed with gravel and small stones. Through its midst ran the tiny river, at the moment nearly dry in an unusually warm December, but with a bed that was many times the width of the stream. For there were times when cloudbursts or sudden meltings of ice in the hills above La Madera spread its bosom and raised the sluggish current to torrential force. Off in the distance the mountains of the Sangre de Cristo Range cut the sky, while up- and downstream small adobe houses like their own, adorned with strings of brilliant chili peppers, stood out against the now bare cottonwoods and the brown fields where crops had been.

For four of Lolla's nine years Don Pedro, the prince of little burros, had been her friend, companion, brother almost, for in those nights when a light layer of snow swirled down from the peaks she had led him inside the house, and he had folded up his legs and lain on the floor beside her cot. In the daytime she often went with him up on the mesas where her father gathered wood, and bound it on the faithful creature's back in neat, round bundles. Sometimes she sat astride him and galloped across the mesas, or climbed laboriously foot by foot up the incline leading away from the river. She was more fortunate than he, because she could express her love to him in words, while he had only ears to twitch in fond signs.

And now it was the day before Christmas, and the hot afternoon was wearing on. "If the heat goes on," her father had said that morning, "snow will melt in the hills, and then look out for the river. And now I'm not too sure about our bridge if the water rises. Part of the foundation was washed out last summer, and it's leaning badly."

By nighttime the heat had not abated. They sat down to supper in the little room where they ate, lived, and slept, attired in light clothes, just as in summer. The father had on his best clothes, a yellow coat and blue trousers. The mother had a print dress from Santa Fe. Lolla wore the gown that a friend had sent her from a store, white, with pictures upon it of burros, and men with large hats, and women with veils and shawls over their heads.

All at once night was upon them. They had eaten early and lightly in preparation for the midnight service, but night comes swiftly in a New Mexican winter, the day leaping away over the mountaintops with the red, sinking sun, and darkness coming up from valleys and canyons to engulf the world. Now the evening star blazed in the sky, and Lolla, running to the door, exclaimed, "The star! The star. It's Christmas!"

Then suddenly she looked about, perplexed. "I don't see Don Pedro." The little donkey was not there. The light through the open door showed only the end of his rope.

"He didn't come back today. It's so warm. He's eating dried grass," said the mother. "But there isn't time to look for him. We'll have to get started soon."

"I'm going to look for him," said Lolla determinedly.

"You can if you want to. Your father and I are getting started." Those pre-service minutes were very valuable to Madre Marta, for in them she met her neighbors and talked over everything of interest that had gone on during the week.

It wasn't far from the house to the church, just down the road and over the bridge and about half a mile up to the small steepled building that had stood there since 1590. As Lolla had been there over this route a hundred times or more in the dark, her mother had no fear for her.

So in a few minutes the older members of the family set out. They went on foot, not owning a horse or automobile. Many of the Spanish families in the valley had cars, most of them old, but all serviceable.

As the parents reached the bridge they saw the headlights of more than a dozen of these bobbing their way toward it, and as they crossed they had to be careful to keep well to one side to give the cars the right of way.

The bridge was not of the best construction, even when it had been new. It was narrow and rough, and the recent floods had loosened the underpinnings on one side so that it slanted badly.

At one point the father looked down at the dark stream. "It's getting higher," he said as the reflection from a passing car lit up the icy water. "We'll have to be careful of this bridge. It'll go down sometime. Then we shall have to use the rougher road to the other bridge downstream."

In the meantime Lolla had roamed up and down the valley looking for the burro.

"Don Pedro, Don Pedro," she called. With every call echoes came back to her from the slanting mesa sides, but there was no sound of scampering feet, no burro voice raised in a deafening bray.

She had searched for more than an hour when she decided to give up hunting and go to the church. It would be such a pity to waste time while the Padre was there. . . . Dear old Padre José, the priest from Española, so kind, so gentle, with such a nice voice and nice hands. She loved him, she thought, almost as much as she did Don Pedro, and that was a whole lot.

Her mother had left a lantern for her beside the door. She took this up and started on her way. When she was on the bridge it seemed to her that it swayed more than usual. Turning to one side, she lowered the lantern a little over the rail, and then sprang back in fright. The water was very high. How black it was, how swift, how silent!

Usually when the river rose there was a roar that filled the valley; the whole flood came at once. That was usually after a cloudburst. But now the stream came rushing on with mighty force, and yet making little noise. It had, as a matter of fact, risen slowly. The melting ice up above had added gradually to its torrent. The river was still rising!

She hurried on, anxious now to get to the other side. But just as she was on the last little span she stopped suddenly and her heart began to beat swiftly. Something was moving at the river's edge, and it was not ice.

At the end of the structure, where it slanted down to the road, she sat down and swung her lantern out. What a curious noise. For a moment she could see nothing. She called out. The noise ceased.

All was silent again except the rushing of the river and the crackle of small particles of ice on its surface. Deep silence lay about the hills and the village. There was nothing to be seen, either, except for the small circle of light from her lantern.

"Who are you?" she called again.

Then without warning came the explosive, raucous accents of a burro.

Don Pedro. She stopped in her tracks. He's under the bridge. What shall I do to help him?

The impulse to action gripped her. Running down the slope, she turned to the right and descended the bank to the water's edge. Raising the lantern, she held it out as far as she could, and there not five feet away were a little brown tail and a pair of sturdy legs.

He's stuck in the mud. Don Pedro!

It came to her immediately to run for help. But then

she realized that all the houses along the road were deserted. Everybody was up in the church.

So, acting on impulse, she waded out into the rising river. It was not very deep here, and the bed was all hard gravel and large stones. Her mind was so set on extricating her burro that she did not notice that the water was icy cold. Don Pedro was in the river, and somehow she must get him out.

"Don Pedro, Don Pedro, I'm coming," she cried, and at the sound of her voice the brown tail began to flip.

It was impossible to get much farther. The gravel was slanting off into soft clay. To reach his head and try to urge him back up was out of the question. She hung her lantern where its feeble gleams threw a pale light on the scene.

Then, deeper in the water, she seized her pet's tail in both hands and tugged with all her might. "Don Pedro! Kick," she commanded. "Kick as hard as you can, Don Pedro."

There was a violent effort, and one leg came clear. "That's it," she said. "That's it. Try again." She threw her whole weight into the force of the pull.

Splash. His front feet were out of the mire. "Now—" He reared up as burros will rear and swung in a half circle. Another splash. Then suddenly by her side in the dim light the little burro went plunging up the bank.

As Lolla turned to wade toward the shore the feeble light disclosed something that made her gasp. She had not noticed it before, for she had been so intent upon

Pedro. Grasping the lantern, she turned and hurried back to the shore.

"Don Pedro, Don Pedro," she called.

He came up, and leaving the lantern on the bridge in the hope that its feeble rays might serve as a temporary warning to travelers, she flung herself upon his back. "Go, Don Pedro. Go. Quick as you can."

They were off over the rutty road, with all the speed the little burro possessed. Sure-footedly, he kept to the even places.

In the old church good Padre José had just completed a talk to the inhabitants of the villages who had come in for the midnight service. He had told them in his kind, firm voice, full of the philosophy of experience and knowledge, what the joys of Christmas Day meant to the world. Of the Child born in the manger in Bethlehem and the Wise Men and Shepherds, people like themselves, who had followed the Star.

The place was crowded. Suddenly in the back of the church there was the sound of voices, exclamations. The rear door swung wide open, and Padre José looked down the narrow aisle and gasped in astonishment.

For through the door and up the aisle, scattering the men in the rear of the church and the children clustering about against the walls, came, of all things, a little burro. He was soggy and wet, his hair was dripping, and the mud was thick about his forelegs.

"What is this?" Padre José was indignant. "Such disturbance in a church!"

But as the burro came up the aisle, almost to the

steps leading to the altar rail, he saw that riding on his back was a small girl. She was as disheveled as the burro. But her eyes were shining with purpose.

"Padre José," she cried. "The upper bridge is all washed out at the bottom. If anybody goes over it in an automobile it will fall. People will be killed. Don't let them, Padre José."

The priest's expression changed. He instantly caught the force of the child's purpose. "You have just come from there?" he asked.

"Yes, Padre José."

The whole congregation had now risen to its feet in alarm. All thoughts were on the girl's words.

Still sitting on Don Pedro's back she blurted out the whole story—how the burro had wandered into the river, how she had gone to get him out, how she had seen one foundation of the bridge so badly washed that it was likely to topple at any moment. As she finished, Padre José came down from the steps and touched the little animal with tender hands.

"God works in ways that we know not of," he said. "Go, Juan and Mario. Take lanterns and guard the old bridge. And we who remain here, let us join in a prayer of thanksgiving that perhaps lives have been saved through this little burro." He smiled down at Lolla. "Welcome, my child. Your lateness was in good cause."

Lolla had slipped from Don Pedro's back and knelt in the aisle. As if sensing the place, and being moreover tired, Don Pedro lay down at full length. As the service went on and Lolla's heart quieted she glanced at the animal lying beside her. Lovingly she scratched the fuzzy little head. She remembered another little burro in a story that she loved.

He has a right to be here on Christmas Eve, she thought.

Weep No More, My Lady

✕✕✕

JAMES STREET

The moonlight symphony of swamp creatures hushed abruptly, and the dismal bog was as peaceful as unborn time and seemed to brood in its silence. The gaunt man glanced back at the boy and motioned for him to be quiet, but it was too late. Their presence was discovered. A jumbo frog rumbled a warning and the swamp squirmed into life as its denizens scuttled to safety.

Fox fire was glowing to the west and the bayou was slapping the cypress knees when suddenly a haunting laugh echoed through the wilderness, a strange chuckling yodel ending in a weird "*gro-o-o.*"

The boy's eyes were wide and staring. "That's it, Uncle Jess. Come on! Let's catch it!"

"Uh, oh." The man gripped his shotgun. "That ain't no animal. That's a thing."

They hurried noiselessly in the direction of the sound

that Skeeter had been hearing for several nights. Swamp born and reared, they feared nothing they could shoot or outwit, so they slipped out of the morass and to the side of a ridge. Suddenly Jesse put out his hand and stopped the child, then pointed up the slope. The animal, clearly visible in the moonlight, was sitting on its haunches, its head cocked sideways as it chuckled. It was a merry and rather melodious little chuckle.

Skeeter grinned in spite of his surprise, then said, "*Sh-h-h.* It'll smell us."

Jesse said, "Can't nothing smell that far. Wonder what the durn thing is?" He peered up the ridge, studying the creature. He had no intention of shooting unless attacked, for Jesse Tolliver and his nephew never killed wantonly.

The animal, however, did smell them and whipped her nose into the wind, crouched and braced. She was about sixteen inches high and weighed twenty-two pounds. Her coat was red and silky, and there was a blaze of white down her chest and a circle of white around her throat. Her face was wrinkled and sad, like a wise old man's.

Jesse shook his head. "Looks som'n like a mixture of bloodhound and terrier from here," he whispered. "It beats me—"

"It's a dog, all right," Skeeter said.

"Can't no dog laugh."

"That dog can." The boy began walking toward the animal, his right hand outstretched. "Heah. Heah. I ain't gonna hurt you."

The dog, for she was a dog, cocked her head from one side to the other and watched Skeeter. She was trembling, but she didn't run. And when Skeeter knelt by her she stopped trembling, for the ways of a boy with a dog are mysterious. He stroked her, and the trim little creature looked up at him and blinked her big hazel eyes. Then she turned over and Skeeter scratched her. She closed her eyes, stretched and chuckled, a happy mixture of chortle and yodel. Jesse ambled up and the dog leaped to her feet and sprang between the boy and the man.

Skeeter calmed her. "That's just Uncle Jess."

Jesse, still bewildered, shook his head again. "I still say that ain't no dog. She don't smell and she don't bark. Ain't natural. And look at her! Licking herself like a cat."

"Well, I'll be a catty wampus," Skeeter said. "Never saw a dog do that before." However, he was quick to defend any mannerism of his friend and said, "She likes to keep herself clean. She's a lady and I'm gonna name her that, and she's mine 'cause I found her."

"Lady, huh?"

"No, sir. My Lady. If I name her just plain Lady, how folks gonna know she's mine?" He began stroking his dog again. "Gee m'netty, Uncle Jess, I ain't never had nothing like this before."

"It still don't make sense to me," Jesse said. But he didn't care, for he was happy because the child was happy.

Like most mysteries, there was no mystery at all about

My Lady. She was a lady, all right, an aristocratic Basenji, one of those strange barkless dogs of Africa. Her ancestors were pets of the Pharaohs and her line was well established when the now-proud races of men were wandering about Europe, begging handouts from Nature. A bundle of nerves and muscles, she would fight anything, and could scent game up to eighty yards. She had the gait of an antelope and was odorless, washing herself before and after meals. However, the only noises she could make were a piercing cry that sounded almost human and that chuckling little chortle. She could chuckle only when happy and she had been happy in the woods. Now she was happy again.

As most men judge values, she was worth more than all the possessions of Jesse and his nephew. Several of the dogs had been shipped to New Orleans to avoid the dangerous upper route, thence by motor to a northern kennel. While crossing Mississippi, My Lady had escaped from the station wagon. Her keeper had advertised in several papers, but Jesse and Skeeter never saw papers.

Skeeter said, "Come on, M'Lady. Let's go home."

The dog didn't hesitate, but walked proudly at the boy's side to a cabin on the bank of the bayou. Skeeter crumbled corn bread, wet it with pot likker, and put it before her. She sniffed the food disdainfully at first, then ate it only when she saw the boy fix a bowl for his uncle. She licked herself clean and explored the cabin, sniffing the brush brooms, the piles of wild pecans and hickory nuts, and then the cots. Satisfied at last, she jumped on

Skeeter's bed, tucked her nose under her paws, and went to sleep.

"Acts like she owns the place," Jesse said.

"Where you reckon she came from?" The boy slipped his overall straps from his shoulders, flexed his stringy muscles, and yawned.

"Lord knows. Circus, maybe." He looked at M'Lady quickly. "Say, maybe she's a freak and run off from some show. Bet they'd give us two dollars for her."

Skeeter's face got long. "You don't aim to get rid of her?"

The old man put his shotgun over the mantel and lit his pipe. "Skeets, if you want that thing I wouldn't get shed of her for a piece of bottom land a mile long. Already plowed and planted."

"I reckoned you wouldn't."

Jesse sat down and leaned back, blowing smoke into the air to drive away mosquitoes. The boy got a brick and hammer and began cracking nuts, pounding the meat to pulp so his uncle could chew it. Skeeter's yellow hair hadn't been cut for months and was tangled. He had freckles too. And his real name was Jonathan. His mother was Jesse's only sister and had died when the child was born. No one thereabout ever knew what happened to his father. Jesse, a leathery, toothless old man with faded blue eyes, took him to bring up and called him Skeeter because he was so little.

In the village, where Jesse seldom visited, folks wondered if he were fit'n to rear a little boy. They considered him shiftless and no-count. Jesse had lived all of his sixty years in the swamp, and his way of life was a torment to folks who believed life must be lived by rules. He earned a few dollars selling jumbo frogs and pelts, but mostly he just paddled around the swamp, watching things and teaching Skeeter about life.

The villagers might have tried to send Skeeter to an orphanage but for Joe (Cash) Watson, the storekeeper. Cash was a hard man, but fair. He often hunted with Jesse, and the old man had trained Cash's dogs. When there was talk of sending Skeeter away, Cash said, "You ain't agonna do it. You just don't take young'uns away from their folks." And that's all there was to it.

Jesse never coveted the "frills and furbelows of the fool folks" and yearned for only two things—a twenty-gauge shotgun for Skeeter and a set of Roebuckers for himself, as he called store-bought teeth. Cash had promised him the gun and the best false teeth in the catalogue for forty-six dollars. Jesse had saved $9.37.

"Someday I'm gonna get them Roebuckers," he often told Skeeter. "Then I'm gonna eat me enough roastin' ears to kill a goat. Maybe I can get a set with a couple of gold teeth in 'em. I seen a man one time with six gold teeth."

Once Skeeter asked him, "Why don't you get a job with the W.P. and A. and make enough money to buy them Roebuckers?"

"I don't want 'em that bad," Jesse said.

So he was happy for Skeeter to have M'Lady, thinking the dog would sort of make up for the shotgun.

The boy cracked as many nuts as his uncle wanted,

then put the hammer away. He was undressing when he glanced over at his dog. "Gosh, Uncle Jess. I'm scared somebody'll come get her."

"I ain't heard of nobody losing no things around here. If'n they had, they'd been to me 'fo' now, being's I know all about dogs and the swamp."

"That's so," Skeeter said. "But you don't reckon she belonged to another fellow like me, do you? I know how I'd feel if I had a dog like her and she got lost."

Jesse said, "She didn't belong to another fellow like you. If'n she had, she wouldn't be so happy here."

Skeeter fed M'Lady biscuits and molasses for breakfast, and although the Basenji ate it, she still was hungry when she went into the swamp with the boy. He was hoping he could find a bee tree or signs of wild hogs. They were at the edge of a clearing when M'Lady's chokebore nose suddenly tilted and she froze to a flash point, pausing only long enough to get set. Then she darted to the bayou, at least sixty yards away, dived into a clump of reeds, and snatched a water rat. She was eating it when Skeeter ran up.

"Don't do that," he scolded. "Ain't you got no more sense than run into water after things? A snake or a gator might snatch you."

The Basenji dropped the rat and tucked her head. She knew the boy was displeased, and when she looked up at him her eyes were filled and a woe-begone expression was on her face.

Skeeter tried to explain, "I didn't mean to hurt your feelings. Don't cry." He stepped back quickly and stared

at her, at the tears in her eyes. "She *is* crying! Be John
Brown!" Skeeter called her and ran toward the cabin,
where Jesse was cutting splinters.

"Uncle Jess! Guess what else my dog can do!"

"Whistle?" the old man laughed.

"She can cry! I declare to goodness! Not out loud,
but she can cry just the same."

Jesse knew that most dogs will get watery-eyed on
occasion, but, not wanting to ridicule M'Lady's accom-
plishments, asked, "What made her cry?"

"Well, sir, we were walking along and all of a sudden
she got a scent and flash pointed and then—" Skeeter
remembered something.

"Then what?"

Skeeter sat on the steps. "Uncle Jess," he said slowly,
"we must have been fifty or sixty yards from that rat
when she smelled it."

"What rat? What's eating you?"

The child told him the story and Jesse couldn't believe it. For a dog to pick up the scent of a water rat
at sixty yards simply isn't credible. Jesse reckoned
Skeeter's love for M'Lady had led him to exaggerate.

Skeeter knew Jesse didn't believe the story, so he
said, "Come on. I'll show you." He whistled for M'Lady.

The dog came up. "Hey," Jesse said. "That thing
knows what a whistle means. Shows she's been around
folks." He caught the dog's eye and commanded, "Heel!"

But M'Lady cocked her head quizzically. Then she
turned to the boy and chuckled softly. She'd never

heard the order before. That was obvious. Her nose came up into the breeze and she wheeled.

Her curved tail suddenly was still and her head was poised.

"Flash pointing," Jesse said. "Well, I'll be a monkey's uncle!"

M'Lady held the strange point only for a second, though, then dashed toward a corn patch about eighty yards from the cabin.

Halfway to the patch she broke her gait and began creeping. A whir of feathered lightning sounded in the corn and a covey of quail exploded almost under her nose. She sprang and snatched a bird.

"Partridges!" Jesse's jaw dropped.

The child was as motionless as stone, his face white and his eyes wide in amazement. Finally he found his voice. "She was right here when she smelled them birds. A good eighty yards."

"I know she ain't no dog now," Jesse said. "Can't no dog do that."

"She's fast as greased lightning and ain't scared of nothing." Skeeter was still under the spell of the adventure. "She's a hunting dog from way back."

"She ain't no dog a-tall, I'm telling you. It ain't human." Jesse walked toward M'Lady and told her to fetch the bird, but the dog didn't understand. Instead, she pawed it. "Well," Jesse said. "One thing's certain. She ain't no bird hunter."

"She can do anything," Skeeter said. "Even hunt

birds. Maybe I can make a bird dog out'n her. Wouldn't that be som'n?"

"You're batty. Maybe a coon dog, but not a bird dog. I know 'bout dogs."

"Me too," said Skeeter. And he did. He'd seen Jesse train many dogs, even pointers, and had helped him train Big Boy, Cash Watson's prize gun dog.

Jesse eyed Skeeter and read his mind.

"It can't be done, Skeets."

"Maybe not, but I aim to try. Any dog can run coons and rabbits, but it takes a pure D humdinger to hunt birds. Ain't no sin in trying, is it?"

"Naw," Jesse said slowly. "But she'll flush birds."

"I'll learn her not to."

"She won't hold no point. Any dog'll flash point. And she'll hunt rats."

"I'm gonna learn her just to hunt birds. And I'm starting right now," Skeeter said. He started walking away, then turned. "I seen a man once train a razor-back hawg to point birds. You know as good as me that if a dog's got pure D hoss sense and a fellow's got bat brains he can train the dog to hunt birds."

"Wanta bet?" Jesse issued the challenge in an effort to keep Skeeter's enthusiasm and determination at the high-water mark.

"Yes, sir. If I don't train my dog, then I'll cut all the splinters for a year. If I do, you cut 'em."

"It's a go," Jesse said.

Skeeter ran to the bayou and recovered the rat M'Lady had killed. He tied it around his dog's neck. The

Basenji was indignant and tried to claw off the hateful burden. Failing, she ran into the house and under a bed, but Skeeter made her come out. M'Lady filled up then and her face assumed that nobody-loves-me look. The boy steeled himself, tapped M'Lady's nose with the rat, and left it around her neck.

"You done whittled out a job for yourself," Jesse said. "If'n you get her trained, you'll lose her in the brush. She's too fast and too little to keep up with."

"I'll bell her," Skeeter said. "I'm gonna learn her ever'thing. I got us a gun dog, Uncle Jess."

The old man sat on the porch and propped himself against the wall. "Bud, I don't know what that thing is. But you're a thoroughbred. John dog my hide!"

If Skeeter had loved M'Lady one bit less, his patience would have exploded during the ordeal of training the Basenji. It takes judgment and infinite patience to train a bird dog properly, but to train a Basenji that'll hunt anything to concentrate only on quail took something more than discipline and patience. It never could have been done except for that strange affinity between a boy and a dog.

M'Lady's devotion to Skeeter was so complete that she was anxious to do anything to earn a pat. It wasn't difficult to teach her to heel and follow at Skeeter's feet regardless of the urge to dash away and chase rabbits. The boy used a clothesline as a guide rope and made M'Lady follow him. The first time the dog tried to chase an animal, Skeeter pinched the rope around her neck just a bit and commanded, "Heel!" And when she obeyed, Skeeter released the noose. It took M'Lady only a few hours to associate disobedience with disfavor.

The dog learned that when she chased and killed a rat or rabbit, the thing would be tied around her neck. The only things she could hunt without being disciplined were quail. Of course she often mistook the scent of game chickens for quails and hunted them, but Skeeter punished her by scolding. He never switched his dog, but to M'Lady a harsh word from the boy hurt more than a hickory limb.

Jesse watched the dog's progress and pretended not to be impressed. He never volunteered suggestions. M'Lady learned quickly, but the task of teaching her to point birds seemed hopeless. Skeets knew she'd never point as pointers do, so he worked out his own system. He taught her to stand motionless when he shouted "Hup!" One day she got a scent of birds, paused or pointed for a moment as most animals will, and was ready to spring away when Skeeter said "Hup!"

M'Lady was confused. Every instinct urged her to chase the birds, but her master had said stand still. She broke, however, and Skeeter scolded her. She pouted at first, then filled up, but the boy ignored her until she obeyed the next command, then he patted her and she chuckled.

The lessons continued for days and weeks, and slowly and surely M'Lady learned her chores. She learned that the second she smelled birds she must stop and stand still until Skeeter flushed them; that she must not quiver when he shot.

Teaching her to fetch was easy, but teaching her to retrieve dead birds without damaging them was another matter. M'Lady had a hard mouth—that is, she sank her teeth into the birds. Skeeter used one of the oldest hunting tricks of the backwoods to break her.

He got a stick and wrapped it with wire and taught his dog to fetch it. Only once did M'Lady bite hard on the stick, and then the wire hurt her sensitive mouth. She quickly developed a habit of carrying the stick on her tongue and supporting it lightly with her teeth. Skeeter tied quail feathers on the stick, and soon M'Lady's education was complete.

Skeeter led Jesse into a field one day and turned his dog loose. She flashed to a point almost immediately. It was a funny point, and Jesse almost laughed. The dog's curved tail poked up over her back, she spraddled her front legs and sort of squatted, her nose pointing the birds more than forty yards away. She remained rigid until the boy flushed and shot, then she leaped away, seeking and fetching dead birds.

Jesse was mighty proud. "Well, Skeets, looks like you got yourself a bird hunter."

"Yes, sir," Skeeter said. "And you got yourself a job." He pointed toward the kindling pile.

The swamp was dressing for winter when Cash Watson drove down that day to give his Big Boy a workout in the wild brush.

He fetched Jesse a couple of cans of smoking tobacco and Skeeter a bag of peppermint jawbreakers. He locked his fine pointer in the corncrib for the night and was warming himself in the cabin when he noticed M'Lady for the first time. She was sleeping in front of the fire.

"What's that?" he asked.

"My dog," said Skeeter. "Ain't she a beaut?"

"She sure is." Cash grinned at Jesse. Skeeter went out to the well and Cash asked his old friend, "What the devil kind of mutt is that?"

"Search me," Jesse said. "Skeets found her in the swamp. I reckon she's got a trace of bloodhound in her and some terrier and a heap of just plain dog."

M'Lady cocked one ear and got up and stretched; then, apparently not liking the company, turned her tail toward Cash and strutted out, looking for Skeeter.

The men laughed. "Som'n wrong with her throat," Jesse said. "She can't bark. When she tries, she makes a funny sound, sort of a cackling, chuckling yodel. Sounds like she's laughing."

"Well," Cash said, "trust a young'un to love the orner'st dog he can find."

"Wait a minute," Jesse said. "She ain't no-count. She's a bird-hunting fool."

Just then Skeeter entered and Cash jestingly said, "Hear you got yourself a bird dog, son."

The boy clasped his hands behind him and rocked on the balls of his feet as he had seen the men do. "Well, now, I'll tell you, Mr. Cash. M'Lady does ever'thing except tote the gun."

"She must be fair to middling. Why not take her out with Big Boy tomorrow? Do my dog good to hunt in a brace."

"Me and my dog don't want to show Big Boy up. He's a pretty good ol' dog."

"Whoa!" Cash was every inch a bird-dog man and nobody could challenge him without a showdown. Besides, Skeeter was shooting up and should be learning a few things about life. "Any old boiler can pop off steam." Cash winked at Jesse.

"Well, now, sir, if you're itching for a run, I'll just double-dog dare you to run your dog against mine. And anybody who'll take a dare will pull up young cotton and push a widow woman's ducks in the water."

Cash admired the boy's confidence. "All right, son. It's a deal. What are the stakes?"

Skeeter started to mention the twenty-gauge gun he wanted, but changed his mind quickly. He reached down and patted M'Lady, then looked up. "If my dog beats yours, then you get them Roebuckers for Uncle Jess."

Jesse's chest suddenly was tight. Cash glanced from the boy to the man and he, too, was proud of Skeeter. "I wasn't aiming to go that high. But all right. What do I get if I win?"

"I'll cut you ten cords of stovewood."

"And a stack of splinters?"

"Yes, sir."

Cash offered his hand and Skeeter took it. "It's a race," Cash said. "Jesse will be the judge."

The wind was rustling the sage and there was a nip in the early-morning air when they took the dogs to a clearing and set them down. Skeeter snapped a bell around M'Lady's neck, and at word from Jesse the dogs were released.

Big Boy bounded away and began circling, ranging into the brush. M'Lady tilted her nose into the wind and ripped away toward the sage, her bell tinkling. Cash said, "She sure covers ground." Skeeter made no effort to keep up with her, but waited until he couldn't hear the bell, then ran for a clearing where he had last heard it. And there was M'Lady on a point.

Cash almost laughed out loud. "That ain't no point, son. That's a squat."

"She's got birds."

"Where?"

Jesse leaned against a tree and watched the fun.

Skeeter pointed toward a clump of sage. "She's pointing birds in that sage."

Cash couldn't restrain his mirth. "Boy, now that's what I call some pointing. Why, Skeeter, it's sixty or seventy yards to that sage."

Just then Big Boy flashed by M'Lady, his head high. He raced to the edge of the sage, caught the wind, then whipped around, freezing to a point. Cash called Jesse's attention to the point.

"That's M'Lady's point," Skeeter said. "She's got the same birds Big Boy has."

Jesse sauntered up. "The boy's right, Cash. I aimed to keep my mouth out'n this race, but M'Lady is pointing them birds. She can catch scents up to eighty yards."

Cash said, "Aw, go on. You're crazy." He walked over and flushed the birds.

Skeeter picked one off and ordered M'Lady to fetch. When she returned with the bird, the boy patted her and she began chuckling.

Cash really studied her then for the first time. "Hey!" he said suddenly. "A Basenji! That's a Basenji!"

"A what?" Jesse asked.

"I should have known." Cash was very excited. "That's the dog that was lost by them rich Yankees. I saw about it in the paper." He happened to look at Skeeter then and wished he had cut out his tongue.

The boy's lips were compressed and his face was drawn and white. Jesse had closed his eyes and was rubbing his forehead.

Cash, trying to dismiss the subject, said, "Just 'cause it was in the paper don't make it so. I don't believe that's the same dog, come to think of it."

"Do you aim to tell 'em where the dog is?" Skeeter asked.

Cash looked at Jesse, then at the ground. "It ain't none of my business."

"How 'bout you, Uncle Jess?"

"I ain't telling nobody nothin'."

"I know she's the same dog," Skeeter said. "On account of I just know it. But she's mine now." His voice rose and trembled. "And ain't nobody gonna take her away from me." He ran into the swamp. M'Lady was at his heels.

Cash said, "Durn my lip. I'm sorry, Jesse. If I'd kept my big mouth shut he'd never known the difference."

"It can't be helped now," Jesse said.

"'Course she beat Big Boy. Them's the best hunting dogs in the world. And she's worth a mint of money."

They didn't feel up to hunting and returned to the cabin and sat on the porch. Neither had much to say, but kept glancing toward the swamp where Skeeter and M'Lady were walking along the bayou. "Don't you worry," he said tenderly. "Ain't nobody gonna bother you."

He sat on a stump and M'Lady put her head on his knee. She wasn't worrying. Nothing could have been more contented than she was.

"I don't care if the sheriff comes down." Skeeter pulled her onto his lap and held her. "I don't give a whoop if the governor comes down. Even the President of the United States! The whole shebang can come, but ain't nobody gonna mess with you."

His words gave him courage and he felt better, but for only a minute. Then the tug of war between him and his conscience started.

"Once I found a Barlow knife and kept it, and it was all right," he mumbled.

But this is different.

"Finders, keepers; losers, weepers."

No, Skeeter.

"Well, I don't care. She's mine."

Remember what your Uncle Jess said.

"He said a heap of things."

Yes, but you remember one thing more than the rest. He said, "Certain things are right and certain things are wrong. And nothing ain't gonna ever change that. When you learn that, then you're fit'n to be a man." Remember, Skeeter?

A feeling of despair and loneliness almost overwhelmed him. He fought off the tears as long as he could, but finally he gave in, and his sobs caused M'Lady to peer into his face and wonder why he was acting that way when she was so happy. He put his arms around her neck and pulled her to him. "My li'l old puppy dog. Poor li'l old puppy dog."

He sniffed back his tears and got up and walked to the cabin. M'Lady curled up by the fire and the boy sat down, watching the logs splutter for several minutes. Then he said, almost in a whisper, "Uncle Jess, if you keep som'n that ain't yours, it's the same as stealing, ain't it?"

Cash leaned against the mantel and stared into the fire.

Jesse puffed his pipe slowly. "Son, that's som'n you got to settle with yourself."

Skeeter stood and turned his back to the flames, warming his hands. "Mr. Cash," he said slowly, "when you get back to your store, please let them folks know their dog is here."

"If that's how it is—"

"That's how it is," Skeeter said.

The firelight dancing on Jesse's face revealed the old man's dejection, and Skeeter, seeing it, said quickly,

"It's best for M'Lady. She's too good for the swamp. They'll give her a good home."

Jesse flinched, and Cash, catching the hurt look in his friend's eyes, said, "Your dog outhunted mine, Skeets. You win them Roebuckers for your uncle."

"I don't want 'em," Jesse said rather childishly. "I don't care if'n I never eat no roastin' ears." He got up quickly and hurried outside. Cash reckoned he'd better be going, and left Skeeter by the fire, rubbing his dog.

Jesse came back in directly and pulled up a chair. Skeeter started to speak, but Jesse spoke first. "I been doing a heap of thinking lately. You're sprouting up. The swamp ain't no place for you."

Skeets forgot about his dog and faced his uncle, bewildered.

"I reckon you're too good for the swamp too," Jesse said. "I'm aiming to send you into town for a spell. I can make enough to keep you in fit'n clothes and all." He dared not look at the boy.

"Uncle Jess!" Skeets said reproachfully. "You don't mean that. You're just saying that on account of what I said about M'Lady. I said it just to keep you from feeling so bad about our dog going away. Gee m'netty, Uncle Jess. I ain't ever gonna leave you." He buried his face in his uncle's shoulder. M'Lady put her head on Jesse's knee, and he patted the boy and rubbed the dog.

"Reckon I'll take them Roebuckers," he said at last. "I been wanting some for a long, long time."

Several days later Cash drove down and told them the man from the kennels was at his store. Skeeter didn't say a word, but called M'Lady, and they got in Cash's car. All the way to town the boy was silent. He held his dog's head in his lap.

The keeper took just one look at M'Lady and said, "That's she, all right. Miss Congo III." He turned to speak to Skeeter, but the boy was walking away. He got a glance at Skeeter's face, however. "Heck," he muttered. "I wish you fellows hadn't told me. I hate to take a dog away from a kid."

"He wanted you to know," Cash said.

"Mister"—Jesse closed his left eye and struck his swapping pose—"I'd like to swap you out'n that hound. Now, course she ain't much 'count . . ."

The keeper smiled in spite of himself. "If she was mine I'd give her to the kid. But she's not for sale. The owner wants to breed her and establish her line in this country. And if she was for sale she'd cost more money than any of us will ever see." He called Skeets and offered his hand. Skeets shook it.

"You're a good kid. There's a reward for this dog."

"I don't want no reward." The boy's words tumbled out. "I don't want nothing except to be left alone. You've got your dog, mister. Take her and go on. Please." He walked away again, fearing he would cry.

Cash said, "I'll take the reward and keep it for him. Someday he'll want it."

Jesse went out to the store porch to be with Skeeter.

The keeper handed Cash the money. "It's tough, but the kid'll get over it. The dog never will."

"Is that a fact?"

"Yep. I know the breed. They never forget. That dog'll never laugh again. They never laugh unless they're happy."

He walked to the post where Skeeter had tied M'Lady. He untied the leash and started toward his station wagon. M'Lady braced her front feet and looked around for the boy. Seeing him on the porch, she jerked away from the keeper and ran to her master.

She rubbed against his legs. Skeets tried to ignore her. The keeper reached for the leash again and M'Lady crouched, baring her fangs. The keeper shrugged, a helpless gesture.

"Wild elephants couldn't pull that dog away from that boy," he said.

"That's all right, mister." Skeets unsnapped the leash and tossed it to the keeper. Then he walked to the station wagon, opened the door of a cage, and called "Heah, M'Lady!" She bounded to him. "Up!" he commanded. She didn't hesitate, but leaped into the cage. The keeper locked the door.

M'Lady, having obeyed a command, poked her nose between the bars, expecting a pat. The boy rubbed her head. She tried to move closer to him, but the bars held her. She looked quizzically at the bars, then tried to nudge them aside. Then she clawed them. A look of fear suddenly came to her eyes and she fastened them on Skeets, wistfully at first, then pleadingly. She couldn't make a sound, for her unhappiness had sealed her throat. Slowly her eyes filled up.

"Don't cry no more, M'Lady. Ever'thing's gonna be all right." He reached out to pat her, but the station wagon moved off, leaving him standing there in the dust.

Back on the porch Jesse lit his pipe and said to his friend, "Cash, the boy has lost his dog and I've lost a boy."

"Aw, Jesse, Skeeter wouldn't leave you."

"That ain't what I mean. He's growed up, Cash. He don't look no older, but he is. He growed up that day in the swamp."

Skeeter walked into the store and Cash followed him.

"I've got that reward for you, Jonathan."

It was the first time anyone had ever called him that, and it sounded like man talk.

"And that twenty-gauge is waiting for you," Cash said. "I'm gonna give it to you."

"Thank you, Mr. Cash." The boy bit his lower lip. "But I don't aim to do no more hunting. I don't never want no more dogs."

"Know how you feel. But if you change your mind the gun's here for you."

Skeets looked back toward the porch where Jesse was waiting, and said, "Tell you what, though. When you get them Roebuckers, get some with a couple of gold teeth in 'em. Take it out of the reward money."

"Sure, Jonathan."

Jesse joined them, and Skeeter said, "We better be getting back toward the house."

"I'll drive you down," Cash said. "But first I aim to treat you to some lemon pop and sardines."

"That's mighty nice of you," Jesse said, "but we better be gettin' on."

"What's the hurry?" Cash opened the pop.

"It's my time to cut splinters," Jesse said.

Elephant Ears

RUTH LANGLAND HOLBERG

Toivo Niemi sat on the bakery steps watching two men put up a poster on a high fence across the street. It was fascinating to watch the great sheets of colored paper unfold. Each sheet was matched to the next sheet and pasted down. Presently Toivo saw that it was a circus poster. There appeared a gorgeous tiger, and soon a white horse with a dazzling young lady standing on his back was seen galloping around a ring. It was like a huge picture puzzle growing before his wide, blue eyes.

All at once a very dark uninteresting sheet of paper turned out to be a magnificent elephant. He wore brightly colored trappings and was by far the finest animal in the circus.

The last paper was pasted on the fence. Toivo read that next week the circus was to be in Gloucester at

Stage Fort Park for three days. Just then he heard his father call him. It was hard to leave the circus poster and go into the bakery.

"Toivo," said his father, dusting flour from his hands, "I want you to take this *nisu* to Folly Cove. Mrs. Lempi is having a coffee party this afternoon."

Toivo looked at the coffeecake the Finnish people called *nisu*. It was baked especially for the party and was shaped like a huge wreath, sprinkled with sugar and chopped nuts, and fragrant with the scent of crushed cardamon seeds.

"My! What a big *nisu!*" said Toivo.

"Yes, it is, and you must be very careful, Toivo. I'll put it on this large cardboard and wrap it loosely," said his father. "Toivo! Are you listening to me?"

Toivo's eyes were filled with dreams.

"Father, the circus is going to be in Gloucester next week. Could I go to see it?"

Mr. Niemi's face grew sober. "No, Toivo, I can't spare the money. The fare on the bus and the admission—no, I can't manage it."

"Oh, Father!" Toivo groaned. "I've never seen a live elephant."

He turned to look out the window at the circus poster.

For the first time his father noticed the gorgeous poster. He looked at it rather longingly, but he shook his head firmly and said, "There are so many things to contribute to nowadays that mean much to our country. I am an American, even if I was born in Finland. Come now, get along with that *nisu* and hurry back, for I'm going to the *sauna* and you must stay here in the bakery."

Up on Squam Hill, near the quarries where the Finnish men worked, was a small hut in which they took the weekly steam bath which they called a *sauna*. Great slabs of granite in the center of it were heated with a wood fire. After the stones were hot and the ashes had been brushed away, pails of cold water were thrown on the stones and the steam filled the small room. There were rows of seats in tiers so one could climb higher where the steam was hottest. Little bundles of birch twigs were used to beat the skin to a wonderful rosy glow, and pails of cold water were poured over the bathers when they had steamed themselves long enough. In winter some of the older men who had been born in Finland would sometimes leap into snowbanks to cool off before getting dressed.

Toivo enjoyed the *sauna*, too, but boys went on a different day.

He trudged slowly and carefully down the road to Mrs. Lempi's. She was delighted with the great wreath of well-browned, sweet dough.

"Here's the money, Toivo. Don't lose it. Can't you stay and play with the boys?" she asked.

Toivo shook his head. "No, my father is going to the *sauna* and I must stay in the bakery."

"But no one comes to the bakery this time of the afternoon," said Mrs. Lempi. "And the boys are playing circus."

Toivo looked wistful. Mrs. Lempi's boys had seen the

circus poster, then, and were most surely going next week. He rubbed the toe of his sneaker in the dirt.

"I never saw a live elephant," he said.

"Oh, but you are going to the circus next week, surely?" Mrs. Lempi said in surprise.

Toivo felt a lump in his throat. He could only gulp, "I must hurry back," as he dashed to the road before Mrs. Lempi could see the spangle of tears in his blue eyes.

Mr. Niemi was waiting impatiently for Toivo. He started down the steps, hesitated, and muttered crossly to himself, "There, I forget about the rest of the *nisu* dough. Oh, well . . ."

Toivo looked at his father questioningly. "What is it, Father?"

Mr. Niemi was already striding down the road to an auto filled with Finnish quarrymen going to the *sauna*. They tooted the horn and called for him to hurry, and in a flash he was in the car speeding toward Squam Hill.

Disconsolately Toivo went into the bakery. He saw the roll of dough his father had left in his hurry to be off. From the window over the breadboard he could see one half of the circus poster. He looked at it a long time. The elephant with his curled trunk and great flapping ears was all he could see. He found a pencil and tried to draw the picture on a sheet of wrapping paper, but it wasn't a very good drawing.

All at once he took the rolling pin and rolled out the lump of dough into a thin sheet, thinking all the time of the elephant's ears. From one end he cut an oval shape about nine inches long and four inches wide. He pressed plenty of raisins into the dough and sprinkled it heavily with sugar. Then he cut out seven more shapes just like the first. The oven was hot. He didn't wait for the dough to rise as usual. He just popped the funny-looking objects into the oven.

It was very quiet. Toivo cleaned the breadboard and rolling pin. He swept the floor where he had scattered flour. But try as he could to keep busy, his eyes would go back to the window and the picture of the elephant.

Soon the bakery was filled with a delicious aroma. Toivo suddenly remembered he had put something in the big oven to bake. He ran and opened the door and took out a long tray of queer-looking cakes. They smelled good and looked good, all studded with raisins and glazed and sticky with melted sugar.

Just then the door opened and a stranger came in. Toivo knew at once that she was a summer visitor. She was friendly and asked Toivo what smelled so good. Toivo was bashful and could only look flustered. The customer asked for some *nisu*.

"I've heard about that famous Finnish coffeecake and I want to buy some to serve in my tearoom," she explained, and looked around at the glass cases to see what was in them.

All she could find were some round loaves of dark Finnish bread and a few jelly doughnuts. There was no *nisu*.

She was disappointed, but kept sniffing the air. "What is it that smells so appetizing?" she said, and stepped behind the glass cases so she could look into the bake room. Before Toivo could say a word she breezed in and stared at Toivo's tray just from the oven.

"What are these?" she cried in amazement.

Toivo was embarrassed. He did not know what to call his queer creations. All at once he could see the circus poster through the corner of his eyes, and he blurted out the first words that came to his mind, "Elephant Ears!"

"Elephant Ears! Wonderful! Why, that's exactly what I want! Elephant Ears!" She kept saying it over and over. Then she broke off the corner of one and nibbled it, and her face broke into smiles.

"At last I have found something different to serve in my tearoom," she was saying half to herself.

Toivo's eyes were popping from his head. She went on, "Wrap them up and I'll give you an order for six dozen a day. How much are they?"

Toivo knew exactly what to charge according to the amount of dough, raisins, and sugar.

"Five cents each," he said in a stunned voice.

The young woman wrote her name and address on a paper, paid for the Elephant Ears with a highly pleased expression, and left Toivo with a broken Elephant Ear to show that he had not dreamed the astonishing happening.

When Mr. Niemi came home and heard about the Elephant Ears and tasted the broken one he was just as astonished as Toivo at the delicious crispness and sweet stickiness of the oddly shaped cakes.

"Elephant Ears!" he kept saying over and over.

"Well, Toivo, I guess a boy who has to bake six dozen Elephant Ears a day surely deserves to see a real live elephant. I want to see one too."

They grinned at each other and began to make plans at once.

Ashu and the Whirlwind

ERICK BERRY

Ashu was a daughter of the Jukons, once a mighty nation of warriors and priests in West Africa. She often thought with pride of her nation and of her tribe, but she was only thirteen years old and sometimes other things seemed more important.

Just now Ashu stood in the little mud house that was her home, with a tiny mirror in her hand. She was trying to see in it the whole of her face at once. But when she saw one bright eye the other disappeared from the little mirror, and when she saw her wide-lipped mouth with its flashing teeth, then her small black nose was out of the picture. She tried hardest of all to see the orange headcloth, folded into a long flat piece and tied around her head like a turban. The ends were left flapping over one earringed ear, and her curly hair stuck up through the center.

She made a face at herself in the mirror. A cotton headcloth! Ashu, daughter of the Jukons, longed for silk. She had seen a certain silk handkerchief hanging in the booth of a trader in the market. She had cast longing eyes on it only yesterday, and the day before, and the day before that. It was a rich orange brocade patterned with magenta—truly a wonderful headcloth. But it cost ten shillings, and she did not have ten shillings!

Soon she came to the market place, the center of the life of every African town. Men from the hills, clad only in breechcloths, were in sharp contrast to the chiefs of the district, who wore flowing white robes and huge spotless turbans. The smell of lemon oil mingled with the odors of dried fish and of freshly killed meat.

Ashu pressed through the market-day crowd, turning her back on the booth where the orange handkerchief hung. A storyteller was beating a drum in one corner of the market while he kept up an endless folk tale to amuse the crowd. Ashu joined the group but with only half an ear for the story he was telling.

Close to her stood two traders, talking quietly. Without meaning to listen, she heard their remarks above the drumming of the storyteller.

". . . Amadu, the thief they call the Whirlwind, is in Wukari."

The Whirlwind! What a curious name! thought Ashu, and pressed closer that she might hear better above the beating of the storyteller's drum.

The first trader, a tall man clad in a long blue robe,

continued. "A large reward is offered for his capture, but the risk in taking him would be great. He has a charm that carries evil. All men know of it. His first wife made it for him, and Allah struck her with blindness. The charm is wicked beyond belief."

The shorter man gave a grunt of interest.

"This charm," went on the other, "he still has, and there is no charm to oppose it. I myself would like the reward, but I also value my life."

Just then the two men moved off, still talking.

Ashu noted that it was already quite dark except for the full moon slowly rising through the trees. Very thoughtfully she turned her back on the market and wandered away. Who was this Amadu whom they called the Whirlwind?

Now she heard the sound of drumming in another part of the town and hastened toward it. Some young people were grouped about two native drummers. They were dancing and shouting and clapping. Anyone who wished might join the dance.

Ashu tightened the cloth about her hips, gave an extra twist to her headcloth, and stepped into the dance. Slowly the full moon rose. The red dust beat up from the hard-packed earth. The voices of singers rose and fell, and Ashu danced on and on.

It was nearing daylight and the moon was about to set when the dancers began to drift away to their huts. Ashu, still not tired, was among the last to leave.

The town was never quite deserted at night, never

wholly asleep. Ashu, having said her good nights in a high sweet voice, ran swiftly down the street. The moon was low now and the street was dark. Ahead of her was a stranger, also moving quickly. She had noticed him some time before as he stood watching the dancers from the shadow of a tree. He had a rapid walk, almost catlike, and the girl wondered who he might be. Her own feet made no sound on the dusty way.

Suddenly the stranger darted down the narrow opening into the small alley that led to Ashu's own house. As he turned he gave a quick glance behind him. Ashu's figure melted into the black shadow of the high wall and he did not see her. She was close behind him now, and she saw him dodge quickly into the entrance of her father's compound. Suddenly remembering what she had heard earlier about a thief, Ashu also remembered

that her father kept a heavy money box buried deep in the earth floor behind the entrance hut.

"Thou!" she called loudly, and rushed in after the man. She saw the figure turn as she came up. She made a grab at him with one hand, but he slipped out of her grasp and was gone through the entrance hut into the dark street.

One might as well try to catch a whirlwind. Whirlwind! This must be Amadu, the Whirlwind! Now she understood the reason for the name. The girl turned and went on into the compound slowly, thoughtfully.

On the following Friday, Gaddo, her father, who was a worker in leather, said that he planned to start for Ibi two days later for a trading trip. Ashu decided to stay at home with the younger children. But the older women in the compound thought that they would go with Gaddo. The hairdresser in Ibi was known to be excellent, and it was many weeks since they had had their hair dressed.

Thirty miles for a new hairdressing, then back again in a day or two—that was just a pleasure trip to an African native. On moonlight nights the roads were busy with an endless stream of travelers and traders. They came across the desert from Egypt, from the snowy mountains of the Cameroons, from French Senegal land, and from the jungles of the Gold Coast, always trading, always moving onward.

When the family had gone, Ashu went back to the compound and made her plans. She was frightened, but excited and interested. If the man she had seen in her compound was the Whirlwind he would come again. No doubt he would hear of the family trip and take advantage of it.

Cleverly, she managed that evening to coax some girls who had started dancing in the next street to come into the compound of her own house. The dance lasted very late. When the drummers finally left, some of the girls stayed on eating mangoes, telling stories, and chattering till daylight. No thief would enter while they were there.

It was late the next morning when Ashu started for market with a plan in the back of her head.

When she reached the market place she joined a group of men who sat talking in the shade of one of the small market booths. Among them was her uncle Ablus, who was her father's brother and a policeman of Wukari. As the morning was hot he had taken off his heavy red turban. It lay behind him as he talked, along with his red cotton shoulder band and the handcuffs Ashu needed for her plan.

She crept into the shade and sat down next to Ablus. He gave her a smile, patted her hand, and went on talking with the other men. Half an hour later, when Ashu got up to leave, he did not even look up. So he did not know that the handcuffs lay in the bottom of her calabash beneath some corn she was carrying.

That evening Ashu did not feel nearly so brave as she had felt earlier in the day. It was all very well to plan in broad daylight to catch a thief and to work all day to set a trap for him. It was another thing to wait at night with a pounding heart, in the dark stillness of the little entrance hut, to carry out the plan. Her mouth was dry. Her knees were shaking. She lay down on the mat which she had dragged from her own hut and pretended to be asleep.

Before long she heard a slight sound. She peered out from beneath her arm. Surely a shadow had crossed the moonlight in the doorway.

She was right. A shadow had. Someone was beginning to dig, softly, in the place just inside the compound wall. Ashu, her heart starting to pound all over again, gave a little sigh, intending it to be heard.

It had hardly been uttered before the Whirlwind, living up to his name, was beside her. He laid a heavy hand on her mouth.

"Who is that?" he asked sharply. Then, realizing that it was only a girl, he lifted his hand that she might reply, but he still kept a rough hold on her shoulder.

"I am Ashu, the daughter of Gaddo!" she answered, and struggled to sit up.

There was silence for a moment. Then a voice demanded, "Are you alone in the compound?"

"There is no one else here but the small children," said Ashu.

The Whirlwind's hand slipped from her shoulder, and Ashu's courage began to come back. Perhaps her plan might work after all.

"Come!" ordered the thief in a whisper. "Show me the place where the silver is hidden."

His hand pulled her toward the wall where, indeed, the money was buried. He let go her wrist and pressed a sharp knife against her side.

"Dig!" he ordered in a low voice. "You know where. Let the work be swift."

Ashu's hands found the small jungle knife with which the Whirlwind had started to dig up the earth. Pretending to work swiftly, Ashu nevertheless took her time. Meanwhile the knife pressed unpleasantly against her side, and pressed even closer when the sound of voices came from the street.

Ashu pushed at the loose earth with swift brown hands, and the Whirlwind, eager and quick, soon laid down the knife to help.

Ashu dug deeper and deeper. The moon rose higher and higher. At last she felt the touch of cold iron, down an arm's length into the cool earth.

"Here is what you seek," she said.

"Where?" said the Whirlwind. "Show me!"

His hand was on her wrist and she guided it down, down in the darkness. There was a little exclamation from him as he felt the iron.

"You'll need both hands," she suggested. "It's all in an iron box, one of the white man's boxes. It is very heavy." Her arm was still in the hole, while he was stretched out beside her to reach both hands after hers. Roughly he pushed her aside.

"Let me be. I will do it alone," he said.

But Ashu's hand was still guiding his fingers. Suddenly there was the sound of a metal click. Ashu sprang up.

Amadu, the Whirlwind, lay face down, his arms in the hole. His wrists were held tightly by the handcuffs Ashu had that afternoon fastened to the handle of the heavy iron box. Her plan had worked!

Hugging herself with delight, the girl ran through the streets in the moonlight, straight to the house of her uncle the policeman. She went to tell him where he could find his handcuffs.

It was a week later. Ashu peered into her little mirror admiringly. On top of her curly hair was a splendid silk handkerchief of flaming orange patterned with magenta. She had received a good reward for the capture of the Whirlwind in the very act of robbing her father. She patted the handkerchief happily.

The Hundred Dresses

ELEANOR ESTES

Today, Monday, Wanda Petronski was not in her seat. But nobody, not even Peggy and Madeline, the girls who started all the fun, noticed her absence. Usually Wanda sat in the next to the last seat in the last row in Room Thirteen. She sat in the corner of the room where the rough boys who did not make good marks on their report cards sat; the corner of the room where there was most scuffling of feet, most roars of laughter when anything funny was said, and most mud and dirt on the floor.

Wanda did not sit there because she was rough and noisy. On the contrary, she was very quiet and rarely said anything at all. And nobody had ever heard her laugh out loud. Sometimes she twisted her mouth into a crooked sort of smile, but that was all.

Nobody knew exactly why Wanda sat in that seat,

unless it was because she came all the way from Boggins Heights and her feet were usually caked with dry mud. Maybe the teacher liked to keep all the children with dirty shoes in one corner of the room. But no one really thought much about Wanda Petronski once she was in the classroom.

The time when they thought about Wanda was outside of school hours—at noontime when they were coming back to school, or in the morning early before school began when groups of two or three, or even more, would be talking and laughing on their way to the schoolyard.

Then, sometimes, they waited for Wanda—to have fun with her.

The next day, Tuesday, Wanda was not in school either. And nobody noticed her absence again, except the teacher and probably big Bill Byron, who sat in the seat behind Wanda's and who could now put his long legs around her empty desk, one on each side and sit there like a frog to the great entertainment of all in his corner of the room.

But on Wednesday, Peggy and Maddie, who sat down front with other children who got good marks and didn't track in a whole lot of mud, did notice that Wanda wasn't there. Peggy was the most popular girl in school. She was pretty; she had many pretty clothes, and her auburn hair was curly. Maddie was her closest friend.

The reason Peggy and Maddie noticed Wanda's absence was because Wanda had made them late to school. They had waited and waited for Wanda, to have some fun with her, and she just hadn't come.

They often waited for Wanda Petronski—to have fun with her.

Wanda Petronski. Most of the children in Room Thirteen didn't have names like that. They had names easy to say, like Thomas, Smith, or Allen. There was one boy named Bounce, Willie Bounce, and people thought that was funny but not funny in the same way that Petronski was.

Wanda didn't have any friends. She came to school alone and went home alone She always wore a faded blue dress that didn't hang right. It was clean but it looked as though it had never been ironed properly. She didn't have any friends, but a lot of girls talked to her. Sometimes they surrounded her in the schoolyard as she stood watching the little girls play hopscotch on the worn hard ground.

"Wanda," Peggy would say in a most courteous manner, as though she were talking to Miss Mason or to the principal. "Wanda," she'd say, giving one of her friends a nudge, "tell us. How many dresses did you say you had hanging up in your closet?"

"A hundred," Wanda said.

"A hundred!" exclaimed all the little girls incredulously, and they would stop playing hopscotch and listen.

"Yeah, a hundred, all lined up," said Wanda. Then her thin lips drew together in silence.

"What are they like? All silk, I bet," said Peggy.

"Yeah, all silk, all colors."

"Velvet too?"

"Yeah, velvet too. A hundred dresses," Wanda would repeat stolidly. "All lined up in my closet."

Then they'd let her go. And then before she'd gone very far they couldn't help bursting into shrieks and peals of laughter.

A hundred dresses! Obviously the only dress Wanda had was the blue one she wore every day. So why did she say she had a hundred? What a story! And the girls laughed derisively while Wanda moved over to the sunny place by the ivy-covered brick wall of the school building where she usually stood and waited for the bell to ring.

But if the girls had met her at the corner of Oliver Street they'd walk along with her for a way, stopping every few feet for more incredulous questions.

"How many shoes did you say you had?"

"Sixty."

"Sixty! Sixty pairs or sixty shoes?"

"Sixty pairs. All lined up in my closet."

"Yesterday you said fifty."

"Now I got sixty."

Cries of exaggerated politeness greeted this.

"All alike?"

"Oh, no. Every pair is different. All colors. All lined up." And Wanda would shift her eyes quietly from Peggy to a distant spot, as though she were looking far ahead—looking but not seeing anything.

Then the outer fringe of the crowd of girls would

break away gradually, laughing, and little by little in pairs the group would disperse. Peggy, who had thought up this game, and Maddie, her inseparable friend, were always the last to leave. Finally Wanda would move up the street, her eyes dull and her mouth closed, hitching her left shoulder every now and then in the funny way she had, finishing the walk to school alone.

Peggy was not really cruel. She protected small children from bullies. And she cried for hours if she saw an animal mistreated. If anybody had said to her, "Don't you think that is a cruel way to treat Wanda?" she would have been very surprised. Cruel? Why did the girl say she had a hundred dresses? Anybody could tell that that was a lie. Why did she want to lie? And she wasn't just an ordinary person, else why did she have a name like that? Anyway, they never made her cry.

As for Maddie, this business of asking Wanda every day how many dresses and how many hats and how many this and that she had was bothering her. Maddie was poor herself. She usually wore somebody's hand-me-down clothes. Thank goodness, she didn't live up on Boggins Heights or have a funny name. And her forehead didn't shine the way Wanda's did.

Sometimes, when Peggy was asking Wanda those questions in that mocking polite voice, Maddie felt embarrassed and studied the marbles in the palm of her hand, rolling them around and saying nothing herself. Not that she felt sorry for Wanda exactly. She would never have paid any attention to Wanda if Peggy hadn't invented the dresses game. But suppose Peggy and all the others started in on her next? She wasn't as poor as Wanda, perhaps, but she was poor. Of course she would have more sense than to say she had a hundred dresses. Still she would not like them to begin on her. She wished Peggy would stop teasing Wanda Petronski.

Today, even though they had been late to school, Maddie was glad she had not had to make fun of Wanda. She worked her arithmetic problems absent-mindedly. "Eight times eight—let's see. . . ." She wished she had the nerve to write Peggy a note, because she knew she never would have the courage to speak right out to Peggy, to say, "Hey, Peg, let's stop asking Wanda how many dresses she has." When she finished her arithmetic she did start a note to Peggy. Suddenly she paused and shuddered. She pictured herself in the schoolyard, a new target for Peggy and the girls. Peggy might ask her where she got the dress that she had on, and Maddie would have to say that it was one of Peggy's old ones that Maddie's mother had tried to disguise with new trimmings so that no one in Room Thirteen would recognize it.

If only Peggy would decide of her own accord to stop having fun with Wanda. Oh, well! Maddie ran her hand through her short blond hair as though to push the uncomfortable thoughts away. What difference did it make? Slowly Maddie tore into bits the note she had started. She was Peggy's best friend, and Peggy was the best-liked girl in the whole room. Peggy could not possibly do anything that was really wrong, she thought.

As for Wanda, she was just some girl who lived up on

Boggins Heights and stood alone in the schoolyard. She scarcely ever said anything to anybody. The only time she talked was in the schoolyard about her hundred dresses. Maddie remembered her telling about one of her dresses, a pale blue one with cerise-colored trimmings. And she remembered another that was brilliant jungle green with a red sash. "You'd look like a Christmas tree in that," the girls had said in pretended admiration.

Thinking about Wanda and her hundred dresses all lined up in the closet, Maddie began to wonder who was going to win the drawing and color contest. For girls, this contest consisted of designing dresses, and for boys, of designing motorboats. Probably Peggy would win the girls' medal. Peggy drew better than any one else in the room. At least, that's what everybody thought. She could copy a picture in a magazine or some film star's head so that you could almost tell who it was. Oh, Maddie was sure Peggy would win. Well, tomorrow the teacher was going to announce the winners. Then they'd know.

The next day it was drizzling. Maddie and Peggy hurried to school under Peggy's umbrella. Naturally, on a day like this they didn't wait for Wanda Petronski on the corner of Oliver Street, the street that far, far away, under the railroad tracks and up the hill, led to Boggins Heights. Anyway, they weren't taking chances on being late today, because today was important.

"Do you think Miss Mason will surely announce the winners today?" asked Peggy.

"Oh, I hope so, the minute we get in," said Maddie. She added, "Of course, you'll win, Peg."

"Hope so," said Peggy eagerly.

The minute they entered the classroom they stopped short and gasped. There were drawings all over the room, on every ledge and window sill, dazzling colors and brilliant, lavish dress designs all drawn on great sheets of wrapping paper. There must have been a hundred of them all lined up.

These must be the drawings for the contest. They were! Everybody stopped and whistled or murmured admiringly.

As soon as the class had assembled, Miss Mason announced the winners. Jack Beggles had won for the boys, she said, and his design for an outboard motor was on exhibition in Room Twelve, along with the sketches by all the other boys.

"As for the girls," she said, "although just one or two sketches were submitted by most, one girl—and Room Thirteen should be proud of her—this one girl actually drew one hundred designs—all different and all beautiful. In the opinion of the judges any one of the drawings is worthy of winning the prize. I am very happy to say that Wanda Petronski is the winner of the girls' medal. Unfortunately, Wanda has been absent from school for some days and is not here to receive the applause that is due her. Let us hope she will be back tomorrow. Now, class, you may file around the room quietly and look at her exquisite drawings."

The children burst into applause, and even the boys

were glad to have a chance to stamp on the floor, put their fingers in their mouths and whistle, though they were not interested in dresses.

"Look, Peg," whispered Maddie. "There's that blue one she told us about. Isn't it beautiful?"

"Yes," said Peggy, "and here's that green one. Boy, and I thought I could draw."

While the class was circling the room the monitor from the principal's office brought Miss Mason a note. Miss Mason read it several times and studied it thoughtfully for a while. Then she clapped her hands.

"Attention, class. Everyone back to his seat."

When the shuffling of feet had stopped and the room was still and quiet, Miss Mason said, "I have a letter from Wanda's father that I want to read to you."

Miss Mason stood there a moment, and the silence in the room grew tense and expectant. The teacher adjusted her glasses slowly and deliberately. Her manner indicated that what was coming—this letter from Wanda's father—was a matter of great importance. Everybody listened closely as Miss Mason read the brief note.

"Dear Teacher:

My Wanda will not come to your school any more. Jake also. Now we move away to big city. No more holler "Polack." No more ask why funny name. Plenty of funny names in the big city.

Yours truly,

Jan Petronski"

A deep silence met the reading of this letter. Miss Mason took off her glasses, blew on them, and wiped them on her soft white handkerchief. Then she put them on again and looked at the class. When she spoke her voice was very low.

"I am sure that none of the boys and girls in Room Thirteen would purposely and deliberately hurt anyone's feelings because his name happened to be a long, unfamiliar one. I prefer to think that what was said was said in thoughtlessness. I know that all of you feel the way I do, that this is both very unfortunate and very sad. And I want you all to think about it."

The first period was a study period. Maddie tried to prepare her lessons but she could not put her mind on her work. She had a very sick feeling in the bottom of her stomach. True, she had not enjoyed listening to Peggy ask Wanda how many dresses she had in her closet, but she had said nothing. She had stood by silently, and that was just as bad as what Peggy had done. Worse. She was a coward. At least Peggy hadn't considered they were being mean, but she, Maddie, had thought they were doing wrong. She could put herself in Wanda's shoes. But she had done just as much as Peggy to make life miserable for Wanda by simply standing by and saying nothing. She had helped to make someone so unhappy that she had had to move away from town.

Goodness! Wasn't there anything she could do? If only she could tell Wanda she hadn't meant to hurt her feelings. She turned around and stole a glance at Peggy, but Peggy did not look up. She seemed to be studying hard. Well, whether Peggy felt bad or not, she, Maddie, had to do something. She had to find Wanda Petronski. Maybe she had not yet moved away. Maybe Peggy would climb the Heights with her, and they would tell Wanda she had won the contest; that they thought she was smart and the hundred dresses were beautiful.

When school was dismissed in the afternoon Peggy said, with pretended casualness, "Hey, let's go and see if that kid has left town or not."

So Peggy had had the same idea! Maddie glowed. Peg was really all right.

The two girls hurried out of the building, up the street toward Boggins Heights, the part of town that wore such a forbidding air on this kind of November afternoon, drizzly, damp, and dismal.

"Well, at least," said Peggy gruffly, "I never did call her a foreigner or make fun of her name. I never thought she had the sense to know we were making fun of her, anyway. I thought she was too dumb. And gee, look how she can draw!"

Maddie could say nothing. All she hoped was that they would find Wanda. She wanted to tell her that they were sorry they had picked on her, and how wonderful the whole school thought she was, and please not to move away and everybody would be nice. She and Peggy would fight anybody who was not nice. Maddie fell to imagining a story in which she and

Peggy assailed any bully who might be going to pick on Wanda. "Petronski Onski!" somebody would yell, and she and Peggy would pounce on the guilty one. For a time Maddie consoled herself with these thoughts, but they soon vanished, and again she felt unhappy and wished everything could be nice the way it was before any of them had made fun of Wanda.

Br-r-r. How drab and cold and cheerless it was up here on the Heights! In the summertime the trees, the sumac, and the ferns that grew along the brook on the side of the road made this a beautiful walk on Sunday afternoons. But now it did not seem beautiful. The brook had dried up. And today's drizzle just sharpened the outline of the rusty tin cans, old shoes, and the

forlorn remnants of a big black umbrella, in the bed of
the brook.

The two girls hurried on. They hoped to get to the
top of the hill before dark. Otherwise they were not
certain they could find Wanda's house. At last, puffing
and panting, they rounded the top of the hill. The first

house, that old rickety one, belonged to old man Sven-son. Peggy and Maddie hurried past it almost on tiptoe. Somebody said that once old man Svenson had shot a man. Others said, "Nonsense! He's an old good-for-nothing. Wouldn't hurt a flea."

But, false or true, the girls breathed more freely as they rounded the corner. It was too cold and drizzly for old man Svenson to be in his customary chair tilted against the house, chewing and spitting tobacco juice. Even his dog was nowhere in sight.

"I think that's where the Petronskis live," said Maddie, pointing to a little white house with lots of chicken coops on the side of it. Wisps of old grass stuck up here and there along the pathway, like thin kittens. The house and its sparse little yard looked shabby but clean. It reminded Maddie of Wanda's one dress, her faded blue cotton dress, shabby but clean.

There was not a sign of life about the house. Peggy knocked firmly on the door but there was no answer. She and Maddie went around to the back yard and knocked there. Still there was no answer.

"Wanda!" called Peggy. They listened sharply, but only a deep silence pressed against their eardrums. There was no doubt about it. The Petronskis were gone. How could they ever make amends?

They turned slowly and made their way back down the hill. It was a relief to be back on Oliver Street again, but they still felt disconsolate, and Maddie wondered if she were going to be unhappy about Wanda and the hundred dresses forever. Nothing would ever seem good to her again, because, just when she was about to enjoy something—like going for a hike with Peggy to look for bayberries or sliding down Barley Hill—she'd bump right smack into the thought that she had made Wanda Petronski move away.

"Well, anyway," said Peggy, "she's gone now, so what can we do? Besides, when I was asking her about all her dresses she probably was getting good ideas for her drawings. She might not even have won the contest otherwise."

Maddie turned this idea carefully over in her head, for if there was anything in it she would not have to feel so bad. But that night she could not get to sleep. She thought about Wanda and her faded blue house-dress and the little house she had lived in; and old man Svenson living a few steps away. And she thought of the glowing picture those hundred dresses made—all lined up in the classroom.

At last Maddie sat up in bed and pressed her forehead tight in her hands and really thought. This was the hardest thinking she had ever done. After a long, long time she reached an important conclusion.

She was never going to stand by and say nothing again.

If she ever heard anybody picking on someone who was funny-looking, or who had a strange name, she'd speak up. Even if it meant losing Peggy's friendship. She had no way of making things right with Wanda, but from now on she would never make anybody else that unhappy again. Finally, all tired out, Maddie fell asleep.

On Saturday Maddie spent the afternoon with Peggy. They were writing a letter to Wanda Petronski. It was just a friendly letter telling about the contest and telling Wanda she had won. They told her how pretty her drawings were and that now they were studying about Winfield Scott in school. And they asked her if she liked where she was living and if she liked her new teacher. They had meant to say they were sorry, but it ended up with their just writing a friendly letter, the kind they would have written to any good friend, and they signed it with lots of X's for love. They mailed the letter to Boggins Heights, writing "Please Forward" on the envelope. The minute they dropped the letter in the mailbox they both felt happier and more carefree.

Days passed and there was no answer, but the letter did not come back, so maybe Wanda had received it. Perhaps she was so hurt and angry she was not going to answer. You could not blame her.

Weeks went by and still Wanda did not answer. Peggy had begun to forget the whole business, and Maddie put herself to sleep at night making speeches about Wanda, defending her from great crowds of girls who were trying to tease her with, "How many dresses have you got?" And before Wanda could press her lips together in a tight line, the way she did before answering, Maddie would cry out, "Stop!" Then everybody would feel ashamed the way she used to feel.

Now it was Christmastime and there was snow on the ground. Christmas bells and a small tree decorated the classroom. On the last day of school before the holidays the teacher showed the class a letter she had received that morning.

"You remember Wanda Petronski, the gifted little artist who won the drawing contest? Well, she has written me, and I am glad to know where she lives, because now I can send her her medal. And I hope it gets there for Christmas. I want to read her letter to you."

The class sat up with a sudden interest and listened intently to Miss Mason as she read the letter.

"Dear Miss Mason:

How are you and Room Thirteen? Please tell the girls they can keep those hundred dresses, because in my new house I have a hundred new ones, all lined up in my closet. I'd like that girl Peggy to have the drawing of the green dress with the red trimming, and her friend Maddie to have the blue one. For Christmas. I miss that school and my new teacher does not equalize with you. Merry Christmas to you and everybody.

Yours truly,

Wanda Petronski"

On the way home from school Maddie and Peggy held their drawings very carefully. All the houses had wreaths and holly in the windows. Outside the grocery store hundreds of Christmas trees were stacked, and in the window, candy peppermint sticks and cornucopias of shiny transparent paper were strung. The air smelled like Christmas, and the bright lights shining everywhere reflected different colors on the snow.

"Boy!" said Peggy, "this shows she really liked us. It shows she got our letter and this is her way of saying that everything's all right. And that's that," she said with finality.

"I hope so," said Maddie sadly. She felt sad because she knew she would never see the little tight-lipped Polish girl again and couldn't ever really make things right between them.

She went home and pinned her drawing over a torn place in the pink-flowered wallpaper in the bedroom. The shabby room came alive from the brilliance of the colors. Maddie sat down on the edge of her bed and looked at the drawing. She had stood by and said nothing, but Wanda had been nice to her anyway.

Tears blurred her eyes and she gazed for a long time at the picture. Then hastily she rubbed her eyes and studied it intently. The colors in the dress were so vivid that she had scarcely noticed the face and head of the drawing. But it looked like her, Maddie! It really did. The same short blond hair, blue eyes, and wide straight mouth. Why it really looked like her own self! Wanda had really drawn this for her. Excitedly she ran over to Peggy's.

"Peg!" she said, "let me see your picture."

"What's the matter?" asked Peggy as they clattered up the stairs to her room where Wanda's drawing was lying face down on the bed. Maddie carefully raised it.

"Look! She drew you. That's you!" she exclaimed.

And the head and face of this picture did look like the auburn-haired Peggy.

"What did I say!" said Peggy. "She must have really liked us anyway."

"Yes, she must have," agreed Maddie, and she blinked away the tears that came every time she thought of Wanda standing alone in that sunny spot in the school-yard, looking stolidly over at the group of laughing girls, after she had walked off, after she had said, "Sure, a hundred of them, all lined up."

The Birchbark Canoe

RUSSELL GORDON CARTER

Kneeling in the bright sand, Hubert Robertson stared across the great marshes to the north of Boston in the Colony of Massachusetts. He wondered at the identity of the white distant object drifting toward him through the main passage. It had the appearance of a birchbark canoe, and it looked empty.

Hubert had come to the marshes to fish for eels, but now he thrust hooks and line back into his pocket and jumped to his feet, shading his eyes against the morning sun. Yes, it was an empty canoe! He could see a paddle slanting upward across the gunwale.

While he watched the craft grow swiftly larger he thought of Seeconnet, the young Indian with whom he had grown up. His throat tightened as he remembered the incident that two days ago had ended their friendship. In Seeconnet's canoe they had been running the rapids of a small inland river when the craft struck a submerged rock and pitched the two of them into the cold water. Hubert, in the stern—and therefore responsible for steering—had not noticed the rock, but his companion had spied it and shouted a warning that came too late.

The white boy recalled clearly how the Indian had looked at him as they pulled themselves out of the water: a bruise upon his forehead, his straight black hair glistening, his dark eyes angry and unblinking. He remembered also Seeconnet's sharp words just before he stepped into the canoe and set off down the rapids alone, "White boy stupid like big owl in daytime. Not know how to paddle canoe!" Then he was gone, and with head bent, Hubert had made his way homeward through the woods.

Now, squinting across the desolate marshes, he said aloud, "I wonder if this empty canoe is Seeconnet's? If so . . ."

At that moment a strong puff of wind swung the craft sidewise, and on the high bow, vivid against the white birchbark, Hubert saw the big star that Seeconnet had painted with the juice of berries the day he had finished making the canoe.

Something surely must have happened to Seeconnet! It didn't matter that the Indian had been angry with him. He still liked Seeconnet. Hunting and fishing together, they had been almost the same as brothers.

While the canoe drew nearer and nearer, Hubert peered far off across the marshes and tried to think where Seeconnet might have gone. Suddenly he knew!

"I'm sure of it!" he exclaimed. For on the morning the two had set out to run the rapids he remembered his companion saying, "Soon we paddle to Dark Island. See birds' nests. Gather shellfish from rocks. Soon we go."

Hubert lifted his head, his hands clenched at his sides. To the east where he could just see it beyond the marshes, lay Dark Island, almost a mile from shore. He saw something else also. The water out there, dark like the rocky island itself, was streaked and specked with white.

Then he said to himself, Maybe Seeconnet found the water too rough for paddling. Yet how account for the empty canoe drifting into the marshes?

It is perhaps like this, Hubert decided at last. Either Seeconnet reached the island and then the wind swept the canoe away, or he struck a reef while paddling and was pitched into the sea. In either case, wind and tide would have driven the canoe into the marshes.

The craft was only a score of yards distant now. Hubert waded into the water, an arm outstretched He knew just what he would do!

A few moments later he was kneeling in the stern, the paddle swinging with sure, strong strokes as he headed for the open sea. He had never paddled a canoe in salt water, and when he reached the broad opening in the marshes and the full force of the wind struck the craft and spun it sidewise he was almost sure he would have to turn back.

Then he regained control, paddling now on one side and now on the other, and he knew he would go on.

Seeconnet is out there alone on Dark Island, and possibly he is hurt and needs help, the white boy said to himself.

It was a struggle now between him and the wind. Again and again a fierce gust swung the bow of the canoe around, but each time, with a thrust of the paddle, Hubert managed to swing it back. Yet he knew the wind was likely to grow stronger as he approached the island. Taking advantage of a few moments of calm, therefore, he inched forward until he was kneeling almost in the middle. With the bow lower, the wind couldn't swing it so easily.

But the farther he drew from the mainland the bigger the waves became. Only Hubert's strength and quickness with the paddle kept the canoe from swamping.

Onward he struggled, refusing to turn back. By the time he was midway to the island he was kneeling in half a foot of icy water. He was glad the wave crests had spilled water aboard, for it made the canoe ride more steadily. He continued to paddle, his face wet and the taste of salt on his lips.

Ahead of him he could see a mass of white water and knew there were reefs beneath it. Twice Hubert felt the bottom scrape against rock. Three times he pushed hard with his paddle against a black outcropping. Then at last the white water was behind him, and he had only the wind and waves to battle.

When he was within two hundred yards of the island

he saw great waves breaking along the western shore where he would have to land, and the sight of them momentarily robbed him of his courage. How, he asked himself, could such a fragile thing as a canoe of birchbark make its way safely through that turmoil of water?

Then he saw something else, and he knew he would have to go on. There at the base of a high overhang of rock, his arms wide-flung, lay a slim familiar figure, motionless under the low gray sky.

Was Seeconnet alive? What had happened to him?

Straight ahead now with all the power of his young strong body, Hubert sent the canoe into the most frightening water he had ever encountered. Deep went the paddle, swinging the bow into the wind. Deep he sank it again, driving the craft forward. Straining and gasping, he paddled as he had never paddled before: swiftly, desperately, while his heart pounded and the water swished about his aching knees.

As a huge wave lifted the canoe he had the feeling that he was racing with the speed of a seagull toward the dark island. On either side wave crests heaved and crashed and hissed while the canoe plunged onward. Hubert knew that the great wave he was riding would break just beyond the reef barrier.

The island seemed to be rushing wildly toward him while he plied the paddle. The sky itself seemed to be rushing down upon him as the wave rose higher and higher.

Suddenly it broke, and amid the thunderous roar of it the canoe was sliding down a long cascade of green water toward a wide expanse of white. With a sense of relief and triumph, Hubert ceased paddling and held himself ready. The moment he felt the scrape of pebbles against the bottom he thrust a leg over the side and, with one hand clutching the paddle and the other grasping the gunwale, splashed forward, hauling the craft well up onto the rocky beach.

Then he turned to look for Seeconnet. To his surprise the Indian, aroused perhaps by the scraping of the canoe on the rocks, had pushed himself unsteadily to his feet. His face seemed to have lost some of its color, and his right arm hung limp. Beside the old discolored lump on his forehead was a deep jagged cut.

"Seeconnet, you are badly hurt," Hubert exclaimed, hurrying to his side. "Tell me, what happened?"

The Indian's brows came together in a frown, and he was silent, his gaze fixed on the far horizon.

Hubert was about to ask again what had happened when he noticed a shattered wicker basket lying at the base of the cliff.

The white boy turned his gaze upward and then said, "I think I understand. If I am wrong, tell me. You fell from the rock. It is slippery, and the wind is strong. Anyone might have fallen. You injured yourself, and while you lay unconscious the tide carried the canoe away. It is not so?"

Seeconnet still remained silent, but by a momentary darkening of the Indian's eyes Hubert knew that his explanation had come close to the truth.

"Anyone might have fallen," Hubert repeated. "Your arm, is it broken? And can I help?"

"Arm get well," Seeconnet responded, and turned away as if he had no wish to talk.

Hubert tightened his lips. He knew that the Indians were often hard to understand. Yet it seemed to him that even though Seeconnet might be ashamed of having fallen he ought at least to show a measure of gratitude. He himself had risked his life to reach the island.

"Well," he said abruptly, "we must return to the mainland. Yet how to launch the canoe in such heavy seas I know not!"

Without looking at him, Seeconnet pointed toward the southern end of the island.

"Yonder, water more quiet," he said.

So Hubert returned to the canoe and lifted it. While he carried it easily upon his shoulders he thought what a wonderful craft it was.

In a shallow cove partly sheltered from the wind he set the canoe upon the water, and Seeconnet stepped into it, seating himself near the bow. Knee-deep in swirling water, Hubert grasped the stern and pushed off, then scrambled aboard and lifted the paddle. With wind and tide in his favor he had no trouble in reaching the mainland.

In fact, he would have greatly enjoyed the passage except for the Indian sitting stern and silent in front of him.

Seeconnet is not grateful, nor does he wish to be friends again! Hubert said to himself bitterly.

Within the marshes the white boy paddled slowly,

following the main passage until at last he beached the canoe at the place where he had planned to fish for eels.

"Shall we leave the canoe here?" he asked.

Seeconnet shrugged one shoulder. His face was without expression.

Hubert clenched his hands hard, wanting to voice his anger. I have taken grave risks for your sake! he almost exclaimed. I have brought you safely from the island where you lay injured and helpless, yet not a word of thanks do you offer! He was indeed on the point of speaking out when he noticed a slight twitching of the Indian's face, and suddenly he knew that Seeconnet was in great pain. All along he must have been making a brave attempt to hide his suffering. That was why he appeared sullen and unfriendly.

"Very well," Hubert said quietly, thankful that he had held his anger in check, "we shall leave the canoe here among the tall grasses."

But Seeconnet shook his head. Then, as if with a powerful effort, he said, "Canoe not belong Seeconnet any more. Belong to Hubert . . . gift of friendship to white brother. White brother know how to paddle canoe good as red man."

"Oh, Seeconnet . . ." Hubert began joyfully, and then was abruptly silent. The Indians were a restrained people and knew how to appreciate restraint in others. So, as he swung the canoe to his shoulders and the two set off together toward the Indian encampment, he merely smiled and added gravely, "This is the very best thing you could have given me, Seeconnet, this beautiful gift of friendship!"

Champion Fire 'n Feather

LAVINIA R. DAVIS

The Coventry dog show was a great success. As
usual, old Mrs. Tatham's great Danes won most of the
ribbons. Her big Champion Bally MacClough won best
dog of the show and her brindle pup led the novice
class.

Jimmy Harris hadn't been taken to the show, but his
family had gone, and told him about it. In the cool of
the evening Jimmy ambled over toward the Tatham
place. He didn't exactly set out for there, but his feet
seemed automatically to move down the soft dirt road
in that direction. Queer old Mrs. Tatham didn't relish
visitors, but surely she'd show off her new litter of
puppies. Jimmy's feet moved faster as he approached
the square white house.

The place was very quiet except for an occasional
barking dog. Jimmy walked up the overgrown front

238

drive with his hands in his pockets. No well-brought-up dog would go after you if you went squarely and openly up the front drive.

The old Ford that carried Mrs. Tatham and her dogs to the show was in the front yard, but the house seemed deserted. Jimmy walked around to the low white kennels and there he found Mrs. Tatham. The old lady was dressed in an old tweed jacket and boots up to her knees. She was feeding one of the yearlings and she didn't seem glad to be interrupted. She looked up as Jimmy came in and her blue eyes were as cold as deep ice.

"Goo— Good evening," Jimmy said, but Mrs. Tatham never softened.

"What are you doing here?" she asked, and Jimmy knew that he was trespassing.

"I—I just came to see the dogs," he said lamely.

Mrs. Tatham finished feeding one of her dogs and stalked back to her quiet house. She was a little woman, as short as Jimmy, but she held herself like a queen.

"When I want visitors I invite them," she said. "The rest of the time my dogs can be seen at dog shows."

Jimmy felt as though he'd been slapped in the face. He wanted to talk, to explain that he couldn't very often get to the shows, and that he was more interested in dogs than anything in the world. Old Mrs. Tatham wasn't interested. She opened the door of her kitchen and Jimmy saw the big face of one of the great Danes. The dog barked once, and Jimmy felt sure it was Champion Bally MacClough. As Mrs. Tatham went in, the dog subsided. The door was shut and Jimmy was left alone.

There was nothing to do but turn around and go home. Jimmy started down the road, thought better of it, and headed cross-country behind the house and over the fields. Perhaps all the stories he'd heard about Grandma Tatham were true and the sooner he got off her land the better. Grandma liked dogs better than humans, and plenty of people in Coventry thought she was a bit touched in the head. She lived alone and except for Jeb Green, who did her chores, few people called on her. She kept herself to herself, and it was only when she drove out in the rusty sedan with the huge dogs filling the back seat that people saw her.

Jimmy slowed up as he neared the orchard. Two robins picked worms on the grass ahead of him and overhead a bird sang. No matter what people thought about Mrs. Tatham, birds and animals recognized her as their friend. A calf bleated as Jimmy reached the trees, and Jimmy jumped. Perhaps some of the Danes were loose to keep out intruders. Perhaps old Mrs. Tatham herself had her eye on him from the house. Jimmy remembered the story he'd heard about her scaring Bill Blaine on Halloween when he'd come to lift her gate off the hinges. Jimmy tried to hurry through the deep grass.

He'd gotten about as far as the woodpile when he heard a twittering in front of him. He looked around and for a moment he couldn't see anything. There was the woodpile and a scrawny overgrown plum tree, and just beyond was the incinerator. Jimmy began to go ahead, and then he saw the little bird in front of him. It lay there quite still like a brown, crumpled leaf.

Jimmy stooped down and picked it up, and the little thing peeped desperately and beat its tiny wings against his hand. It had a downy orange breast and barred wing feathers. It might be an oriole, Jimmy decided, and wondered if he could find its nest. He didn't dare take it home. Bill Blaine said Grandma Tatham knew every kitten that was born in her stable. The chances were good that if there were birds nesting in her orchard she'd know about them too.

Finally Jimmy saw the nest in the plum tree. He climbed up and put the little thing inside. There was nothing else he could do. He hoped that the parent birds would come and care for it, and stood for a moment watching the nest. As he stood there he heard the sharp snap of a window being shut. He looked at the Tatham house but the empty windows stared back at him blankly. Jimmy felt uncomfortable and hurried on.

He headed southward through the meadows toward the Blaines's farm. Bill Blaine had plenty of stories about Grandma Tatham. Jimmy didn't especially like Bill Blaine and he'd never paid much attention to the stories, but now his interest was thoroughly aroused. He wanted to hear everything the Blaines had to say.

Bill was in the barn watering the overworked team. Jimmy couldn't help noticing the collar galls on both of the horses. Jimmy's father would have had a fit if any horse on his farm had looked like that, but the Blaines didn't seem to mind. They had a big radio and two shiny new cars, but the livestock on the place was down at the heel. A yellow mongrel barked furiously as Jimmy appeared, but Bill cuffed him into silence.

"Hi, Jim," he said, "how's things?"

Jimmy said that he had been over at the Tathams' to look at the dogs. Bill laughed before he finished his sentence. "Bet you didn't get to first base. The old woman's crazy."

Bill turned his horses into a paddock and gave the old mare a swift crack with his hand as she passed. "Sure she's crazy," he said. "Babies them dogs as though they was people."

Bill settled down into the haymow to talk, and Jimmy seated himself nearby to listen. It was an hour and a half later before he realized that he ought to go home. By that time Jimmy was half certain that Grandma Tatham was crazy and a witch.

When Jimmy finally said good-bye and started for home the early summer twilight was nearly over and it was quite dusky. Something stirred under a quince bush on the Blaines's place and Jimmy jumped. It was nothing but a mangy-looking cat, and Jimmy laughed to himself. Bill's stories had made him creepy.

He skirted the Tatham place and then he saw the fire. It was just at the edge of the property and Jimmy knew that it must be the incinerator. For a minute he hesitated. If you had your incinerator right by your woodpile you deserved a fire. There was nothing else nearby to catch, and the grass was drenched with dew.

Suddenly Jimmy thought of the bird and he started to run. He stumbled through the daisies and hawkweed. It was silly to care, but when he'd saved that bird once he couldn't let it die now.

By the time Jimmy reached the fire the flames lapped at the edge of the woodpile. His heart pounded. There was no water nearby. There was not even time to get help.

Jimmy lunged forward and began to separate the long logs. They had not been sawed yet. That was in his favor. The smoke caught his throat, stung his eyes. His hands ached as he hauled the hot logs. He danced up and down on the flames, scattered the wood with his bare hands. Once he felt the searing of fire on his forearm, but it was no time to stop. The flames were still near the plum tree; too near for the bird's safety.

"Help!" Jimmy shouted. "Help!" The sound was empty on the quiet air. He kept on fighting until he knew that the fire was no longer gaining. He stopped for one moment to suck the fresh air into his lungs. Then he shoved forward blindly, his arm in front of his face. He was beating, yanking, tearing the fire, when there was a sudden spurt of steam. He looked up. Old Mrs. Tatham threw another bucket of water at the fire. One of her big dogs barked at her side.

"Give me those pails," Jimmy gasped, and ran toward the kennel. By the time he was back again the fire was nearly out. With the last swish of water the wood was black and charred, but there wasn't a spark left. Jimmy glanced at the incinerator and saw the wire basket blown over on its side. So that had started it. He looked past it at the plum tree and saw the nest still safe and untouched. He breathed deeply, and for the first time he was really aware of old Mrs. Tatham.

She did look like a witch in the soft darkness. Her long white hair streamed down her neck and she had an old dark coat thrown over her shoulders. She had her hand on her dog's collar, and the big dog seemed turned to stone.

"You did a good job," she told Jimmy. "Come back tomorrow and see me."

Jimmy got out a hurried "Yes, ma'am." Then he ran for home.

The next morning when he woke up he remembered that he had something ahead of him. For a minute he couldn't think; then he knew that he was going to see Grandma Tatham. After Bill's stories Jimmy didn't relish another visit, but he had said he would go.

In the broad daylight the house was less spooky. Jeb Green was cutting the grass near the house. Three big great Danes thumped their tails on the wooden porch as Jimmy approached. Mrs. Tatham was waiting for him at the kitchen door.

"You're a good boy," she said when she saw him. "You saved that woodpile. Come and I'll show you my new litter."

Jimmy's heart lifted. He wanted to see those puppies more than anything in the world. He felt he was sailing under false colors. He wanted to save the bird, not the woodpile, but what could he say without being rude? Mrs. Tatham led the way to the big whitewashed kennel and went in. The mother dog wagged her tail and, when Mrs. Tatham spoke, allowed Jimmy to get close to her puppies.

They were wonderful puppies, brindle and brown and gray. They had long soft ears and the biggest, floppiest feet Jimmy had ever seen.

"Golly," Jimmy breathed. "Golly."

"Which one would you pick if you were judging a show?" Mrs. Tatham asked briskly. "Which one's worth a blue ribbon?"

Jimmy studied them carefully. They were all good, and to a boy who had always longed for a dog they seemed perfect. How could anyone choose a best among such perfection? Finally, one by one, he discarded the biggest, the smallest, one with bent legs, and picked on a brindle with a round face.

"I'd give that the blue," he said, and Grandma Tatham picked it up.

"He's yours," she said shortly. "I owe you that for the wood."

For a second Jimmy fought with himself. She need never know about the bird. Suddenly he squared his shoulders and told her. "It wasn't the wood, ma'am," he got out. "There was a bird in that plum tree. . . ."

Mrs. Tatham nodded at him and her old eyes were soft now and gentle. "I know, son," she said. "I saw you from the house."

Jimmy remembered the click of the window that had

sent him scampering, and grinned. Dad was right, as usual, about old Mrs. Tatham. She might be queer, she might like dogs better than people, but she was quicker and fairer than most people. More than that, she was generous. He turned back to the pup.

"You call for him in another week," she said. "I'll have him weaned by then."

Jimmy stroked the puppy, wondering if it could be true. This little dog, the son of champions, really his?

"What are you going to call it?" old Mrs. Tatham asked, and Jimmy shook his head. He was beyond speech, beyond thanks. He could do nothing but hold the soft, marvelous creature and hope he was not dreaming that this beautiful dog was truly his.

Mrs. Tatham lifted the pup gently away from Jimmy and handed it back to its mother. "Call it Fire and Feather," she said crisply. "That's how you won him."

Jimmy nodded. "Champion Fire 'n Feather," he said slowly. "It sounds swell."

Hatsuno's Great-Grandmother

FLORENCE CRANNELL MEANS

Hatsuno Noda walked alone in the crowd of girls and boys pouring out of school. She held her head so straight that her chubby black braids spatted her trim shoulders, and her step was so brisk that you would have thought she enjoyed walking by herself. Hatsuno could not bear to let anyone guess how lonesome she felt in the gay throng.

Brother Harry and six-year-old brother Teddy were deep in clumps of their schoolmates, but the girls from Hattie's class streamed by her without pausing. Behind her Patty White, whom she liked best of all, skipped along between Sue and Phyllis, giggling and talking. Hattie wondered what they were talking about. Often they were chattering about Hattie's secret dream; but today it sounded as if they were discussing the Mother's Day tea next month. This morning the teacher had appointed Patty chairman of the decorating committee.

Hattie could have helped decorate. Her slim fingers knew how to fold amazing Japanese paper birds, flowers, dolls. And at the old school the teacher would have had her do colored drawings on the blackboard, along with Tommy Lin, who was Chinese, and Consuelo, who was Mexican. The three drew better than any of the "plain Americans." But in this new school, where almost all were "plain Americans," no one knew what Hattie's fingers could do.

No, the girls were not talking about the tea.

"If you join now," Patty was saying, "you can go up to camp this summer . . ."

Oh, if only Patty were saying it to Hatsuno! But she wasn't. She broke off as she danced past with the others.

"Hi, Hattie!" she called, wrinkling her tiptilted nose in a smile and tossing back her thistledown curls.

Hattie smiled a small, stiff smile, though she ached to shout "Hi!" and fall in step with Patty. Then maybe Patty would think to ask her.

"Join—camp": those words were the keys to one of Hattie's dearest dreams.

Hatsuno had never been in the mountains. All her life she had lived where she could see them stretching like a purple wall across the end of the dingy downtown street. They were beautiful, with snow-capped peaks shining pink and lavender and gold in the sunrise, and Hatsuno had always longed to explore them; but though they looked so near, they were miles and miles away.

The new school had given her hope. In the new school

there was a Camp Fire group; and every summer it spent a few days at a camp far up in the mountains. Hattie had seen pictures of its bark-covered lodges climbing steeply among the tall evergreens beside a sparkling stream. She had heard Patty tell of the camp-fires and the horseback rides. For Patty was a Camp Fire girl, and Patty's mother was the guardian of the group. Yet, friendly though Patty was, she never spoke of Hattie's joining. And Hattie was far too shy to bring up the subject.

In her old home she had not been so shy; but the old house had grown too small, and they had had to move to a larger one. Hattie, the first Noda baby, had been followed by five boys, and, as Harry said, each child shrunk the house a little bit more. This spring brought not only a new baby but a new grandmother, and the house was as small as Hattie's year-before-last coat. Even Mother couldn't let out its hems enough to make it do.

Mother could manage almost anything. During the depression, when Father was out of work, Mother had kept the children neat as wax and even stylish. She was always up, working, when Hattie awoke in the morning; always up, mending and making over, when Hattie went to sleep at night. Mother was proud that even in the bad years Denver had few Japanese-Americans "on relief": almost as few as in jail.

Even Mother could not stretch the house enough for the new baby and Great-Grandmother. So the Nodas had moved, uprooting the children from neighborhood and school. The new school was pleasant; Hattie's teacher, Miss Bender, was lovely; Patty White was the gayest, prettiest girl Hattie had ever met. But Hattie didn't fit in.

So here she was, walking home alone, with Camp Fire and the mountains as far away as ever. Teddy overtook her, making noises like a machine gun—like a railway train—like an airplane. Teddy's face was as round as a button, his eyes as black as coal, his teeth as white as rice.

"Last one home's a lame duck!" he chirped at her.

She did not hurry as she once would have done. Home was a changed place now; changed by Grandmother as well as by the new house.

Though Great-Grandmother had come from Japan ten years ago, Hattie had never seen her till this month. Great-Grandmother had lived with Aunt Kiku in San Francisco until Aunt Kiku's death had left Grandmother alone.

She was not at all what Hattie had expected; not at all like grandmothers in books—comfortable, plump people who loved to spoil their grandchildren. No, Grandmother was not that kind.

Hattie slowly opened the door which still quivered from Teddy's banging it. Little gray Grandmother sat stiffly erect, only her head bent toward the sock she was darning, her small feet dangling.

"How do you do, Grandmother?" said Hattie.

"How do you do, Elder daughter?" Grandmother

responded. There is no easy way to say "granddaughter" in Japanese.

Under their folded lids Grandmother's eyes traveled down Hattie. Hattie, feeling prickly, smoothed her hair, straightened her collar, twitched her checked skirt, and finally shifted her weight to one knee as Grandmother reached her feet.

"A cold day for bare legs," Grandmother observed. Hattie thought her look added, And a great girl twelve years old should wear long stockings.

Self-consciously Hattie's eyes pulled free from Grandmother's. "Oh," she cried, "Dicky's climbed on the piano again." She ran over and replaced the box of satiny white wood in which her latest—and last—doll always stood on view, fairly safe from the six boys. It was an enchanting doll with glossy black hair and a silk kimono. "The other boys at least keep off the piano," Hattie scolded, "but not Dicky."

Grandmother's cool eyes seemed to say, Boys have to be excused, since they're so much more important than girls. And why should a great girl of twelve care about dolls?

Hattie hurried on into the good-smelling kitchen. "Mother," she complained, "Grandmother doesn't understand that we're Americans, not Japanese. I bet she'd like me to flop down on my knees and bump my head on the floor the way you used to have to, and say, 'Honorable Grandmother, I have returned.'"

"Wash your hands," said Mother, "and help me get dinner on the table."

Hattie slapped her shoes down hard as she went to the sink to wash. She wished her heels weren't rubber; they didn't make enough noise to express her feelings.

"Of course you will give proper courtesy to the old," Mother said quietly.

"Why? She doesn't even like me." The question was useless. Hattie had grown up knowing that politeness to the old was as much a law as honesty, industry, self-control—and minding parents.

Mother only said, "Stop and buy grapefruit on your way from school. Be sure to pick out heavy ones."

"Of course," Hattie grumbled. Hadn't she known how to choose good fruit and vegetables since she was nine?

Dinner was Japanese-American. Seven Nodas—and Grandmother—crowded around an ordinary American table; but the utensils were chopsticks instead of knives and forks. The fish soup and the pickled radishes were Japanese; the *pakkai* were American spareribs, and the fluffy white rice was international. Bread and butter were pure American, and the dessert was Japanese gelatine, too firm to quiver. "It's not so nervous as American jelly," Harry said, and made Teddy laugh till his eyes went shut.

Only Grandmother seemed all Japanese: in the way she sipped her soup and tea, with a noise that was polite in Japan but not in America; in the way she refused bread and butter; in the way she greeted an old neighbor of the Nodas who came in as they were finishing the meal.

Grandmother shuffled across the room, toeing in,

because for sixty-five of her seventy-five years she had worn clogs; and she bowed the deep bow of old Japan, her withered hands sliding down to her knees. Why couldn't Grandmother be more American?

The neighbor had come to remind them that tonight was the festival called Buddha's Birthday. Grandmother's eyes brightened at the news. But Mother apologized: she could not go with Grandmother, for Saburo the new baby was feverish, and she could never bear to leave her babies when they were sick. Father? He had to work tonight. Thoughtfully Grandmother looked at Hattie. Hattie excused herself and hurried back to school.

Right up to the time school opened she kept seeing Grandmother's eyes brighten and grow dull. If Hattie had been with Patty and the others on the school-ground, as she longed to be, she might have forgotten Grandmother. But sitting lonesomely at her desk, pretending to read, she could not forget.

Maybe it was good, after all, to have a rule about being kind to old people whether they like you or not. Hattie thought of Mother taking care of her and her brothers when they were young and helpless. How dreadful if, when Mother grew old and helpless, they did not take turn about and care for her! Hattie frowned at her book, thinking.

"Mad, Hattie? My, but you're scowling!" teased Patty, pausing as she came in from the schoolground.

Hattie shook her head and smiled. If only Patty would sit down beside her and say the thrilling words, "Oh, Hattie, wouldn't you like to join Camp Fire?" If she would even say, "Can't you come over after school?"

But after school Hattie walked home alone as usual, stopping for the grapefruit on her way. When she had put them in the home cooler she hunted up Grandmother and ducked her head in a shy bow. "Grandmother," she said, "if you want to go to Buddha's Birthday tonight, I'm sure Mother will let Harry and me go with you."

The Nodas were Methodists, so the Buddhist church was strange to Hattie and Harry. Tonight it was crowded, and all through the program small children trotted in and out and climbed over people's feet, with nobody minding. There were songs and dances and pantomimes, graceful kimonos, stately poses, dignified steps; and voices in the high falsetto which was the proper tone for Japanese actors, but which gave Hattie a funny, embarrassed feeling. "Such squeaky doors!" Harry whispered comically.

Coming home by streetcar and bus, the three arrived so late that all the house was sleeping. Harry bade Grandmother good night and stumbled drowsily to his room, but Grandmother lingered, eyes bright and cheeks flushed.

Hattie hunted for something to say. "The dancing was lovely," she said. "And the kimonos."

"I have one old kimono," Grandmother said, turning toward her door. With Hattie at her heels she opened a dresser drawer and took out a silken bundle which she unfolded and held out, smiling faintly at Hattie's gasp of admiration.

"Chrysanthemums, for your aunt's name, *Kiku*— Chrysanthemum," said Grandmother. Gorgeous blossoms in many rich colors grew across the heavy blue crepe. "It was the only one she saved from the great San Francisco fire. She wrapped it around one of her doll boxes." Grandmother motioned toward the drawer and a white wood box that lay there.

"Could I see?" Hattie stuttered.

"You may," Grandmother answered.

When Hattie slid open the box a breath of the Orient puffed out into her nostrils. She lifted the bag that protected the doll's hair and face, and gazed at the miniature lady, exquisitely molded and robed in brocades, padded, corded, embroidered. Clasping the box to her breast with one hand, Hattie pulled out a chair for Grandmother. "I don't know much about the doll festival," she coaxed shyly. "Here in Denver we don't."

She curled up on the floor at Grandmother's feet. "O Kiku San brought her doll set with her," Grandmother said, "when she married and came to America. This one is more than a hundred years old. We were taught to take care of things. The girls' festival—O Hina Matsuri—was a great day. It was play, but it taught us history and manners."

Looking from the doll to Grandmother, Hattie listened with all her might. She missed some words, for the Japanese the Nodas used at home was simple, and to Hattie's relief there had been no Japanese Language

School for some years now. Still, she could follow the story, and it made pictures for her in the quiet night: little-girl-Grandmother wearing enchanting kimonos in charming rooms carpeted with cushiony mats; spending long hours learning to serve tea just so, to arrange flowers just so, to paint the difficult Japanese letters just so; learning to hold her face and voice calm no matter how she felt. Girl-Grandmother, writing poems with her friends and going to view the full moon, valuing beauty above riches. Grandmother, hearing about America and longing to go where life was free for women. Grandmother, never able to come until she was too old to fit herself into this new land.

When the parlor clock struck one Grandmother stopped short. "A girl of twelve should be asleep!" she said severely.

Next morning Hattie wondered if she had dreamed that companionable midnight visit, for Grandmother looked coldly at Hattie's bare knees and said, "Since you must run and jump like a boy, I suppose those ugly short clothes are necessary." But even while Hattie was biting her lip uncomfortably Grandmother added, "Hatsuno, the chrysanthemum kimono and the doll are to be yours. After all, you are our only girl."

Home was beginning to seem homelike again.

That was fortunate for Hattie, since neighborhood and school were still strange. It was a relief to go back to their old district on Sundays to the Japanese Methodist Church. And once Mother took the older children to an evening carnival at their old school. On the way they stopped at the store where they used to buy Japanese food, dishes, cloth. Clean and bright itself, it was jammed in among grimy secondhand stores and pawnshops. It was queer, Hattie thought, but no matter how clean people were, or what good citizens, if they happened to be born Chinese or Japanese or Mexican they were expected to live down on these dirty, crowded streets with the trucks roaring past. Yes, the new neighborhood and school were far pleasanter than the old—if only Hatsuno could fit in.

As Mother's Day approached, Hattie felt lonelier than ever. When she came into school two days before the tea, Patty, Sue and Phyllis were huddled around the teacher's desk. Miss Bender smiled approvingly at Hattie, who was already top student in Seventh Grade. Patty smiled, too, and looked at her expectantly. Hattie's heart thumped with the wish to push herself in among them. But how could she? She smoothed her starched skirt under her, sat down, and pretended to clean out her desk.

"It's such a late spring," Miss Bender was saying, "the lilacs aren't out. But I'll bring sprays of cherry blossoms. And we must find out how many mothers to expect. I hope your mother is coming, Hattie."

"No, ma'am," Hattie said soberly. "The baby has chicken pox, and Mother just won't leave a sick baby."

"Haven't you an aunt or grandmother who could come in her place?"

Oh, dear! Grandmother would be so different from the rest. What would Patty think of her? Then Hattie's head came up. "I'll ask Great-Grandmother," she said.

She thought Grandmother would refuse. She hoped Grandmother would refuse. Instead, Grandmother asked, "Every girl should have mother or grandmother at this tea?"

"Yes, Grandmother."

"And your mother will not leave the baby. Elder daughter, you went with me to Buddha's Birthday. I go with you to school."

Hattie swallowed a lump in her throat. Grandmother was doing this because she thought Hattie wished it. Tea—Grandmother would sip it in Japanese fashion. Would she notice if the girls giggled? She would hide the fact if she did. Hattie thought of Grandmother's long training in the concealment of pain or disappointment. Well, that was a good heritage for anybody. Hattie would use it now. "Thank you, Grandmother," she said. "I will come and get you Friday after school."

When the two came into the schoolroom that afternoon the mothers were all there and having their tea, and it seemed to Hattie that everyone stopped talking and turned to gaze. Well, she and Grandmother must look pretty funny, Hattie thought.

Hattie was dressed like the other girls, in white sweater and short white skirt, her white anklets folded neatly above her oxfords and her black hair out of its braids and done in another favorite style of the season. Grandmother, as short and slim as Hattie, wore a dress nicely made over from a kimono but looking a little strange; and her gray hair was combed straight back from the withered little face with its slanting eyes.

Politely Hattie introduced Miss Bender to Grandmother and pulled up one of the visitors' chairs, since Grandmother had never been to tea where people stood up and balanced the dishes on their hands. Patty brought her a plate, Phyllis the sandwiches, Sue a cup of tea. Then Patty returned, pulling her mother after her. "Mom," she said, "here's Hattie. And here's her great-grandma." Patty dropped her mother's hand and stood beaming.

Hattie looked anxiously at Grandmother. She could not speak a word of English, or the others a word of Japanese. But instead of words, Seventh Grade and its mothers were bringing sandwiches and cakes till Grandmother's plate was heaped. And Grandmother sat there, as stately and self-possessed and smiling as if she went to seven teas a week.

Hattie studied her more closely. Others might think Grandmother's little face a mask, but Hattie saw that the eyes were bright again and that the wrinkled cheeks were pink. Grandmother liked it! Grandmother felt happy and at home!

Maybe even a great-grandmother could be lonesome, especially when she was too old to learn the ways of a new land. Thinking so happily of Grandmother that she forgot all about her own shyness, Hattie squeezed Patty's arm, just as she might have squeezed Teddy's on some rare occasion when he was sweet instead of maddening.

HATSUNO'S GREAT-GRANDMOTHER

Patty squeezed back—quickly, as if she had been waiting for the chance. "Mother!" she stuttered in a voice that matched her gay fluff of curls. "Mother, I think maybe I was mistaken. I think Hattie might like to . . ." She looked eagerly up into her mother's questioning eyes. "You ask her, Mother!" she begged.

"About Camp Fire? Hattie, would you like to join our Camp Fire group?"

Hattie was silent from pure joy and astonishment.

"If I got your name in this week," Mrs. White continued, "you could go to camp with us. A camp in the mountains; do you know about it?"

"Oh, yes, ma'am, I know," Hattie said with shining eyes. "Oh, yes, ma'am!"

The Horse That Saved a Million Lives

WYATT BLASSINGAME

She may have been a daughter of a granddaughter of the Justin Morgan horse. We do not know. By the first decade of the nineteenth century some of the Morgan's offspring had been brought into the Kentucky wilderness, and this small, dark mare had all the qualities of Old Figure: tremendous endurance, gentleness, intelligence. She understood the danger of the flooded stream in front of her and she stood, head held high, looking at it, waiting for her rider to decide what to do.

The rider was a big, rawboned man wearing a coonskin cap and heavily dressed against the damp cold. His name was Ephraim McDowell. Though still in his mid-thirties, he was already recognized as the most skilled surgeon west of the Allegheny Mountains.

McDowell had already traveled forty miles. He and his horse were bone-tired and their destination was still far ahead. As had happened many times before, a human life depended on the doctor's getting there in time to operate. Now, over the head of his horse, he looked at the swollen river, wondering. The yellow, rushing water was filled with logs and debris. Even as he watched, a huge tree swept downstream, turning slowly as it moved past him.

"Well," the doctor said aloud, reaching out and patting the horse on his neck, "there's no way around. I guess we've just got to go across." With that he touched his heels to the horse's sides and lifted the reins.

The little horse moved delicately down the slope of the bank. Where the yellow flood ate at the mud she turned her head and looked back at the doctor. "Go on, girl," said McDowell. "You can make it."

Slowly, feeling her way, the little horse waded into the river. The water sucked at the earth under her hoofs. It came up around her knees, moving so swiftly that it piled in high ridges on both sides. Now the water touched her belly. She stopped, letting a half-submerged tree limb sweep past, then went on.

The river was filled with floating logs. Standing in his stirrups, the doctor leaned upstream, fending off the debris that rushed at them.

Suddenly there was no bottom under the horse's feet. For an instant she went completely under. Then her head was above the surface again and she was swimming, the doctor still in the saddle, still fighting off the tree limbs brushing against them.

The horse swam strongly, but the far bank seemed

to her rider to rush upstream past them. There was a bend in the river, and horse and rider were swept past it. For a moment they were out of the main current and the little horse moved steadily toward the opposite bank. Then the current struck them again, pushing them downstream.

But the bank was close now. Another minute and there would be ground under the pawing hoofs. Then it happened. The rolling log rushed at them. The doctor tried to reach it to push it aside and could not. The end of it crashed into the horse's chest with a sound the doctor could hear above the roar of the flood. It smashed the horse backward and under.

For what seemed to the doctor hours, the yellow water rushed over him. Instinctively he clung to his horse. He knew that, burdened with his heavy clothing, he would never be able to swim in this current. The horse, stunned from the blow, was being swept downstream like the log that had struck her.

Then somehow the little horse began to swim again. She got her head above water. She fought against it, her powerful legs beating steadily. Moments later her hoofs touched bottom. Slowly, shivering in all her muscles, she staggered out of the river and up the bank. McDowell's medical bag, soggy but intact, still hung from the saddle horn.

Shakily the doctor dismounted and looked back at the stream they had crossed. He had been raised in a strict religious home where he had been taught justice and to give credit where credit is due. Now he put his hand on the horse and thanked it for saving his life.

What neither the little horse nor the man could know was that in saving the doctor's life the horse had also saved the lives of untold thousands of persons not yet born. Ephraim McDowell was to become not only one of America's great surgeons, he was to make one of the most important discoveries of medical history, a discovery that would influence surgery throughout the world and save more lives than a Napoleon or a Genghis Khan could destroy.

In this, too, the little black mare would play a part.

It was early one December morning in 1809 when a man in buckskin, his face pinched with cold, knocked on Dr. McDowell's door in Danville, Kentucky. He had ridden sixty miles through the wilderness, he said, to ask the doctor's help. The wife of a friend and nearest neighbor, a Mrs. Thomas Crawford, was seriously ill. She was expecting a baby, but something had gone wrong. The man who served the wilderness settlers as doctor had no idea what to do and he had sent to ask if McDowell would come and help.

The doctor did not hesitate. He asked directions, pulled on his heaviest clothing, and while his wife prepared food for him to take he went out and saddled the little black horse.

The weather was bitterly cold. There had been rain, and now icicles hung from the trees. They glittered in the early morning sunlight as the doctor rode out of Danville and into the forest. The little black horse moved

steadily—not at a run, for there were sixty miles to go—
but at a fast walk. She kept going hour after hour while
the doctor sat hunched in the saddle, coonskin cap
pulled low against the cold.

At noon man and horse rested a few minutes, the
doctor eating the food his wife had prepared, the black
mare munching on corn. Then they moved on again. The
road that had at first been a well-marked wagon trail
was now only a path through the trees, but eventually
it led to a small cluster of houses. Dogs ran out barking
and the black horse shied away from them.

The dogs' barking brought several men and women
from the houses, and the doctor asked directions from
them. A man pointed; one of the women asked,
"You're the doctor from Danville?"

"Yes."

"You better hurry, Doctor. Mrs. Crawford's in real
pain."

"All right." He touched his heels to the horse, and
though over fifty miles lay behind them, the weary
mare broke into a long lope. Her hoofs made a crackling
sound on the frozen path. The sun was gone now. The
winter twilight was thick under the trees.

At the Crawford cottage the wilderness doctor stood
in the yard with Tom Crawford and two of the Crawford
children. They heard the sound of the horse before they
saw it, and Tom Crawford's face grew bright with hope.
As the little horse topped the slope and came pounding
down toward them the wilderness doctor said, "That's

McDowell. If anybody can save Mrs. Crawford, he can."

The horse pounded to a stop, blowing hard and flecked with foam. McDowell dismounted, aching with weariness. He knew how the little mare must feel, and told one of the Crawford boys, "Take her in the barn and put a blanket over her." Then, carrying his medical bag, he and Thomas Crawford and the wilderness doctor went into the house.

A roaring fire lit the single room with red and yellow light. McDowell crossed to the bed where Mrs. Crawford lay. He asked her how she was feeling and she smiled wanly at him. "Not too good. I'm glad you came."

"We can thank that little mare of mine for getting me here as soon as she did," said McDowell. "It's a long ride." He took off his coonskin cap, his greatcoat, and turned back to the bed to begin his examination.

A few minutes later he stood up and, taking the doctor aside, spoke to him in whispers. "Mrs. Crawford isn't pregnant," he said. "She has an ovarian tumor."

The face of the wilderness doctor grew drawn. "Then there's no hope?"

"There may be."

The wilderness doctor stared at him. "How?"

"There is a chance. I want to talk to Mrs. Crawford in private. The decision will have to be hers."

The wilderness doctor looked at him as if he were mad, then shook his head and went outside. Slowly Mr. Crawford followed him.

When they were gone McDowell sat down beside Mrs. Crawford's bed. He told her as gently as possible that she had a tumor and that this kind of tumor had always proved fatal. Even so, there might be a chance. In the past no doctor had ever dared to operate and try to remove the tumor because it was believed that if the abdominal wall were opened the patient would not live. No doctor wanted to be accused of murdering his patient, so women with such tumors were simply allowed to die of them. However, McDowell said, he had performed abdominal operations on dogs, and they had lived. He believed, against all the warning of the medical profession, that the operation could be performed on a human being.

For a minute the sick woman lay there beneath her blankets, looking upward. Then she turned her face toward the doctor. "I want you to operate," she said.

McDowell did not dare to try an operation as difficult and delicate as this except in his own home, where all his instruments were at hand and he had an assistant to help him. But how could he get Mrs. Crawford to Danville, sixty miles away? There was no road over which a wagon or buggy could possibly pass. She would have to travel on horseback, and there was only one horse McDowell felt he could trust to carry her safely. That was the little black mare.

Early next morning they set out. They rode slowly, the doctor going ahead, the little mare picking her way gently. Even so, Mrs. Crawford was in pain.

The journey McDowell had made in one day's hard

riding took several days. In that time the black mare did not stumble once. When dogs ran out of the wilderness cabins to bark at her heels she did not shy. It was almost as if she understood the serious condition of the woman she carried.

Perhaps in some strange way she did understand. Already she had saved McDowell's life. It may be that the gentleness with which she picked her way through the wilderness helped Mrs. Crawford to survive until the doctor could operate.

McDowell performed the operation on Christmas morning, 1809. He chose Christmas, he said, because on that day, "all the prayers of the world" would be rising to God, and he needed God's help. While he operated, a mob gathered outside his home. They believed that the doctor was operating only to satisfy his own curiosity. It was deliberate murder, they said. Even while McDowell worked they stormed the door of his house, but the sheriff turned them back. Then they hung a rope from a tree out front, saying they would have it ready to hang the doctor when Mrs. Crawford died.

But Mrs. Crawford did not die. Five days after the operation McDowell entered her room to find her standing up, making the bed. In a few weeks she returned home to join her family.

This time there was no need for her to ride the gentle mare that had carried her to Danville. She was a well woman. In those weeks medical history had been made. Even though the medical profession was slow in admitting it, Ephraim McDowell had proved that the abdominal wall could be opened and human lives saved by such surgery. Today every time such an operation is performed, every time even an appendix is removed, the doctor and patient owe a debt of gratitude to Dr. McDowell. And a debt of gratitude to McDowell is a debt of gratitude to the little mare that saved his life and helped make his work possible.

Katie Catches
a Ghost

KATHARINE KOCH

It was so still in the schoolroom that Katie could hear the clock ticking its slow way through the afternoon. Sunlight flickered through the maple trees outside the west windows and danced on the dusty blackboards. There was a drowsiness in the air, an invitation to daydreaming.

"Katie, are you studying your geography? What are you thinking about?"

Startled at the teacher's voice, Katie withdrew her gaze from the dancing lights on the blackboard. She had been thinking so hard that she forgot, for the moment, that she was in school, and answered as though Mom had asked the question.

"I'm thinking about ghosts."

A gale of surprised laughter from the children brought Katie to her senses. She glared indignantly at Jimmie

271

Green who sat across the aisle. He was whooping aloud and his face was turning alarmingly red with his efforts.

He's only laughing like that because he likes to make a lot of noise, thought Katie. Why are boys so silly?

"That's enough, children," said Miss Clearson, tapping her desk with her ruler. "Put your mind on your lesson, Katie, and don't waste you time on silly notions."

Obediently, Katie fastened her eyes on the map in her big brown geography. "Ohio is bounded on the south by the Ohio River, on the west by Indiana," she whispered. But she felt resentful at the children who had laughed. She *had* been thinking about ghosts. In fact, she had thought of little else for the last week. And it was mostly Jimmie Green's fault too.

It had all started last Saturday, Katie remembered, as her thoughts drifted once more from Ohio and its boundaries. She had been getting ready to go to the library and she was having a dreadful time with her shoes. As usual, she had skipped a button, and when she reached the top of the long row she was a button short. But before she had time to get as cross as she usually did Papa came home with the news that he had finally found a house and that they could move into it the next week.

"As soon as I heard about it this morning I went over to look at it," said Papa. "It's a good location, much closer to the newspaper office, and near the school. There's a fine big yard for the children and it's a quiet street. There won't be many teams racing past and stirring up the dust on Saturday nights." Then, with a teasing look at Katie, he added, "And there are plenty of trees for our tomboy to climb. I believe she still has a few teeth that haven't been knocked out."

Papa hesitated a moment, as if making up his mind about something. Then he went on. "But there's something I think you ought to know before you decide about moving. The fact is—well—there's some talk around town about the place being haunted."

Mom paused in her ironing to look at Papa in astonishment. She banged the flatiron back on the kitchen range and tested a hot one with a wet fingertip while Katie waited anxiously for her reply.

"Do you mean to say that in the year 1906 there are people who actually believe such—such twaddle?" Mom asked. "How on earth did a story like that ever get started?"

"From what I can find out it started with Mrs. Peters, who's been living there the past few months. She claims she heard footsteps and rattling noises, and she's positive there are spirits up in the attic. I suppose on windy nights she heard the usual moans and groans."

Papa grinned at Mom. Then he picked Katie up on his knee and finished buttoning her shoe.

"Now, Katie," he cautioned her, "you'll probably hear some wild tales about haunted houses from your school friends. But you just remember that only foolish or ignorant persons believe such things; and don't scare your sister Francie with such silly stories."

Katie nodded gravely. She trusted Papa and was sure

that he knew everything there was to know. Besides, Katie rather liked the idea of living in a haunted house. It would be exciting. Why, it would be something like a storybook!

To Katie's surprise, her friends did not share her enthusiasm. Some of them acted *scared,* and Susie Thompson actually seemed to feel sorry for her.

But Jimmie Green was the worst. Every day at recess he hunted for Katie to tell her the new and alarming things he had learned about ghosts.

"They float through the air and they touch you with cold and clammy fingers," he informed her. "Then you start to pine away and pretty soon you die."

Katie looked at him coldly. "My Papa says only ignorant people believe in ghosts," she stated with dignity. "You must be an extremely ignorant boy, and I feel very sorry for you."

But a little gnawing doubt began to nag at Katie's mind. Maybe there really were ghosts and Papa didn't know about them. That was the doubt which had grown bigger and bigger during the week, and that was the reason Katie's thoughts were far away from the quiet schoolroom and her geography lesson.

"Close your books, children, and get ready for dismissal."

Katie jumped as the teacher tapped her desk. She jumped again when Jimmie Green put a cold finger on her neck and whispered, "Spooks!" as soon as they were out of doors.

Katie's quick temper flared, but before she could

think of a suitable way to get even, she remembered that Mom had told her to hurry home from school. Today was moving day and there would be things she could do to help.

The empty rooms at home had an unfamiliar and lonely look. Papa was directing the packing of the last load of furniture.

"Your mother's over at the new house," he told Katie, "and I've a job for you and Francie. I've piled some of my favorite books in your coaster wagon. Baby Barbie can sit on this big copy of Shakespeare, and you girls can pull. Take your time and be careful of the books."

Aside from a little argument with Francie about who was pulling harder, the first part of the journey was uneventful. When they reached the blacksmith shop they stopped to watch a horse being shod. Sparks flew in a red shower as the smith shaped the shoe. He thrust a piece of heated iron into a tub of water and wiped drops of sweat from his face. He grinned his jolly grin at Katie and boomed, "Don't suppose I'll be seeing you again, Katie. I hear your pa's moving into the haunted house. Watch out for the spooks!"

The men in the shop laughed, and Katie looked at the blacksmith closely. Surely he must be joking! Could he be serious?

"What did he mean, Katie?" asked Francie, as they moved on. "What are spooks?"

"He was just joking," answered Katie. "Here's the place we turn. Let's walk as far as that big tree in front of the yellow house. Then we'll stop to rest. This wagon is getting heavier all the time."

As they paused, panting, there was a terrific *yap, yap, yap* and a black-and-white terrier dashed out of the yard. From his perky ears to the tip of his stubby tail he quivered in a frenzy of indignation over these trespassers who lingered on his sidewalk.

Skidding to a stop a safe distance away, he braced himself firmly against the ground and barked furiously. Francie scrambled to safety on top of the books, and baby Barbie scowled at the barking animal through the ragged locks of hair that fell over her eyes.

"Maybe he thinks Barbie is another dog," laughed Katie. "She looks pretty fierce with her hair hanging like that."

"It's your fault she looks the way she does," reminded Francie. "You're the one that cut her hair so she'd have bangs. Mom didn't like it."

The memory of how angry Mom had been when she had discovered Katie's attempts at barbering was not a pleasant one, and Katie hastily changed the subject.

How are we going to get past this—this bloodhound? she wondered. She took a tentative step forward but backed quickly as the dog broke into a fresh spasm of sound.

Baby Barbie took matters into her own hands. "Bad doggie!" she cried, and burst into anguished howls.

"Oh, my gracious!" exclaimed Katie anxiously. But Barbie's wails brought immediate results. The door of the yellow house flew open and a woman came running.

KATIE CATCHES A GHOST

"Stop it, Muttsy! Be quiet! He won't hurt you, children. He just likes to act brave. You're strange in the neighborhood, aren't you? My goodness, what's that you've got in the wagon? Where are you going? Are you lost?"

Katie waited politely until the woman stopped for breath. Then she answered, "No, ma'am, we're not lost. We're helping move Papa's books. We're going to the white brick house up the street."

"What, the house where Mrs. Peters lived? My goodness, what can your mother be thinking of to take three defenseless children into that house? You poor little lambs! Well, run along, children. I'll call on your mother soon and see if there's anything I can do to help."

Katie's heart sank. The woman didn't look like a foolish or ignorant person, even if she had called them poor little lambs.

Deep in her disturbing thoughts, she forgot that Francie was still sitting in the wagon, and plodded gloomily on until her aching arms reminded her of the extra passenger.

"Francie, you stay on top and hold Barbie and guide the wagon. I'll push for a piece," she suggested.

The wagon rolled smoothly along, with Katie puffing a little until she stopped beside a lilac bush to catch her breath.

At the same instant a bicycle shot around the corner. It was pedaled by a small boy who was leaning far over the handlebars.

Crash! The wheel struck the edge of the wagon and the boy somersaulted into the air and landed on the grass. As Katie watched in speechless horror, he sat up, rubbed his head, and demanded, "Gee whiz, why don't you watch where you're going?"

Katie's fear turned to indignation. "Why—why—*me* watch where *I'm* going!" she sputtered.

"Oh, well, maybe you couldn't help it," admitted the boy generously. "Here, I'll help you pick up some of the books. Where you going with a wagonload of books, anyway?"

Katie understood that this was a peace offering and accepted it as such. "We're moving to the white brick house in this block."

"The white brick house? Gee whiz, you mean—the *white brick house?*"

"Yes," snapped Katie, "and you don't need to tell me it's haunted. I know it's haunted, so there!"

The boy picked up his bicycle and wheeled it up the street, turning several times to look back and making an expressive gesture with his hand across his throat the last time.

Katie looked at Francie's puzzled face. "Just like a silly boy," she said scornfully, hoping that her own growing uneasiness didn't show. "Come on, Francie, help me pull. We're almost there."

When they reached the house there was so much to keep Katie busy that her vague fears slipped from her mind. She carried bundles of clothes upstairs, unpacked some of the dishes, and helped Papa put his books on the shelves.

Presently Mom called them to supper on the big, screened porch which ran the length of the kitchen. It was queer how much better the food tasted when they ate on a porch. An apple tree brushed its branches against the screen and a wren chattered the latest bird gossip to them, her tail teetering up and down with the force of her remarks.

A sleek red squirrel scampered up the trunk of the tree and sat balancing himself with his bushy tail. His whiskers twitched as he looked at them with bright, inquiring eyes. Baby Barbie pointed her spoon at him and sang, "Bad doggie! Bad doggie!" and they all laughed—Barbie the loudest of all. The squirrel gave a jump and landed on the roof overhead, and they could hear his feet pattering across the shingles.

"He must have a nest around here some place," said Papa. "Maybe if we watch we can find it. No, not to-night, Katie. It's time for you children to get some sleep."

Mom had fixed the bedroom with clean white curtains and fresh rag rugs. Katie's favorite *Alice* and her *Chatterbox* books were on the shelf, and Francie's rag doll lay staring solemnly at them as they got ready for bed.

Papa came in to say good night. "Your mother's had a hard day, and she's gone to bed with a splitting headache," he warned them. "Be as quiet as you can. No chattering to each other tonight."

Francie was asleep almost before Papa closed the door, but Katie lay thinking of the events of the day. Thoughts of ghosts—Jimmie Green—the red squirrel—supper on the porch—blurred together, and finally she drifted off to sleep.

Some time later Katie awoke. The room was in heavy shadow, and for a moment she lay dreamily wondering where she was and letting her sleep-filled eyes wander around the unfamiliar room. Suddenly she froze in terror. A white shape hovered near the foot of the bed. It rose and swayed back and forth, drifting closer, then moving slowly away. Katie inched closer to Francie and then let out her breath in a gasp of relief as she realized that it was only the window curtain fluttering in the night breeze.

"Well, you great big silly!" Katie scolded herself. And then she thought, It's a good thing I didn't yell. Wouldn't I have felt foolish now? I s'pose if I were Mrs. Peters I'd tell everybody I saw a ghost.

This was a pleasing thought, and for a time Katie lay basking in a smug feeling of superiority over foolish people who believed in ghosts. But her satisfaction was short-lived.

Suddenly she sat upright. What was that? Footsteps upstairs! And queer rattling noises! Just as Mrs. Peters had said!

Katie sat rigid, holding her breath and listening. Was it only her imagination? Mom always said she had the wildest imagination of any child she knew. No, there were the light footsteps again!

KATIE CATCHES A GHOST

What should she do? Should she close her eyes, hide her head under the covers and wait for the morning? Was she going to be a fraidy-cat, scared by a few strange noises?

Should she call Papa? But that would wake Mom, and Papa had said they must be quiet and not bother Mom. Francie stirred in her sleep, and Katie remembered that Papa was depending upon her to keep Francie from being scared.

Resolutely Katie forced her shaking knees to slide out of bed. Tiptoeing across the room, she picked up the lamp and turned up the wick. She felt a little braver as the light glowed brightly, sending the shadows running into the corners.

Softly Katie crept up the attic steps. Now she could hear more plainly the rattling sounds, but she wasn't sure whether they came from the attic or from her chattering teeth. At the attic door she paused a moment. Then, summoning all her courage, she thrust open the door.

The mysterious sounds stopped abruptly as the rays of the lamp made a golden circle in the darkness. Fearfully Katie peered into the attic.

Crouched in the light, a red squirrel stared back at her, a hickory nut clutched in his paws.

"So this is Mrs. Peters' ghost!"

It was Papa's voice behind her, and Papa was taking the lamp from her hand, his arm holding Katie comfortingly close.

At the sound of Papa's voice the squirrel gave a bound and disappeared behind the rafters. Soft footsteps pattered down the porch roof, and the hickory nut, knocked by flying feet, went rattling across the attic floor.

Katie's knees felt strangely weak as Papa helped her back to the safe haven of the bedroom. Papa picked her up in his arms and sat down in the rocker.

"You spunky little thing!" he said.

Katie snuggled close to Papa and shut her eyes. Papa had been right. Only foolish persons believed in ghosts.

"I was scared," she confessed in a small voice.

"Why, of course you were, Katie," said Papa. "But you did just the right thing. Instead of running away from your fear, you faced it. Most fears are pretty much like your ghost, you know. They're mostly imaginary, and if you run away from them they get bigger and bigger. But if you're brave enough to face them, they fade away. They haven't a chance—not even a ghost of a chance," added Papa with a chuckle.

He bent over to catch Katie's sleepy murmur. "I caught a ghost," mumbled Katie. "Just wait till I tell Jimmie Green!"

Little Red

❋❋

PEARL S. BUCK

Little Red was called Little, because his father was Big Red, and he was called Red because, like his father, he always wore something red. Big Red and Little Red, father and son, had always lived, since they were born, in a village on the edge of a small lake in the mountainous country of Lu, in the province of Kiangsi, in China.

The reason the two, father and son, so loved the color red was a simple one. Big Red had been the only son of his mother, and for that reason she kept him dressed in red until he was too big, and then she gave him a red kerchief to wear around his neck.

"I can see you a long way off," she always said, "because of the red kerchief."

So Big Red grew up wearing the red kerchief.

When Little Red was born, he looked exactly like his father, and his mother, who was a sweet and gentle woman, was the first to see this. She loved Big Red, and as a sign of her joy in the little son, she kept him dressed in red until he was too big, and then she gave him a red kerchief, but a little one.

"I can always see where you both are, father and son, Big and Little, with your red kerchiefs," she said.

It was true that when the farmers were working in their fields she could see her two, and when they went to town she could see them coming home, for when she looked out of the door there were the two spots of red, which were their kerchiefs.

They lived happily in the village until the Japanese came, and they never even imagined that someday an enemy would come and take their beautiful country. Some people might have called them poor, for no one in the village had ever seen an automobile, much less owned one, and the houses were small, and none of the fathers ever had much money in his pockets. On the other hand, some people would have called them rich, for they had good food to eat, rice and vegetables, and very fine fish, and chickens and pork, and certainly the best eggs. And they had clothes enough to keep them warm in winter, and in summer Little Red and his playmates went swimming in the ponds, or they climbed the mountains behind the village and spent the day exploring. In autumn they gathered chestnuts from the trees on the mountains and roasted them over charcoal. Altogether it was a good life.

When the Japanese came it changed so quickly that it was hard to believe that it was the same place. The village had been such a safe and pleasant one, where babies played in the street, and where mothers sat in the doorways sewing and watching and talking to one another and laughing at what their children did. As soon as school was over, the school children played in the street, too, and Little Red was always one of them. They played hopscotch and shuttlecock and toss-pennies, and then skipped home to early suppers, and if there were actors in town visiting, they might go to a play in the temple court afterward.

It was as pleasant as that one day, and the next day all was changed. The villagers had heard something about the war, of course. People in the village did not read newspapers, but they listened to other people traveling by, and they heard about the Japanese and how they wanted to take the whole of China. But almost as soon as they heard it, it really happened. For the next day the whole village was in confusion. An army of men came tramping through. Some of the men were on foot, but some rode in the cars which the village had never seen. Little Red happened to be home from school for lunch, and he had taken his bowl to the door and stood eating as fast as he could because he wanted to get back to school in time to play before afternoon work began. He was pushing rice and cabbage into his mouth with his chopsticks when suddenly he felt his father pull his shoulders, jerk him back, and slam the door shut and bar it.

Inside the house everything went wrong at once. His father dropped his bowl on the tile floor and broke it, his mother spilled the tea she was pouring, and the baby began to cry.

"The dwarfs are really here," Big Red gasped to Little Red's mother.

"You must run out of the back door up the mountain," she gasped back. "You should have gone yesterday with the other men, when we first heard the dwarfs were near."

"I did want to get the cabbage planted before I went away," he groaned, "so that if I didn't get back you would have something to eat with the rice."

Before anything could be done, there was a great noise and clatter at the door.

"Shall I open the door, Father?" Little Red asked.

Before anyone could open the door it crashed in, and there stood the strange men who were the Japanese. Big Red and Little Red and the mother and the baby could only stare at them. They were all terrified, and the baby was so frightened that he stopped crying, his mouth wide open.

"You," one of the men yelled at Big Red. He was an officer and he carried a sword as well as a pistol. "Come out here! We want able-bodied men to carry loads for us!"

The moment he spoke the soldiers behind him seized Big Red by the hands and legs and jerked him out in the street. There was already a long line of villagers tied together with ropes, and to this long line Little Red now saw his father tied too. He ran and clung to his father's waist, and his father bent and whispered in his ear, "Get back into the house, bar the door, and take care of your mother!"

He dared not disobey his father, and yet how could he bear to see him go? He obeyed and he disobeyed. He ran into the house, barred the door, and ran out the back door again. There from a distance he watched what happened to his father. The line of villagers was driven down the road like oxen, and the enemy soldiers whipped them if they went too slowly and pricked them with their bayonets. At the head of the line Little Red saw his father march steadfastly away southward. Hiding himself in the bushes, he followed until he was sure of their road, and then he ran home to tell his mother.

You can imagine how his mother cried when she heard what had happened to Big Red. She put the baby in his crib and sat down on a bench in the kitchen and cried and cried, wiping her eyes on her blue cotton apron.

"We will never see him again," she sobbed. "He is such a big strong man, he is so good, he is such a fine worker, they will never let him go. And now he is a prisoner! Oh, if I had only made him go to the mountains yesterday!"

"What is in the mountains, Mother?" Little Red asked. Then his mother told him, "In the mountains there are men from many villages gathering together in an army to fight the enemy. They wanted your father to come yesterday and lead them, and he promised to go as soon as the enemy drew near. This morning, even, he might have gone and been safe if he had not stayed to plant those wretched cabbages. How can I eat them now? They would choke me, for it is because of them he is taken prisoner."

Little Red listened to all of this and said nothing.

He was at this time twelve years old and he knew that there are times when it is better for a boy to listen and say nothing, especially when he is planning something very big. He let his mother cry until she was tired, and he held the baby when that small one began to fret, and he burned the grass under the caldron in the stove when his mother stopped crying after a long time and sighed and said, "Well, I suppose we must eat, even if he is gone. But you eat—I can't eat a thing."

She was rather astonished when he ate an unusually big supper, and she was inclined to be a little cross with him for it. "I am glad you have a big appetite," she said, "but I am surprised, when you know how your poor father is suffering."

He still said nothing. He went to bed very early and so did she, and they had not opened the door since he barred it shut at noon. The mother had cried so much that she went to sleep, although she had not thought she could. But Little Red did not sleep. In his bed he had put a bit of broken brick, and he lay with it in the middle of his back. He lay a long time thus, purposely to keep awake, and when at last he began to hear his mother breathe as though she were sound asleep he rose and made ready to carry out his plan. In his belt he thrust the kitchen chopping knife. In his red kerchief he tied some bread, rolls, and salted cabbage, and two hard-boiled salted duck eggs, which his mother always kept on hand. Then he felt in the broken teapot and took out half of the family money which they kept there. It was never very much, but he thought half would be enough for him in case he did not get home for a long time.

He wished that he could tell his mother where he was going, but she could not read, and there was no use in writing her a note. So he had to go without a word.

He opened the back door and slipped through. The moon was bright and better than any lamp, but he walked softly just the same. He had a long way to go and he set out swiftly and steadily southward. He knew exactly what he was going to do. He was going to find out where his father was, and with the knife he would cut the ropes that bound him and help him to get away.

He thought exactly how it would go. They would have to stop for the night somewhere. Probably the prisoners would all be lying on the ground. Of course they would be guarded by the soldiers. But he would creep forward carefully, making use of every shadow. Perhaps there might be a shadow over the moon by then to help him. Often enough clouds came out of the mountains in the night and spread up over the sky. But the sky was clear now.

He had never been out in the night alone before and he did not like it very well. The frogs were croaking loudly in the ponds, and a bird wailed out of a bamboo grove. But he went on. Two hours passed and he came at last to a village, where he hoped to find his father. It was empty. On the silent street every door was barred. His dream of finding Big Red there was only a dream.

He was so tired that for a moment he was discouraged. Where now should he turn?

But if they were going south, his reason told him, they would still be going south.

He got down on his knees and looked at the road in the bright moonlight. Like all the roads of that province, it had a stone path down the middle, made of flat stones from the mountains and polished smooth by people's feet. If many people had walked down the road today the dust would be tramped away and it would be a sign of which way his father had gone. Sure enough, the polished stone was smooth and clean of dust. He got up again and followed it. When the road forked he followed the one which was clean of dust upon its stone path. It led steadily south.

Now Little Red knew that if you keep going south far enough you reach the great river, and if the prisoners and his father reached the river they would be put on boats, and then there would be no way of following them, for the water could give him no hint and no clue. He began to run instead of walk, dogtrotting along on his tired feet.

I must take the nearest way to the river port! he thought.

He had been to the river port twice with his father,

because that is where the fair is held every year, and he knew the way. But of course the gates of the city would be locked at such an hour, and a country boy with a red kerchief full of bread and cabbage and two duck eggs would certainly not be let in or even listened to if he knocked.

There's nothing to do but go around the city, Little Red now told himself.

So he went around the city to the river's edge and crawled along in the mud for a long way. The city wall came right down to the river, and he had to step into the water to get past, but he did that easily enough, and was indeed quite ready to swim if the water were deep. But at this season the river was low, and he was able to walk around the wall.

Now he knew that the boats were all tethered to iron rings fastened in the stones of the river wall on either side of steep stone steps that went to the river, and so to the steps he went. There was not a sign of anyone. The moonlight shone down on the wet steps, and the quiet boats bobbed up and down on the slight swell of the river, and the whole city slept.

He had a dreadful moment of dismay. Suppose they had not come here at all! Perhaps he had guessed entirely wrongly! Then he remembered that he had come around the city, and they perhaps would come another way. And he had come quickly, being alone, and they would come slowly. He sat down on a corner of the step and made himself very small, and waited. He was so hungry that although he tried not to, he felt compelled to eat a piece of the bread he had brought for his father, but he would not allow himself to eat one of the duck eggs.

Scarcely had he done this when he heard a loud noise in the city. Shots rang out in the night, men yelled and cursed, and he heard the heavy squeak of the city gates.

I am right, he thought wildly. I shall see my father! And he squeezed himself very small against the wet wall, into a shadow which the parapet just above his head cast down on the steps. The red kerchief of food he hid between his knees.

Sure enough, in a few minutes of heartbeats so loud that they sounded in his ears like drums, he saw the weary line of men drag themselves around the corner. His father was still at the head of them. He knew his father, for he held up his head, and besides there was the red kerchief about his neck, clearly to be seen in the white moonlight. It was all Little Red could do not to call out, not to press forward. But he knew this would never do. So he sat small and close in the shadow.

It was well he did, for now the soldiers rushed after the prisoners and herded them down the steps together, and Little Red lost sight of his father entirely. A soldier brushed past him as he hurried down to the boats, and for a moment he was terrified. The soldier looked down at him, saw him, and gave him a kick and then went on. Little Red sat motionless while the prisoners were pushed on the boats.

Now he was glad that his father was Big Red. For he

watched the spot of red on the tall man who got into
the boats with all the others. Then Little Red put down
his kerchief but he kept the knife in his belt, and
silently, as the boats left the shore, he crept down the
steps. Into the water he went as cleanly and deeply as
one of the river animals that live along the shores of
rivers. He paddled softly after the boats and after the
big man who sat on the edge of one of them, his red
kerchief fluttering in the night wind.

The boats were rowboats, sampans, and small cargo
boats, and the men to whom they belonged rowed
slowly and unwillingly, knowing that they would get no
pay for what they did. It was not too hard for Little
Red to paddle along like a small dog and reach the side
of the boat where Big Red sat, his head in his hands,
tied to the other prisoners by the rope around his waist.
Little Red dared not call. He hung onto the boat by one
hand and with the other he reached for the knife and
slipped it to his father's foot. Then he pounded lightly
on that foot.

Big Red looked down from under his hands. He saw
a kitchen knife—nothing else. Then he saw something
bob up out of the water, a dark, wet little face. He
could not see who it was, and before he looked again the
head was bobbing away toward the shore.

For Little Red had very sensibly reasoned that he
would go back and wait on the steps so that his father
would have only himself to save. Purposely he did not
let his father see who he was.

If he knows it is I, he thought, he will stay to see

that I am all right and then maybe we'll both be caught.

So he took care of himself and dragged himself out of the river and sat on the steps, very wet and a little cold. The red kerchief was still there, to his joy, for he had been afraid a dog might find it. The food smelled delicious, and he had to be very stern with himself and not even open the kerchief lest he eat more of it. He simply sat and waited.

Big Red, when he saw the knife, could not imagine how it had got there. If he had believed in strange things as some people did, he would have said a river god had come to his help. He was so astonished that he was almost ready to believe it. But he knew that he must not waste time wondering. He took the knife, which was very sharp, and softly cut his ropes. Then quietly he laid it on the foot of the next man and slipped into the water without a ripple. It was easy enough, for the boat was so laden with prisoners that its side was almost level with the river. He sank under the water and began to swim, holding his breath as long as he could. And then one of those clouds came out of the mountains, as they so often did just before dawn, and covered the face of the setting moon. When he came up again he was quite safe. No one could have seen his dark head against the muddy water of the river.

Little Red sat in the darkness on the steps and shivered. Now he could not see his father and he must listen carefully. Yes, in a few moments he heard a man breathing heavily and trying not to breathe. He called out softly, "My father!"

There was no answer. The breathing stopped suddenly. His father was afraid. Little Red understood at once.

"Big Red!" he whispered loudly. "It is Little Red!"

"Little Red?" his father whispered. "Then where are you?"

Feeling for each other along the step, they found one another and each gave the other a big hug.

"Why, you Little Red," his father gasped in a whisper. "How did you come here?"

"I brought the kitchen knife," Little Red whispered back.

But Big Red did not stop while he listened. With the father's arm about his son's shoulder, they went around the city wall and struck over a narrow path to the hills. And all the time Little Red told his father exactly what had happened, and Big Red laughed and hugged Little Red and said over and over again, "You see why the enemy can never conquer our country—no country can be conquered whose boys are like you!"

When they had reached the mountains they went into a little cave and now they felt safe.

"Here is the food," Little Red said proudly. Then he felt he must tell the worst. "I did eat one piece of bread because I was so hungry," he confessed, "but I would not allow myself to have a duck egg."

His father took the kerchief and opened it and divided the food exactly into half. "You are a brave man," he said, "and brave men must eat. Moreover, they must share equally all that they have."

So they ate, and Little Red ate the duck egg, and it tasted even better than he had imagined.

"Now," his father said when they had eaten, "I must go up higher into the mountains and stay there."

"Oh," cried Little Red. "Let me come with you, Father!"

At this Big Red looked grave. "Who will look after the family?" he asked.

It was now Little Red who looked grave. "I should so much like to live in the mountains," he begged, "with you, Father! Because the baby keeps me awake at night when he cries."

His father laughed and clapped him on the shoulder. "Now," he said, "here's a compromise. You shall be the messenger between home and mountains. One night at home, one night in the mountains—how is that? Messengers we must have."

And that is how Little Red became what he is today, a messenger between the men on the plains and the men in the mountains. He stops often to see how his mother and the baby are, but he never stays more than one night. But sometimes by coaxing his father he stays a couple of nights and more in the mountains in an old ruined temple, where the villagers have made a fort. From there they go down into the valley and fight the enemy, and, as often as he can, Little Red tells them where the enemy is. He is too young to enlist, but how can Big Red do without him?

The Willow Basket

CAROL RYRIE BRINK

"They're shiftless—that's what they are!" said Mrs. Woodlawn decidedly.

Shiftless was a terrible word in pioneer Wisconsin. Caddie, Tom, and Warren exchanged discouraged glances. They had been delighted to see the McCantrys come back—even if the father, mother, and four children had returned on foot, wheeling all of their possessions in a wheelbarrow.

Mr. and Mrs. McCantry and the four children were standing in the road now, casting wistful glances at the Woodlawns' cozy white house while they waited for Tom and Caddie to inform their parents of their old neighbors' return.

"But, Mother," said Caddie, "Emma is so nice, and all they've got left is what they can carry in a wheelbarrow."

"They had just as good a chance here as the rest of

us," said Mrs. Woodlawn severely. "They had a farm, but they must needs sell it for what they could get and go on to something finer. And now, it seems, they are back with nothing but a wheelbarrow."

"We must not judge people too hastily, Harriet," said Mr. Woodlawn mildly from the doorway.

"Oh, Father, we may ask them in for the night, mayn't we?" begged Caddie.

"Well, now," said Mr. Woodlawn, with a pleasant wink at Caddie over his wife's smooth dark head, "we'd better let the McCantrys go on to the next farm. The Bunns or the Silbernagles will take them in for the night, and that will let us out of any obligation."

Mrs. Woodlawn whirled about with a suspicious look in her eyes and was just in time to catch her husband's smile and the tail end of his wink.

"Go along with you!" she said, beginning to laugh. "I never intended to let them go without supper and a night's rest, and you know that. But I do feel better for having said what I think of them!"

Tom and Caddie and Warren raced away to invite the McCantrys in to supper and comfortable beds. They were a dispirited-looking lot as they sat along the roadside, waiting for the hospitality of a former neighbor. The bottom of Mrs. McCantry's dress was draggled with mud and dust, and the two boys were barefoot; but Mrs. McCantry had a bonnet of the latest fashion trimmed with purple velvet pansies, and Pearly, the little girl who was next to the youngest, had a new gold ring.

Emma, the eldest of the four and Caddie's own age,

slipped a warm, brown arm through Caddie's and gave her a squeeze. Emma didn't have gold rings or bonnets with pansies; but she was brown and solid and comfortable, and Caddie liked her best of them all. When a bird called out in the meadow Emma could pucker up her lips and imitate it. It was Emma who looked after the little ones as much as her mother did.

Now Mr. McCantry picked up the handles of the wheelbarrow, and Caddie thought that his shoulders looked rounder and more bent than they had when he went away. The wheelbarrow creaked as he trundled it up the path to the front door. Caddie could see that it contained some patchwork quilts and cooking utensils, a set of Mrs. McCantry's hoops, and a clock which was not running.

"Why don't you wind your clock?" asked Caddie. "I hate to see a clock that doesn't go."

"It's broke," said Emma. "We still carry it around, but it's like most of the rest of our things. It won't work any more."

"That's too bad," said Caddie, but it gave her an idea. Mr. and Mrs. Woodlawn met the McCantrys at the front door.

"Well, well," said Mr. Woodlawn heartily, shaking his former neighbor's hand, "so you have come back to us again, McCantry? Dunnville is a pretty good place after all."

"It is that!" said Mr. McCantry. "I'm glad to be back. We've been a weary way."

"Now, Josiah, why do you say that?" cried Mrs. McCantry sharply.

Caddie looked at her in surprise and saw that she had lost her discouraged look of a few moments ago and was quite the fine lady once again.

"We have had a most edifying journey, really," she said, "and spent some months with my brother, who has a most elegant house which puts anything you have here in Dunnville quite to shame. Of course we were most elaborately entertained, and it is only by the merest chance that you see us in these circumstances. An unforeseen accident happened to our horse and carriage, and we just thought how healthful it would be to come along on foot."

"Yes, yes, of course," said Mrs. Woodlawn hastily. "Now do come in and wash yourselves for supper."

The two little boys went along with Tom and Warren— while Pearly was taken in charge by Caddie's little sisters, Hetty and Minnie.

Caddie squeezed Emma's arm.

"Come up to my room," she said.

"Wait," said Emma, smiling mysteriously. "I've got a present for you, Caddie."

"A present for me?" Caddie was incredulous.

"It's not very good," said Emma shyly, "but I made it myself. An old lady who took us in one night, when we hadn't any money, showed me how."

She fumbled through the untidy bundle of quilts and skillets in the wheelbarrow and brought out a little willow basket.

"Why, it's ever so pretty!" cried Caddie, sincerely pleased. "But you'd ought to keep it for yourself."

"Oh, I can make lots more of them," said Emma. "Big ones too; but we don't have room to carry them, and I thought you'd like this little one."

"I'd love it," said Caddie. "Thank you, Emma."

Meals were always good at the Woodlawns', but any sort of company rallied Mrs. Woodlawn to extra effort. Tonight, besides the supper which she had already planned, she went to the smokehouse and took down one of the hams which had come from their own well-fed pigs and had been salted and smoked under her own direction. With a sharp knife she cut the tender pink slices and fried them delicately brown before heaping them on the big blue china platter. Each slice was half ringed around with a thin, crisp layer of fat—just enough to give variety to the lean. Mr. Woodlawn filled the plates of the hungry-looking McCantrys with the generosity of a good host, and Emma and the littler boy fell to with a will. But Pearly set up a thin wail of protest.

"I can't eat this," she said, pointing an accusing finger at the fat.

"Me neither," said Ezra, the littlest brother.

"You can't eat that tender bit of fat?" cried Mrs. Woodlawn in surprise.

"They've got aristocratic stomachs," Mrs. McCantry said proudly.

For a moment Mrs. Woodlawn was speechless.

"Maybe Mama could cut the fat part off for you, Pearly," began Mrs. McCantry doubtfully.

Mrs. Woodlawn's earrings began to tremble as they always did when she was excited.

"No," she said, with that gleam in her eye which her own children had learned to obey. "If you can't eat that good ham just as it is, fat and lean, you're not very hungry. My children eat what is set before them with a relish. They know if they don't they can go to bed empty. Anyone who eats at my table can do the same."

Over her tumbler of milk Caddie saw with twinkling eyes that Pearly and Ezra were eating their fat with their lean. Personally she thought the fat was the best part when it was all crisp on the outside and juicy on the inside, as Mother fried it.

The McCantrys were not there for one night only; they stayed on for many days, but there were no more complaints about their meals.

Caddie and Emma enjoyed the time very much. Together they went down to the swamp where the young willows grew thickly, and the boys helped them cut slender, pliant shoots to weave more baskets. The Woodlawn land and Dr. Nightingale's land came together here at the edge of the swamp, and beyond their fences the swamp stretched away in a fairyland of tiny hummocks and islands on which grew miniature firs and tamaracks. There was wild rice in the swamp in the autumn and quantities of wild cranberries.

"What a pretty place this is!" said Emma. "If I were you, Caddie, I would build a little house on this hill overlooking the swamp. I like the nice spicy swamp smell, don't you?"

A red-winged blackbird, swaying on a reed, uttered a throaty call, and Emma answered it.

Caddie remembered this later when she heard her father and mother talking about a home for the Mc-Cantrys.

"Really, Harriet," said Mr. Woodlawn, "I've talked alone with McCantry, and they have reached rock bottom. He hasn't any money left."

"To hear her talk, you would think they were millionaires."

"I know, my dear, but she's a foolish woman. It's her foolishness that's brought them where they are, I think. But we can't let them starve, for all that, and we can't have them living with us always either. Somehow we've got to set them on their feet once more."

"Well, Johnny, grumble as I may, I suppose that you are always right about such things. What had we better do?" sighed Mrs. Woodlawn.

"I thought we might give them a little land at the edge of our place somewhere. Perhaps one of our neighbors on the other side would contribute a little, too, and then all of the neighbors could get together and help build them a house. We could make a sort of raising bee out of it."

"A raising bee!" repeated Mrs. Woodlawn, her eyes beginning to shine. "Yes, we could do that."

"Oh, Father," cried Caddie, forgetting that she had not been included in the conversation so far, "that would be lots of fun! And I'll tell you the very place for the house."

"You will?" laughed her father. "So you've already picked the site?"

"Yes, I have! It's that corner down by the swamp. Emma loves the smell and the redwing blackbirds, and they could get all the cranberries and wild rice they needed, and maybe they could sell what they didn't need, and they could make willow baskets out of the willow shoots and sell those too."

"Willow baskets?" asked her father. "Sell willow baskets? You're going a little too fast for me, daughter. I'm lost in the swamp."

"Oh, wait!" cried Caddie. She was in one of her eager moods when ideas came too fast to be expressed. She flew out of the room and returned in a moment with Emma's basket in her hands. "Look! Wouldn't you pay money for a big basket if it were as nicely made as that?"

Her mother took the basket in her own slender hands and looked it over carefully.

"Yes, I would," she said. "I believe a lot of people would. We've never had anyone around here who could make baskets."

"Well, we have now," said Caddie. "Can't we set the McCantrys up in business?"

"Where's my bonnet?" cried Mrs. Woodlawn. "I'm going to call on the neighbors!"

Dancing with excitement, Caddie ran for her mother's tasteful gray bonnet.

"Thank kind Providence, it doesn't have purple pansies on it," said Mrs. Woodlawn as she went to the barn for a horse.

There was nothing like another's need to rally the pioneers of that day. Dr. Nightingale joined Mr. Woodlawn in donating a good-sized strip of land at the edge of the swamp. Another man, who had plenty of timber on his farm, offered enough logs to build a cabin if others would cut and haul them. Men and boys who had nothing to give but their time gladly did the cutting and hauling. One neighbor offered a pig, another a cow, and a third the use of his horse and plow to break a garden spot.

On the day of the "raising," men and boys on horseback arrived early from all the country around and went to work on the cabin. The women and girls came along later in the morning with covered dishes and jars of pickles and preserves.

Mrs. Woodlawn and Mrs. McCantry, with the help of the children, had made tables by putting long planks on sawhorses near the site of the new house. Over an open fire were great pots of coffee and stone jars full of Mrs. Woodlawn's choice baked beans.

It was not often that the neighbors came together for a common purpose. They were a settled community now, and it had been a long time since one of them had had a raising for himself. There had been the time of the Indian "Massacre Scare" when they had all come together under the Woodlawns' roof for several days; but then they had been filled with fear and distrust.

Now they came together in a spirit of friendship and helpfulness.

The children raced about, playing tag and Blindman's Buff and I Spy, while the men laid up stones for a fireplace and hewed and raised the logs one upon another to make the McCantrys' walls. The women unpacked baskets and laughed and chattered as they spread the feast. They were seeing friends and neighbors they had not seen for weeks, perhaps for months or years.

There was one thing which Mrs. Woodlawn and Mrs. McCantry had in common: they both loved a party. With happy, flushed faces they moved about among the neighbors, shaking hands, filling coffee cups, and urging more beans or gingerbread on people who had already eaten their fill.

The swamp echoed with the ringing of axes and mallets and the cries of men as they heaved the upper logs into place. By sundown the McCantrys had a house of their own. All the hard work was done and only the finishing was left for Mr. McCantry. As the neighbors prepared to depart other gifts came out of their wagons: a sack of potatoes, a rocking chair, a bushel of turnips, a goosefeather pillow, strings of dried apples, a couple of live chickens.

At the last moment Mr. Woodlawn nailed up a shelf by the new fireplace. No one knew why until Caddie and Emma came breathlessly over the fields from the Woodlawns' house carrying the McCantrys' clock. Caddie and her father had sat up late the night before to take it all apart, clean it, and coax it to run. Now it ticked away on the shelf as gay as a cricket.

"There!" said Caddie triumphantly. "A house is ready to live in when a clock is ticking in it!"

"My land!" said Mrs. McCantry. "That clock hasn't ticked for years—just like us, I guess." Her bonnet was all crooked with excitement and the purple pansies bobbed and trembled over one ear, but for once her eyes were perfectly frank and honest. "I know what you've been thinking of us, Mrs. Woodlawn," she said slowly. "Shiftless, you thought, and I guess you were right. But we've seen what neighbors can be like today. We're going to set right out to be good neighbors ourselves. You won't ever regret all that you have done for us!"

The two women looked at each other and for the first time they smiled in sudden understanding. Caddie and Emma smiled, too, and hugged each other.

Caddie knew that Mrs. McCantry might often forget her good resolutions, for she was that kind of person; but she knew also that Emma would always make up for Mrs. McCantry's shortcomings, for Emma was a person to trust.

The McCantrys would be good neighbors.

Whitey and the Prairie Fire

GLEN ROUNDS

When Uncle Torwal left for town right after breakfast, Whitey thought some of going along with him. But finally he decided to stay home and fix a new cinch for his saddle instead.

"Sure you won't change your mind and come along?" Uncle Torwal asked as he finished saddling Black Eagle, the best quarter horse in the country. "Somebody might even stir up a horse race."

"No, sir, I reckon I'll stay here this time," Whitey answered. "I have a few little odd jobs to do."

"Well, take care of things. I'll be back sometime this afternoon." And Torwal rode the dancing black horse out through the gates.

Uncle Torwal treated Whitey much the same as he would any rider that might have been working for him. And as far as Whitey could see, he did almost a man's share of the ranch work. Even so, he enjoyed staying alone on the ranch now and then, working around by himself as if maybe he really owned the place.

But now he felt uneasy when the first thin traces of smoke started drifting in from the hills toward Elk Creek. This time of year the whole country was tinder dry, and a prairie fire might burn for miles if it got a good start. So far there was no way of telling how far this smoke was coming. It might be from some big fire twenty miles away.

All morning Whitey kept interrupting his work every little while to watch the smoke and wonder if it was getting thicker. After a while he lost interest in oiling his gear, and went to the house to fix himself some dinner. Instead of making a batch of biscuits as he'd been planning, with ham and gravy to go with them, he got a couple of cold flapjacks left from breakfast. Making a sandwich with a piece of cold bacon, he sat on the steps to eat. But somehow he didn't feel very hungry and fed most of it to the old cat that was rubbing around his boots.

For a while after he'd eaten, the smoke didn't seem to thicken any more, and Whitey began to think that it wouldn't be long before Uncle Torwal came. But even so, he was restless and couldn't settle down to do any of the things he wanted to, so after a while he went down to the windmill and climbed to the top of the tower. From there he could see a long way in all directions. Looking off toward Elk Creek, he could see that the fire was somewhere not too far beyond the ridge. As he watched, a big fuzzy cloud of yellowish-white smoke began to boil high up into the sky. Apparently the fire had been burning slowly through short grass until it had reached a swale where higher grass or buckbrush had suddenly blazed up to make the big smoke cloud.

A fire that size would soon make its own draft and begin moving faster. Looking in the other direction, Whitey wished Uncle Torwal would hurry back from town. But there was no sign of anything moving as far as he could see. Ordinarily there would have been ranchers coming from all directions to see about a fire of that size. But today everybody in that part of the county had gone to town.

Earlier in the summer Whitey and Uncle Torwal had plowed fireguards around the ranch buildings and around the stackyards on the flats where all the winter's hay was stacked. But a fire with a fair wind behind it could easily jump the narrow plowed strips. It had been a dry year, and on all sides of the ranch the range was grazed off short. But the big winter pasture running to the fence just this side of the ridge next to the fire had grass almost knee high. If a fire once got into that, nothing could save either the ranch buildings or the stacks of winter hay.

So after a last look toward town Whitey saddled Old Spot and rode out to get a better look. From the top of the ridge he was able to see the fire itself. The black path it had burned stretched half a mile wide, clear across the valley below him, and disappeared over the ridge beyond. Nearer by, the flames—in little creeping lines—were working their way slowly up the gullied slope toward him. It was much too big a fire for him to try to fight by himself. And from the way it was heading, Whitey figured it might miss the big pasture entirely and burn itself harmlessly out on the bare, hardpan flats along the river behind him.

However, there was always the chance that the wind might change, or one of the unpredictable updrafts might carry a burning brand off into the high grass.

So after another look in all directions, Whitey turned and rode back to the ranch. At the windmill he quickly filled the water barrel that sat on the stoneboat by the tank. When he'd finished he threw some gunny sacks and pieces of old canvas into the barrel, and fastened the rope from the stoneboat to the saddle horn, and started back for the ridge.

Old Spot grunted and complained at the weight of the barrel dragging behind him over the dusty ranch-yard. But Whitey was in no humor to listen to him, and when they got onto the grass the going was easier. As they rode, Whitey anxiously watched the smoke. Sometimes it thinned out to an almost invisible thread, and then again it would suddenly billow up in great, fat clouds.

At the pasture gate Whitey unhitched the rope from the water barrel and tied Old Spot to a gatepost. Taking one of the wet sacks with him, he hurried up to the ridge. Down the far slope there were a dozen brisk fires burning where brush in the rain-washed gullies had caught fire. But for now there was nothing for him to do except watch for sparks that might blow overhead. Between the place he stood and the pasture fence below there was a hundred yards or so of close-cropped grass, crisscrossed with deep-cut cattle trails. And on down the ridge it was only a quarter of a mile to the fence corner and the farther edge of the pasture. As he'd guessed, the main part of the fire was going to cross the ridge safely beyond that.

But he would have to watch for tongues of fire that might work up the slope against the wind along the bottoms of the brushy gullies. If he could catch them while they were still in the short grass he might be able to beat them out with the wet sacks before they reached the high grass.

As Whitey watched, a little whirlwind swept a shower of sparks this way and that, high overhead, finally dropping them close by where he stood. Hurrying with the wet sacks, he quickly beat out the smoldering spots. But from then on, as fast as he beat out one patch he'd see another somewhere else.

The smoke was getting thicker so that his chest hurt when he breathed, and his eyes smarted and watered. The sacks quickly dried and began to smolder in their turn, so he hurried to the barrel to get others. As he turned back he saw that a line of fire had broken out of the head of a gully and was creeping down the slope behind him.

Dropping the sacks, he hauled one of the bigger pieces of canvas out of the water and started tying it to the end of the rope still fastened to the saddle horn.

Excitement and the smarting of his eyes made him clumsy, but he finally made his knot secure. Now he mounted Spot, who was rolling his eyes suspiciously at the thickening smoke. Once in the saddle, Whitey had to fight the old horse's head around to move him toward the burning line. Drumming with his heels and using his reins for a quirt, Whitey finally managed to get him alongside one end of the blaze. Turning then, he urged the horse to a trot along the very edge of the burned ground so that the wet canvas was dragged over the burning grass. Turning again at the other end, Whitey managed to drag the canvas along the fire once again before Spot refused to go any farther. Whitey dismounted near the barrel, and after taking Spot's bridle off, turned him loose to go back to the corrals.

Snatching a couple of wet sacks, he ran back to the fire. The dragging canvas had not put out the blaze, but had broken it up into many little individual fires that moved much more slowly than the solid line. The heat seemed to sear Whitey's face, and now and again he had to stop to beat out sparks that settled on his clothes. But soon he'd put out the last of the little fires in the grass, and straightened up to look around him.

Seeing no danger anywhere else, Whitey went to the barrel and for a while alternately dropped his arms in the water and splashed his face and head. When he'd rested a little he tied the handkerchief mask-fashion around his face and turned again to watch the fire. Here and there little flickering places showed where sparks had been missed. Working carefully, he went back and forth along the burned edges until he was sure the last one was entirely dead.

By that time the smoke seemed to be thinning a little and he could see the wide path where the main front of the fire had burned over the ridge and gone on safely past the fence corner. As he stood there feeling too tired to move, a sudden gust of wind swept up over the ridge carrying a flaming tumbleweed. It was rolling and bouncing straight for the pasture fence and the high grass beyond—scattering small, blazing scraps behind it.

Running and stumbling after it, Whitey swung at it with the wet sack, trying to pin it to the ground. But it bounced this way and that, and each time he missed it by inches. Just when he thought he could go no farther the tumbleweed struck the fence and tangled for a minute in the barbed wire. Before it dropped off, Whitey had wrapped it in the sack and was stamping out the sparks that were already starting to smolder inside the fence.

When the last one was out he leaned against the fense post with his eyes tight shut to ease their smarting. He was too tired to move.

Suddenly he heard a noise and opened his eyes to see Uncle Torwal getting off Black Eagle close beside him.

"How are you doing, boy? Are you all right?"

"Yes, sir," Whitey said, straightening up. "I was just resting a minute."

"Looks like we'd have been burned out for sure if you hadn't been here," Uncle Torwal said, looking around at the burned streaks that came down so close to the fence.

"It was close for a while," Whitey agreed. "But the main part of the fire went on by, so this was mostly set from sparks."

They both sat for a while with their backs to the water barrel, waiting to be sure there was no more danger from sparks.

"Well, it looks like it's all safe enough now," Torwal said after a while. "Let's go home and fix up some of those blisters on your hands. You take my horse and I'll walk."

Whitey looked surprised for a minute, for Black Eagle was Uncle Torwal's special horse and he never let anyone else ride him for any reason.

"Go ahead, climb on," Torwal repeated, noticing that Whitey hesitated. "You've earned a ride on a good horse, I expect."

Whitey forgot his tiredness and his blisters as he felt the springy lightness of the big horse under him, so different from Old Spot's heavy lumbering gait. Pushing his hat a little to one side, he sat as tall as possible in the saddle, thinking maybe Uncle Torwal would let him get a horse like this before long.

Adventure on Ice

WANDA NEILL TOLBOOM

Spring had come to the little Alaskan village. The sun, which had remained hidden most of the winter, now rose high in the sky. Shallow pools of shining water lay upon the blue-gray sea ice. The sky was very blue, and everywhere melting snow reflected the bright sunshine.

There was great activity in the village. Parka-clad men, women, and children hurried about. Dogs howled as sleds were loaded. Almost every Eskimo who lived in the village was out-of-doors.

Koonuk helped his father lash a flat-bottomed skin boat to a long sled. He worked quickly and well, feeling proud that at twelve years of age he was doing a man's work. His sister, who was only ten, busied herself packing pots and dishes into the traveling box.

This was one of the most exciting times in the year.

The men of the village were going out to hunt the great bowhead whales that passed by each spring on their way to the Arctic Ocean.

For weeks now Koonuk had been busy helping to clean and mend the boats and paddles and to sharpen boat-hooks and harpoons. Sourrah had sewn her father a fine new pair of waterproof boots. No one had been idle.

Each day Koonuk had become more excited as he looked out across the frozen sea. Now, at last, a great wide crack had opened up. Fields of ice were breaking away from the main ice which was still locked firmly to the land. Through this crack in the ice the whales would travel on their northward journey.

There was now no time to be lost. The capture of many whales meant that the village people would have plenty of food for a long time to come. The skin and bones of the huge animals had many uses too.

Soon the boat was made quite fast. Sourrah handed her father the traveling box and he packed it in with the tent and sleeping robes. She, too, was very proud and happy. This year she was going with her father and brother to the hunt.

As they began to hitch the dogs Koonuk saw that his father was putting a harness on the old dog, Toto.

"Surely we do not take Toto with us," he cried out. "That old dog can no longer travel quickly. She is of no use."

His father was not pleased that Koonuk had spoken out so boldly. "This dog is wise as well as old," he replied. "She has not missed going to the whale hunt for many years. This time she will not be left behind."

"That is true," said Sourrah, stooping to pat the dog's shaggy head. "We cannot go without Toto."

Koonuk said no more, but he felt a little cross with the others.

Soon all the teams of the village were ready, and with much howling and shouting they all set off together with the dogs' noses pointing toward the far-off place where mist rose from the open water.

It was great fun. Koonuk and Sourrah ran beside the sled, as did their father. Sourrah thought of the little cakes that she would fry in the tent, and Koonuk thought of great whales and his new harpoon which lay on the sled.

Thinking these fine thoughts, they did not notice that the sled had slowed until they were far behind the others. Suddenly their father shouted at the dogs to stop. The old dog Toto was limping very badly.

"She has a badly swollen leg. We must travel very slowly," said their father after he had examined her.

"Poor old dog," said Sourrah.

But Koonuk spoke not a word because he was so angry and ashamed. Now the other teams were almost out of sight.

When at last they reached the edge of the ice several tents had already been set up. But only the women and girls were there. Far out on the water they saw the other hunters. Rifleshots rang out. Whales had already been sighted.

Quickly Koonuk and his father unhitched the dogs and set up the little tent for Sourrah. Then taking their hunting equipment, they slid the boat into the water and paddled hastily out to join in the hunt.

Koonuk forgot his anger and disappointment. Out in the water among the large pans of floating ice a great bowhead whale threshed about in a frantic attempt to escape from its enemies. Men in boats were firing upon it from all sides.

As they drew near, Koonuk and his father could see that the whale was going to get away unless someone harpooned it at once. Hastily they dropped the paddles and took up their harpoons. Then they stood upright and allowed the boat to drift.

Suddenly the whale broke away from the hunters and headed straight toward them. It seemed as if they would be upset and thrown into the water. Koonuk's father dropped his harpoon and snatched up the paddle. Frantically he tried to move the boat out of the whale's path, but he was not quick enough.

Luckily the monster swerved at the last moment. Koonuk hurled his harpoon with all his might. The next instant he found himself clinging to the end of the line while the harpoon's head was firmly lodged in the whale. The boat was on its side and both he and his father were soaking wet.

Soon the other hunters were all around them. There were more rifleshots and the flashing of harpoons through the air. Everywhere was shouting and confusion. The hunt was over. The first whale of the season had been captured and Koonuk's harpoon had been the first to find its mark.

That night as he lay in their little tent out on the ice Koonuk could scarcely sleep for thinking of the day's exciting events. He hoped that many more whales would soon be caught so that they might return to the village for the big celebration that always followed. There would be feasting and games and much talk about the first harpoon. How proud he would feel.

In the morning Koonuk did not go hunting. A stiff wind was blowing and his father asked him to stay behind with Sourrah because his sister was afraid the little tent might be swept away. Toto's leg was very lame, and although the old dog dragged herself between the traces, she was not allowed to go. Both Koonuk and Toto watched longingly as the hunting party set off farther up the edge of the ice.

As the day passed the wind grew stronger. Out to sea the pans of ice began to break up and move about. Still the hunters did not return.

In the late afternoon the tent began to shake over their heads and the ice to move beneath them. Then there was a bump and a cracking sound.

They looked outside and were terrified at what they saw. Between them and the rest of the camp was a widening stretch of water. The piece of ice on which their tent sat had broken away and was drifting out to sea.

Sourrah began to cry.

"We must be brave," said Koonuk. "The others in

the camp have seen us and will send a boat for us soon."

But Koonuk did not feel brave. He knew there was not a boat left in camp, and the men were far away.

Carefully he checked everything that floated with them on their pan of ice. There were only the tent, the sleeping robes, a small supply of food, and little else. Behind the tent was old Toto who looked up and wagged her tail.

Hour after hour they drifted. The wind lessened, but the air became very cold. On the horizon they saw only the white line of shore ice and the hills beyond. They ate a little and talked a little. Sourrah brought Toto into the tent to keep her company. Still they saw no sign of rescue.

The sun set and rose again. On the second day the weather grew even colder. Once they were blown very close to land but they drifted out to sea again. When night came they had no food left. Cold and hungry, they lay down to sleep.

Koonuk woke in the twilight of the Arctic spring night. For a moment he could not remember where he was. Then he heard Toto whining outside the tent. He found her crouched at the edge of the ice pan. Everything was strangely still. New ice had formed upon the surface of the water.

We have again drifted close to shore. If we could only get across, thought Koonuk.

Then he saw Toto slide from the pan and drag herself a little way out onto the new ice. Whining, she looked back at the boy as if asking him to follow.

Was it possible that the new ice would hold? In some places it would be stronger than in others. If only they knew where to go. Perhaps Toto would guide them. Quickly he woke Sourrah, and although she was very frightened she agreed to take the chance.

Slowly and carefully, on hands and knees they followed the dog. The new ice was like a thin sheet of rubber and it bent beneath them. At any moment Koonuk expected to drop into the sea, yet on and on they went. The tent was soon left far behind. Toto half walked, half crawled, all the while sniffing the ice with her nose. Now she went this way, now that.

Koonuk lost all track of time. His hands and feet became so cold that he could scarcely move them. Sourrah began to cry, but still they moved on.

Suddenly he heard voices. He thought he must have been asleep. The first thing he saw when he opened his eyes was the rough surface of a rock. They were safe on land. His father and several of the other hunters were helping him and Sourrah to their feet.

"Toto brought us safely across the ice. She is truly a wise dog," whispered Koonuk as soon as he could speak.

"She is wise indeed," replied his father. "Day and night we have searched. It was the howling of the old dog that brought us to you here. Many whales have been caught. Let us quickly return to the village."

"Yes," shouted the others joyfully. "Now let the celebration begin."

Old Sly Eye

RUSSELL GORDON CARTER

It was a May evening in the year 1675. Alone in his father's log house on the northern edge of Dover township in the province of New Hampshire, Alben Hastings lit the lantern and opened his worn copy of the *Pilgrim's Progress*. Suddenly a loud commotion sounded in the direction of the barn—mad squeals and frightened bellowings, and the hollow thudding of hoofs. Leaping erect, he seized his musket, and lantern in hand, went racing outside.

He was within a dozen yards of the barn, the wind singing in his ears, when the moon rolled from beneath a formation of ragged clouds and he checked himself abruptly. There beside the shed lay the recently born calf, and over it crouched a big catlike creature, its solitary eye gleaming, its great, round tufted tail weaving savagely to and fro—a panther.

Dropping the lantern, Alben raised the musket and fired, only to see the creature leap sidewise, apparently unhurt. The next instant it swept past him and vanished in the deep shadows.

The boy clenched his teeth. "Old Sly Eye!" he muttered angrily, and his thoughts went swiftly back to the morning two weeks earlier when his father had set forth with Mr. Stephen Wainright on a prolonged trapping expedition beyond the Piscataqua.

"Yes, my lad," John Hastings had said then, "I know how much you would like to come along, but 'tis your duty to stay behind and look after your mother and sister. And mind ye keep a good watch over the livestock! I wouldn't want to come home and find Old Sly Eye had done to us what he's done to others."

Alben strode to where the calf was lying. It wasn't his fault that Old Sly Eye had somehow managed to break into the barn, for his father himself had said the barn was reasonably secure against varmints. The calf lay motionless—there was no question that it was dead. Within the barn the cow and the two oxen were still stamping about and letting out occasional bellows, but the boy was not so much concerned with them; they were safe and unhurt.

As Alben continued to stare at the calf he thought of other plunderings within the township—cattle and swine slain by the big one-eyed panther that often killed for the mere sake of killing. Ever since the previous autumn Old Sly Eye had eluded the bullets and traps of the angry settlers—and tonight he, Alben Hastings, had had an easy shot at close range and had failed to bring the beast down!

Well, regrets wouldn't help. Since the calf was dead, it would serve as food, and therefore the thing for him to do was to hang it on a tree or against the barn, high enough so that nothing could get at it. At the cabin —up in the loft where he and his father were accustomed to sleep—there was a coil of rope he could use. Returning to the lantern, which had gone out, he picked it up and started at a slow walk for the house.

In the south, silver-edged clouds were racing past the moon. He wondered what the hour might be. Perhaps his mother and Rebecca would soon be coming home from the Wainright cabin, a mile or so to the west. They had gone over to help care for old Mrs. Wainright, who had fallen and broken a leg.

The door to the log house was swinging and creaking on its hinges, and as he shouldered his way inside, the wind caught it and thrust it shut behind him. Striding to the fireplace, he groped for the powder horn and bag of shot on the high mantel and reloaded the musket.

On the frontier a loaded musket sometimes meant the difference between life and death. After he had set it down, resting the muzzle against the wall, he crossed the hard-packed earthen floor to the ladder leading to the loft. It would be as black as midnight up there, but there was no need to bother with flint and steel. He knew exactly where the rope was hanging.

With quick, sure steps he started up the ladder, but as his hands closed on the top rung he felt his heart tighten and his throat go suddenly dry. Something was in the loft—something heavy enough to cause the boards to creak! He was about to back downward when there was a snarl and a rush of padded feet, and the next instant a heavy body thudded against his shoulder and then hurtled past him, knocking the ladder violently sidewise. With a desperate lunge Alben clutched at the edge of the loft, and for several seconds after the ladder had crashed to the floor he clung there, his legs dangling. Then he succeeded in swinging himself upward.

Old Sly Eye! Crouching on the edge of the high platform, Alben felt the tumultuous pounding of his heart as he stared downward into blackness. The panther was over near the door; he could hear it crooning and snarling. He could hear the occasional thump and swish of its long, heavy tail against the wall. Presently it moved, and he had a partial glimpse of it in a narrow band of moonlight slanting through the opening in the shutter across the south window. He saw its solitary gleaming eye, the other lost perhaps in an encounter with another panther. Then it vanished again in the blackness, and now he could hear it going around and around the room, hissing and muttering, and making other catlike sounds deep within its throat.

Why had Old Sly Eye entered the house? Alben asked himself the question while he was groping about for something with which to defend himself. Was it in hope of finding another victim? Panthers as a rule kept

away from humans, yet Old Sly Eye was no ordinary panther. Or was it perhaps curiosity that had prompted the creature to enter the partly open door? The boy could not be sure. He knew only that the panther was down there, unable to get out, and that he himself was in danger.

The loft held no weapon or heavy object that could be used as a weapon. In his two hands he held the rope. It was a stout new, half-inch Portsmouth rope, more than a score of feet long—but what good was it? As he finally tossed it aside he thought longingly of his loaded musket down near the fireplace.

The panther continued to move here and there, now and again passing through the band of moonlight. Every little while it would snarl in a way that made Alben shiver, and once he thought he heard it sharpening its claws on one of the logs. Or was it trying to reach the loft? The logs that formed the walls were unevenly placed—it might come slithering upward. And he was utterly defenseless, lacking even a knife.

Suddenly, with a feeling of icy water cascading down his spine, he remembered his mother and sister. Why had he not thought of them before? They, perhaps more than himself, were the ones who were in danger! Even at that moment they might be approaching the house. They would open the door and then. . . .

Perspiration bathed his face and neck and armpits. With cold hands clutching one of the posts, he stared downward, lips drawn tightly across his teeth. What could he do to warn them? Of course, if he should hear them coming he would shout; yet even so Rebecca might think he was joking. He remembered with regret some of the jokes he had played in the past. But it was possible that they might reach the door before he heard them. The thought of the two of them unsuspectingly entering the cabin sent a chill through him. I must do something! he said to himself.

Yes, but what? He was a virtual prisoner in the loft. There were no windows, and the only way to get down was either to jump or slide down the rope secured to a post. In either case the panther would be waiting for him. Again he thought of his musket. Was there any way he could reach it, perhaps with the aid of the rope? No, the weapon was too far away.

The more he pondered, the more he became convinced that the only thing to do would be to go down the rope and then make a rush for the door. It would perhaps take three seconds to go down the rope and another three seconds to reach the door—but during that time Old Sly Eye was not likely to be sitting quietly on his haunches! Alben drew his sleeve across his moist forehead. He was strong and active, but what chance would he have in a barehanded struggle with a powerful panther? Nevertheless there seemed no other way.

Knotting an end of the rope securely round a post, he gathered up the rest of it, ready to toss it downward. His eyes had by now grown more accustomed to the darkness, and he thought he could make out the panther directly below him. He let the rope drop, and an instant later the house resounded to a frightful scream that set his teeth to chattering. He saw the creature bound like a ghost through the band of moonlight, and then heard it snarling over near the door.

While he waited, listening, he fancied he heard distant voices, as if his mother and sister coming through the forest might be talking to each other—or was it merely the sound of the wind? Raising his own voice he shouted, "Mother! Rebecca! Keep away, there's a panther in the house!" There was no response. He waited a minute or two and then shouted again. Still there was no response. He had the sudden unhappy feeling that perhaps no one could hear him outside the stout log house—that no matter how much he might shout it would do no good.

The night was silent now save for occasional gusts of wind and the snarling of the panther and the thumping of its tail against the door. Supposing the door should suddenly open and Rebecca should call, "Alben, are you asleep?" Then the panther would leap and strike—and then. . . .

It was more than he could endure! He must risk his life. He mustn't remain idle another moment. But if only he had a weapon of some sort—anything, even a short stick with which he could thrust! Maybe he could find a stick. He would make another search. It would take only a few seconds.

As he was feeling about in the darkness his hands encountered the blankets that on cold nights he and his father used for sleeping. There they were, neatly folded against the wall. With a quick exclamation he seized one and shook it out. Here was something perhaps better than a stick! The blanket was thick and heavy—at least it would protect his face.

Holding it loosely over his left arm, he seated himself on the edge of the loft, ready to descend. The panther was still over by the door, and he imagined it waiting for him, teeth bared, claws prepared to strike and to rip. Again he thought of the musket. If only he could get his hands on it!

Still holding the blanket loosely over his left arm, he started downward. His feet had hardly touched the floor when a nerve-shattering scream filled the house and a glistening body flashed toward him through the band of moonlight. Crouching, he flung the blanket out protectingly almost at the same instant the snarling panther was upon him.

Perhaps for half a minute it seemed that he and the panther and the blanket were all hopelessly entangled. He could feel the rough wool against his face. He could feel the weight of the creature upon him and smell the strong unpleasant odor of it. Then needlelike claws, caught in the folds of wool, were raking his back and shoulders. Lashing out with hands and feet, Alben tried desperately to free himself. A corner of the blanket covered his head. He reached upward, tore it loose, then rolled sidewise, all the while kicking and struggling.

Suddenly he was free! Rolling twice over, he sprang

to his feet. The musket over there by the fireplace! Darting across the room, he snatched it up.

At that moment, above the snarls of the panther still with claws entangled in the blanket, he heard voices outside. It was not the wind, it was not his fancy—the voices were real. With musket raised, he hesitated. Should he risk a shot in the darkness? If he were to miss it might be fatal, not merely to himself but also to his mother and sister. No, he must not miss! Racing to the door, he flung it wide and leaped outside into the night.

His mother and Rebecca were crossing the clearing from the western edge of the woods. Catching sight of him in the moonlight, the girl shouted, "Alben, what are you doing?"

He paid no heed to her. He was half a score of yards now from the open door of the cabin, musket raised, jaws set. The seconds passed while he waited, listening to the thumping of his heart.

"Alben!" This time it was his mother. "What's wrong?"

At that moment a great, tawny, glistening shape appeared in the doorway, its solitary eye gleaming. It swung its head first to the right and then to the left. It raised its voice in a prolonged scream. Then spying the boy, it came bounding forward.

A tongue of flame flashed from the musket, and the crash sent the echoes flying. They continued to tremble across the moonlit clearing while the panther lay twitching on the grass.

Alben strode to where it was lying. Dead, he said to himself. As dead as the calf! But there were two bullet marks on the panther, one on the throat and the other on the side of the small, narrow head, close to one of the rounded ears! Suddenly he understood. His first shot had not missed, after all! Probably it was that first bullet, momentarily bewildering the creature, which had caused it to seek shelter in the house.

"Alben, Alben! Oh, Alben!"

He turned to confront the others. Both were talking to him at once. "Your shirt, 'tis torn to shreds! And you are bleeding! Oh, Alben, are you badly hurt? Tell us what happened!"

He took a deep breath and then smiled. It was easy enough to smile now! "Not so very much happened," he replied slowly. "Yes, I know I'm a bit scratched an' torn, but after all, nobody could expect to fight Old Sly Eye barehanded and not get himself hurt a little!" And then while they gazed at him, wide-eyed, he told them the whole story.

An Extra Indian

MARION HOLLAND

If the new boy had come into Miss Gowdy's room at any other time, Miss Gowdy might have paid more attention to him. The other children might have paid more attention to him too. But it was the week before the Thanksgiving pageant and they were all very busy.

Miss Gowdy had the janitor bring in an extra desk and chair and set them at the back of the room; then she asked the new boy if he could see the blackboard all right from there, and he said, "Yes."

And that was all he did say for a long time. His name was Jed Black, and he just sat quietly, taking in everything that was going on with dark, watchful eyes.

Plenty was going on, but not the usual things like reading, spelling, and arithmetic. Miss Gowdy's room had had plenty of reading, looking up everything in the library about the First Thanksgiving; and plenty of spelling, writing a play about it and copying out all the parts. And plenty of arithmetic, too, figuring out how many yards of material had to be sent home for the costumes the Pilgrims' mothers would make. The Indians, of course, were just going to wear khaki pants and blankets and a few feathers, which was a break for the Indians' mothers.

Now they were all busy finishing up a life-sized deer upside down. That is, the deer was upside down, hung by the feet from a long stick, which two Indians were to carry onto the stage as the Indians' contribution to the feast. Of course there had really been five deer at the First Thanksgiving. But then there had really been ninety Indians too. As there were only fourteen Indians in the play, they figured that one deer would do.

They had a wire framework of a deer which they were padding out with paper and paste and paint. The new boy stayed in his seat and watched. When they were finished, everybody admitted that one side looked more like a cow; but the other side was a pretty fair deer. So they stuck the arrow in that side and warned the two Indians who were to carry it to keep that side toward the audience.

Then they got on with their rehearsing. Everybody had a part. All the girls were Pilgrims; they had to be, because all the Indians at the First Thanksgiving were braves. Only three of the boys were Pilgrims, and they were Pilgrims because Miss Gowdy had told them they had to be. She didn't want the audience to get the idea that all the Pilgrim Fathers had been Pilgrim Mothers.

Finally Miss Gowdy remembered the new boy. She said that he had better be a Pilgrim, too, and they could write in a few lines for him to say.

Diana Carr, who had the most important Pilgrim part next to Governor Bradford, said quickly: "Oh, but we all know our parts, and it would mix us up. Besides, there isn't time for him to get a costume fixed."

"Let him be an Indian," said Johnny Schmidt, who played Massasoit, the leader of the Indians. "We can always use an extra Indian."

So for the last few rehearsals Jed was an Indian. He was the Indian who came on the stage last, behind all the other Indians, and didn't say anything. But that didn't matter, because quite a lot of the other Indians didn't say anything either, which was one of the reasons all the boys wanted to be Indians.

"It's a good thing we didn't have to write in a part for him," said Diana to Joan, her best friend. "He'd never have learned it. Why, I don't think he can even talk."

"Maybe he's a foreigner," suggested Joan kindly. "He sort of looks like one."

"Well, if he is, of course he can't help it," admitted Diana. "But naturally the Pilgrims ought to be Americans."

"But they weren't. Anyway, not yet. They were English," Joan pointed out.

At the dress rehearsal everybody was in costume except the new boy. He just wore the same T-shirt and faded blue jeans that he wore to school. He stood so far in the back that Miss Gowdy didn't notice; but Johnny did, and he was worried about it. After all, he was Massasoit and he was responsible for these Indians.

He stopped Jed after school. "Look, I can lend you some things to wear for the play tomorrow," he said, speaking very slowly and distinctly. "If you don't have any."

"I'll have something," replied Jed. "Anyway, I hope so. My brother sent away for some things, and they probably came in the mail today."

Why, he talked just like anybody! Imagine that dumb Diana, going around and telling everybody that the new boy was some kind of a foreigner and didn't know a word of English!

"Why don't we go home with you and see if the things came?" suggested Johnny. "Then if they didn't, we'll go over to my house and I'll fix you up with some feathers. We'll go over to my house, anyway, and shoot a few baskets, if you like basketball. O.K.?"

"O.K.," said Jed.

By 9:30 the next morning, all the seats in the school auditorium were filled and people were standing up in the back. Behind the drawn curtains on the stage the Pilgrims were all in their places, but the Indians were still in the dressing room, rubbing brown paint on their arms and faces.

Just as the audience finished singing "America the Beautiful," Johnny stuck his head out of the dressing room and said, "Ready!" to Miss Gowdy, and she hurried to one side of the stage and pulled the curtain.

There were the Pilgrims, seated at a long trestle table piled high with corn and pumpkins and fish. They talked about what a hard year they had had, the first year in the new country. They talked about how they had finished building houses and had gathered a good harvest, and how thankful they were for these blessings.

Then Governor Bradford stood up and reminded them all about how helpful the Indians had been and how they might never have survived the terrible winter if it hadn't been for the Indians. He said he had invited their friend Massasoit to bring some of his braves to share the Thanksgiving feast.

This was the Indians' cue to enter. First came Johnny Schmidt, then after a little jostling at the entrance, the two Indians with the deer. Then came the other Indians, and last of all Jed.

But Jed didn't stay at the back as usual. The other Indians parted left and right, and Jed walked forward to stand beside Governor Bradford at the head of the table.

A noisy gasp of surprise went up behind the Pilgrims, but the audience didn't hear it because the audience was gasping too. There was a confused rustling sound from the auditorium as everyone leaned forward to get a better view.

Jed was dressed in fringed deerskin embroidered at the neck and sleeves with porcupine quills. On his feet were beaded moccasins; on his head, a sweeping war bonnet with silver medallions that glittered beside his thin cheeks. No dyed turkey feathers, these, but proud white-and-gray eagle feathers.

He raised his right hand, palm outward, and spoke. He spoke Johnny's lines, Massasoit's lines; he spoke them quietly, but so clearly that everyone in the audience could hear every word.

He said that his people, too, always gave thanks for a good harvest. He said that now the white men and the red men were brothers, and they would remain brothers as long as each kept his word when it was given. He said all the things that Miss Gowdy's class had written down for Massasoit to say, but now they listened to it as if they had never heard it before.

He ended: "This country to which you have come is a beautiful country, full of good things. If we share the good things fairly there is room for all."

Governor Bradford was supposed to reply, but his words were drowned out in a thunder of clapping from the audience; so the Pilgrims and the Indians just bowed their heads in grateful thanks and Miss Gowdy pulled the curtain.

Backstage everything was confusion. The deer was dropped, and several people stepped on it, but nobody needed it any more, anyway. Everyone crowded around Jed and Johnny, asking questions, and Johnny answered them as fast as he could talk.

"Jed's a real Indian, a full-blooded Indian, and his whole name is Jed Black Horse Running. So when I went to his house yesterday and saw his clothes I knew he ought to be Massasoit, not I. He learned the lines in a flash. Knew most of 'em already, just from listening."

"Do you wear these all the time at home?" asked someone, fingering the deerskin fringes.

Jed just shook his head, but Johnny said: "Of course not. These are extra special, just for the most important ceremonies, and when Jed told his brother about the play they decided it was an important ceremony and sent for 'em, back on the reservation. That's where Jed used to live, but now he's living with his brother so he can finish school here and be an engineer like his brother."

Diana said to Joan as they went into the dressing room: "So that's what he is, an Indian. I knew he was some kind of foreigner."

Johnny shouted after her: "Listen, you! If you went somewhere else you'd be a foreigner, did you ever think of that? Besides, compared to Jed, everybody in this whole school is a foreigner. And hurry up with that dressing room because us Indians have an important date to play basketball as soon as we get the paint washed off."

The Wish Book Dress

A Story of the Southern Highlands

MAY JUSTUS

"Whoa, Beck! Whoa, there, Heck!" Glory, in the cabin kitchen, heard Uncle Bildad Cooley's shout and ran out to the gate where the mail wagon had stopped.

"Howdy, honey. You want this wish book?" The old man held out to her a mail-order catalogue. "There's no wrapper on it—no address—and I thought you might like it."

"Oh, yes!" Glory replied eagerly. "Much obliged," she added, speaking in a mannerly way.

"Don't mention it," Uncle Bildad said. "Get on, Beck. Get along, Heck!"

Glory hastened into the house again. It was nearly time for dinner, she could tell by a glance at the sun plank in the kitchen floor. No time for looking at the wish book now. She must get the corn pone in the oven and give attention to the sallet pot on the chimney crane.

342

She would get the table set, too, so as to be ready when her folks came in from planting the new-ground field. Grandy, Mammy, and Matt had left home long before the sun had risen over Little Twin. They'd be hungry enough to eat chips. She hoped they would like the dinner and say a praiseful word about it. They'd be surprised for certain over one thing: the sallet, for they were expecting beans, this being bean day. Yesterday they had had potatoes—the last mess, for the rest Mammy said must be saved for seed. She had gathered the sallet first thing after they had left this morning—a little here and a little there—for the poke, wild mustard and dandelion made as yet but a sprinkle of green along the creek bank. Later on there would be a God's plenty, as Mammy said.

When the corn pone was baking on the hearth and an extra gourdful of water had been added to the pot, Glory sat down on a stool to feast her eyes on the wish book.

What a sight of fanciful frocks there were—page after page of them—girls' dresses and boys' suits, beribboned hats, shiny shoes! Glory was bewitched by a dress on the back of the wish book—a blue flowerdy dress marked ninety-eight cents. Oh, how she wished that it could be hers. If it were midsummer she could save huckleberry money and order it. Down at Cross Roads store huckleberries sold for as much as fifteen cents a gallon. Glory sighed. Huckleberries wouldn't be ripe for a long, long time.

A bark and a shout outside warned her that Matt

and Barney were rushing on ahead of the others. She dropped the wish book by the stool and got up to fix dinner.

"I'm ready to eat raw bacon rinds!" shouted her brother. "I'm so hungry I could sop the pot and lick my fingers too!"

"Humph—I reckon you better not let Mammy see you!" Glory said, smiling at him. "Go on out and wash. I'll have dinner on by the time you get the dirt off."

Mammy and Grandy came in a few minutes later, and soon they were sitting around the table.

"Look-a-there!" cried Mammy. She had seen the bowl of sallet before Grandy had asked the blessing. And then they were all so pleased that they could scarcely shut their eyes till he said "Amen."

There was a good helping for everyone, and a gourdful of potlicker which was given to Grandy, who liked to crumble the corn-pone crust in the savory broth.

"Seems good to have spring stuff again—I declare it does," said Mammy. "A month back there was snow on the ground, and now it's getting green."

"A passel o' herbs are up," Grandy said. "Star root and May apple and sang and Solomon's-seal. I mean to go herb hunting," he added, "as soon as corn is planted. Some herbs fetch a goodly price in cash money down at Cross Roads store."

"Seems like a sin," Mammy said, "to sell suchlike for money. The Good Man planted herbs for medicine. Seems like they ought to be free to outlanders as well as to we 'uns. Maybe the Good Man would like it better if we gathered herbs to give away."

"No, He wouldn't," Grandy said. "The Good Man knows the outlander people need herb medicine and we need money—it's naught but a fair exchange."

"Maybe so," agreed Mammy, and Glory was glad, for all of a sudden a notion had popped into her head.

The next day Mammy stayed at home to get the dinner, for it was hominy-making day and Glory couldn't tend to that, so she went to the field with Grandy and Matt. On the way down the Hollow she watched for herbs and found star root and May apple. She marked the places where they were growing, using sassafras sticks which had been tossed aside from a brush pile because it was thought bad luck to burn them. After the morning's work was done she would dig up the herb roots. Her apron would do for a poke to carry them home, and her folks would think she was carrying wood for kindling. She had a mind to keep her plan a secret from everybody until she was certain-sure that she could carry it out. She would gather herb roots here and there and sell them and save the money till she had a dollar. She could order the wish book dress herself—she could write well enough to do *that*. And wouldn't they all be surprised when she diked herself out in that pretty, flowerdy, wish book dress?

Glory smiled above her hoe handle, her mind in a far meander, and all of a sudden she overreached the next hill of corn and came near whacking Matt's near heel —he was on the row ahead of her.

"Watch out what you're a-doing, Missy! A body would think you meant that lick to addle a copperhead snake."

"I'm mighty-much sorry," Glory said, and to put Matt in a good humor she began to sing, as if to herself, his favorite ballad song, knowing that he would join her in a few moments.

> "Tom Bolyn was a poor man born,
> His shoes were ragged, his socks were torn.
> The calf of his leg hung down to his shin,
> But nobody's noddy was Tom Bolyn."

Matt began to whistle as she sang the next verse:

> "Tom Bolyn had no britches to wear,
> So he took him a sheepskin and made him a
> pair.
> The wool side out and the skin side in,
> 'It's cooler for summer,' says Tom Bolyn."

At the third verse, Matt began to sing with Glory:

> "Tom Bolyn bought an old gray mare,
> Her sides were bony, her feet were bare.
> Then away he cantered through thick and
> thin,
> 'I'm off for a journey,' says Tom Bolyn."

Matt sighed. "I've got a hankering to go to the Big Sing on Far Side. An all-day singing it's going to be— Noah Webster said so. His folks are going, and Noah asked me to go along with him." Glory sighed too.

"I wish you could go," she told him. "I wish you could get you a pair of store-boughten shoes."

Matt covered another hill of corn. "I may have 'em— I *may*," he muttered, almost as if he were talking to himself.

Glory pricked up her ears, but asked no questions. Matt had secrets of his own sometimes, and she wasn't one to be nosy. If she waited long enough she would find out.

Spring hurried on its way, coming up Darksome Hollow with bouquets of redbud and dogwood and wild plum. May apple tents were thick in the coves; star root bordered the valley that ran like a ragged ruffle at the foot of Little Twin. Solomon's-seal, bloodroot, and wild ginger grew in unexpected places.

Glory spent all her spare time hunting wood treasure these days, gathering it and hiding it away. When she had a great heap of herbs gathered she would take it down to Cross Roads store. The wish book dress was coming true, that flowerdy dress, just as she had planned.

One day she missed the wish book from the shelf where she had put it, and after searching high and low she found it wedged in a chimney crack of the cabin corner where Matt kept all his belongings—clothes, playthings, odds and ends. The wish book, she saw, was folded back to the page which showed all the shiny shoes. Down in the corner was a thumbmark which rested like a shadow above the price mark: $1.98.

Glory looked and looked. She turned the pages of the

wish book over till she came to the picture of the blue flowerdy dress. There were two dreams instead of one inside that book, she was thinking, but she wouldn't let on to her brother that she knew!

A day or so later as she came out of Darksome Hollow with her apron of herbs she ran into Matt with a poke under his arm. No questions were asked and no explanations were given by either, though they had to walk side by side toward home.

She never ran into Matt again on an herb hunting, but now and then he disappeared, and she guessed where he had gone. When she saw him start out in one direction she always took the other.

One day Glory came in from the woods to find Mammy much distressful over Matt.

"He just keeled over when he got in from a wild scramble," she told Glory. "Some kind of a fever he's got, I reckon. He's looked dauncy for a long time."

She made a big brewing of tansy tea, and when he got no better she added spicewood and boneset to the pot and dosed him for a day on that. When she had to leave the cabin she left Glory in charge as nurse, and Glory did her best. She persuaded him to drink the bitter tea out of the black kettle by promising to read the story of Joseph or to sing a ballad to him. Glory had her hands full. Mammy and Grandy had to work in the cornfield these days. There was no time now to hunt herb roots. The wish book gathered dust on the mantel till one day Matt asked to look at it. Glory knew he was feeling better then.

Noah Webster came over one Sunday, wearing a pair of shiny new shoes.

Matt eyed them admiringly. "They look p'int blank like a pair o' wish book shoes!"

"They are," said Noah. "I ordered them to wear to the Big Sing," he added. "It's not far off now, you know—just a week from today. I wish you could go—maybe you can. You say you feel a sight better."

Matt looked so woeful that anybody might have thought him worse instead.

"We'll come by on our way to the Big Sing," Noah promised, "and see if you want to go along."

"Much obliged," was all Matt said.

After Noah had gone home Matt said to Glory, "I won't go to the Big Sing barefoot. I had planned to buy a pair o' shoes—wish book shoes like the ones Noah had. I was gathering herbs for the money—but the handful I have wouldn't more'n buy shoestrings—much less shoes."

His eyes wandered to the cabin wall where a brown tow sack was hanging. Glory looked at it, too, and that very minute the big plan came ready made.

Glory and Matt sat side by side on the steps with Old Barney the dog frisking about and sniffing now and then in a most supicious way. New smells were in the air. It must mean that somebody was going away from home.

"Your shoes are a sight to behold," said Glory.

349

"They're as pretty as the picture in the wish book and prettier too!"

Matt wiggled a shiny toe. "They are, certain-sure," he answered. Then he laughed. "I can't get over the surprise I had yesterday when Uncle Bildad brought 'em. You could 'a' knocked me over with a feather when he handed me that box."

He wiggled the toe of the other shoe. "And I'm much obliged to you," he said.

He knew all about Glory's secret now—how she had saved her herbs to buy a dress; how later she had sold hers and his together and ordered these wish book shoes. "I'm mighty much obliged," he said.

"Don't mention it," Glory replied, not only for good manners but because she was glad her plan had turned out so well.

Matt went on. "I know," he told her, "where a sight o' herbs are a-growing. Come next week we'll gather a whole passel and buy you a wish book dress."

Caleb's Luck

LAURA BENET

"Could I sit here a spell, ma'am?"

Miss Cranston looked up from her desk and saw a drooping, small figure in one of the seats. So noiselessly had the boy entered that she had not even heard him come. After school that day she had settled down in the empty schoolroom to plan examination questions. The first of June spelled closing time for the High Ridge Community School in the North Carolina mountains.

"Who is it?" she asked quickly.

The tired voice replied in deep satisfaction: "This is the finest sittin' I ever sat."

"Did you want to see me?" asked the teacher kindly.

"I reckon so," was the placid response. Still the boy made no motion to get up.

Pushing aside papers, Miss Cranston walked down the

351

aisle. A glance had already told her that this twelve-year-old mountaineer was completely exhausted.

"What's your name?" she said.

"Caleb Waters."

"Have you come far?"

"Nigh onto fifteen miles. It's a long way to Turkey Creek Bottom."

"Have you had anything to eat?"

"Piece o' corn pone, ma'am."

She brought him the remains of her lunch, and his eyes brightened. "It's a purty place here. I'm comin' for schoolin' next year."

"That's good news," said Miss Cranston encouragingly. "We think it's a nice place, but it's too far for you to walk. Is some neighbor going to drive you in to school each day?"

His face fell. "No; ain't nobody to fetch me. Say, ma'am, can I stop here by the week?"

"Yes, if you pay for your board, Caleb. The people who could board you are poor, too, you know. Could you pay a little?"

"No," he answered decidedly. "I can't pay anything."

The teacher reflected: "Could you take a job this summer—or"—a bright idea occurred to her—"do you know the rock near High Ridge called Garnet Rock? Summer visitors are interested in the garnets."

"I've heard talk about it."

"While you're here, Caleb, go to see Ed Jones who runs the hotel. He'll have someone going out there, I'm sure. Pick up a big sackful of the best stones and you

can sell them." And she added: "I'll have my landlady fix
you up at our house tonight." She gave him directions
as to how to find the place. "Can you read and write
and do easy sums?"

"No'm. That's why I want to go to school."

Miss Cranston sighed. They shook hands, and Caleb
limped wearily off to the Jones House, the country hotel on High Ridge's one long street. Ed Jones, the pro-
prietor as well as postmaster, eyed him curiously. Yes,
he said, a farmer was riding out Garnet Rock way, and
maybe he could get a lift behind him on his horse.

Caleb got the lift and when he arrived at the Rock
he used his time well. He had quick eyes and nimble
fingers and spent the afternoon diligently mining garnets, getting together a packet of really good ones.

The farmer returned for him good-naturedly. "Right
smart lot o' stones ye have there," he remarked.

Caleb gave him one of the largest in return for the
ride.

"It's a purty place here," he said, repeating his stock
phrase amiably.

"Well, son, you take them garnets to Ed Jones. He'll
advertise 'em for ye 'mong the summer folks."

Caleb hurried off to see Ed Jones, a close bargainer,
who appraised the garnets slyly. "Not worth a sick
chicken's crop," he said, "but rub 'em up and I'll trade
'em for ye at a few cents apiece. Come by in a week."

Caleb ached with disappointment. He had pictured
himself making several dollars from his finds. It would
take quite a few of those scarce dollars to get him

through the winter. Ma wanted that he should have learnin'. Well, he'd go back to that teacher lady.

At her boardinghouse he had supper, a good night's sleep, and breakfast. Then the fifteen miles home seemed less difficult. And Miss Cranston told him that ten dollars in his pocket would cover the whole winter's schooling.

"I'll try to help you," said Miss Cranston, "when I get back from vacation. The schoolbooks will be free. You must have one whole suit and a pair of shoes and some board money. I'll help you all I can." She waved a friendly good-bye.

Caleb tugged at his bleached hair badly in need of cutting. Then he set off for his far hills without a backward look. On the outskirts of High Ridge, the county seat and highest point in these mountains, he paused for the view before descending into the bottom land. Leaning against a stalwart rock, he looked his fill. Fragments of the rock had broken off and a large white piece of quartz lay at his feet. His eyes rested on it eagerly. Ma had asked him to fetch a stone for propping the cabin's door, for there were few good-sized rocks to be had on their own acre of muddy ground. This shining stone was mighty pretty and not too large to carry. He picked it up and went on his way.

It was dark night when he reached the hillock where the home cabin adjoined those dense woods where his father ran a still.

"Caleb!" his mother's voice said. "So it's you, boy? I was studyin' the ridge since sundown. Thought you was fixin' to come back last night. You ain't forgot th' rock?"

"No. But Ma, I can't make th' winter schoolin'." And Caleb's eyes flashed in despair.

"Sit a spell, Caleb. Tell me about it. I got some black-eyed peas for you."

They talked in whispers. The moon rose over the cabin, which, with its spring and a rickety shed for the cow and chickens, stood alone in a clearing. The cabin was lonely, but the pungent pines and balsams, the sound of Turkey Creek, and Ma's burned-out patch of flowers spelled home as much as did Ma herself.

"You got to git schoolin', Caleb. Your skullpiece is better'n your Pa's and ye're twelve and can't read nor write. No sense in knockin' round these hills makin' stills and shootin' up revenue men like your Pa has. Mebbe I kin slip ye some o' the egg money."

Caleb shyly laid his hand on hers.

Before they went to bed Ma propped the cabin door open with the new stone. "Such a purty, shiny one," she said.

"I brung you a garnet too, Ma. I want you should wear it in a gold ring someday."

"Mercy, what could I do with a fancy piece like a gold ring, Caleb? Hush your talk. We're nothin' but rabbits. When the sheriff's gun goes bang we run for cover."

A week passed. Caleb had to do the several chores that made up daily life. But one day when his father was at the still and his mother at a quilting bee down the creek, two miles away, he was left to tend his small sister. He sat at the cabin door, contemplating the piece of white quartz. It would set a little firmer if he tilted it over on the side—so. As Caleb did this, something caught his eye—a sharp glitter from the quartz. The bright speck was embedded too deep for him to pick it out.

Going to the shed, he fetched Pa's ax. Whack, whack! After half an hour of work he detached the glittering bit that had winked at him. It was encrusted with other material but its color was a deep greenish blue. He hid it carefully away.

That evening Pa came home in a temper. "Someone is watchin' my still," he said. "I got to move it farther off into the cave by the stream. We got to lay low. Caleb, don't ye let me hear ye say ye'r a-goin' to High Ridge! Sheriff's men might catch ye."

"But, Pa, my garnets . . . ?"

"Just let me find ye gone and I'll—" He raised his hand threateningly.

Ma was silent. Often in the days that followed, her eyes met her son's—the same question in both. But when Pa had wild spells like this it was best to lie low.

The long hot summer days dragged on, each one more bitter than the last. But the sheriff never did find the still, and after some weeks they could relax. When Caleb needed courage he looked at the blue stone—for he couldn't go after his garnet money. But now it seemed as if Pa was possessed to discover the piece of white quartz—it had been so handy for the door. But Caleb kept the pretty blue stone well hidden, for it was his one bit of hope. He put it in a hollow tree, then moved it from there on account of thieving squirrels who might mistake it for a nut.

One day a dreadful thing happened! The stone had finally been placed in an empty tobacco sack hanging from the peg where he kept his few clothes. His father, in a tantrum, found the tobacco pouch, shook it out, and, since there was no tobacco in it, tossed it away.

Caleb heard the precious blue stone rattle on the floor boards of the cabin before it slipped through a crack. Then followed a frantic hunt. While Ma was at the spring he spent an hour under the house, half sobbing as he frantically clawed up dirt with his hands. A skunk and her family had found a home there. Just as Caleb finally spied the treasure beside one of the upright posts that supported the cabin, the mother skunk deluged him with her scent!

There was a reckoning. When Pa came home he cut a hickory switch from the grove, a stout new one that would hurt, and took his son out to the shed to be whipped "for turnin' thet skunk loose." Then Caleb, along with his scented shirt and trousers, was put to soak in a tub for dismal hours. But he'd put the stone safely in a new place.

When but two weeks remained before the High Ridge School was to reopen for the fall session, Pa announced that he was going away to do some "hoss-swappin'" in Cutter County.

"Yer cousin at the Falls kin take you-all in for a night or so," he decreed. "I aim to be gone a short spell."

Ma's face was hard to read. When her husband had gone to get in the corn she said, "Caleb, boy, here's your chance. We'll go along to Cousin Cassie's. Ye make tracks tomorrow for High Ridge. Ye might get a lift."

Sure enough, Caleb met a mountaineer who was taking his wife to the doctor at High Ridge. Never had the boy imagined that it would be so easy to ride in one of those Fords. The miles melted away. When they got to the county seat he was promised a return trip at the end of the day. Caleb ran to the Jones House but found its owner was at the post office. He made tracks across the mountain-village street. What if—what if he should get two dollars for those garnets? Schooling seemed nearer and nearer. Life wouldn't be so lonely any more.

Ed Jones, postmaster, looked at the ragged mountain lad as though he had never seen him. "Well?"

"I aimed to get the—what the summer folk gave for my garnets I left with ye," gulped Caleb.

"Garnets! Left 'em months ago, ye young rascal! Never sent no word nor come after 'em. I sold some and threw the rest out. Give ye twenty-five cents for the lot." Grudgingly he pushed two dimes and a nickel over the sill.

"Ye mean—ye cast them away?" Caleb asked darkly.

Caleb's spirits fell like the charred stick of a skyrocket. Out went a hard fist. In another instant Ed Jones's large nose would have been double its size. But the postmaster slammed down the window. "Git out o' here, varmint, or I'll have ye run out of town!" he shouted.

The mountain boy sat down on the post-office steps heavily. He felt very sick at his stomach and dizzy too. It was the hot time of the day and few people passed in and out for letters. At last he heard a deep unfamiliar voice saying to him: "You're from these parts. Whereabouts is the Garnet Rock?"

He opened his eyes and saw a broad-shouldered, middle-aged man who looked very wise. In a dazed voice Caleb answered: "I can't rightly remember."

"But I am interested in stones, you see." The man bent down toward him. "Have you mined garnets 'round here in your hills?"

"I ain't from here. I'm from Turkey Creek Bottom." Then Caleb fumbled in his shirt and brought out the blue stone. "Can ye tell me what it is?" he mumbled.

The man's eyes brightened: "Let me examine it," he said.

The boy clutched it distrustfully. "He cast away my garnets," he stammered, chest heaving. "Them garnets I was aimin' to get schoolin' with."

"This isn't a garnet." The man knelt down beside him on the steps. "This is something very different. Come over to my workshop."

They went across the street to the shop—a more comfortable-looking place than Caleb had ever seen. While his new friend, who was a geologist, occupied himself with a magnifying glass and tools, Caleb munched chocolate and crackers.

At last the examination was finished: "Looks very favorable," the man, whose name was Wilkinson, announced. "Caleb, you're a lucky boy. You've got a precious stone here—a rare blue beryl, as sure as I'm alive."

The owner of the stone looked up languidly: "A—burril? I ain't never heard o' them. Is it a kind o' garnet?"

"Better. What did that postmaster give you for your garnets, boy?"

"Twenty-five cents."

"I'll pay you ten dollars for this stone, just as it is."

Caleb stared at him. His face grew dark red. "Ten dollars? You're foolin', mister. Pa'd take it fer a hoss for sure."

"Tell me a little about yourself," Mr. Wilkinson said, and listened to Caleb's story of the summer. "I'm staying here several weeks longer," Mr. Wilkinson said. "I'll see that teacher and arrange about your winter term." And Caleb knew by his voice that he meant it. "Here's the ten dollars—but you'd better let me be your banker. Some day you'll show me where you found the stone?"

"Sure," said Caleb with satisfaction. "This here"—he fingered his change—"it'll buy my ma a new calico dress length. And say, mister, we got to chip 'nuff off the ten dollars to buy her a ring. More garnets are easy to come by."

CALEB'S LUCK

Henry Wilkinson looked hard at Caleb and smiled. "Easier than some other things," he said. "A lot easier than courage and patience and really working for an education."

Gloucester Boy

RUTH LANGLAND HOLBERG

It was the Sunday in June when all the fishing boats were in and the captains and crews gathered in the square before the church for the ancient crowning ceremony brought over from Portugal by the forefathers of the fishermen of Gloucester.

Herrick Court went up in several flights of steps with houses on each side. Manuel Madieros lived in the last house on the top floor, and from the kitchen window he could look far out to sea beyond the lighthouse.

Manuel's mother did not look out to sea, for it made her feel sad. When Manuel was a baby and his sister Palmagra was three years old Papa Madieros' boat had not come home from a fishing trip to the Georges Banks.

But Manuel watched for his Uncle Joe, and when he saw the schooner *Philomena* coming in he would clatter down the stairs of Herrick Court, across Main Street, and down Union Hill to the wharves.

"Hi, Uncle Joe!" Manuel yelled.

Uncle Joe climbed up on the wharf and said, "Hi, Manuel! Going out with us next trip?"

Manuel wanted to shout "Yes, Uncle Joe!" but he remembered how sad his mother was when he begged to go with Captain Joe on a trip. She wanted him to be a postman so she would know just where he was at every hour of the day.

One day Uncle Joe said to her, "If Manuel wants to be a fisherman how can he keep his mind on addresses and streets and numbers when his thoughts are only of boats and fish? Why not let him take one trip with me?"

Mrs. Madieros said nothing for a long time, and Manuel and his uncle looked glumly at each other. At last she said, "If you go on a trip and find that you are the right sort of boy to take to fishing for the rest of your life, I will not stand in your way. But if the work is not as pleasant as you think it is, will you be a postman when you grow up?"

Manuel promised, but he knew in his heart that he would be a fisherman like his father.

When he went on board the *Philomena* he had a duffel bag, oilskins, all the sweaters he owned, and boots reaching to his hips.

"Why should I take sweaters and warm clothes when it is summer, Uncle Joe?" questioned Manuel.

"Ho, ho!" laughed Uncle Joe. "You'll learn something

about cold weather on the open sea, even if it is summertime."

There were twelve men in the crew. The engineer was called the Chief and the cook was called Tony. Manuel went down to the galley to have his duties explained, for Uncle Joe had said, "It is a strong man's work to go dragging, but the cook can use a lively boy in the galley."

The routine of two hours off and two hours on duty was begun, and Manuel stowed his dunnage away in the upper bunk that was his and began his work of peeling potatoes and vegetables and getting the table ready for dinner.

He wondered at the number of steaks he saw being cooked.

"Ha!" bragged Tony. "Best food on earth isn't too good for fishermen. When you see how they work and how little sleep and rest they get, you'll know they need good food."

Going to the Georges Banks was like one long fete day. But the morning Uncle Joe cast out the sounding lead a very different feeling came upon everyone, and there was an immediate stir of action.

Heavy doors bound with iron weighted the great net at each end. As they went overboard the net with its glass floats to keep it apart sank rapidly.

"How far down will it go?" cried Manuel, watching the place where it sank.

"Maybe fifteen fathoms—the cod stay within three fathoms of the bottom."

"But how do you know there is cod down there?"

"The sounding lead shows us that. We know from long years of fishing just what fish belongs to certain kinds of sea muck."

Suddenly the net was dragged in, with the winch screeching as it drew close to the schooner.

The doors heaved up and a squirming mass of fish came into view. In no time the fish were dumped into the open hatches, and one of the crew shoveled ice between the layers as fast as they came down.

"Heave her out again!" commanded Captain Joe.

Manuel began to wonder why the cook did not give him any kitchen duty. He was hungry too.

But no one paid any attention to being hungry, it seemed. The net went down over and over again.

Manuel made some sandwiches and brewed coffee, and with a basket of cups he managed to give each man a steaming drink. He went below and cleaned up the galley and sat on his bunk and all at once fell asleep. How long he slept he did not know.

On deck again, he found everything just the same as when he had left hours ago. At last, as the net came up with only a small catch, Captain Joe called, "Guess we cleaned up this ground all right."

The next day was cold, and Manuel, not being as active as the men at work, went below to warm up and listen to the radio. The announcer gave the time. Then came the weather report.

"Storm warning Eastport to Sandy Hook. Storm is

moving with marked intensity. Small craft take warning!"

At once he went up to Captain Joe and repeated the
announcer's words.

"Go below and listen to the next report. We must get
all the fish we can before that storm breaks."

Again the warning came. The storm was moving
southeasterly. At the same time the schooner gave way
to a different motion. Manuel dashed up and found the
men hauling in a full net, with water pouring over the
decks, fish slipping into the hatches, and ice being
shoveled over them. The holds were full.

"Batten down the hatches!" cried the Captain.

The waves began to lift and spill across the deck, and
rain fell.

"Go below and stay there," ordered the Captain with
a sharp look at his nephew.

Manuel was thrilled with the tossing of the schooner,
but he obeyed the orders like a good seaman and
crawled safely down the companionway.

Some of the crew were snoring in deep sleep. In the
hot forecastle Manuel found it hard to remember how
icy and stormy the winds were.

He listened to the radio for quite a while. At last he
said to himself, Maybe, if I take just one look to see
Uncle Joe standing at the wheel like the statue at home,
he won't mind.

He put on his sweater, but left the boots and oilskins
at the side of his bunk, and made his way to the deck.

At that moment no waves were pouring over. There was a lull in the storm. He clung to a rope dangling from a mast and breathed the wild air. Then, before any one of the crew busy on deck knew what was happening, a huge wave thundered over and swept Tony overboard with it. He tossed for an instant on the water. No one rushed to throw him a line.

"It's no use, his clothes are so heavy he will sink," cried Captain Joe with a terrible groan.

Like a flash Manuel dove overboard, remembering his lessons in lifesaving on the Gloucester beach. In another flash Captain Joe threw a line after him.

The devout Portuguese crew prayed to Our Lady of the Good Voyage for the safety of the rash boy. Like men watching a miracle, they saw Manuel next to Tony, holding his collar in one hand, reaching for the line with the other.

Someone began to pull in the rope with Tony holding fast. Manuel was keeping his head above water and struggling with the waves.

Another anxious moment. He was gaining toward the schooner, toward a second line that tossed always beyond his reach. In that instant of peril there came to Manuel a vision of the statue of Our Lady between the twin towers at home, looking out to sea; he saw her eyes bent on him, and her brave words were whispered in his ears. He kept on struggling, and it seemed as if her arm reached out to give him the line. He clenched it fast in his fist.

Ages passed. He was being hauled on deck. He was carried below and hot milk was given him.

He breathed naturally again, and all at once he was asleep.

When Manuel awoke the schooner was rocking gently. There was Tony grinning at him. "Ho—so you are awake and hungry, too, eh, Mannie?"

He sat up.

"Did I oversleep? Is it time for me to peel potatoes?"

"Peel potatoes? Ha, ha!" laughed Tony. "A real seaman like you peel potatoes!"

It all came back to him.

"Oh, Tony, I did not obey the Captain's orders."

"Well, this time I guess he will let it go."

ALL KINDS OF COURAGE

Later on Manuel thought of his promise to his mother. "Will my mother mind very much because I am going to be a fisherman?" he asked his uncle.

"Not when I tell her that you are strong and fearless and have the salt sea in your veins. I think she will be proud and glad to have you like your father was."

As the *Philomena* drew into harbor once more they could see Our Lady of the Good Voyage off in the distance above the roofs of Gloucester town.

"Your mother will be happy when she sees you crowned," said Uncle Joe.

It was the Sunday in June when all the fishing boats were in and the captains and crews gathered in the square before the church for the ancient crowning ceremony brought over from Portugal by the forefathers of the fishermen of Gloucester. Hundreds of children were there also. The girls were dressed in white, like Palmagra, with broad red ribbons across their breasts. The boys were dressed like Manuel in their best clothes, with red ribbons across their chests and red ribbon bows on the right arms.

There were two bands, three drill teams of young women, and an escort of Coast Guards and policemen.

Palmagra and three other girls formed a square with red staffs, and an older girl carried a beautiful banner with the words DIVINIA ESPIRITO SANTO embroidered on it. A silver dove tipped the staff of the banner. Suddenly the parade began as the children were shoved into place. The smallest ones, dressed in white, led it. The fishermen in their Sunday clothes joined it and the band played and they all marched in and out the streets of Gloucester under American and Portuguese flags until they came to a little house all decorated with banners where Captain Joe Madieros lived.

Uncle Joe looked so handsome and solemn that Manuel hardly knew him. His heart nearly burst with pride as the Captain came down the porch steps carrying a crown covered with a piece of silk and walked into the square made by the girls with red staffs.

Captain Madieros led the parade back into the church square, and the tiniest girls threw paper rose petals at his feet and the band played a slow hymn.

Overhead the famous carillon began to ring. The bell tunes floated over the town and scattered across the sea like far heavenly music. The sun was bright and warm, and Manuel could see the statue of Our Lady between the twin bell towers, holding the little fishing boat in her arm.

Soon the church was filled and the ancient ceremony began. The priest told how, in the thirteenth century, Queen Isabel of Portugal, against the King's will, took baskets of bread to her poor people.

One day he stopped her and angrily asked what was in the basket.

"Roses," she said.

The King looked and saw the basket was filled with roses, and at the same time a dove from the sky flew down on the Queen's head.

Though Manuel knew the story by heart, he never

tired of hearing how the Portuguese made a saint of Isabel and how, whenever they were in trouble, they prayed to her and pledged themselves to the ceremony of the Crowning if they were rescued.

Now the choir was singing softly and the priest was placing the shining crown for a minute on Uncle Joe's head as he knelt. He had been a good man all the year, as everyone knew, and that was why he had been chosen for the honor. Then the crown was placed on the heads of those who had been delivered from some danger during the past year and, of course, Manuel and Tony were among them.

When the ceremony was over everybody marched across the square to the hall for dinner.

Many of the fishermen's wives had been baking bread for days and had even stayed up all night to see that it raised properly. The fishermen and their friends ate upstairs, and the children were downstairs where they could make as much noise as they wanted. Manuel ate his *sopas,* a fine flavored meat broth with sprigs of spearmint and spongy chunks of bread swimming in it, until he could eat no more.

But somehow he had room for the delicate sweet bread called *resquillas.* The loaves were round and made with a hole in the center so that many could be carried on the arm to give to the poor.

The older people listened to speeches and the children played in the square after they had taken the left-over food to the sick and those who were kept at home.

There was an auction of donated lobsters, fruit,

wine, and bread tied with red ribbons and decorated with flowers.

When evening came Uncle Joe said, "Well, Manuel, you earned a share in the profits of the trip. Shall I put it in the bank for you?"

Manuel nodded his head.

"What are you thinking of?" asked the Captain.

"I will save it to buy a schooner some day," Manuel said in a choked and happy voice.

"You are a chip off the old block. A real Gloucester boy," said Captain Joe.

Rounding up the Sheep

ELIZABETH YATES

"Stoppa!" Father called, after they had been riding an hour on the trail that led up to the mountains. Tucking into his belt the silver-handled whip which he only used to snap in the air, he tossed the reins over his pony's neck and slid off the saddle.

Finnur, Gudrun, and Hans slipped from their saddles and stood quietly while the ponies moved a little away from them to feed where the grass was green.

"How big the world is!" Gudrun exclaimed, thinking of all that lay ahead of them beyond the mountains—thinking of the stony roads over which they had come, the rivers they had crossed, and the wild grandeur of the countryside.

"It's not the world," Finnur reminded her. "It's just a part of Iceland."

Soon they tightened the strap of a saddlebag here and

a blanket roll there and remounted. Leaning low over the heavy manes, they patted the ponies and whispered in their ears, for everyone knew that ponies went better if you loved them. The ponies pressed their noses forward and pricked up their ears, as if answering the call of the mountains; then they were off, single file, over the stony trail.

The time for the ingathering of the sheep had come, and the three children were going with their father to Cousin Olaf's farm to help with the work. Next to fish, sheep were most important in Iceland—giving food, wool for warm clothes, hides for shoes, horns for implements, bones for toys.

When Father called "Stoppa!" again, they halted by a tumbling brook where the ponies could drink, pushing their soft noses around in the cool water.

"Your saddlebag has the sandwiches," Finnur reminded Gudrun, "and here's the milk." He took from his bag a bottle wrapped in layers of wet newspaper to keep it cool.

"I'm as hungry as a pony," Hans exclaimed.

"Then eat as well as one," Father said. "We've a long way to go."

In the late afternoon they reached the great rift leading down to the Plains of Thingvellir. They reined up their ponies to look with pride on the spot where over a thousand years ago the first parliament in the world had met.

"If I had a hat on, I'd take it off," Hans said, for there was something noble about this great open plain bound by snow-streaked mountains, with a lake at one end and a river filling the silence with sound.

Even the ponies stepped softly as they reached the shore of the lake where they were to camp for the night. Two little tents were quickly set up, and Gudrun gathered sticks and dried moss to keep the fire going while the others went to the lake to see what they could angle for their supper.

"The fish are certainly in a hurry to be eaten," Finnur shouted to Gudrun as they soon came back to the camp with four salmon trout.

"This is the best kind of supper ever," Gudrun said when there were only piles of clean bones on their plates. Then she yawned, and Father said it was time for everyone to go to bed.

The ponies were hobbled, the fire was put out, blankets were unrolled and one tired traveler after another rolled up in them. The ground might be hard, and darkness far from settling on the world, but sleep came quickly to them all.

The next day the country grew wilder and rockier. The rivers were deeper, and some of the ponies had to swim, their riders clinging to them. Of course they got wet, but people could shake as well as ponies, and the fresh wind soon dried them off.

"We're getting into the high mountains now." Father looked around him. "See how much greener the grazing is than farther south!"

They reached Cousin Olaf's farm by noon, and Cousin Anna had a hot luncheon ready for them—mutton stew and boiled potatoes, with rhubarb jam and bread for dessert. Then, with Olaf leading and the two sheep dogs winding in and out among the ponies, they started up where the pastureland stretched high and far and the sheep were grazing.

"We part here," Cousin Olaf cried out when they reached a certain point; and taking Gudrun and Hans with him, he went up one trail while Father and Finnur took the other.

"*Bles!*" they called to each other as the trails parted. There were more than three hundred sheep with their lambs up in these high meadows. Cousin Olaf had thought that he would round up most of the flock and that only a hundred or so would be where Father and Finnur were going. Then they planned to meet again the next afternoon at the farm in the valley.

"We've got ninety-nine," Father said, when near evening he made his count, "and I don't believe there are any more to be found."

"It's been very easy," Finnur said almost regretfully. "The sheep have all come together so well."

They herded the sheep into a small enclosure between the rocks, with Bruni the dog standing guard at the opening. Then they built their tiny campfire, heated some soup and sipped it slowly before rolling up in their blankets for the night.

Finnur had heard bleating so much of the day that he was not surprised to hear it at night. He was not surprised until he woke up and found the short night was over and the morning gray and dew drenched about

him. On the far peaks the sun was glinting. At hand
the sheep in their enclosure were lying so close that
they looked like a rough woolen rug left out all night
and sparkling with dew. Bruni lay stretched across the
opening, his nose between his paws; and though Finnur
saw him only from the back, he knew the dog was alert.

There was such stillness everywhere that Finnur began to think he had been very silly to let a dream awaken
him. Then he heard the bleating again. One sheep in
the flock gave answer, hoarsely, pitifully. Finnur lay
still and tired to find with his eyes the spot on the
mountain which his ears told him must be a lost lamb.

Bruni was troubled. He knew there was a lamb left
on the mountain, but he had been told to guard the
flock so could not go in search of it.

"Never mind, Bruni; we'll find the lamb," Finnur said,
and Bruni's tail wagged feebly.

Sharp eyes, trained to see the speck of a cormorant's
egg on a cliff face or to spot the tiny sail of a boat on the
shimmering horizon, scanned the mountain. There, high
up in a place which seemed part of the world of
clouds and sunshine, was the lamb.

There was only one thing to do—go for it. Finnur never
thought how it could be done. He knew only that it
must be done. "Father!" He nudged the still form sleeping nearby.

Father turned and opened his eyes slowly.

"Will you take Bruni's place watching the sheep so
that I may have him to go up the mountain? There's
a lost lamb."

Father nodded sleepily, hardly realizing what he was doing until he saw Finnur unroll himself from his blanket, give a shake to his body and a toss to his head like a pony coming out of its stable. Finnur started off, Bruni bounding to his heels at a word.

"Finnur, where are you going?" Father was awake now.

"Up there." The boy pointed.

"But you can't—the rocks are too slippery; it's too early . . ." Father called, shaking himself from his blanket.

Then the sheep, knowing Bruni had left them, began to move around in their enclosure and would have been all over the mountain again if Father had not turned to them.

The wall of the mountain rose above rocks and crumbling stone that slipped and slid as feet tried to trace a way on them. Finnur knew that his hope of ascent was to find the way the lamb had gone. Bruni was doing everything to help, sniffing back and forth, trying to pick up one trail from a dozen intercrossing ones. Suddenly he looked back at Finnur; then started up the mountain.

Finnur followed quickly—up, straight up. More than once he wished that he had four soft padded feet instead of two in clumsy shoes. Still, hands could be as good as feet, and placing them on the rocks, now here, now there, he pulled himself up.

Bruni was a long way ahead, but his excited yelps were a good guide up the steep slope. Now the tone of his barking changed. He was cross. The sharp tone dropped again to a wail. Something had happened to make Bruni very angry, then very sad.

Higher and higher up the steep face of the mountain Finnur climbed until he reached Bruni. Crouching on a ledge, ears laid back and tail pressed between his legs, Bruni had reached the point where he must stop. There was no way up, no way sideways, only down. But the lamb had come that way, for there was the imprint of its cloven hoof.

"Good Bruni, it was clever of you to find the way," Finnur said consolingly, his arms around the dog.

There was another ledge near them, only a little more than out of reach, and on it was the lamb—looking at them with curious eyes, so interested that it had forgotten to bleat.

A strange stillness hung in the air; then from far below in the valley Father's voice came faintly, "Don't do it, Finnur."

At that moment the sun came over the mountains and lit up the whole valley. It shone brightly on the rock walls, and in that new light the distance from ledge to ledge looked greater. Finnur's heart felt heavy. Then a shadow came over the sun and lay on the mountain, a shadow of two wings widespread. An eagle had sighted the lamb. Hovering in the sky, it was waiting for the moment when it might descend on its prey.

"I must do it, Father," Finnur shouted down to the valley.

Putting his face to the mountain, Finnur counted the

cracks between the ledges where fingers might go, the places where feet might lodge. Not for nothing had he scaled the cliffs near home ever since he could walk.

Slowly he eased himself along the rock. There was no sound anywhere, from Father or the sheep below, from Bruni nearby, or the lamb he was approaching; no sound save the dull thumping of stones that became loosened. But there was always the shadow of the eagle drawing nearer and nearer.

Finnur reached the lamb and comforted it; then he waved his arms to free the air of the swooping bird. Picking up a stone from the ledge, he hurled it toward the eagle which hissed angrily and soared skyward.

"How shall I ever get you back?" Finnur whispered softly to the lamb.

Then he remembered a picture in a book at home, a picture of a man who went out to find a lost sheep and returned with it over his shoulders. Finnur hunched back and pushed the lamb up into the air, gripping its legs. Holding them with one hand, he reached into his pocket for some string which he had brought with him to mend his saddle, should it need it. With this he quickly tied the lamb's legs together around his neck. The lamb was safe now, and Finnur's arms were free.

He faced the mountain again, seeking the familiar crevices for his hands, and because of the added weight he was carrying, making his feet doubly secure in each niche they fumbled after. The eagle still overshadowed them, but its circular flight was winging higher and higher. Back on the ledge with Bruni, Finnur looked across at where the lamb had been. How easy everything seemed now that it had all been done!

Bruni led the way down the mountain, the lamb following and Finnur behind them both. As they approached the enclosure the sheep began to bleat joyously; the ponies were neighing; Father was cheering.

It's just like the story in the Bible. Finnur smiled to himself. Because one lost lamb was being returned there was great rejoicing, as if only the lost one mattered.

The afternoon sun was lengthening over the valley when they joined the others at the farm, driving the sheep before them. Father told how the lamb had been brought down the cliff, and Cousin Olaf thanked Finnur warmly.

"Such a fine little ram he is too," he said. "He will be the head ram of our flock, and all the rest of his days shall walk the mountainland like one who has done great things."

"And we'll always call him 'Finnur's ram,'" said Cousin Anna.

Gudrun and Hans had had a busy time rounding up the two hundred sheep that were their charge, but there had been no great adventures in doing it. They were proud of Finnur and shook hands with him.

Cousin Anna called them in from the sheepfold to their meal. Spread around the table were bowls of *skyr*, a bowl for each one, and in the center of the table was plenty of sugar and rich yellow cream to mix with the *skyr*. It was good, this dish of curdled milk that had been a favorite in their land for so many centuries, and nothing could have pleased them more.

"It's the Icelandic *skyr* that makes us strong," Cousin Olaf said with a wink at Finnur as they took up their spoons.

Gray Fox and the Eagles

❧❧

CLAIRE DUTER

The Indian braves sat close around the fire. Big Chief Beaver quietly smoked a pipe. Tomorrow they would start on the big hunt.

Young Gray Fox sat in the outer circle. He watched the smoke from the campfire, curling lazily on its way up to the sky. Now he listened to the legends of the hunt. The braves had many stories to tell of their great prowess.

Soon the fires burned low. The braves left, one by one, to rest before their long journey. Before sunup they would be well along their way.

Gray Fox waited until the last Indian brave had left the campfire. He crawled over and sat down beside his father, Big Chief Beaver.

"Father," said Gray Fox, "I, too, wish to hunt with the braves. I am strong. My arrow shoots more swiftly than the wind."

GRAY FOX AND THE EAGLES

"Even the son of a chief must prove his courage before he can hunt with the braves," said his father. "First you must bring me the feather plucked from the tail of a fierce, live eagle. Only then can you go on the hunt."

Early the next morning Gray Fox started on his long, difficult journey. He knew where to find the nest of the mighty eagle. It would be hidden high up on the mountain.

He walked many days before he reached the foot of the mountain. After more days of climbing he was above the timber line. Now he went more slowly, picking his way carefully, examining the crags and ledges with his keen eyes.

Then he saw it! There was a coarse nest of twigs and branches high up on the rocky ledge.

Gray Fox climbed the sharp rocks until he was above the eagle's nest. He looked down. Something was terribly wrong. The two baby eagles in the nest looked sick, their heads drooped low. Beside the nest, on a ledge, was a wounded mother eagle. An arrow had pierced her wing. The broken shaft was still stuck in it.

Gray Fox knew in an instant that tragedy had struck. The father eagle was most likely dead, for the baby eagles were starving. The great mother eagle lay helplessly on the ledge, watching her hungry babies but unable to bring them food.

Gray Fox climbed back along the crag. He knew what must be done. He read the signs left by passing animals readily and truly, and knew the jack rabbit was nearby.

There it was! A perfect target standing on a rock.

Gray Fox took a stone from his belt. He threw it. Straight and true it sped to find its mark. Then Gray Fox carried the rabbit over the rocky trail above the ledge. Slowly he climbed down until he reached the eagle's nest. The ledge was wide. He put the rabbit down, took his knife, and skinned the animal. He cut strips of meat and fed the young eagles.

The mother eagle, though weak, helpless, and very near death, tried in vain to struggle toward him, her fierce spirit ready to protect her young. Gray Fox continued to feed them, being careful at first to stay out of reach of her beak and talons.

Then slowly a wondering sort of understanding began to show in the mother eagle's eyes. She ceased her struggle to reach her young and watched quietly while they were fed.

Gray Fox was watching her. Now he was sure she would accept his friendship. With no thought of danger he cut a strip of meat and gave it to the mother eagle. While she tore hungrily at the food Gray Fox pulled the broken arrow from her wing. Then with deft fingers he set the broken wing, using strong twigs to brace it and coarse grass to tie it in place.

For several weeks Gray Fox stayed with the eagles. He went out each day to hunt for their food. But there came a day when he hunted long and far in search of food. Toward sundown he started back, emptyhanded. As he neared the nest he heard the cry of the mountain lion stalking its prey. Gray Fox ran swiftly, thinking only of the danger to his eagles.

When he neared the rocks above the nest he saw the lion pacing nervously back and forth. Gray Fox silently drew his bow. He took an arrow and aimed carefully. Swiftly the arrow flew and buried itself in the big cat's back. The animal, enraged with pain, leaped toward Gray Fox. But again an arrow flew. It hit deep in the animal's shoulder and made him falter.

Gray Fox started to circle toward the rock above the ledge. But before he reached safety the mortally wounded animal charged toward him. Without hesitation Gray Fox stepped to one side, and the enraged beast plunged over the cliff to the ledge below.

Gray Fox climbed cautiously down the steep rocks. The mountain lion was dead. He skinned the carcass and hung the skin to dry. Now there was food a-plenty for the eagles.

One morning, when Gray Fox awakened on the ledge, the mother eagle was gone. He waited, talking to the young eagles who were now strong and well fed. Soon he saw the mother eagle returning, and in her talons she carried a wild pig. She dropped the prize at the feet of Gray Fox. He knew she was showing gratitude for his kindness.

Now the golden eagle was well again. She could fly out each day for food to supply the needs of her family. Gray Fox knew his usefulness here had ended. He could rejoin the tribe. But first, as the grateful mother eagle stood at his side, he plucked a red-gold feather from her tail.

Wearing the lion skin over his shoulder and the prized

feather in his belt, Gray Fox started the long trek homeward. But as he neared the end of the journey he became filled with doubt.

"A feather from the tail of a fierce, live eagle," his father had said. By the time he arrived home with his trophy, tired and discouraged, he realized his was not a fierce eagle.

Quickly Gray Fox sought his father. He showed him the beautiful feather and told his story.

When the story was finished, Big Chief Beaver asked, "But was it you, alone, who killed the mountain lion?"

"No," said Gray Fox, "I only wounded him. He was killed when he plunged over the mountain cliff."

Big Chief Beaver lowered his head in thoughtful silence. Finally he raised his head. "I will hold council with the wise men of the tribe," he said. "I will hear what they advise."

The wise men were called together and Big Chief Beaver spoke. "My son has brought his prize, a tail feather from the mighty golden eagle, and he wears the skin of the mountain lion as a trophy. He is ready to hunt with the braves, but first you must hear his story." And he motioned to Gray Fox.

Again Gray Fox told his story. He waited breathlessly for the wise men's decision. There was a long silence.

Then White Cloud, the oldest Indian, spoke, "You will join the braves. Your trophy was won by skill and agility. You have tamed the fierce golden eagle with your kindness. It takes far greater courage to show kindness to a fierce opponent than to pluck his tail and seek shelter from his wrath."

The wise old Indians of the council nodded their heads in agreement.

Gray Fox treasured the memory of his eagles. But he treasured even more White Cloud's wise words: "It takes far greater courage to show kindness to a fierce opponent."

The Jar of Tassai

❦❦❦

GRACE P. MOON

DREAMS

Tassai lived on the top of a mesa that looked far out over the Painted Desert. The air was clear as thin ice. It made even the farthest mountains and blue hills look nearer than they really were. Tassai was a Pueblo Indian girl, brown as a nut that has dried in the sun. She liked to lie on the edge of the mesa and look over the desert and dream long dreams.

But Tassai did not often have time for dreams. There was too much work for her to do. It was not hard work, and it had magic in it. It had the magic of watching green things spring up out of the ground where only brown earth had been before. For Tassai worked with her mother in the little fields at the foot of the mesa.

Tassai brought water, too, from the spring at the foot of the mesa, carrying it up the steep trail in jars. For hours each day she ground the red and blue and yellow grains of corn. She cooked when her mother needed her help, and she knew where to find the grasses that her mother wove into baskets.

There was one thing Tassai did that no one knew about, for she did it only at times when no eyes were watching. She was making a jar from clay that she had found in a secret place where the earth was smooth as honey to the touch, and rich and dark in color. Not even her mother knew that Tassai was working at this jar. She had a very special reason for making it.

She shaped and smoothed it just as she had seen her mother do, until one day the most beautiful jar of all seemed to form itself in her hands. She could hardly believe her own eyes, it was so beautiful. And when she had added a design of little black lines and baked it a golden brown, she thought again that never had a jar been so lovely as this one. She wrapped it in a piece of blanket and hid it away carefully until the time should come to show it.

All through the hours when she worked in the fields, Tassai thought of her jar. In her thoughts a little song sang itself over and over again until her feet danced to the music of it:

It is so beautiful,
My big, round jar!
So round and beautiful!
Only the Moon,
When it walks on the edge of the world
At harvesttime

Is like my jar.
Round and smooth it is,
And has a shine that sings!
Maybe the Moon has come to me
To be my jar!

Not long before Tassai had made her jar, the Governor of the Pueblo called the people of the town together in the little open place where meetings were held. He told them that the people of three towns were going to meet for a time of dancing and feasting. He asked that each man, woman, and child bring to the feast something he had made. This was because a great White Man who had visited the Indian towns had said that the Indians could not make any good things. The White Man had also said that, since this was so, the Indian children would have to go away to the White Man's school to learn the White Man's ways.

The Indians did not want their children to be sent away. They planned to show all the finest things that they could make so that the White Man would change his mind. Prizes would be given for the best things brought to the feast.

There was much excitement at the Governor's news and much talking and planning of what should be done. Tassai was excited from the first. She could hardly wait for the time to come.

THE JAR OF TASSAI

THE BIG DAY

The day itself was wonderful. There was a feel in the air that was different. Tassai felt that she could not walk or talk or even breathe as she did on other days. The open place in the town was bright with color. It was like a fair.

There were good smells and different sounds everywhere. There were baskets and pottery and woven things all spread out for everyone to see. There were silver bracelets and rings and belts. There were bright blankets and things of leather and wood. There were great pumpkins and squashes and ears of corn that were bigger than any Tassai had ever seen before. There were beaded moccasins and sandals for the feet, and nets for carrying things. There were fruits piled high in baskets, and little cakes made of pine nuts and seeds. There was good food cooking in pots.

Tassai was one of the very last to come into the open place on that big day. She had been busy since dawn, helping her mother make their home ready for strangers to see. When at last she was free she picked up the blanket in which her jar was wrapped and ran to the open place. There she stood, holding tightly to her bundle.

The old Governor of the Pueblo, with two White Men from the big White School, moved from place to place. They looked long and closely at each of the many things that had been brought. These three men were to say which were the best of all and to give the prizes.

A little white girl, daughter of one of the men, danced ahead of them as they walked. She looked at everything with bright, eager eyes. Her father looked at her proudly as often as he looked at the shining things the Indians had made.

When the men had seen everything else Tassai came close with her bundle and touched the blanket with trembling fingers. She was frightened now. Perhaps they would not think her jar was beautiful. Others crowded close. They had not known that Tassai would have anything to show.

"Maybe it is not very good," she said in a voice that was so low no one heard her. "Maybe it—" Then her words would not come at all, for when she opened her bundle the beautiful jar was not there. She had not noticed that there were two bundles of blankets in the room of her home. The one she had picked up in her excitement held only an old corncob doll.

There was a big laugh from those who stood near. The words of Tassai, explaining her mistake, were lost. Quickly she pushed her way through the laughing crowd and ran home. She did not know that the little white girl, eager to see again that queer doll, was following close behind her.

The house of Tassai was the last one in the little town, on the very edge of the mesa top. She ran into the door and did not notice that the little white girl who had followed her had stopped suddenly just outside the doorway. The child was watching, with wide, frightened eyes, a snake that lifted its head from beside a big stone. It was a rattlesnake, and it moved its flat, ugly head closer and closer to the little girl. She gave one sharp cry as Tassai came out of the door with the jar in her arms. Tassai had thrown aside the blanket and held the jar unwrapped in her arms.

There was no time to think. There was no time to call for help. Tassai did the only thing she could do. With all her strength she threw the jar at the snake. It broke into many pieces on the rock, and the snake lay flat and still.

The little girl did not make another sound. Her father, who had heard her first cry, came running. He held her tightly in his arms.

For the first moment Tassai thought only that the snake was dead. Then she thought of her jar. No one would call it beautiful now. She picked up a little broken piece. One of the White Men took it from her hand.

"It must have been a mighty pretty jar," he said. "Did you make it?"

Tassai nodded her head.

The father of the little white girl looked at the piece of jar, too, and then at Tassai.

"That was a beautiful jar," he said slowly. His voice shook a little so that he had to clear his throat. "I am sorry that we cannot give the prize for a broken jar— but—" He cleared his voice again. "For what you have done for me I will give you anything else you ask." He closed his arms more tightly around his little girl.

At first Tassai could not answer. In her surprise the words would not come. Then she said, "There is nothing I wish but to stay here in the Pueblo. Could it be that we need not go far away to learn the ways of the White Men?"

The man smiled. "You will not have to go away," he assured Tassai. "The White Teachers are coming here to learn from the Indians instead. Today your people have shown what beautiful things they can make—like your jar. There will be a school here where the Indians and the White Teachers will work together."

Tassai was very happy now. It did not matter that her jar was broken. She could make another, even more beautiful.

The Green Hat

❧❧❧

VERA L. DAYE

Len Corbett hit the trail with long, easy strides. Behind him came the rest of the Robin Hood Patrol— Jim, Don, Roscoe, Larry, and the others. Ed Harley, the patrol leader, brought up the rear.

The slightly crusty snow glistened in the sun. Len adjusted his goggles more carefully against the glare. He was going to win the Serpent Run again this year, he just knew he was. The other fellows were good skiers, but none could match him except perhaps Red Skinner, his best friend. And although Len felt Red would give him a good race, he had no doubt he could beat him.

Each winter, as soon as there was enough snow for skiing, Ed Harley, leader of the Robin Hood Patrol, took his boys out to the Serpent Run. The boy who won the race down the sloping, twisting run also won the Green Hat, Robin Hood's Hat. His was the privilege of wearing the coveted hat for a day, his the honor of leading the patrol on its cross-country hike. And he was the one to read the signs in the snow, the rabbit tracks, the imprint of an alighting hawk, the tracks of a frightened field mouse.

For two years, ever since Mr. Harley had held the race, Len had been Robin Hood. Behind him now he could hear the boys talking.

"Len's a cinch to win again," said Jim.

"Oh, I don't know!" retorted Don. "Red is better than ever this year."

"Yes. He's been out practicing every day."

That was Roscoe, and at the sound of his voice Len felt a tiny shiver go through him. He knew Red had been skiing more than ever this winter, but not every day! He might prove to be a real threat.

The troop began to climb toward the crest of green marking the top of the run. Mr. Harley was beside Len now and drawing ahead on the flowing ski run. At the top he stood against the backdrop of evergreens and waited until the last straggler had come up.

"Everybody ready now?" called Mr. Harley.

The boys stopped talking and milling around, and listened carefully to the instructions their leader was giving them.

"We all know Len and Red are our best skiers," he was saying, "so we'll race them last. First, though, I'm going to divide the troop into two teams of five boys each. The winner of the first team will race the winner of the second team. Then the winner of that run will race Red. The final winner will meet Len, our last year's Robin Hood."

Every boy in the Robin Hood Patrol eyed the soft green felt hat Len was wearing. As last year's Robin, it had been Len's to wear to the Serpent Run. Now he took it off and handed it to his leader. For the actual race he would wear a small visored cap like the rest of the boys.

"Roscoe, Jim, Don." As Mr. Harley called out their names, the boys took their places at the edge of the slope.

At the starting signal they were off, one after another, down the tricky course. Len saw Don flounder, lose his balance, and sprawl and slide on the glittering snow.

"Don's out," he cried.

With a sheepish grin the loser struggled to his feet.

"Tough luck!" whispered Len.

The excited boys watched the rest of the flying skiers, thin plumes of white marking their progress toward the flag-marked pole, where John, Mr. Harley's second in command, waited to clock the winner.

"It's Roscoe," shouted Red, "Roscoe's won. I saw his yellow sweater flash past the pole."

The second race proved even more exciting. There were spills and thrills in plenty. Then Deane Jones met Roscoe. The boys were yelling themselves hoarse by this time. The sound deepened when Roscoe and Red met for the semifinals. The former tried hard, scorning the easy stems he had used before. But he was no match for the more brilliant Red.

399

As the tall, sandy-haired boy herringboned his way back up the Serpent Run, Len stood quietly in the center of the excited throng. Red was good! More than that, he was extra good! Len felt a tingle of fear run through him. What if Red should be good enough to beat him?

By now Red had reached the small plateau where the Robin Hood Patrol waited. His eyes were bright, his cheeks crimson in the cold air.

"That was a good run," Mr. Harley said.

"Tough luck, Roscoe," called Jim, while the others echoed him.

"Now, the final race," called the patrol leader.

Len moved across the snowy ground to the starting point. Red followed, then bent down to adjust the ski harness on his left foot. Len watched him carefully.

Presently, Mr. Harley spoke quietly. "Ready, boys?"

"Ready," returned Red as Len merely nodded.

Then they were off and away in a whirl of flying snow. Both took the first drop down in easy stems. But when the long steep incline in the center was reached, they were flying along in a half crouch, knees bent, and arms taut on their poles. Inch by inch Red began to creep past his chum. The cheers at the top of the hill grew louder.

All at once Len saw Red lurch to one side. He struggled to regain his balance, his arms flailing wildly. In that instant Len shot past him and went on down the Serpent Run, eyes and body intent on navigating the tricky turn to the finish.

The groan that had gone up at the top gave way to

cheers as Len streaked home. Then, slowly, as he turned to herringbone his way back, his eyes went to Red. The other boy was picking himself up out of the snow.

"Sure thought I had you that time." He managed to grin wryly as Len came abreast.

"Did you hurt yourself?" the victor stammered.

"No, just my pride," returned Red. "Guess my harness came loose."

Silently the two chums went back to the plateau.

"Hard luck, Red," shouted Roscoe. "Better luck next year, old fellow."

"Len won. Len's Robin Hood again this year," the troop called happily. They liked Len.

Then to the amazement of the troop, instead of taking the Green Hat from Mr. Harley, Len handed it back.

"That wasn't a fair test," he said quickly. "Red's harness worked loose. In his excitement he didn't get it fastened right before we started. I saw it."

Mr. Harley faced Len squarely. "Well, Len, it's up to you. You decide."

"We'll race again. That was just a warm-up, anyway," said Len quickly.

"Boy! Do you mean it?" cried Red.

Mr. Harley nodded and bent to adjust and tighten the harnesses of both skiers. Then he waved to John, waiting below and wondering what the fuss was about. When all was ready, the two friends, grinning happily at each other, went over the top and down the long serpentine run.

At first there wasn't the breath of a sound from the rest of the patrol. Then, as they saw the boys racing knee to knee, neck to neck, they began to cheer—a wild cheer that sent the echoes ringing.

"It's Red—no, it's Len—"

In a whirl of snow they watched the skiers streak to a finish.

"It's Red!" shrieked Roscoe, his new bass breaking into treble. Red had beaten Len at last!

This time nobody waited for the skiers. They all came sliding down the run helter-skelter, even Mr. Harley. When they reached the panting, rosy-faced skiers the patrol leader held the Green Hat toward Len.

He took it happily. Turning to Red he removed the visored cap and replaced it with the coveted Green Hat.

"I christen thee Robin Hood for a day," he said soberly.

With eyes like stars, Red turned to lead the Robin Hood Patrol on its annual cross-country hike. As he followed close behind his pal, Len wondered why he felt so queer, so sort of sad, and yet so happy all at the same time.

A Spear for Omar

𝕏𝕏

HEDDY RADO

Omar knelt at the bottom of the small dugout canoe and let his hand drift in the balmy water of the Red Sea. He loved this hour of the day, heading homeward with the keel of the canoe deep in the water, heavy with a day's catch of fish. It usually made him feel peaceful to watch the sun sink slowly behind the jagged mountains that lined the dry, hot desert.

Today, however, there was no peace in Omar for he had failed again. As if in answer to his shame came his father's soothing voice, "Do not worry too much, my Son. Tomorrow you will be able to hold your breath underwater longer than you did today."

Omar's father was known to be the best spearfisherman from Suez all the way down to Port Sudan. He was a big man with strong muscles rippling underneath his tanned skin. Clad only in a loincloth, he squatted in

the canoe and paddled homeward with even, powerful strokes.

Omar's brother Gomez, who knelt in the stern of the
canoe, cleaning and drying his underwater goggles with
the tail of his galabia shirt, started to laugh. "Tomorrow
Omar will be bobbing up for air every few seconds just
like he did today," Gomez mocked. "How can he ever
be a spearfisherman if he is afraid he might drown as
soon as he is underwater for more than a few seconds?"

"Tomorrow I shall stay underwater for hours, you will
see!" cried Omar. Deep inside he was thoroughly
ashamed of his fear of drowning.

With an angry motion Omar's father jarred the paddle
against the canoe. "There will be no more fighting between you two," he said. "And as for you," he added,
turning around to Gomez, "it would not harm you to
exercise some more caution. It is not well to show fear,
but also it is not wise to disregard danger altogether
as you so often do. The sea is full of danger for the
reckless spearfisherman." After that he took up his paddle, and no one spoke again.

Omar sighed and looked with deep longing at the
spears at the bottom of the canoe. His father had
promised him a spear of his own as soon as he had
conquered his fear. The spears were slender, long shafts
of smooth wood with metal points that gleamed dark
red in the last rays of the sinking sun. To Omar the
spears looked beautiful and well worth the effort he
silently promised to make.

The next morning Omar's father announced that he would stay behind. "I want you two to go to sea alone today," he said. "Gomez is well able to do some spear-fishing alone, providing he will be careful. And as for you, Omar," he continued, "I expect you to keep your promise and do some real diving today."

Omar respected his father too much to argue, although he did not want to go without him. Silently he nodded, and then the two boys went on their way.

Gomez smirked at Omar and said, "Let's go. I'll race you to the beach."

The minute the two brothers jumped into the crystal-clear water Omar forgot his disappointment that his brother had won the race over the burning sand. As much as Omar resented his brother's teasing, he felt great admiration for him. Now he admired the way Gomez gripped the heavy spear and shot downward with the ease and grace of a dolphin. It took only a few seconds until he bobbed up again with his first catch. He threw the fish into the canoe and grinned at Omar.

"How about coming down yourself?" he asked.

Omar held onto the canoe. "I will, I will," he said hastily. "But, Gomez, please don't take any chances and stay down too long. You know that father warned you yesterday."

"You worry about yourself," Gomez called. Then he flipped back his hair, took a few deep breaths, and down he went again.

Now came the big moment for Omar to dive himself,

and he was determined to dive well today. He let go of the canoe and submerged quickly.

A few feet below the surface the very water seemed to be alive with fish. The trembling rays of the sun penetrated the clear water and illuminated the colorful fish in a soft, mysterious light. Yet the whole scene seemed almost unreal because no sound broke the deep silence.

By now Omar's breath began to give out and he felt like darting to the surface. However, he forced himself to overcome his panic and swam deeper toward the pink coral reef. It was covered with flaming red sponges and the curiously nodding heads of purple worms. Scattered over the coral like precious diamonds were thousands and thousands of sparkling sea gems.

But the sight of numerous clams half hidden in the reef dampened Omar's enthusiasm a little. With their wide-open jaws they seemed to be just waiting for Omar. If he swam too near they would close their shells as quick as a flash over a finger or an arm. Omar kept well away from the gaping jaws of the clams, swimming with smooth, careful strokes.

When he finally came to the surface he was very happy. His father would be proud of him when he heard how well Omar had dived today.

Gomez emerged a few feet away with another catch. He was panting for air but nevertheless didn't linger long. After treading water for a few moments he took a deep breath and went down again.

A slight breeze had come up and sent gusts of hot air

from across the desert. The water, however, was still as cool and smooth as flowing silk.

Omar turned on his back and paddled slowly to the canoe. He held onto the crudely carved wood which gave him a funny, tickling feeling in his palms. Then as he hung onto the canoe he suddenly went limp all over. The water around him became cold as ice.

Before Omar even saw the motionless shadow he knew that a shark must be near. With a quick glance he scanned the water below him and saw that most of the fish had disappeared into the countless alcoves of the reef. That was all he needed to know. In one smooth motion he slipped into the canoe.

The shark slowly emerged from the deep water and started circling the boat. He had a huge, silvery, stream-lined body, small, murderous eyes, and a set of teeth that made Omar shudder. The boy leaned over the side of the canoe and looked frantically about for his brother. The water was almost deserted. Only a few herring fish darted about.

There was no sign of Gomez.

Omar scanned the water from the other side of the boat. About fifteen feet below, half hidden by the pro-truding ridge of a deep alcove in the reef, he saw his brother.

Omar's hand went to his mouth to stifle a cry. He saw that his brother's hand had been caught in one of the many clams and he was trying desperately to free himself. But he was already weakened by lack of air and seemed unable to pry his hand loose.

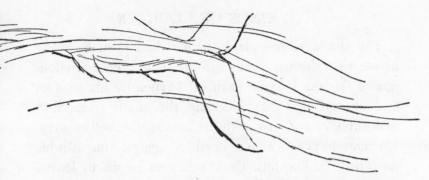

"Oh, how could he have been so careless," moaned
Omar. He knew that he had only a few precious seconds
in which to save his brother.

There was a slim chance that the shark might not
attack if Omar could disregard him completely. He felt
his mouth go dry as he lowered himself into the water.
He did not turn his head when the shark moved in
closer. Without any outward sign of his deadly fear he
went straight down.

Never before had Omar dived as deep as that, and
he felt as if his lungs would burst. For a second everything went black before his eyes.

But then he saw his brother in front of him. His
body was swaying, helpless from the terrible lack of air.
His hand was caught in the closed jaws of the clam.
If he had not stayed underwater until there was hardly
any breath left in him, he might have been able to
free himself somehow. The cocky expression Gomez
usually wore was gone. He looked at Omar with horror in his eyes.

Omar acted quickly. With deft fingers he pried the
clam loose from the coral. He left it attached to Gomez's
hand because he didn't want to waste precious time.
He could attend to the clam when they were safe in
the canoe, if they ever reached it.

The shark, whose giant shadow had been hovering above their heads, swam toward them. Omar tried to ignore the shark as he grabbed Gomez by his armpits and started upward. Suddenly the shark seemed to look directly at Omar with his murderous, yellow eyes. He came in closer, almost brushing against him with his powerful, fanlike fins. Omar's fingers began to loosen their grip on his brother, and they started to sink. The water around them had grown murky with waves churned by the shark.

If it was true that a shark might not attack if his victim showed no sign of fear, then Omar knew what he had to do. He tightened his fingers around his brother's arm until he could feel his nails sinking into the soft flesh. Then he turned his back on the shark and began to swim upward in calm, slow motions.

The effort took all Omar's strength and courage. Only a few feet more and they would be safe. A few feet more was all they needed.

When their heads broke the surface the shark came in for attack. He made a sharp turn and shot directly at Omar through the boiling waves. For a split second they were face to face, the shark a dreadful sight with his huge set of razor-sharp teeth.

In desperation Omar took the last measure his father had taught him in an emergency like this. He let go of Gomez, raised his right arm and slapped the shark across its pointed nose. Then he struck again and again and again.

For a long moment the shark seemed stunned and

motionless. Then he churned about, brushing against Omar's face with his rough fins as he turned toward the deep water.

Omar grabbed Gomez and pulled him into the canoe. Gomez sank to the floor, too exhausted to move, while Omar fell forward on his knees. His breath came in painful gasps and his eyes felt as if they would burst from their sockets. For a moment he gave way to the wave of faintness that washed over him, and supported his head against his arms on the seat in the boat's stern.

But only for a moment. Then he felt for his brother's arm. He took a knife and with its strong handle chipped away part of the shell. Although Gomez winced with pain, Omar worked fast until he could press the knife in and pry the clam open.

"It's only a flesh wound and will heal fast," Omar said after he had examined the wrist. He wrapped his dry shirt around it to stop the bleeding.

His brother opened his eyes weakly. He smiled at Omar and his smile was full of love and admiration. "Thank you, my brother," he said, "thank you."

Omar gave the makeshift bandage a last tug. "Shhh," he said, "do not speak now. You must rest."

Suddenly he felt very weary. His whole body ached and his right hand was bruised from fighting off the shark. However, it was not time for him to rest yet. Slowly he took the paddle and brought the boat in safely to the dock.

The next morning when Omar awoke he found a spear next to his sleeping mat. His father stood looking

down at him, warm approval in his eyes. Omar jumped
to his feet, gripping the spear tightly in his hand.

"You will be a fine spearfisherman, my Son," his father
said and Omar lowered his head, a great surge of happiness rushing through him.

Yukon Trail

WILLIS LINDQUIST

Under the lowering Alaskan sky young Steve Woodford stepped from the train at the snow-covered outpost of Nenana. He looked anxiously around for his Uncle Jim, the famous "Flying Doctor" of the Yukon of whom he had boasted so much at the orphanage.

For years he had dreamed of going to the Yukon. Now he was on his way and he was happy. He was going to have a real home and belong to a family. He hoped Uncle Jim and Aunt Bess would like him.

The young Indian who came up grinning couldn't have been over sixteen. "You're Steve?" he asked in perfect English. "Well, I'm Sam Ketchum. I've got a letter for you. There's been a lot of sickness up in the Yukon, and your uncle couldn't fly down for you."

Steve's heart sank as he took the letter. It was short. Uncle Jim wrote about how busy he was and that he might not be able to fly down for two or three weeks.

"Sam Ketchum is a young Indian guide who works for me," the letter went on. "I've told him to make you comfortable at the hotel. In a day or two he will be starting back for the Yukon with my new dog team. You could go with him if you wish, but I would not advise you to do so. It is a 350-mile mush through wilderness and tundra, and it would be a hardship for a boy accustomed to the soft life of civilization."

Steve read the letter several times at the hotel. It disturbed him that his uncle should think he was soft.

When he joined Sam for a dinner of venison roast he said, "I wanted to come up here last year, Sam. But Uncle Jim wouldn't let me. He wrote that I was too young. He said that the Yukon was a man's country and it was no place for a boy. So he made me wait a year. And now he thinks I'm soft. I'm going to show him, Sam. I'm going with you and the dog team."

Sam laughed. "It won't be easy," he warned. "But you have to learn about dogs sometime if you're going to be of any help to your uncle. We'll start at dawn."

It frightened Steve to think of the trip when he went to bed. He had never seen the big sled dogs. Some were part wolf and said to be dangerous.

It was still dark when the hotel man came with a set of fur breeches and a hooded parka, fur boots, and a fur sleeping bag.

Sam was waiting for him at the sled, with eleven mighty huskies straining at their harnesses, anxious to be off.

"Better meet some of your dogs," Sam said. "This first one, your leader, is Mutt. He's been to the Yukon before, and he knows the trail."

The tawny big brute lowered its head and watched Steve with suspicion. Steve fought down his fear and leaned over to pet the dog. Its fangs bared in a snarl.

"Not too close," Sam warned. "Mutt doesn't know you yet. And you better stay clear of Kooga—this big Malemute. He's a real troublemaker."

"Why is the sled tied to a tree?" Steve asked.

"Because otherwise they'd be off like a flash and we couldn't stop them," Sam explained. He pointed to an iron rod suspended above the ground at the rear of the sled. It looked like a narrow rake. "That's your brake. You step on it and the prongs dig into the snow and stop the sled."

They packed, and Steve got on top of the sled.

"Hold on!" Sam warned as he untied the rope from the tree.

The dogs were off, eleven big brutes harnessed in pairs except for Mutt who took the lead. They raced over the snow in full gallop. The sled bounced and flew, and it took all of Steve's strength to hold on.

Standing on the runners in back, Sam gave a hearty laugh. "Dogs are always wild to get started. They'll soon slow down."

They did. For hours they went, skirting great slopes of spruce and Norway pine, and on and on into the still white wilderness.

At midday they stopped for a few minutes' rest and a bite to eat.

"Now you drive," suggested Sam. "I'll run behind for a while to get warm. But whatever you do, don't fall off the sled. You'll not be able to stop the dogs, and you'll lose them and the sled and all your food. It's not a good way to die."

Steve leaped on the runners. "Get going!" he shouted. Mutt turned his head back and looked at him, but nothing happened.

"Holler *mush*," Sam suggested. "When you want to go right, holler *gee*, and for left *up*. And swing the sled around corners so it doesn't tip."

Steve nodded. "*Mush!*" he screamed. It worked. He stood proudly on the runners. He was driving a dog team!

There was real work to it, he soon discovered. Keeping the sled upright at curves was tricky, and he had to be careful to avoid the stumps and rocks that might smash the sled. On the down slopes he stood on the brake to keep from running over the dogs.

But suddenly it happened. He made the mistake of looking back too long at Sam who was jogging half a mile behind them. He hit a slope, and his feet slipped from the runners. But he held on, dragging as the sled gathered speed downhill until it pushed the dogs forward into a wild, scrambled heap. Then the sled tipped.

It started one of the wildest dog fights Steve had ever seen. Each seemed to be blaming the others for what had happened, and they snarled and slashed with white-fanged fury.

"Stop them! Stop them!" yelled Sam.

Steve stood frozen with fear. He didn't move. He didn't dare venture close.

Sam came up full speed, screaming at the dogs. He pried them loose one by one with a snowshoe, and straightened their harnesses which had become badly tangled. Then he mopped the sweat from his face.

"You'll have to learn how to do that quick," he gasped. "If you don't you'll lose a dog or two before you know it."

For five days they went on, and then Sam began to have chills and fever. "I was in the hospital for a week before you came," he explained. "Maybe I left too soon. It's coming back."

By noon he was groaning with pain and could not leave the sled. "There's a settlement over on Carlson Creek," he whispered. "You'd better get me there fast."

Steve reached the hollow among the bluffs in three hours, and only the women and children were there to meet them. The men were out on a week-long hunt.

"This one needs the doctor," said an old woman.

Steve went cold with dread, but he knew what had to be done. "Sam says my lead dog knows the trail well. I'll go get the doctor."

Sam mumbled in protest. "You'll stay here," he gasped. "Your uncle flies to this settlement every so often for a check."

"It might be weeks," said the old woman, "there is much sickness."

"I'll go," said Steve. He had no choice. Soon he found himself alone on the trail with a fierce pack of Malemutes and Eskimo huskies, and he felt panic rising within him. He began to wonder if he could handle the team.

He began talking to the dogs, calling them by name as Sam had told him to do. He stopped for the night under a sheltering cliff near a staggering thicket of birches. Now the moment he dreaded most had come. He had to handle the big dogs.

Steve tried not to show his fear. The big leader dog watched with yellow eyes as he approached, its ears flattened to the massive head. As Steve reached down to unfasten the harness the wolf dog snarled.

"Easy, Mutt!" Swiftly, Steve unharnessed the dog and led it to the nearest birch tree and tied it up. He came away weak but bursting with a happiness he had never known. *He could do it!* The other dogs, even the big Malemute Kooga, were easy after that.

One day followed another with perfect weather. The dogs were beginning to know him, some even licked his hand. But Mutt, the leader, remained sullen.

Then he saw the plane in the sky one morning. It circled above him, his uncle waved, and Steve, forming big letters in the snow, told him to go to Sam at Carlson's Settlement.

A howling Arctic blizzard started that night and kept him in his sleeping bag for two days. The third morning dawned clear, and he looked out on a white world. No dogs were in sight. They had all been buried by the snow.

As they mushed north that afternoon he became careless. He did not see the low branch until it struck him with a stunning blow in the face. He was falling. "Don't lose your sled or you die!" Sam's words came roaring back to his ears.

With all his strength he tried to hold on. But it was no use. His fingers slipped and he lunged headlong into the snow. He floundered. He tried to rise to his feet, but the earth seemed to tilt on end, and he couldn't tell which side was up.

The dogs and the sled were speeding away. He could see them vaguely. In a few moments they would be gone. There was nothing he could do to stop them. His food, his sleeping bag, even his snowshoes were on the sled. A man couldn't live very long on the lonely white tundra without them.

In that reeling instant of terror he seemed doomed. His mind cleared a little, and instinctively he cried out at the top of his lungs.

"Gee! Gee! Gee, Mutt!"

He held his breath. For a terrible instant nothing happened. But suddenly the big lead dog swung to the right. He waited until the whole team had turned. Then he screamed again. "Gee! Gee, Mutt!" Once more the lead dog turned.

They were coming back now. Steve got to his feet and stumbled to meet them, waving his arms. He tripped over a snowdrift and sprawled before the on-rushing team. That was all he could remember for a long time.

When he opened his eyes finally it seemed that a miracle had happened. Mutt, towering over him, was licking his face.

He threw his arms around the big dog, buried his face in the heavy fur, and let the tears come. Even a man could cry in Alaska if there was no one to see his tears.

From that day on his uncle paid daily visits to watch his progress and to drop sandwiches and food from Aunt Bess. In the first of these packages he found a note.

"I have seen Sam," wrote his uncle. "He's doing fine, thanks to you. If you keep up your good speed you should reach home in three days. We'll be waiting."

Steve felt a deep inner excitement. Home! In three days! He could drive a dog team now, and he felt sure that he could be of real use to his uncle. They would not find him soft and useless. They would like him.

Near sunset, three days later, as he came down the slope into the small settlement of Unison in the Yukon, his uncle and half the village came out to meet him. They were cheering and waving and smiling. His tall uncle wore a large smile and threw an arm over his shoulder.

"Good boy, Steve," he said warmly. To the people

of the village he said, raising his voice, "I'm mighty proud to introduce you to my nephew Steve. He mushed all the way from Nenana in fifteen days, and that's a record for any of us to shoot at."

When they entered the log cabin which was to be his new home there were gifts from almost everyone in the village—snowshoes, parkas, beaded reindeer pants, a beautiful Malemute pup, a carving from a walrus tusk, and bows and arrows.

Steve mumbled his thanks to the smiling villagers who stood before him. They were a strange mixture of old sourdoughs, Eskimos, Indians, and boys and girls.

One young man spoke up. "The Flying Doctor has cared for us and saved many of us from death. We love him as a father, and we are glad to welcome another of his blood."

It was not until later when Aunt Bess and Uncle Jim and Steve were alone that Uncle Jim spoke.

"I want to confess, Steve, that I've been worried about having you here. I wanted you to be happy, but I knew that a soft white boy from civilization would soon be looked upon by these people with contempt."

He smiled and took Steve firmly by the shoulders. "But I see now I was wrong. I need not have worried. You did what had to be done. You've got the makings of a real Yukon man."

Steve turned quickly away to play with the pup— and to hide the mist of happiness that had come into his eyes.

Index

Index

INDEX

INDEX

INDEX

I26